Sarah J. Daley

THE
VIOLENTLY DEPARTED

ANGRY ROBOT
An imprint of Watkins Media Ltd

Unit 11, Shepperton House
89-93 Shepperton Road
London N1 3DF
UK

angryrobotbooks.com
The hunter and the hunted

An Angry Robot paperback original, 2026

Copyright © Sarah J. Daley 2026

Edited by Simon Spanton Walker and Alan Heal
Cover by Sarah O'Flaherty
Set in Meridien

All rights reserved. Sarah J. Daley asserts the moral right to be identified as the author of this work. A catalogue record for this book is available from the British Library.

This novel is entirely a work of fiction. Names, characters, places, and incidents are the products of the author's imagination or are used fictitiously. Any resemblance to actual events, locales, organizations or persons, living or dead, is entirely coincidental.

Sales of this book without a front cover may be unauthorized. If this book is coverless, it may have been reported to the publisher as "unsold and destroyed" and neither the author nor the publisher may have received payment for it.

Angry Robot and the Angry Robot icon are registered trademarks of Watkins Media Ltd.

ISBN 978 1 91599 825 5
Ebook ISBN 978 1 91599 824 8

Printed and bound in the United Kingdom by CPI Group (UK) Ltd, Croydon CR0 4YY

The manufacturer's authorised representative in the EU for product safety is eucomply OÜ - Pärnu mnt 139b-14, 11317 Tallinn, Estonia, hello@eucompliancepartner.com; www.eucompliancepartner.com

9 8 7 6 5 4 3 2 1

PRAISE FOR SARAH J. DALEY

Abandon ennui, all who enter here and descend into the hellish, lyrical delights of The Violently Departed *– half literary epic, half thriller, entirely a masterpiece!*
Patricia A. Jackson, author of *Forging A Nightmare*

With charming wit and masterful craft, Sarah J. Daley presents your new favorite half-demon detective Hero Viridian, a uniquely complex and ferocious character I'd follow to Hell and back. Atmospheric prose, seamless worldbuilding, and clever, buddy-cop hijinks make The Violently Departed *a fast-paced fun and darkly delightful read."*
Salinee Goldenberg, author of *Way of the Walker*

In The Violently Departed, *Sarah J. Daley has constructed yet another world I want to visit populated by characters I'm not sure I should hug, shake, chat up, or flee. It's wonderfully confusing!*
R.W.W. Greene, *Mercury Retrograde*

A murder mystery with small town secrets, demons and demon hunters, and gentle commentary on class and prejudice: this one is a real page-turner. The reader is swept along by Daley's silky-smooth prose, and by the time I got to the breathless conclusion, I realized I'd been up all night. Yes, it's one of those. Captivating.
Khan Wong, author of *The Circus Infinite* and *Down in the Sea of Angels*

"A fantastic, blood-curdled howl of a book. I would follow Hero Viridian into whatever dim doorway she led me to and walk into the dark with a smile on my face. A refreshing, heavy metal tour-de-force. A barnstorming pandemonium of devils, bar-fights, and battle-nuns, but above all, a hell of a good time."
S.K. Horton, author of *Gorse* and *Ragwort*

What a blast! I raced through this book, gripped by the dark mystery at its heart and its cast of compelling characters. With humour, pathos, and not a little arson, The Violently Departed *is a spellbinding whodunnit filled with twists, turns, and infernal machinations.*
M.K. Hardy author of *The Needfire*

A curious case of brilliance in Sarah J. Daley's latest adventure, that's equal parts Sherlock Holmes and Constantine, propelling you into a grim, witty, thrilling mystery as a demonic inspector and a blunderbuss-wielding demon hunter team up to investigate a most unholy murder. It's so much fun, there will be Hell to pay if we don't see more Hero and Keen in the future!
Dan Hanks, author of *Swashbucklers* and *The Way Up Is Death*

If David Lynch was given a season of Supernatural *to play with, you'd get something close to* The Violently Departed. *Gloriously macabre, wonderfully off-kilter, endlessly entertaining – you won't forget the rampant genius of Sarah J. Daley easily.*
David Green, BFSA Award-nominated author of the Empire in Ruin series, Hell in Haven (The Holleran Files) series and *Magic, Maps and Mischief*

The Violently Departed *by Sarah J. Daley is a gory delight of a genre mash-up. Daley's effortless prose keeps the tension up from the first page to the last in this demonic police procedural-meets-murder mystery. In a world where demons not only walk the earth, but leave demon-blooded babies in their wake, the atmosphere of prejudice and fear pervades all. Clever, entertaining and imaginative, this was a wholly enjoyable read.*
Gabriela Houston, author of
Binding the Cuckoo, The Second Bell and *The Bone Roots*

A fast-paced, stylish crime thriller stabbing into the heart of a vicious dark academia.
Cameron Johnston, author of *First Mage On The Moon*

For Fat Steve, the best boy, departed too soon

CHAPTER ONE

Blood painted the walls. Great, vibrant swaths of crimson. The blood spoke to her, an epic poem of violence. Of murder. Hero touched her tongue to the back of her teeth, sucking in a shallow breath. The air held the bitter tang of copper. Luckily, the tastes and smells lacked the rancid foulness of decomposition. There was still time to Speak with the recently departed spirits. One of them might know the answers she'd been called upon to find.

She moved deeper into the house, a multi-storied affair in a prestigious neighborhood known for its fancy dwellings and wealthy families. A family of five lived here. *Had* lived here. Three of them were dead on the floor – the mother, the father, and the eleven-year-old daughter. A fourth victim, the teenaged son, was in the sanatorium barely clinging to life while the fifth member of the family, the eldest daughter, wept outside with a trio of peacekeepers holding back the curious public. The girl had returned from a trip to visit her grandmother only to discover her entire family slaughtered. Shocked and grief-ravaged, she would be questioned thoroughly once she'd calmed down. Hero had given her a glance as she'd entered the domicile. The hysteria had seemed genuine.

So far there were no suspects, and the peacekeepers were at a loss. This was a good neighborhood. Nothing had been stolen, which should have been the first logical expectation – a robbery turned foul. But to Hero, at least, the violence told a different story. She trod carefully on the fancy woven rug, worth more than she made in a year, then stepped around a tipped ottoman, scattered cushions and spilled lamps. Blood had soaked into the rug and she crouched by it, sniffing deeply. Everything was cast in a haze of softness by her green-tinted, wire-framed glasses, and she slid them down to the tip of her nose to get a clear look.

The other peacekeepers in the room shifted uncomfortably as they observed her at work. With her glasses concealing the color of her eyes, they could at least pretend she was fully human, but once those green-tinted spectacles were lowered, her true nature was undeniable. A softly muttered prayer slipped from one of the PKs, and Hero wrinkled her nose. She knew what they thought of death speakers, her especially. The demented nun. Demon sister. Cursed half-demon arsonist.

Perhaps they'd hoped she would come in, wave a hand, immediately announce the identity of the killer, then politely piss off? It wasn't quite that easy. But it had been just one killer here; she already knew that by the feel of the place, the echoes left behind. Her demon half could sense evil intent like a hound smelled a fox. Evil intent smelled delicious. And the person who'd killed this family had been motivated by selfishness and lust, traces of which hung in the air as clearly as the blood painted the walls.

"Sister Viridian," said one of the peacekeepers, a young, uniformed bloke with narrow eyes and a baby face. "Have you found any answers? The captain said..." He let his words trail off, stuttering into silence when she turned her gaze upon him. That baby face took on a pasty hue and she smiled, letting her slightly elongated canines touch her lower lip. They weren't exactly fangs, but they weren't *not* fangs either. A look from her had that effect on people. No one cared to be under the scrutiny of a red-eyed she-devil.

"Inspector," she said. "Inspector Viridian."

The man blinked and removed his custodian helmet as if she were a lady he was courting. He bowed. "My apologies."

"And your captain will get his answers right after I do."

"Yes, yes, of course, Inspector Viridian."

Without the shield of her glasses, she could see the room, as well as everything and everyone in it, far better. The blood and corpses screamed their story in a glance. The murders had been carried out by a single individual. A surprise attack. The father had been stabbed in the heart while he slept on the sofa – the pink velvet cushions were sprayed with blood. The mother had been ambushed from behind, her throat slit, as she'd sat at her sewing machine in the corner, and the middle-aged woman was now slumped over it, the dress she'd been mending soaked in her blood. Her foot still rested on the pedal.

Hero stood, moving to the third victim. The child. She had fought back, and it was mostly her blood painting the walls. It was clear where she had stumbled over the footstool while trying to flee. Hero didn't even need to Speak with the girl's spirit before deducing the cause of her demise. Defensive wounds on the girl's hands indicated the violence of her death, but it was the righteous anger searing Hero's eyes which revealed the truth. She had fought, both angry and terrified at the unexpected attack. The terror was over now, but the rage remained.

"The boy, the one who survived," she said, straightening to turn to the peacekeeper in charge – an older woman, trim and proper in her deep-blue uniform, a nightstick at her belt and a saber on her hip. Standard issue. "What is his condition?"

The woman, unfazed by Hero's blood-red gaze, cleared her throat before answering. "Beaten bloody, Inspector. Stabbed eight or nine times. He fought like a wildcat from what we can tell."

So. The boy and girl had managed to fight. Good. Though how the boy had survived, Hero had no idea. The will to live had to be strong in that one.

The authorities could have waited and questioned him when he awoke, but most seemed certain he never would. And you couldn't have an entire family laid waste and not bring a suspect to judgement. Not in Evergreen Heights. Important people lived here. Rich people. Doctors, barristers, judges and police chiefs. Bishops and politicians. Titans of industry.

Bloviating assholes, in Hero's opinion. The absolute dregs of society. But these were the neighborhoods where her talents were put to most use. When someone was murdered here, the city actually gave a shit.

"Hmm. The boy and the girl managed to fight back. Poor planning on the part of the murderer, I'd say. Left a mess behind, which makes it that much easier for me, praise the Goddess."

The peacekeeper – Bresnahan? Brennan? – rubbed her chin and cast her eyes around the room, looking uncomfortable at Hero's comment, the predatory gleefulness of it. The "mess" was a room full of corpses and blood-splattered walls. The PKs had wanted to move the bodies, take them to the morgue, but Hero had forbidden it. Spirits tended to linger near their old shells – for a time, at least; you had to get them fresh. Why call her at all if they wanted to do things the old-fashioned way, with forensics and questioning of the living and all of that nonsense? She was trained for such work – a condition of her service – but her peculiar skills were innate, even if it was her demon blood which gave her the power and not the Goddess Infinite or her Branch.

Death speakers were rare, of course, and their abilities varied. Some could barely get a word out of the dead, or none at all, only sensations or echoes or vibes. Being half demon and not just possessing a little demon blood somewhere in your ancestral lines, like so many posers out there, made Hero special.

So special, in fact, that her own mother had tried to gouge her eyes out when she was a defenseless child. Again and again. No one liked looking into those swirling crimson flames which passed for irises, especially the woman who'd been raped by a roving incubus and given birth to a half-demon monster.

Hero remembered every one of those incidents vividly – the fear, the pain, the healing. Her eyes always grew back, like obnoxious weeds, sending her mother into fits of rage and driving her father to drunken benders. Such a lovely family. The attacks stopped only when she was old enough and big enough to fight back. She didn't have to fight for long. The day after she punched her mother in the jaw and broke it, she was sent to the abbey two towns over. Out of sight and out of mind.

Hero went to the dead girl first, ignoring the two adults, whose deaths had been shocking, certainly, but not terribly traumatic. Their spirits milled about in a fog of confusion, half believing they still lived, judging by their futile attempts to talk to the peacekeepers crowding their fine parlor. When had they ever let so many commoners into their gilt-edged, rosewood-furnished, velvet-wallpapered abode? Was this some charity event?

An errant whisper from the father distracted her from the slaughtered girl. A mention of a "dirty-necked boy daring to think he might be good enough."

Hero's ears pricked up even as she prepared to open the Gate to the Underworld and Commune with the girl's shade. Did the father's stray comment bear some meaning? Was there a clue in his words? To the identity of the murderer, perhaps? She would know more once she reached the Land of the Dead. Righting the overturned foot stool, Hero took a seat and prepared to hear what the dead had to say.

"I need silence," she ordered the officers processing the crime scene. Her words were hard, clipped. "Disturb me and don't be shocked when Hell pays a visit."

It was best to invoke Hell when seeking compliance; the Underworld, even the Land of the Dead, didn't inspire dread the way mention of Hell did. Most of the living envisioned a land of eternal suffering, fire and brimstone and tortured spirits. In fact, that wasn't far from the truth – the flames and brimstone, anyway – but Hell was merely a passageway for most shades on their way to their final rest. The only real threat in Hell was demonic in nature, and she tended to avoid Pandemonium if she could help it. No need to poke the hornets' nest.

The shuffling steps and murmured conversations ceased. A wise bunch, these particular peacekeepers. Hero settled her cane across her knees, straightened her scapular and removed her glasses entirely. She focused on the dead girl's body and called upon the fires of Hell.

PK Commander Tyka Brennan watched the death speaker at work with a sick feeling in the pit of her stomach. Demons were evil, pure and simple, an affront to Creation and the enemies of the Goddess Infinite. Yet here one sat, communing with the victim. Disturbing the dead, more like. Forcing a child to relive the worst thing that had ever happened to her. And all she herself could do, a decorated commander and skilled investigator, was stand in mute witness to the travesty.

The half-demon was so obviously not *one of us*, Tyka wondered how she managed to walk down the street without being accosted, spit upon or punched, or what have you. What was one supposed to do to walking evil? Cast a few warding signs in her direction? Call a priest?

Though her face was unlined, the inspector's hair was pure silver, wrapped into a sleek chignon at the base of her narrow skull. And she was tall, too tall for a proper woman. Lanky like a lad, almost sinewy. She moved like she had no bones. Smooth like a serpent. Her skin had a porcelain cast to it, an alien paleness. It made Tyka's skin crawl – proper skin, skin with tones of pink and brown, skin with flaws. Real skin, not a facsimile.

Tyka could have overlooked all of that, if the half-demon speaker had at least acted human, but her supercilious attitude, her strange enjoyment of blood and death, and her manner of dress brought out a deep hatred, a natural hatred of an *other* – an other who chose to mock religion and comport herself in a sacrilegious way. She dressed like a Celestial nun, or some twisted version of one, in a simple cream-colored shirt under a long scapular paired with wide, flowing pants gathered at the ankles. All in shades of emerald, cobalt and ivory rather than the canonical white, black and crimson. It was an odd mishmash of fashion that set her apart as much as her strange hair, physique and – blessed Branch – her eyes. Her Goddess-cursed eyes of crimson flame.

I would have gouged them out, too, if my child had such eyes.

The mother never faced charges for her cruelty, Tyka knew, and she understood why. Most mothers would have killed a demon-bred child. Most *decent* mothers. What she should have faced charges over was shipping the girl-child off to an abbey, her eyes covered as if she were merely blind and not a devil incarnate. Those poor nuns raised the girl in the faith, gave her a good home, a roof and food and education, trained her as a heavenly Shield of their finest battle order, only to discover her demon half by accident. Only to have their abbey burned to the ground.

For that, Death Speaker Hero Viridian had served ten years in prison.

And now she works for us. As a damnable inspector, no less.

PK Commander Tyka Brennan had never been able to pass the qualifying test to be raised to an inspector.

Not that she was bitter about it.

Her nose had an itch, but Tyka didn't move. She wanted to – oh, how she did, to shift a bit and run a hand across her face. As much as she disliked the inspector, she also had a healthy respect for her ability. When Hero Viridian warned you about Hell, you'd be a fool not to listen. Who would know best about Hell but a disgraced, half-demon ex-nun?

The air had a subtle tension to it around the speaker. She herself was absolutely still, holding on to the cane across her knees – it hid a slim sword; Tyka had seen such covert weapons before – and staring at the dead body. A lurid light shone from her creepy eyeballs and the tip of her tongue protruded from between her red, red lips like a cat's. The moment, the silence, the tension stretched, grew rigid, then snapped.

Hero smiled, her fangs on full display, and Tyka thought they might have gotten longer. The inspector turned to her, and Tyka shifted at last, scraping at her itchy nose while she gave a quick, respectful bob of her head. The other PKs around her shuffled and sighed, as relieved as Tyka was to be given their freedom back – and relieved that the ex-nun had turned her cursed eyes on Tyka and not them.

"Send in the survivor," she said, sounding satisfied and eager all at once. "I need to talk with her a bit."

"The other daughter?" Tyka exclaimed. "Why, she's quite traumatized, Inspector."

Hero chuckled and rose to her feet, unwinding with feline grace. She stretched her arms above her head, her cane held high, as if she'd just woken, then collapsed back into a normal stance and leaned on her cane. "Yes, I imagine plotting to have your entire family slaughtered will traumatize a girl. Send her to me. And start looking for her friend, James Durram. He'll be trying to get rid of a bloody knife, I suspect."

Murmurs of doubt and surprise erupted from her fellows, but none of them were looking into the woman's damnable eyes. Tyka was. She saw the truth writ large within them. Her lips pressed together and she nodded sharply. "As you command, Inspector." She turned to an underling. "PK Gris, bring the girl inside. Now."

CHAPTER TWO

The eldest daughter, sixteen-year-old Claudia Coffee, broke quickly once Hero confronted her. Her own little sister had recognized the boy she'd sent to kill them, a ne'er-do-well of dubious upbringing but with fine black hair and a charming smile – the boy Claudia loved with all her heart yet was forbidden to even see, let alone marry. Though he'd been dressed in stiff new clothes, his face hidden by a mask and his telltale hair tucked under a knit cap, the little girl had known him by his blue eyes – cold and crystal, peering at her with pure malice from a face blackened with coal powder.

He'd done a good job with his killing. He'd left no clues – no fingerprints, no shoeprints, no hair or blood scattered at the scene, and the knife was gone before the peacekeepers apprehended him. The new clothes, too. Every trace of evidence had been removed. The boy who'd survived the attack might have been a witness, had he lived, but Hero learned after dealing with the guilty daughter that he hadn't survived after all, succumbing to his wounds and shock – a shame, but not really important. She'd found the killer through the dead, not via witnesses.

There were no thanks after she was done with the daughter. The weeping confession, the claims she was "forced into it" by her beloved – Hero cared nothing about any of that. As far as she was concerned, her part was done. She didn't need to know the why, only the who. Let the barristers sort it out. For her, it was back to the station.

"Another case solved. Very good, Inspector. Yet again, you've earned your keep."

Her keep. Hero kept her face carefully composed. Captain Culpepper hadn't just called her into his office to congratulate her. He was reminding her that she owed him. He was the one who'd given her this job, this chance. What other jailbird left prison to land a cushy job with the Inspectorate Division of the peacekeepers of the Realm? Most paroled prisoners were lucky to scrape by begging on the streets. Many returned to their lives of crime or left the area completely to start anew elsewhere. Hero did not have that option. It was hard to hide eyes made of fire, and she had grown tired of being hunted.

"My pleasure, Captain," she said, tapping the brim of her dainty top hat with her cane and giving him a fangless grin. "It wasn't a difficult case."

"Right. No evidence, dead witnesses. A grieving daughter of upstanding character." He returned her grin, an edge to his. Culpepper didn't like it when she was modest. He considered her abilities a skill like any other, one she'd cultivated through hard work and practice. A skill *he* had recognized before anyone else.

He'd been the one who'd brought her into the fold in the first place. He never liked to think he might have made a mistake giving a remorseless arsonist a second chance. But it wasn't really that great a risk; they both knew the truth of why she had started that fire. Deep down, he loved her for it. Constrained by his position, by the law, by life, he would never have been free to do the same. A half-demon pariah, on the other hand... What did she have to lose?

"It wouldn't have been the first time someone of means managed to get away with murder," he said, reaching for a scroll from the pile atop his worn desk. Cases upon cases, all needing inspectors. Only a select few would be tempting enough to unleash Hero. The one in his hands was brand new, the parchment blazing clean but the seal broken – which meant he'd read it – and it was important enough for her attention.

Culpepper held it almost reverently, peering at the crest embedded in the bits of broken wax. Hero couldn't quite make it out.

"You got another for me?" she asked politely, her ears pricking with the possibility of something grand, something challenging. Her skills were impressive, and she liked using them. Opening the Gate to the Underworld gave her a high she never stopped chasing. The flames filled her with power, made her feel alive – ironic in the halls of the dead, maybe. Even more, Speaking with the dead was titillating, their lives and souls laid bare to Hero. Rooting out their secrets, witnessing their last moments on earth, tracking them through the fiery corridors of that chaotic place, skirting the Spheres – especially Pandemonium, where her kin slavered to possess their wayward daughter – affirmed her very existence. She was meant for this.

"I might," Culpepper admitted. His craggy forehead deepened into canyons, sending his bushy brows dipping toward his nose. She didn't understand his reluctance; the captain enjoyed a good case as much as she did, the more gruesome the better. "It sounds like they desperately need a death speaker. They have suspicions, maybe a few suspects, but not much else."

Hero dropped into a rolling chair across the desk from him and spun in a circle using her cane as thrust. "Tell me." She faced him, then rolled again. By the time she turned back around, he had the scroll open.

"A young woman went missing for six days," he began, peering at the document, scanning its contents. "They found her in the woods in pristine condition, as in no insect activity or animal predation or other signs of decomp. Nude. Ligature marks on her neck, possibly. No defensive wounds. Some signs of trauma, but no fluids left behind."

Hero hissed low. She knew what he meant by *trauma*. "So, rape, strangulation, then a body dump." She shrugged, tapping her cane rhythmically against the floorboards. "This sort of case isn't difficult. She'll most likely have known her attacker."

"Her tongue was removed."

A twist. Lovely. "So, rape, strangulation, and a message. Makes it even easier. I'll be in and out in a day. Where am I going?"

"Don't be so quick, Hero. There's more you need to know."

"So tell me. I haven't got all day."

He grunted, amused. "Where else do you have to go?"

Another spin, this one to hide her annoyance. Just when she thought they were friends, he reminded her she was property. No, she had nowhere to go but to her little dormer room two streets over. Maybe to the tavern for a drink or two. Either way, she couldn't go far. She was at their beck and call, waiting to be summoned. Her chains might be invisible now, but they were there, nonetheless.

Better than prison, by a far pace.

"The young woman is a nun," he said when she was facing him again.

Abruptly, she stopped spinning. Her body tensed. She didn't like nuns, seeing as she'd been raised by them.

And she'd thought her mother had been cruel.

"She was a teacher," he continued, staring at her intently, trying to read her face. *Good luck with that.* Her bright eyes were dimmed by her tinted, wire-rimmed glasses and she kept her pale skin smooth, expressionless.

"Where?" she prompted.

"At the Archbishop Clementine Preparatory School of Excellence."

Her cane thumped heavily against the floor but otherwise she revealed nothing of her inner turmoil. "The one in Havenside," she said flatly. "Or is there some other school with the same pompous designation?"

"No, that's the one. I knew you'd have a problem with this. And not just because a Celestial nun of the Shield is involved."

"And why would I have a problem? A case is a case, right?" *Whether or not it involves my former order.* "It'll be quick." She twirled her cane, feeling her lips curve into a frown. It was an entirely human reaction, and she hated it. She had tried to blend in over the years, at home, at Blackstone Abbey – everywhere. Forcing smiles, laughter, tears – reactions she thought would be normal, human. At most, she'd merely made people uncomfortable. Her attempts to subsume her demon half only made her strangeness more glaring. In prison she had rolled into her heritage, her otherness, and the inmates had respected her true nature, its power, its strange beauty. In a tangle of misfits, she'd found her place. Now, she preferred to keep her humanity in check.

"They wouldn't have called for a speaker if this was a simple case, Inspector." He shook the scroll at her. "This letter indicates they suspect something foul at work, some deeper evil beyond a ravaging murderer. There are layers to this case. Secrets."

Havenside was full of secrets. Full of family, too, which was why she wanted nothing to do with it. *She* hadn't been allowed to attend the most prestigious school in town. *She* hadn't been welcomed into the inner circles of the wealthy and privileged, despite her father being a barrister of some renown. (Well, he hadn't been her real father, had he?) *She* hadn't got a debutante ball or invitations to yacht-club regattas. People in Havenside had given her rude gestures to ward off the evil eye, and their spit when she passed them on the street.

"Who sent the letter?" she asked, and couldn't help holding her breath as she waited for the answer. Her brother wouldn't have sent it, she was sure, although once they had been close.

"Their chief peacekeeper, Roger Dewey. He's a friend of mine. We went to the Academy together." He scanned down the scroll once more, his eyes skittering back and forth across the words. "He's sharp, ole Dewey. Sharp enough to know when he's outmatched. Havenside is a cushy job. Not much happens there, you know. Not like here."

"So, maybe he's seeing conspiracies and mysteries where none exist?" It would be an easy job, she told herself firmly. In and out. A little chat with a dead nun and she could be on her way. "Bored police get that way, I've heard."

"I wouldn't know," he said wryly. "Nevertheless, we can't say no to them. Havenside has gone through the proper channels, greased the right palms, so to say. The body was found only a day ago, so Speaking to the shade should be easy. And at the moment, since you resolved our last case so quickly and thoroughly, you are free to take on something new."

"Efficiency returns to bite me in the ass," she muttered. Her gaze wandered to the lone, greasy window behind Culpepper's head which looked out on a blank brick wall. They were on the ninth floor. From the roof it was quite the view, but from the captain's office they might as well have been underground. Still, she loved the city. The vibrancy of it. The vastness and complexity. The filth. So much life in one place, so many souls and spirits. It was almost like walking the halls of Hell.

Havenside, on the other hand, was a collection of lovely, gargantuan homes on tree-lined streets, a pretentious town square of frou-frou boutiques and upscale bistros and taverns, green swards and open parks, seaside piers and a harbor containing the toys of the rich. Peaceful, quiet, wealthy. Cruel. She would be exposed in Havenside, no longer one of the crowd but a standout, a stranger. Worse, a stranger daring to return to the place she'd once called home.

Culpepper let her stew in her thoughts for a long moment, but she knew that even he had his limits, and she was only one of many inspectors awaiting assignments. None of them had much choice, either. What made her special?

I am a speaker. That's what.

"So," he said – a demand, not a request.

She considered rebellion. What could he do? Drop her in solitary? Clap her in leg irons? Give her a lashing in the yard? No, despite her criminal past, despite her current enslavement to the Realm, she still had choices. Refusing a case would get her suspended for a bit, maybe, sent to do a beat walk, or something odious like transcribing, but nothing worse than a slap on the wrist. She had choices. Why expose herself to something as hateful as going home?

"What was her name?" she asked.

"Sister Catarine Cisco."

A sister. A nun. She sighed. "How old?"

"Twenty-two."

Another sigh.

"And who does this Dewey think killed her? And why?"

"He doesn't know. That's the issue."

"What makes her so special?"

"Here." He tossed the scroll across the desk. It slithered toward her, and Hero snatched it up reflexively. "Read the letter."

Hero did as he asked, then read it again. Her ruby lips pursed. Now she knew why Culpepper wanted her to take the case. "Book me a train," she said, then rolled the scroll up into a tight tube and tucked it beneath her cobalt scapular. She cast him an accusatory glare. "You buried the lede."

"Did I?" His bushy brows rose in surprise, but she saw right through him and scoffed.

"This has the stink of demons about it, Chief. I'm not the best inspector for this job; I'm the only one."

CHAPTER THREE

Demonhunter Oleander Keen adjusted his spanking new jacket, making sure to center the line of brass buttons and keep his bright sash perfectly level around his slim waist. He cut a fine figure, he decided as he observed himself in the looking glass, freshly washed, his dark hair slicked to his scalp in a proper soldier's cut – the sides shaved short, the top rakishly long – his navy coat spotless, gingham trousers tucked in his high, black boots but bloused just the right amount. A shining saber rested at one hip, a blunderbuss at the other, the brass fittings polished to mirror brightness. Both looked brand new, though the saber had been put through its paces. He was no dandy, untried or untested, no demonhunter in name only. He'd faced more than one – many more. Demons didn't frighten him, not First Rank DH Keen.

"Oh, look at you, my brave boy! Such a dashing young officer!"

His mother's excited utterance brought a shade of rose to his high cheeks. He spun away from the mirror, nearly knocking into it with his saber before adjusting his belt to hide his embarrassment. Of course, his mother would catch him mooning over himself in the mirror. She was always about. Always concerned for him. Always underfoot in her worry.

It's her house. Guilt tempered his embarrassment, and he swallowed the annoyed retort he felt on his tongue. Mrs Keen did not truck with any backtalk.

First Rank DH Keen did not fear demons, but he had a healthy respect for his mother.

His assignment to Havenside had been so rushed and unexpected he'd had no choice but to stay with her. He couldn't afford to live anywhere else in the city on his pay grade, and by the Branch he'd tried to find a place in the few hours' head start he'd been given. Alas, returning home had been his best option. Maybe next year he'd be able to afford a place of his own – if he remained assigned to Havenside, of course. Demonhunters went where they were called, fulfilling their noble duty.

"Come have breakfast, Boo," his mother said, giving him a little wave as she turned and headed down the hall. "Can't have you hungry on your first day. Ack, can you imagine having a growling stomach in front of all those tough PKs?"

"All right, Mother. I'll be right down."

"You'd better! Don't want you to be late because you spent all morning fussing with your outfit like some debutante on the way to a cotillion."

Oleander sighed, but he took one last look at himself before following her. In a way, he felt like a debutante, about to be presented to polite society, to the real world. This was his first official job since leaving the Citadel. His first assignment not as a cadet, but as an officer. He wanted to be proud; he deserved to be proud. Even to be a little full of himself.

It would be a lot easier if he weren't living in his boyhood home, the papered walls and carpeted steps worn and familiar, the rooms looking smaller than he remembered, crowded with pictures and secondhand furniture, thick with memories both good and bad: a doting mother, a grim and distant father forever angry and stressed, always struggling to pay the bills, to put food on the table, reeking of gin.

Oleander Keen had always wanted more than this. Even as a child, he'd known his house was smaller than the houses of his school chums. His house was nowhere near the ocean, with its pleasant breezes and popular beaches. His house sat on the wrong side of the railroad tracks. His neighborhood had long ago been dubbed "Otherside". He was set apart always by circumstances, by location, by birth.

Nevertheless, peacekeepers did well for themselves sometimes, so it was his hope he would too. One day.

His mother had laid out a feast for him: grits and biscuits, thick slabs of bacon, fried eggs and hot tea. He grimaced, both repulsed by the sight of so much food and tempted by it. The aromas tickled his nose and set his mouth to watering. He tugged at his sash, tightening it. He'd earned his trim figure through hard work and privation. Spurred by the cruelty of his classmates at Clem Prep, he'd fought to shed his soft layers and reveal the athlete beneath. His mother had never understood why he'd suddenly hated her cooking.

"I usually eat a slice of toast and have a cup of black coffee, Mama," he said, dithering beside the kitchen table, the same one he'd sat at as a boy, his hand on the back of a wooden chair with uneven legs and a creaky seat. He dithered because, Goddess damn him, he wanted to *eat*.

"Nonsense." She moved about the tiny kitchen, putting eggs and raw bacon back into the ice box, stacking dirty pots by a sink full of steaming soapy water. Efficient in her efforts, bustling happily. She'd been smiling since he'd appeared on her doorstep the night before, orders in one hand and a rucksack over his shoulder. She'd been living here alone for nearly a decade now. Tall and rangy like him, her silver-shot hair in a high ponytail, wearing a house dress he recognized and the apron he'd given her for one of her birthdays, she looked no different than he remembered but for a few more lines around her eyes and mouth. She hadn't changed. Nothing had changed. Just him.

"I can't send my only child off on his first day of work without a full belly," she scolded him gently, then came to the table and pulled out his chair. "Sit. Eat. Enjoy a good meal. I know the Citadel makes you all live on scraps."

Oleander found he couldn't disobey a direct order from his mother. He sat. He ate. And it was as glorious as it smelled.

Which was why when he stood before his new chief for the first time, it was with a belly fit to burst through his smartly tied sash.

"First Rank DH Oleander Keen." The chief was reading through Oleander's orders and sounded both curt and vaguely pleased. "You're from Havenside?" he added after scanning the rest of the papers, his eyebrows lifting.

"I am, sir." He clicked his heels together at attention. "Grew up in Otherside."

"Ah, a townie," the chief murmured in an offhand sort of way, not registering the insult. Luckily, Oleander didn't need to hide how the term made him stiffen as he was already at attention. His stomach gurgled unpleasantly.

Chief Roger Dewey was a relatively young man to have achieved such a high rank, his short hair still dark brown, his shoulders firm and square, his belly flat and his chest full. Here was a man Oleander could proudly serve.

"You went to Clementine Prep?" It was somewhere between a question and a statement. There was doubt in his tone as he peered at him, but also a hopeful lift, as if it would please him to know Oleander went to Havenside's most prestigious school. Even if he was a townie.

"I did, sir." Oleander understood his doubt. Most students went on to become barristers or surgeons or businessmen, not PKs, even elite PKs like demonhunters. But university had been out of reach for the likes of him, even with a degree from Clem. The Citadel, however, had been a viable path. "I attended under a scholarship," he added, feeling the explanation was necessary even though it filled him with vague shame. But why should he be ashamed? He'd earned that fucking scholarship, every cursed coin.

"You must be quite clever."

"I did well at my studies, yes, Chief."

Dewey grunted. He tossed the orders onto his pristine desktop. The varnished wood sparkled in the sunlight from the leaded windows looking out over main street. Carriages and horses passed by below, orderly and polite. Like all of Havenside. Even the rougher districts like Otherside exuded a certain charm with its clapboard houses and tree-lined avenues, peeling paint and crumbling curbs notwithstanding.

"Well, I need a clever DH right now," Dewey said. "Which is why I requested one, among other things. You've heard about the missing sister, I'll assume."

"I have, of course. A terrible business."

"She's been found."

Oleander blinked, inferring immediately from the chief's grim tone that this was not a happy thing. And he'd been specifically requested? A demonhunter was not often sent to such a peaceful town, and he'd been wondering at his assignment. For a while, he'd thought it a sick sort of joke, or even a punishment, sending him to the hometown he'd fled – a quiet place ill-suited for an ambitious demonhunter – but now he understood. "Murdered, I presume. You suspect a demon had a hand in her death?"

Dewey pushed back in his chair and stood. "Sorry you won't have much of an orientation, DH Keen, but this case takes utmost priority. If a demon is involved, as I suspect, we cannot let it lie. Once an incursion gets a foothold in a place like Havenside, it's almost impossible to root it out."

Oleander nodded, still processing his circumstances when the chief blew past him and out of the office. He scrambled after him, catching up to him in the bullpen, crowded with uniformed PKs and secretaries in civilian dress manning desks and clacking on noisy, newfangled print machines. Havenside might be a sleepy town, but it was rich, and money bought all sorts of advancements.

"I've dealt with incursions before," he said, matching the chief's long strides, though it took some effort. Damn his full belly. He ignored the ache at his belt. "In Fairview. Rooted out a nest of serpentines under a basilica. They had the bishop there in thrall to them. Nasty piece of business, I can tell you."

"Yes, well, can't say we've had much demon trouble here. But I did the required supplementals at the Citadel, so I recognize the signs."

Oleander held his tongue, reserving judgement. Sometimes people saw demons where none existed, afraid of every bump in the night or every shadow in the corner. Confusing normal human depravity with demonic activity was often the case, too, and a dead nun – a murdered nun – might prompt those unused to regular human fiends to see something supernatural in the death. He would be able to assess the truth quickly enough. In his sharp-looking sash, and in the bandolier across his chest, were stashed vials and potions vital to his work, and his own instincts had been honed to razor sharpness. If any demon had touched the dead woman, he would know.

And if any human was in thrall to demons, he would know soon enough through rigorous questioning and examination. First Rank DH Oleander Keen knew how to do his job.

Chief Dewey led him down a flight of narrow stairs at the end of a hallway lined with interrogation rooms, down into the cool depths of the building. Moisture glistened on the exposed brick walls. Oleander's hackles rose, along with a bitter taste of bile as the contents of his stomach did a little dance. Morgues were cold and grim places, sterilized and detached. Better to deal with the corpses out in the open air, raw and real. Even the most brutal of crime scenes was preferable to the chill finality of the morgue.

"Just to warn you," Dewey said when they reached a door at the end of a long, ill-lit hallway, "you aren't the only one I've called in to deal with this case. Like I said, we are making this our top priority. The entire town is on edge. Women are afraid to leave their homes. The Highborn and the more affluent of our citizens are demanding action. Demanding answers."

Oleander nodded, more distracted by his gurgling stomach than anything Dewey was saying. Goddess, you'd think he'd eaten rotten meat the way his body was reacting, not good bacon, eggs and grits.

Impatient to get this over with, he gestured at the chief – rather brusquely, he'd reflect upon later – to open the blasted door, grimacing at the rising sick he had to swallow. Was it nerves? He felt some stress since this was his first assignment, but he didn't consider himself a particularly high-strung man. There was something in the air, some strange rankness he couldn't place. It wasn't the proximity of dead bodies. The corpses were kept in iceboxes. There was no rot in PK morgues.

The room beyond the door was an examination room, a vast chamber with tables and medical equipment, a bank of coolers stretching along one wall with rows of innocuous latched doors no bigger than the one to Ma's icebox at home. It was shadowed in the far reaches, tables and instruments draped in sheets to keep off dust. Gas lamps blazed closer to the door, illuminating the immediate area, which contained a desk and wooden filing cabinets.

A person sat at the desk, or on it. Lounging, really, while they spun a sleek cane of ebony and silver. A woman, by appearance. Slim and tall, hair as silver as the clouds slicked tight to a narrow skull. She wore peculiar garb, a cream shirt with flared sleeves under a dark blue scapular and trousers that looked wide enough to be skirts, shimmering in a lovely emerald flecked with gold. The outfit tugged at his recollection. Then it hit him – the stranger's outfit was a mockery of a Celestial nun's.

First Rank DH Oleander Keen made these observations – the strange woman, the clothes, the shrouded equipment, the lamps, the desk, the bank of coolers – in the space of a breath. His gut flared angrily, and he understood at last that it wasn't mere indigestion plaguing him. He cursed himself even as he began to move, to leap and spin, his saber whispering from its scabbard, aimed for the stranger's neck.

To kill a demon, one had to act fast and act first. Removing the head was the best way to start.

Demonhunters spent years honing their skills, their art. It was a calling that required training almost as intense as that needed to join a religious order. Your first and most important duty was to protect humankind from demonic influence. Only a skilled demonhunter could spot demons through their glamour.

This one hadn't even bothered to mask her demonic heritage. How had Chief Dewey not seen it himself?

A clang of steel against steel. The woman had barely moved, but she'd stopped his saber with her cane, to his great shock.

No, not the cane, but the slim sword hidden within it. She'd drawn and parried preternaturally fast.

The impact shuddered up his arm, into his shoulder. Immediately, he drew back and countered with a backhand swing. She parried effortlessly, showing her bright teeth at his useless efforts. His eyes met hers through green-colored lenses as their blades met again – demon eyes behind a thin shield of tinted glass. A pathetic attempt to appear normal. He sneered at her, and she landed a blow on his hip with the ebony half of her sword before shoving him back with it.

They faced off, and Oleander was vaguely aware of Dewey calling for them to cease their foolishness, but instinct and training drove him. His saber danced toward the woman, keeping her occupied while he slipped his other hand into his sash for a potion. An acid bomb would slow her down–

"Now, now," she said, sounding irritated. Her teeth grew into fangs, and her sword-and-cane combo spun at him with lethal intent. "None of that nonsense."

Her cane struck his elbow even as she countered his sleek saber with her blade. His hand went numb and he lost his grip on the glass vial in his sash. The demon-woman disarmed him with a twirl of her blade, sweeping a leg from beneath him at the same time.

First Rank DH Oleander Keen found himself on his right hip on the cold tile floor, his saber spinning away beneath a nearby exam table. A needle-thin blade hovered between his brows, so close that looking at it made him cross-eyed. His gaze traveled up the exquisite steel, swirling with the markings of the finest blademasters, to find the demon-woman staring down at him, looking consternated but unruffled.

"This is Inspector Hero Viridian," Dewey proclaimed with peak exasperation, red-faced and flustered. "She is a level-one death speaker from New Savage City. She is here at my request, DH Keen!"

Hero Viridian. He knew the name. Everyone knew the name. As many rumors as leaves on the trees surrounded her, the half-demon disgraced nun turned death speaker. Some claimed she was full demon and tricking all of them. Others thought she was barely clinging to sanity and would snap and commit rampant violence one day. Speculations about her speed and strength and her uncanny nature were popular topics among the peacekeepers of the Realm. Everyone was curious about the former nun who'd hidden her demonic nature from her order, tried to murder a priest of the Branch, then spent ten years in the pen for burning down her abbey.

"A little warning would have been nice," Oleander snapped at his new chief, too flustered to be politic. "You do know what I am, what I do, don't you?"

"Relax, kid," the demon-woman purred. She disturbed his hair with a flip of her blade, sending a few locks across his eyes, then returned the bright sword to its ebony sheath. He was too shocked by her speed to even flinch. "Should have gone for the blunderbuss," she said matter-of-factly. "Even I can't dodge a spray of shot at this range."

He sputtered, unable to come up with a decent retort. He swept his hair back from his forehead and scrambled to his feet. He was half tempted to pull his gun, but she was on alert now. It would be suicide. And even if he did manage to kill her, he'd be swinging from the end of a rope as a reward.

His cheeks grew red hot at her amused regard – or disregard, really. Lips pinched, his mouth filling with saliva, he smoothed his coiffure again, adjusted his sash, turned and politely vomited in the nearby wastebasket.

CHAPTER FOUR

While her new partner noisily emptied his stomach, Hero approached Chief Dewey. The aroma of sick made her nostrils curl, and she imagined the young Hunter was regretting the bacon and grits he'd had for breakfast. It certainly was a dramatic reaction to her presence, and she wasn't sure why a queasy stomach made for good demon detection. It had to be why they fed their cadets such sparse fare at the Citadel. His youth probably didn't help, either – fresh out of the Citadel, she had no doubt, all nerves and eagerness. A fucking squirrel.

"He's shiny new, isn't he?" she said to Dewey as she sauntered past him to the coolers. "I guess I'm lead then, hey?"

"You are the senior on this case, Inspector. But please understand, a Citadel-trained demonhunter is always required when demonic activity is suspected. I made the request, and this is who they sent me," he added, waving in the youth's general direction. It almost sounded like an apology. *Ouch.* Not exactly a ringing endorsement.

She paused before the bank of coolers and tapped her cane against the tiles, waiting. Dewey cleared his throat, tossed a grimace toward the retching officer and then joined her. "Let's allow DH Keen a moment to compose himself, shall we?" he said.

"Certainly. I don't need him for this part anyway." *I don't need him at all.*

Dewey nodded, chose an icebox door at waist height, yanked on its metal latch and opened it. Solemnly, he grasped the table within and eased it out. The rollers beneath it were well oiled and the shrouded corpse glided soundlessly free along with a blast of chill air. Hero approved. The body would be well preserved. By the description she'd read, the nun couldn't have died too long before her body was discovered. It would explain the lack of decomposition, even given the cool weather, and the absence of signs of animal predation.

"The coroner preformed only a cursory examination at the scene, and the diener hasn't been at her yet for autopsy preparation," Dewey said. "We were waiting for you to see her first."

"Hmm, yes, very wise. Once the autopsy begins, the soul tends to become confused. I've lost a number to overeager coroners, let me tell you. Poor devils just wander off into Hell never to be seen or heard from again." She gave him a quick smile, seeing how her words had left him a bit pale-faced. Even dedicated PKs didn't like discussing Hell. The flash of her canines didn't seem to put him much at ease.

"Uh…yes, well. We tried to do our best and preserve as much as we could for you, though the killer left little behind for us unfortunately."

"Have you determined cause of death?" Hero asked, gesturing for him to draw back the sheet. So far, she hadn't felt much spiritual resonance lingering about the corpse. Had this woman even died by violence?

At first sight of the murdered nun, Hero let out a very uncharacteristic gasp. It wasn't often she was confounded, but by the Branch, she was about as flabbergasted as she'd ever been.

The girl beneath the shroud was pristine, her face plump and pink, eyes closed as if in peaceful slumber, pale lashes against flawless cheeks. Her blonde hair fanned out beneath her head, held steady by a stiff riser which might as well have been a pillow in a four-poster bed going by how serene she looked. The only observable marks were around her throat, a strange ring which caught the light in glittering flashes and raw scrapes on her knees, revealed as Dewey stripped away the sheet entirely.

A single trickle of blood had leaked from the corner of her slightly parted lips. Hero was tempted to pull down the chin and observe the gaping hole where Catarine's tongue had been, but it would only further compromise the body. And right now, it was an empty vessel. Hero sensed nothing from it, not even the slight residue of a soul torn too soon from its home. That was what had prompted her gasp.

She drew her lips back from her teeth and sucked in a breath, trying to taste the death in the air, to filter out the nun's soul from the general malaise of the cadaver-filled room. Where was it?

Every other dead person stored in the bank of coolers possessed a shade of themselves, the glimmer of a soul. Most had died slowly, from age or illness, or quite suddenly in various accidents, yet Sister Catarine had no shade hovering near, no obvious sign of a soul. If she had been killed the day she'd disappeared, she must have been dead for six days at most, yet her soul had fled completely? Impossible.

"She has the stink of demons upon her."

Hero started, letting out an unintended hiss. The wretched boy had snuck up on her. She whipped her head toward him, glaring through her tinted glasses, but he wasn't watching her. His eyes, full of sadness and revulsion, were on the dead nun.

"Obviously," she snapped. "The marks on her neck are spectral in nature, a sure sign of Pandemonium involvement. And her soul…" Her lips pinched closed in frustration. Sometimes when a trauma was so great, a soul might become snarled in the halls of Hell. Possibly, she could chase it down.

"What of her soul?" DH Keen asked, the words seemingly dragged from him as if he had no desire to engage her in conversation. He kept his eyes on the body, moving around the table, examining every inch of it in a methodical fashion. Not touching it yet. Good. At least he understood the assignment. Too many hands on a corpse confused the situation, left residue and echoes.

"It is lost, I suspect. Confused. Demonic influence might have sent her screaming into the void. Nuns can be touchy about such things."

"You mean immortal evil? Yes, most people are touchy about such *things*."

His wry tone made Hero chuckle, and he glanced at her, eyebrows pinched as if he thought she was mocking him. She blinked at him innocently. He'd made a joke, hadn't he? At times, humor went right over her head.

"Can you find her, Speaker?" Dewey asked, a bit plaintively. "It would help if the girl knew her killer, or at least got a good look at him. Right now, our suspect pool is shallow and our evidence suboptimal."

Suboptimal. Hero clucked her tongue. That meant nonexistent. "This will require concentration," she announced abruptly. "I must open the Gate. I must delve into Hell."

Keen started and stepped away, his hands twitching, as if he wanted to go for his weapons.

Hero ignored him and removed her tinted glasses, hoping briefly that she'd made a mistake and all would be revealed under her true Sight. But alas, the situation remained the same: the girl's shade was gone.

She focused. The real world faded into grays and browns. Lifeless. Ripples of flame ate at the edges of the room. She stood still, relaxed but alert, letting her mind open. Letting Hell leak into her perceptions. It was always there, the Underworld, just beneath the surface. It was dangerous for her to open the Gate, to stand at the doorway, the edge of the river. There was always a risk she might be pulled inside and swept straight to Pandemonium, never to escape. But the risk was the reward – the elation of escaping, the taunting power in her blood. She was of Hell, but free. Free to roam among the angels, among the pure souled.

The flames grew, eager as always to consume her. Her body didn't move, but her mind took a step. Her disembodied spirit delved into chaos, searching corridors of flame and ash, of blood and rot. The clinging miasma of demon stink became more apparent as she let Hell surround her. To demons, Hell was a passageway and their playground. She had no doubt a demon had had a hand in this nun's murder, had laid its chains upon her. But what demon?

The stench of sulfur filled her nostrils. She sucked it in through bared teeth, tasting, discerning. Did she know this particular demon? She doubted it; there were too many to count. They all knew her, unfortunately. She chased the smell, dashing through the shadows, searching for the source. Would she find the nun's shade hidden beneath it? It wouldn't be the first time a demon had tried to hide their victim from her.

The heat and fury of Pandemonium roared around her the deeper she delved, the closer she ventured to that particular Sphere. Hatred and need beat at her. She was not welcome here, even if the place wanted desperately to consume her. She held on to her human half with a tenuous thread of psychic silver, keeping herself grounded in the morgue, in reality. Even as she roamed through a twisted Hellscape, she was aware of the cold tiles beneath her feet, the nearness of the demonhunter and his pulsing dislike of her, the stolid presence of Chief Dewey, whose alarm and worry for her was actually a bit touching. But nowhere did she feel the aura of a dead, confused, frightened nun, the thing which should be most apparent.

A tremor shook Hero, both in the real world and in the Hellscape. Unease. There was no sign of Sister Catarine. Not even an echo. Just a blankness. A hole in the Underworld. As if... as if everything which had made up this person's entire being had been consumed.

She's been eaten.

The thought exploded through her mind like a bullet. She winced, suddenly feeling the heat of Hell rage all around her, but she held on, unwilling to leave just yet. Yes, the nun's spirit was gone – eaten – but what had eaten her remained. She saw the signs of its teeth in the ether. Judging by their size, it had to have been terrible and powerful, a beast of immense strength, of unfathomable age. A creature older than bone... rising...

Hero gasped – Goddess, her second in one day! – and came back to herself, demon and human reunited as one. She knew her pale face must have gone pure white by how the other two stared at her. Even the DH had a look of concern.

"You have charge of the body, DH Keen," she said. "Let the coroner know he can begin his autopsy."

"Did you find her?" Dewey asked eagerly. "Did you Speak with her?"

Hero shook her head. "Sister Catarine is gone. I do not understand how, but I can assure you it is not good for us, or for this case. Something very old and very strong has taken her soul. I have never seen anything like it."

"Then I suppose we have to do this the old-fashioned way," Keen interjected, somewhat smugly, to Hero's vexation. "Through good police work, exacting diligence and deduction."

"The slow way," she growled, irritated beyond reason. Hell still clung to her, and the familiar stench coating her tongue made her hackles rise.

"I suppose without a shade to spill its secrets, a death speaker is hardly necessary given the circumstances," he continued, oblivious to Hero's rising temper. "It's good you called me in, Chief. A demonhunter is just what this case needs."

"Speaking to the dead is not my only skill, DH Keen. I am lead on this case. You will defer to my command, or you can find another assignment. The demon that did this won't be impressed with your rank."

He bristled, his ears turning pink at her tone. "Maybe *you* should find another assignment, Viridian. I am not afraid of any demon, no matter how terrible. I'll root it out and expose whatever human called it here."

"DH Keen, *Inspector* Viridian has vastly more experience than you," Dewey said, throwing Hero an apologetic glance. "She remains lead, and you will do everything she asks of you. Do you understand?"

His lips, plump and red, thinned at the command and the pink on those too-big ears of his deepened. But he was Citadel trained, and he knew how to take orders: mindlessly. He nodded sharply. "Of course, sir. I beg pardon for my insolence. I just wished to do what was best for the case."

"You are forgiven, Officer. This one time. Now, let's call the diener in to prepare the body. Dr Virchow is eager to begin the autopsy once the body has been cleaned and weighed."

The body. It had such a sound of finality to it, a bitter rebuke – to Hero, at least, vaunted death speaker with absolutely no one to talk to. The dead nun lay in peaceful repose. There was nothing left of her, this Sister Catarine, but an empty shell. A body. Flesh and bone and nothing more.

"Is he skilled, this Dr Virchow?" Hero asked, hooking her glasses over her ears once more. The world faded to a peaceful green.

"He wrote the book on the procedure," said Dewey. "Literally. Soon, I suspect all PKs will follow his protocols for post-mortem examination."

"Impressive." Her gaze cut to Keen. "You will stay and observe. Make sure all remaining blood, all her organs, every hair and fiber anywhere on her, are examined and preserved. Can you do that, DH Keen? I mean *everything*."

Her sharp tone had the opposite effect to what she'd expected. Instead of the defensive air of before, he snapped to, his heels clicking smartly. "Yes, Inspector. I understand."

She huffed, surprised. *Citadel trained*, she reminded herself. They beat the insubordination out of their cadets. A firm hand might work best with this one. Hopefully, his training hadn't rendered him a useless automaton. He was good with a sword, at least. Nevertheless, she hadn't asked for a partner, and she didn't want one. Especially not a Goddess-cursed demonhunter.

Fucking Culpepper should have warned me.

Her jaw clenched. It had taken ten experienced demonhunters to bring her in after she'd run from the smoking ruins of her old abbey. One young buck was hardly a threat. Still, she didn't like the way he looked at her, like he was just waiting for her to turn her back on him. She kept him in her sights as she backed toward the exit. Casually, of course.

Nothing to see here, just a half-demon arsonist disgraced ex-nun jailbird.

"I need to see her file, Chief Dewey," she said. "As DH Keen pointed out, we'll have to do this the old-fashioned way. And gather all witnesses or potential suspects. I will need to speak with them. In fact, I'll want to speak with everyone even remotely involved with this case, including every teacher at Clementine and all of Catarine's students."

Dewey cleared his throat. "That's... that is a tall order, Inspector. Some very important families in Havenside will most likely protest their children being part of a murder investigation."

"Those are the ones we'll start with, then." She gave her cane a quick twirl, her spirits rising. This might actually be fun. She remembered a few of those "important" families. She would enjoy putting them under the spotlight.

A whiff of foulness cooled her amusement, tickling her memory but skittering away when she tried to examine it more closely. She left the morgue with Chief Dewey, an unsettled feeling lodged in her gut.

CHAPTER FIVE

A hush had fallen over the venerated halls of Clementine Preparatory. The polished wood gleamed as brightly as ever, the lemon-scented oil a constant perfume, and sunlight streamed through narrow clerestory windows of stained glass. Students filled the halls at every mark, streaming from classroom to classroom, flitting in and out of light and shadow, light and shadow. The usual boisterousness and chatter was diminished, sunken into whispers and the occasional giggle or laugh that were quickly muffled by shame and embarrassment in the current atmosphere of gloom and grief.

Sister Catarine was dead. The news had circulated within a few hours of the discovery of her body, high on a lonely hilltop meadow, far from where she should have been. How could she have ended up there? What diabolical monster had dragged her to her doom? Nay, what demon had led her so astray?

Speculation ran rampant among the student body. Sister Catarine had been popular, some would go so far as to say beloved. Always there for her students with a kind word or a joyful smile. Fair and honest. Trustworthy. But everyone knew she did things her own way. Some of her ideas about school, teaching and the world in general were strange and, horror of horrors, modern. Perhaps the Church might ease up on its condemnation of those with demonic blood? After all, it wasn't anyone's fault how they were conceived, or to whom they were born. And maybe the Celestial nuns' requirement for celibacy might be outdated. Backward, even. There was perhaps more wiggle room in serving the Goddess and the Branch.

Had such beliefs led to her death? Maybe.

Or maybe she'd just fallen in with the wrong crowd, or the wrong man. Everyone knew she'd been acting strangely those few days before her disappearance – distracted and upset. She'd argued with the headmistress, the Revered Mother Francesca, on the quad in full daylight. She'd been angry, something Sister Catarine never was – not with her students, anyway. She adored them, looked out for them.

Molly Franke's heart had broken when she heard the news about Sister Catarine's death. For six days, she had held on to hope for her teacher's safe return. She'd wept and prayed. Her knees ached from the hard kneelers in the school's chapel, but she had gone there every evening with many of her classmates in vigil. When the news had come, a collective wail rose, even from the older nuns, the mean ones who thought nothing good about anyone. The youngsters in their charge, especially, had gasped and cried and shouted pleas to the Goddess and her blessed Branch.

Now, returning to everyday ordinary life seemed like a dream. How could they learn the history of the Great Exodus or solve math equations or participate in field exercises or pray to the Goddess when their hearts were broken? Molly certainly struggled to do it – to comprehend the cruelty of the world, a world which could take away her favorite teacher.

The only bright side was she wasn't alone. She wasn't the only student with tear-stained cheeks, messy hair and a disheveled uniform. It was hard to care about maintaining a proper dress code when you could barely get out of bed in the morning. The fear of getting a demerit for an untucked shirt or a crooked hem was a laughable worry at this point. She and her friends stuck together in the hallways, though there was a distance among them as they processed their own grief. Julie and Bennett leaned on each other openly, which would usually earn a stern rebuke, but even the class monitors let it pass today. And Cassie had disappeared somewhere. Again. She was probably under the stairs in the main foyer, crying quietly in a broom closet. She'd been particularly close to Sister Catarine, and Molly suspected they'd shared some sort of secret, having seen them in deep conversations in the sister's homeroom, heads bent together, Cassie looking distressed and Catarine soothing her. Nothing terribly unusual. Lots of students confided in Sister Catarine.

The warning bell rang for second period, and there was a sudden silence in its echo as if everyone had forgotten what it meant. Five minutes to get to your next class, or there would be Hell to pay. Even today, in the solemn hush, footsteps quickened to reach the next class in time. All but Molly's. Her steps slowed. Her scuffed Mary Janes turned down the wrong hall even though she knew she'd be late.

Hugging her books to her chest, Molly sped up until she was nearly running. She had to find Cassie, convince her to get to class instead of moping around beneath the stairs. Her friend couldn't afford any more demerits. She might get sent to Bright Renewal Academy with all the other troubled kids if she didn't shape up! She could be a pain sometimes with her withdrawn ways and strange jumpiness, but she was Molly's friend, and had been since primary school. She, like Molly, was one of the few kids at Clem whose parents didn't live in a mansion. But the Grahams, like the Frankes, had deep ties to Havenside, being members of the founding families. Perhaps they lacked generational wealth, but they possessed undeniable history.

"Come out, Cassie, please!" Molly whispered as loudly as she dared through the wood-paneled door that blended with the paneling beneath the grand staircase, concealing a mundane broom closet. Every student at Clem Prep knew it made for a good hiding place when the janitors were occupied. She gave the door a sharp tap, then glanced around to see if the coast was clear. The halls had emptied around her. She sighed. Maybe she should just hide out here with Cassie until lunchtime? Pretend she'd been sick or something? Lots of kids hadn't even come to school today.

Cassie should have been one of them, Molly decided as the sound of muffled weeping greeted her when she slipped into the closet. She pulled the door almost shut, leaving a narrow crack for light. It seeped into the dark space, casting shadows in the corners. The closet stank of ammonia and bleach, mildewed mop heads and the ever-present lemon scent that pervaded the halls. She took a step forward. Cassie's weeping turned into a strange, huffing keen, almost like an animal's whine, and a shiver rolled up her spine. Chilled, Molly mouthed the prayer for protection and absolution.

"I had to tell. I had to tell *someone*."

Cassie's words were faint, wheedling, and silenced Molly instantly. Her prayer lodged in her throat and cold sweat sprang out beneath her wrinkled cotton shirt. Cassie sounded terrified, as if speaking any louder would draw all of Pandemonium into the room.

Perhaps it would. There was a rumor of demonic involvement circling about the campus, a suspicion that Sister Catarine had drawn the wrong kind of attention... or summoned it.

"What did you tell?" Molly asked, keeping her voice to a harsh whisper. She took another step closer to her friend, her eyes slowly adjusting to the dim lighting. "Cassie. Please. What's the matter?"

Lips pressed tight, Cassie shook her head. She sat lodged between a tin mop bucket and a bevy of brooms, her knees drawn up to her chin – a terribly unladylike pose.

Molly wavered, torn between wanting to be away from the sniffling girl and to know why Cassie was so upset. A crawling suspicion made her think it had something to do with Sister Catarine, her favorite teacher. With her silky golden hair and easy smile, she'd been so beautiful, so *alive*.

"Tell me," Molly said, a little more firmly. She crept closer and dropped to a crouch to face her friend. "Does this have to do with Sister Catarine?"

Cassie started, her whole body jerking. She turned wide eyes on Molly. They looked black against the ghostly paleness of her skin. "They *warned* me not to talk." She wheezed as if fighting panic. Her fingernails dug into her scuffed knees, leaving little crescent marks. "But I couldn't help it. Sister Catarine was so kind, so understanding. She seemed to know already anyway, you know? By the way she was acting. She insisted I say something. So... I – I told her things I shouldn't have. And now... and now she's dead because of me!"

"Because of you?" Molly scoffed. Cassie tended to be dramatic, moody and withdrawn or crazy with laughter and recklessness. Was she really making Sister Catarine's death about her? It was an uncharitable thought, maybe, but sometimes it was hard being Cassie's friend. "Who are 'they,' Cassie? What do you mean?"

Again, Cassie shook her head, her reddish curls swinging wildly. "I can't say! You'll be marked if I do, like me, like Cole was. They're going to send me away now. I know it!"

"Marked? I don't get it. Who marked you?"

Another wild shake. "I can't tell you!"

Molly glanced toward the door, growing a bit impatient. This had to be some ploy for attention, Cassie's way of acting out in her grief. It was understandable. Up until now, their lives had been simple. The worst disaster to hit Clementine Prep had been losing the championship game to Szent Boynton Academy. This tragedy was something none of them knew how to process – a dead teacher, a dead nun, a dead *friend*. No, not just dead, but murdered. Things like that didn't happen in Havenside.

"Who?" Molly asked again, curiosity getting the better of her. "What is this all about? Tell me *something*."

Cassie bit her lip and her eyes cut to the side. Then she grew very still and spoke in a low, monotonous tone. "I gave her a letter Cole sent me. From Bright Renewal."

Molly sighed. *This again.* Cole was Cassie's brother, her twin brother. He'd been the first student from Clem sent to the Academy in ages, after he and some other boys broke into the school one night on a dare. His co-conspirators ended up earning a few demerits, but Cole was sent to Bright Renewal Academy. It wasn't fair, and it had devastated Cassie. Still...

"I know it stinks, Cassie, but it's for his own good, right? It won't be forever. Just remember: 'Bright Renewal Academy rescues children from themselves.'"

"No, it doesn't," Cassie said flatly. "I can't tell you any more than that. I mean, I won't. It's not safe."

"I think you're being dramatic," Molly said, a bit harshly, but she was starting to get fed up. Cassie always made mountains from mole hills. She rested her arms across her knees and frowned at her friend. Her calves were starting to ache in this position. "You want attention or something, and all you're going to do is get us both in trouble. I don't know why I was even worried about you."

With a low moan, Cassie covered her face with her hands and almost seemed to sink into herself. She looked so small and frightened, Molly felt immediately sorry for being so mean. "Cassie, I–"

"I saw her body."

A hiss of a whisper. So soft, and so terrible. Molly dropped onto her bottom, not caring that she landed in a puddle of dirty water. "What?" Her face felt numb. It had to be a lie.

"I saw her. In the woods. Under a full moon. She was so white, so limp. Like a doll left in the rain, tossed away and forgotten."

"You're lying!"

"Her tongue was gone, Molly. Torn out." Cassie pulled her hands away from her face and reached for her friend. Those clasping desperate fingers closed on Molly's wrist and it was all the other girl could do not to yank her arm away. Cassie dragged her closer, her eyes wide and her cheeks chalk white. "I told her something I shouldn't have, and it got her killed. They'll make me pay, they said, make me pay if I tell anyone else!"

Her sheer terror was contagious. Molly's heart thundered and she was sweating again. She wanted to wrench herself away and flee. She wanted sunlight and warmth and a crowd around her. Stuck in here with her mad-eyed friend spewing nonsense – frightening nonsense – she felt trapped in a nightmare. Frozen, as if a demon sat on her chest.

"It's okay, you don't have to tell me," she said, trying to pull back without seeming like it. "Come on, calm down. Let's go find a teacher. Sister Violetta will write a note for class, and you won't be in any trouble. Okay? You're just upset, that's all. It was probably just a dream. I have strange dreams sometimes, too, about Sister Catarine. She was so nice."

"She believed me when no one else would," Cassie said. "Who would believe a Graham?" she added bitterly, and Molly winced. Despite their deep ties to Havenside, the Grahams were a very… colorful family, known for tall tales and exaggerations. "They slaughtered her to shut me up, and to send a warning to Cole. They need him, or I think he'd be dead, too."

Her friend sounded insane. Talking about some mysterious "they" who murdered nuns and were conspiring to do… what, exactly? And what did any of it have to do with Bright Renewal Academy? Maybe Cole was just complaining about his circumstances and Cassie had blown it all out of proportion. Had it gotten Catarine killed? She doubted it. She doubted all of this. The only thing she knew for certain was that she wanted to be anywhere but here right now.

The door swept open behind her and light poured in. Cassie winced, her eyelids fluttering, and released Molly to lift a hand against the glare. Molly scrambled to her feet, almost grateful to whoever had caught them.

"Here, now! What are you girls doing? Get out of there at once!"

Cassie bounced to her feet while Molly whirled around to stand at stiff attention before the headmistress herself. The woman was all of five feet tall, with cherubically round cheeks and eyes like a fawn, but her voice was whipcrack sharp and she wasn't afraid to redden her palm on a recalcitrant child. Every student lived in fear of her, and not a few grown men and women, too. There wasn't a teacher on campus Molly wouldn't rather deal with than Revered Mother Isabel Francesca.

"Well?" the revered mother demanded, hands clasped at her cincture, knuckles white as if she were restraining herself from striking one of them. Her soft eyes had turned to shards of black diamond and her cherubic cheeks burned red, giving her a truly terrifying visage.

"We – we..." Molly stammered uselessly. What excuse could she give? Shockingly, her throat closed with a painful ache, and she felt hot tears well in her eyes. No, no, this was not the correct response to such a question from the revered mother. Blubbering girls did not evoke any sympathy from this nun. Beside her, Cassie dissolved into inconsolable weeping, which didn't make it any easier for Molly to fight back her own tears.

But then, a miracle. The revered mother, abbess of the Celestial Order of the Shield Convent, headmistress of Clementine Preparatory, a woman with no discernible heart, unclasped her hands and spread her arms wide. "My poor dears," she said, her sharp voice suddenly honey. "There, there. I know we're all upset this terrible day."

And Molly found herself gathered against the mother's plump shoulder, Cassie collapsing in a puddle against the other. For a moment, though shocked to her core, she let emotion overwhelm her and gave in to her grief. Not for long, though; her sobs quickly turned stiff, muffled, and she pulled herself together and was released from the revered mother's embrace. Her friend remained sheltered in the mother's comforting arms while Molly stood sniffling and scrubbing away her tears.

Mother Francesca caught her eyes above Cassie's head. "Go to class, Miss Franke, and tell Father Kellan I held you back for a private talk." Those eyes of hers grew deep and soft. "I'll take care of Miss Graham. I think she needs a moment to pull herself together. Don't you agree?"

"I – y-y-yes, Mother. I – thank you!" She blurted out this last part, already turning on her heel to escape. She gave them one last glance before rushing down the main hallway and saw Revered Mother Francesca escorting Cassie in the opposite direction – taking her to the school nurse, no doubt, for a drop of calming tincture or a balm of mint. Hopefully, Cassie would keep her strange confession to herself and not drag the mother into her fantasies. With any luck, she'd avoid being sent to the Academy like her poor brother.

Most of the kids at the Academy deserved to be there, troublemakers and malcontents from Otherside, and Molly had little sympathy for them. What kind of future did they have, anyway? Bright Renewal might just manage to mold them into good citizens. But Cole Graham was different. He'd been one of *them*, a Clem Prep student, a promising scholar and athlete. Nevertheless, he should have known better. Molly felt bad for him, but not *too* bad. Whatever he might have told Cassie could only be nonsense. It had nothing to do with Sister Catarine.

She told herself this and pushed everything else out of her mind. Cassie had to be lying!

Getting to her next class happened in a blur of wood and glass, light and shadow, and Father Kellan either didn't notice her slip in late or didn't care. He was writing on the blackboard, his hand moving precisely, producing a swirl of neat, even text outlining the last battle of the Great Civil War. She took her seat in the back corner of the room beneath the tall windows that looked out onto the quad, struggling to slow her pounding heart and stop panting before he turned around.

She needn't have worried. A dull and listless mood hung over the classroom. No one, not even the ever-spiteful Shane Goody, took the opportunity to call out her tardiness. And when Father Kellan turned around at last, his eyes red-rimmed and his cheeks dark with stubble, he seemed hardly aware of his own surroundings let alone the antics of one wayward student. He even stumbled a little as he returned to his desk, drawing a small gasp from some of them.

"No talking," he muttered – well, slurred, really. He flopped into his chair, and it rolled back from his desk a foot or so. Instead of pulling it back into place, he scrubbed his hands through his mop of chestnut hair and stared at the ceiling, his head resting on the back of the chair.

An uncomfortable silence descended. The students waited. Molly caught the attention of her friend Julie, and they exchanged identical looks of consternation. Had Father Kellan been that close with Sister Catarine? Why else would he be so distraught? Usually, he was one of the more enthusiastic instructors at Clementine, a man in love with history and service to the Goddess and her Blessed Branch.

A rustle of papers broke the stillness, a shifting of chairs, a few quiet sighs.

Abruptly, Father Kellan stood, his face unusually pale. "Mr Faraday," he said, pointing to Simon Faraday, the smartest kid in school and a notorious brown-noser. "Take over a second, please. I–" Astonishingly, he dashed from the room. A startled murmur arose among the students.

"Quiet!" Simon ordered, only too happy to be a martinet, the little turd. He stalked to the vacated desk and took a seat, hands folded on the blotter. "No talking until Father Kellan returns. I'll tell if anyone gets rowdy."

A few sniggers greeted his pronouncement, but the perpetrators were quickly hushed. Simon would gleefully rat out any agitators. Shane made a slashing motion across his throat to his sneering buddies, but even he remained compliant.

The uncomfortable silence returned, growing long, then longer. Restless, Molly stared at the clock tower through the tall, arched windows. It was why she liked to sit where she did. Not only was the ornate stone-and-brick edifice beautiful, it also held a massive bronze bell in its rounded cupola. The tolling of that bell meant one more hour closer to freedom, and she liked to watch the hands of the clock creep closer and closer to when it would ring.

So, as it happened, she was staring right at the clock tower when a figure appeared in the cupola, small and pathetic beside the great bronze bell – a student, judging by the plaid, pleated skirt and crisp white blouse. She was too far to see their face, but Molly knew that head of curly red hair.

Cassie? What was she doing up there?

The girl wavered, one hand on the bell, every line of her body taut as she looked over her shoulder. Whatever she saw sent her running – right off the edge of the tower.

Molly screamed, half-rising, arm outstretched, pointing at the windows. A dozen heads whipped round in the same direction, just in time to see Cassie Graham plummeting to the quad.

CHAPTER SIX

A soul. This body had a soul. Quite excellent. Hero took a knee beside the twisted wreckage of a once living, breathing child. She ignored the blood, the flattened skull leaking brain matter, the white bone sticking through a tear of red flesh, and focused on the agitated energy of the violently departed spirit, wild and terrified even in death, when terror should have faded into the background.

But no, this spirit practically radiated fear, as if death hadn't released her from whatever had driven her over the edge of the clock tower. A very unusual circumstance.

This whole case is unusual circumstances.

She'd come to Clementine Prep to visit Sister Catarine's apartment when her investigation had been interrupted by this new tragedy, a suicide by all appearances. More than one witness had seen the girl jump. No one else had been in the tower, or at least no one anyone could see. There was no reason to think the girl had been murdered but for the unusually agitated shade.

She'd been in Catarine's apartment when it had happened. Since she'd been unable to Commune with her dead shade, Hero had been forced to learn about her through more prosaic methods. The simple apartment sat in a cloister attached to the school within whose sheltered walls all the nuns who served as teachers at Clem lived, joined by the other avowed sisters of the Shield, a battle order against Pandemonium at least in theory. Hero found the designation laughable. They battled nothing beyond humans cursed with demon blood, and those they mostly shunned or abused. Entering the convent was like stepping back in time; her knees ached with the memory of hours spent kneeling on hard stone or, worse, on tiny grains of rice scattered across those stones. The very least of her punishments, albeit the most tedious.

Nevertheless, she needed to know Catarine Cisco, and the best way was to put herself in the woman's shoes. With the permission of the abbess – a certain Mother Francesca, who was also the headmistress – Hero was allowed access to the cloisters, accompanied by a watchdog, an elder nun with a sour face, silver prayer beads clutched in one hand and a vial of blessed elixir in the other. Ready to smite the half-demon inspector should she make a wrong move, no doubt. Hero chose to ignore her as she investigated.

Sister Catarine's residence was a simple flat with two tiny bedrooms and a common area, shared by her and another nun – a novice, actually. The roommate had been interviewed by Havenside PKs and taken off the suspect list, though Hero had resolved to speak with her and decide for herself. The cramped living room contained little furniture beyond a lumpy couch and two mismatched chairs in opposite corners. There was a small ceramic stove right inside the door providing heat and a convenient place to boil water for tea. The Book of the Goddess sat in a place of prominence beneath the one window facing the outside world. The gilded tome was on a wooden stand with a kneeler below it for prayer and contemplation, and had been opened – a velvet ribbon laid between the pages – to the Book of Chains, specifically the verses detailing the most forbidden of demonic summonings. Plenty of *thou shalt not*s and *eternal damnation*s. A book of warnings, but also an instruction manual in the wrong hands. Interesting.

The bookshelf against one wall was of interest to her, too. You could tell a lot about a person by what sorts of books they read, books beyond the requisite. Hero scanned the titles, finding interesting works on philosophy and art among the expected religious manuscripts and devotionals. A few novels were tucked among the rest, slim and unobtrusive. Happy tales of finding love, and an adventure story or two. They were Catarine's, all marked with a "CC" on their inside covers. The roommate didn't seem to have a single book in the collection besides the religious ones her order required her to have.

Not a few of the volumes belonging to CC concerned people like herself, those cursed with demon ancestry. It seemed Catarine had a very strong interest in studying Hero's kind. Most of the books championed their humanity despite the dark nature of their heritage. Interesting indeed.

"She was very nearly a radical," Hero commented as she ran her fingers over the spines.

The old nun made a sound. Not a particularly nice sound, either.

The couch and chairs were old and well used, even threadbare, but lace doilies decorated the arms and backs to hide the flaws, all handmade. No newfangled machine-produced accents for these two ladies. A stack of crocheted blankets lay nestled in a basket beside the couch, and one was draped across a fat, overstuffed chair in the corner. A book lay face down on the arm of the chair as if someone had been interrupted in the middle of reading, never to return.

Catarine's book, Catarine's chair. Hero could almost picture her curled up beneath her blanket, engrossed in... what? She checked the title on the book's spine: *Love Poems of the Second Age*. Dear Goddess. A radical *and* a romantic.

A few personal items graced the room. Small portraits of family members hung on the walls. An ivory cameo left on a table. Celestial pendants and silver prayer beads. A horsehair brush and a pewter comb. Hero touched them all then moved to Catarine's bedroom – a very typical cell for a cloistered nun, spare and plain, furnished with just a narrow cot against the plastered wall, a nightstand and a washbasin. No mirrors, of course. She stepped carefully across the floorboards, testing each one.

There. A little give in the wood, creaking beneath the pointed toe of her lace-up boot. She knelt and ran her finger down a slightly larger seam than all the others. Taking a slim knife from her belt, she thrust it into the gap and prized the board free.

"There you are," she murmured as her eyes feasted on a treasure trove within the hidey hole. Letters, an entire stack of them, tied with a velvet ribbon. The same sort of ribbon that marked the page in the Book of the Goddess. She removed the correspondence and tucked it into the evidence bag she'd brought from the station. She would read through the letters back at the stationhouse. She might even let Keen have a look–

A shriek of horror sliced through her skull. Pure terror made her breath come fast and her heart race. The world went white. A sensation gripped her. She was falling.

No! No, no, no–

Hero staggered, released abruptly from the vision. Someone very near had died suddenly, violently. She spun on her heel and rushed back into the common area. The old nun jerked at her sudden appearance and raised the bottle of elixir as if to throw it, but then the sound of screaming filtered into the room and her escort's eyes went wide. Hero strode past her to the door, not caring if the old bag kept up, and broke into a run once she was outside.

By the time Hero had reached the quad and the dead girl, the nuns in charge had pushed back the crowd of onlookers – students, mostly, distraught, many weeping, already traumatized by the loss of their beloved teacher, and now this. Sad, but a distraction Hero didn't need. She found a short nun, hovering over the dead girl like a fucking buzzard.

Goddess be damned, she fucking hated nuns.

"Clear the quad," she said, a bit too sharply. She'd whipped off her glasses as soon as she'd reached the body, and the world had too-sharp edges. Fire nipping at the periphery. Hell reaching for her. "I need to concentrate. This spirit is a twirling ninny."

The nun stiffened. "Mother Francesca," she said loftily, clearly offended by Hero's lack of respect.

"Right. Sorry. You all look the same to me." She shrugged dismissively, giving the nun her back.

"You of all people should know a revered mother when you see one, Sister Viridian."

Hero bristled and showed her fangs. "Inspector. Inspector Viridian."

The revered mother sniffed, but she bustled away, her hands clasped beneath her scapular and her back stiff. A few gestures and a few sharp words had the other teachers herding the children back to their studies. No day off for a dead friend, apparently.

Whatever. Hero settled into a cross-legged position on the graveled courtyard directly beneath the clock tower. That sensation of falling. So obvious what had happened. A patch of blood lay at her knee, and she was careful not to touch it. She didn't need the lingering echoes still attached to the body's humors. She needed the departed, the body's released soul.

So she opened her flame-red eyes wide and entered Hell.

Demonhunter Keen followed his new partner to Clementine Prep after the coroner had finished with the body. Eager to be of use, and eager to see what his partner would think, he'd gone to find her rather than wait for her return. It was always best to be proactive, on the ball. The autopsy had been thorough – so thorough, in fact, he'd nearly lost the rest of his breakfast. Watching the doctor carve up the girl with clinical precision had somehow been worse than witnessing brutal murder.

Every part of the unfortunate nun was weighed and measured. Samples were scraped and collected from beneath her fingernails, off of her skin. Hairs were plucked from her head and catalogued. A strange silvery substance was taken from that shimmering ring around her neck. Tiny pebbles and crystalline shards had been extracted from where they'd been embedded in her scraped knees. All her blood and bodily fluids were placed in jars and vials. It was grotesque, but everything was considered a potential clue which could lead them to her killer. The coroner had exclaimed over each finding in a particularly gleeful fashion that had left Keen unsettled.

"The organs weigh less than half what they should. Why, her heart is as light as a feather!" Virchow had said this while hefting said heart in his palm, as if it were a melon he was intending to purchase.

Tasting bile, Keen had asked, "Have you seen anything like this before?"

"Only once," the doctor admitted, a line etched between his brows. "Long ago, in New Savage. Only demons of immense strength manage to drain the very essence of their victims. It's what killed her, I'm afraid. No human weapon touched this woman."

Drained of her essence? Her very soul, if Viridian were to be believed.

And if that revelation hadn't been bad enough, they'd also discovered Catarine's tongue had been torn out, not just cut out. Virchow had announced this grim discovery as if his sandwich had come with extra pickles.

"Torn out by a very strong and determined sort," he'd murmured, fingers deep in Catarine's wide open mouth. He'd pushed down her jaw so Keen could see, and the sight would haunt him to the end of his days. "The tongue is a particularly tough muscle. Smart move, really. Knives leave marks we can trace."

I'm working with ghouls.

Keen shuddered as he came back to himself beneath a clear sky and a bright sun. His first day on the job had been rather eventful so far. And now he had to return to his old alma mater. Oh, he'd known the nun was a teacher at Clementine Preparatory; it just hadn't occurred to him that he would need to set foot on campus so soon. Not on his first day. And yet here he was, walking down the familiar street beneath the shade of huge, graceful elms, approaching the wrought-iron gates of his old school feeling like he was walking back in time.

Nothing had changed. Not the stone arch emblazoned with the school's name nor the brick pillars and yew hedges stretching along the walls. Except... were they taller, perhaps? It had been some time, after all. How many years now? Five? No, six years since he'd last walked down this flagstone pathway, beneath the welcoming arch. Alone now rather than in a flow of classmates. A surreal moment.

But even then he'd been alone, isolated from the others by class and wealth or, rather, the lack of it. They'd looked down on him for his shabby shoes and the secondhand uniform someone's older brother had left behind for "needy" students. He could almost hear the derisive snickering poorly hidden behind elegant, soft hands which had never known a day of roughness, an hour of want, a moment of need.

Beyond the gateway, inside a manicured courtyard, stood a statue of Saint Clementine dressed as a novitiate of the order she would found, one emphasizing the importance of knowledge and study. The original school had occupied the small chapel now relegated to the outskirts of campus, now used only by the older nuns. On the plinth was the school's motto:

Service. Community. Devotion.

A worthy maxim. Clementine's stone eyes were lifted toward heaven, her palm raised for a benediction from the Goddess. On one of her shoulders sat a stone-carved crow – a creature known for its intelligence – while around her feet curled two serpents, representing demonic forces, both squashed beneath her simple sandals.

As he passed by the statue, Oleander gazed up at its benign face, remembering how he'd taken comfort in this faithful servant of the Goddess, one so lowly and poor yet who had risen to impossible heights. Saint Clementine had started out as a mystic and a poet, an itinerant preacher, then became revered mother of the Clementine order, with thousands of adherents. They'd even bestowed an archbishopric upon her just before her death and then canonized her for her many miracles. Her story had inspired young Oleander, filling him with ambition and religious fervor, and he'd vowed back then to follow a righteous path, to do good works and rise above his station. He was bright, a quick-witted lad full of potential – it was how he'd earned a scholarship in the first place – and with such gifts, anything might be possible.

Armed now with a blunderbuss, a fine sword and a calling, he let himself experience a swelling of pride. Not too much, of course. That was no way for a righteous man to act. A demonhunter's life was about service, not accolades. But he settled a hand on his saber's hilt and stood a little straighter as he strode along the path, confident in his abilities and secure in his status. He was here as a representative of a prestigious organization, a respected professional. Not the most lucrative of callings, maybe, but one deserving of respect, even admiration.

The entrance, however, daunted him. Memories flooded his mind, not all of them pleasant. Honestly, most of them were in fact *un*pleasant. He grasped the cold iron door handle, the interior concealed by the bright sunshine reflecting off the leaded-glass panes, and hesitated. Would anyone inside remember him? Would they see the boy he'd been in the man he'd become?

His pause was brief – a calming breath. Then he opened the door.

It was cool in the old building, much cooler than outside, where false summer had trampled on the belly of autumn. Judging by the emptiness of the hallways, classes must have been in session. In front of him stood the grand staircase to the second floor, leading to the math and science classrooms, the administration offices and the nurses' station. To his left, down and around the corner, was literature and art, history and the cafeteria. To the right stretched a long passageway to the gymnasium. Every inch of the place felt familiar and strange all at once.

The stillness raised gooseflesh on his arms. There was a sense of dread in the air, a gloom that was palpable. Not surprising, perhaps, considering a beloved teacher had just been found murdered.

His footsteps echoed on the polished floorboards as he made his way down the hall, muscle memory directing him. The entrance to the quad was at the end of the east wing, right past the classroom where he'd taken ethics. The cloisters were on the other side of the quad. His partner would still be there, hopefully.

"Excuse me, good sir! The campus is closed to visitors."

He turned. A young woman was hurrying down the hallway toward him dressed in a neat gray frock, a white headscarf holding back sleek black hair and a white apron pinned to her front – a nurse, if he had to guess. He froze, staring. Her cheeks were flushed and her eyes rimmed red as if she'd been weeping, but that wasn't what caught him in a vise. Years vanished and he was a boy again, watching the girl he'd adored approach him with a look of need in her eyes, as if he were a hero come to save the day.

He *was*, Goddess bless him. He was a first-rank DH. He was *someone*. He wasn't that awkward boy from so long ago, fat and ashamed. He snapped his heels together and gave her a bow, taking the opportunity to stare at the floor and gather his wits.

"Ma'am," he said briskly, straightening. "DH First Rank Keen at your service. I am here on official business."

"Oh, praise the Branch," she cried, coming to a stop very close to him, hands reaching out as if she might clutch his arm. "You've come just in time. The inspector is with the… the body. It's so awful! Everyone is beside themselves with shock!"

The body? He blinked. "Please forgive me. I don't... Are you saying there's been another death?"

"There's been a terrible accident," she said, tears glistening in her cornflower eyes. "A student has fallen from the clock tower. I was... I was nearby when it happened. I tried to help, but..." Her voice choked off.

Oleander felt a wave of sympathy, and his heart skipped. He wanted to hold her, to comfort this petite woman with shining hair and perfect skin. Not a nun, but a nurse. Strangely, this pleased him immensely. Abigail Primm. Abby. The girl he'd watched from afar. So bright and lively and fun. Everyone had loved Abby, especially him, an outcast boy from the wrong side of the tracks. She'd been kind to him and decent like so few of his classmates, casting him the occasional smile, complimenting him on an exceptional grade, asking for his help with her studies.

"I'm so sorry. I had no idea."

"Of course not." She waved off his apology. "I'm the one who's sorry. It's been such a terrible time lately. First Cat, and now poor Cassie." Her face scrunched prettily, and her hand went to her trembling lips, ruby red and plump. But in a flash, she gave him a brave smile and pulled herself together. "The students have been gathered for prayer in the cathedral. That's why it's so quiet. I'll take you to the inspector, DH... Keen, you said?"

He nodded, his eyes pinned on her. Did she not remember him? Disappointment swelled in his breast, but then–

"Wait. Keen? Are you... I think I might– Oh, my! Charity Keen!" she exclaimed suddenly, brightly. "It's you, isn't it? Do you remember me? I'm Abigail!"

His good feelings vanished, swept away like so much dross before a bitter crest of emotion: pain, embarrassment, hatred. Flames beat at his cheeks, and he knew his ears had gone red. "I do remember you," he said, his voice hard. "But my name is Oleander."

Her happy expression faltered. "Oh, I know. Sorry, really. I thought you preferred your nickname." Her fair cheeks flushed red, and she lifted a hand to her mouth again, looking flustered. "I didn't mean to insult you, DH Keen. Please forgive my rudeness."

Instantly, he softened. He understood she hadn't meant to be cruel; he'd just hated that name so much. Poor Ollie the scholarship kid, the charity case. He didn't belong and everyone made sure he knew it. His time at Clementine Prep had been some of the worst years of his life, and being here in these gilded halls brought back every miserable memory. But *she* had never done anything to hurt him. It wasn't fair to take out his anger on Abigail.

"No, I must beg forgiveness, Lady. My reaction was uncalled for. I know you meant no disrespect. It just shocked me to hear that old nickname again." He forced a laugh. "Reminds me of how old I've gotten, right?"

She shook her head. "I should know better than to call a grown man – a distinguished officer, no less – by his childhood moniker!"

"Really, it's no bother. I really never minded when *you* called me Charity, Miss Primm."

It was true. And it was altogether too apparent in his tone. He bit down, teeth grinding, wondering if he'd revealed too much of his feelings.

"Oh, please call me Abigail. We're old friends, after all." She reached out to take his hand and an electric thrill passed through him. So this was what it was like to bask in her attention. He'd never experienced it as a youth. She'd been kind, yes, but in a distant sort of way, breezy and distracted. His heart swelled. This was now, and he was so different. A successful man. A *man*, not a boy. He squeezed her hand companionably, forgetting the real reason he was there – to deliver his report to Inspector Viridian – and letting himself experience a moment of hope. She was as lovely as she'd ever been. Perhaps–

"And it is Mrs Hollander, now, DH Keen," she said as she released his hand and crushed his heart simultaneously.

Hollander? Goddess, he knew that name. Dirk Hollander had been his tormentor, his nemesis. The boy who'd made his life a living hell. Fucking Dirk Hollander had married Abigail Primm? The sweetest, kindest, loveliest girl in school?

For a moment, he decided the Goddess did not exist and the world was a joke. Let the demons have it.

"You married Dirk?" he blurted before he could stop himself. And every bitter feeling he'd ever had painted those words.

"I did," she replied, pulling back. She straightened her apron. "He's joined his father in the family business. Hadn't you heard? We've all grown up quite a lot." Her tone held a mild rebuke.

He searched for a response. Dirk had been an unremarkable student, yet he'd attended one of the top universities in the Fifth District. The "family business" was selling rifles and cannon to the military – very lucrative. The Primms were one of the oldest and most respected families in Havenside, but Hollander wealth dwarfed their meager fortune. Money always made for a good match, but it had never occurred to him that Abby would care about such things. She'd always talked about how she might serve the Goddess best. Becoming a nurse was a commendable calling, but marrying someone like Dirk? It was flabbergasting.

All he could think of was the time he'd managed to best Dirk at fencing. That miserable monster had waited for him after school and beaten him bloody.

Oleander opened his mouth, trying to find something nice to say as she grew uncomfortable, her eyes seeking a way out of this conversation.

They were saved by the appearance of Revered Mother Francesca. Oleander recognized her immediately and it was all he could do not to hunch inside himself as he would have done years ago. Only the urgency of her steps, her white face and panicky expression kept him composed. His training asserting itself. *Danger*.

"Demonhunter!" she cried. "Come at once. That accursed nun has gone mad. She's whirling like the Devil and has called the flames of Hell to Earth!"

CHAPTER SEVEN

Hero was in trouble. She truly hadn't expected to confront a full complement of hellhounds when she'd opened the Gate, and the shock threw her for a moment, so focused had she been on catching the dead girl's shade. She refused to let another soul get *eaten*. Not on her watch. Never mind that the thing which had done the eating made her stomach flutter. It wasn't fear – not really; fear was an emotion she'd long since abandoned. Getting one's eyes gouged out on a regular basis made for a strong constitution.

So here in this place, surrounded by holy sisters of the Order of the Shield and a bastion of innocent children, she'd felt nothing but eagerness. Catching such a recently departed soul should have been a simple task: fresh corpse, newly dead – perfect.

What a fool she'd been to be so complacent! She should have paid more attention to her twisty innards. Something quite powerful was at play here. Even at the best of times, the Underworld was dangerous, a place of fire and rot and hidden traps – especially for her, a living being, only half demon.

Naturally, when she rushed, she landed in the hottest of water.

Individually, hellhounds were no worse than large, rabid dogs. In a pack, hot for blood, they were something else entirely. Luckily, she was still on edge after her earlier failure, keyed up and tense and braced for a new disaster, and she reacted with preternatural instincts, spinning out of reach of slavering jaws, and attempted to slam the Gate shut behind her. But the hounds burst through, dragging Hell with them.

She slammed back into her physical self, cross-legged on the ground, and rolled to her feet in sulfurous mist. Her Sight blurred as the two planes of existence merged, one calm and full of confused nuns, neat brick pathways and crushed gravel, the other fiery and grim and rife with slavering hounds.

Hero bounded in great leaps up the clock tower – simultaneously a crumbling, decrepit facade and a solid brick edifice – fingers and toes smashing into the wall for purchase, leaving burning divots behind her as she climbed. The unnatural creatures pursued her, leaping and snarling. Her half-demon flesh was particularly delicious to a hellhound.

"Goddess burn me!" she cursed as one of the beasts snapped at her heel. She kicked it, sending the lean, black-coated monster tumbling to the courtyard. The few nuns remaining on the scene didn't seem perturbed as the dead dog exploded into bits of rancid flesh practically at their feet; their eyes were on her while she clung to the tower like a madwoman. She hissed and launched herself backward off the bricks, executing a perfect flip to land lightly on her feet behind the snarling pack and in front of the two disapproving nuns.

"Have you quite lost your mind?" the pudgy revered mother asked her, outraged at her antics. The other nun stared at her white-faced and shrank back when Hero turned on both of them with a snarl.

"Get out of here!" she roared, whipping her slim sword free of its ebony sheath. She clonked a charging hound on the head with the cane half of her weapon, spilling its brains before it could rip into the clueless nun. "You're in grave danger, you stupid hags!"

Spinning, she sliced through another of the creatures and black blood splattered the paving stones. This, at least, the nuns could see, even if it appeared as sparkling effluvium. The revered mother spat a prayer like a curse and her colleague ran screaming. It took only a heartbeat for the mother to follow her. Good. No chance for casualties now, even accidental ones should her blade strike askance.

"Me? Kill a nun?" she muttered, already leaping and twisting her tall, angular frame away from savage fangs and claws. Her scapular flared and twirled around her, whipping at the beasts, and her voluminous pants caught more than a few of her attackers' claws, saving her skin from damage.

She managed to kill three more of the miserable beasts, bouncing around the courtyard and drawing even more of Hell through in the process. Not her best work, really, but it couldn't be helped. She caught sight of a pale shade among the flames and chaos, weaving through the hellhounds and random stalagmites sprung from nothingness.

"You!" she screamed, trying to draw its attention. Even a half-human voice attracted a spirit – so unexpected in Hell, where demons reigned supreme. "Cassandra Graham! I am here for you!"

The pale form wavered, began to coalesce. Hero felt a swelling of relief and fought her way through the ravenous dogs to reach the spirit of the dead girl. Her silver sword, a bright needle of destruction, tore through the hellhounds like scissors through paper. But they kept coming, determined. They did not want her to reach the shade!

"Sorry, bastards. Not today."

She was close to the glimmering soul. It was watching her with luminous eyes. The dogs swarmed, howling and snapping, barely kept at bay by the devastating sweep of her razor-sharp sword and the heavy club of ebony.

"Speak to me, spirit, and I will Speak for you!"

Its head turned, eyes fixing on her, growing brighter. The mouth opened, stretching as if it was screaming. Whispers floated to Hero's ears and the Communion began. Too late did she realize the danger Speaking would plunge her into as her limbs locked and her entire being focused on the dead spirit.

Well, fuck me.

Frozen, she broke out in a cold sweat. The hellhounds let loose a sound that seemed remarkably like laughter and her concern for Speaking with the girl's shade took a distant second place in the scheme of things.

With a frenzied howl, the hellhounds pounced.

Oleander wasn't sure what he'd been expecting, but he'd run to the quad with his weapon in hand – his blunderbuss this time; the inspector's words still haunted him: *"Even I can't dodge a spray of shot."* And he was damn glad he'd arrived prepared when he found the inspector locked in a grim battle with hellhounds.

Well, sort of. As far as he could tell, she stood frozen in the midst of an entire pack of ghostly specters. Was it fear? Somehow he doubted it, but what else would explain her strange catatonia?

Luckily, he had no such compulsions. Though his heart pounded with excitement and blood rushed in his ears, his entire body felt as alive as it had ever been. He moved with speed and strength, every part of him in harmony, his weapons extensions of his will, his soul. It was always like this when he faced demonic beings, that thrill of the hunt. To do what he was trained to do was the ultimate drug.

The blast of his blunderbuss shattered the afternoon calm. No one else could see or hear the creatures of Hell outside of him and the cursed nun – not in this permutation, at least, half in and half out of the Gate to the Underworld – but he could because of his rigorous training and a cocktail of "special" drugs. His gun and saber were also Goddess-blessed and designed for piercing the veil between worlds. Demons always kept one toe in the Underworld to stay safe from conventional weapons, though this move was useless against a demonhunter's arsenal.

Distantly, he heard the excited cries of students – the commotion had drawn a few white-faced bystanders from the cathedral – and a few screams here and there from nearby sisters. But he blocked out all distractions, reloaded with lightning quickness, calmly fired at another of the hellhounds and watched in satisfaction as it disintegrated like the first ones. The spray from the short, heavy gun was remarkably effective at close range, but in the thick of things reloading the one-shot weapon became nearly impossible. He drew his saber and used the blunderbuss as a club, laying about with it generously while stabbing creature after creature with his blade.

The inspector hadn't even flinched when he'd fired his blunderbuss, but he could see her eyes sliding frantically from side to side and her lips moving. Ah, so she wasn't frozen with fear, then; she'd managed to catch a shade. Perhaps they could learn something useful for their case.

Or maybe the girl had simply fallen from a tower as Abigail thought?

Then why the hellhounds, Keen? Don't be a dunce!

Oleander focused on doing his job. Hellhounds were demonic creatures, and he was very, very good at killing demons.

It was a veritable bloodbath, though the blood in this case was sparkling demonic humors, strangely beautiful as it cascaded onto the paving stones, the grass, the gravel, only to vanish in a twinkling of light. The flames of Hell licked at the edges of his vision, but whenever he turned his head they vanished as quickly as the ethereal blood and viscera. It was satisfying to unleash his talent but frustrating to witness supposedly hallowed ground being desecrated so blatantly. He was fighting demon dogs called by a demon nun! Or, at the very least, she'd given them access to the mortal plane by her recklessness.

He crushed the skull of a whining, injured hound with a stamp of his boot and eviscerated two more before checking on the inspector again. She was blinking her flaming eyes, coming back to herself bit by bit. The flames at the edges of the compound, always at the periphery of his sight, flickered and died, and the last of the shadowy hellhounds snapped out of existence. His new partner staggered as the Gate closed, cutting her free.

He was a step too late to catch her arm and she went to her knees hard on the pavement. Heart pounding fast and hard in his chest, Oleander holstered his blunderbuss and offered her a hand. She stared at it as if she didn't quite know what it was before she grasped it and let him haul her to her feet.

"Well," she said, pulling her glasses from a pocket in her pants and hooking the wire frames back over her ears. Thankfully, her unholy eyes were dimmed once more. "That was interesting."

"Was she murdered, Inspector?" he asked breathlessly, fascinated despite his initial reticence at being teamed with her. He'd never worked with a death speaker before, especially one with her vaunted reputation. She might prove a valuable partner even if she did have the terrible habit of summoning Hell to earth.

"Oh, most definitely." Her green-shaded gaze went to the unfortunate dead girl. "Poor child," she murmured. "Someone very much wanted to keep her silent. I don't believe they intended to kill her, but it ended up that way all the same."

"Do we have our killer?" He tried not to sound too disappointed. It couldn't be this easy, could it? But for a death speaker, maybe it was.

"Unfortunately, no. Something powerful is at work here, Demonhunter. The shade tried its best to speak to me, but unknown forces kept the Communion muddled." A frown, fierce and angry. "It's time to begin interrogations. Tell the revered mother to gather her students and staff."

He cringed, imagining the formidable woman's reaction to such a demand. "Should we... should we wait and see what the chief has to say?"

Hero lifted an eyebrow. "This is *our* case. We run it the way we think is best." She adjusted her glasses and gave him a look. "Are you up to the task, Keen?"

"Yes, Inspector." He clicked his heels, embarrassed by his own hesitation. "I am."

"Good. Let the mother know she's on my list, too."

His stomach sank. Goddess save him!

CHAPTER EIGHT

Her arms were bleeding where the hounds had scratched her. She would heal; she always healed – one of the benefits of her demon birthright. She was never spared the pain, of course. Suffering was inevitable no matter what your heritage.

Blood stained her cream-colored sleeves, now torn and tattered. She seethed at the loss. There were only so many shirts in her valise and her daily stipend wouldn't cover a visit to a tailor in hoity-toity Havenside. The rest of her outfit reeked of Hell after two dips in one day, but a good washing would take care of that. It didn't help with her mood, though. She was seething.

The victim had jumped to her death rather than face whatever was coming for her – terror had driven her off that ledge more than any human hand – but it would be difficult to call it murder. The details weren't quite clear. The Communion wasn't like a normal conversation. Usually, Hero had more to go on – visions and vibes, even a glimpse of the killer. This particular shade had been desperate to communicate, to Speak of its deep, terrible fear. It had wanted her help, *needed* her help, even in death. No girl so young should be so desperate.

The hellhounds had been sent to stop her from reaching the shade, from enjoining a full Communion, but they'd served as a warning, too: *Back off.* It wasn't the first time some angry demon had come after her in the Underworld – her meddling attracted quite a few monsters, all determined to be the one who got her, the half-demon hag who dared to dance between the living and the dead – but this had felt decidedly personal, as if the beast behind the attack knew her and wanted to thwart *her* specifically.

Well, aren't I full of myself? She smoothed her ruined sleeves and leaned forward. The unpleasant nun had given them use of a faculty board room to conduct their interviews, and now she and Keen sat at a long meeting table at its center. Shelves lined the walls, heavy with leather-bound books, golden trophies and grim marble busts of past educators presumably worthy of remembrance. Floor-to-ceiling windows, heavily curtained to protect the precious tomes, comprised the fourth wall. The only light came from tabletop lamps.

It was a dim and intimidating space, the weight of years and privilege making it almost intolerably stuffy. The DH sat hunched over, scribbling furiously in his notebook. She'd related all she could about her aborted Communion with the dead girl's shade – names, sensations, the terrible, terrible fear – though she'd left out the personal nature of the unforeseen hellhound attack. That was her problem; what could he do about Underworld demons? Only when they crossed the threshold into the real world did they become his problem. Although his arrival *had* been fortuitous; the well-timed spray of hot lead had saved her from a good mauling.

"She couldn't name this unseen assailant?" he asked again, pressing her. "Say whether it was a man or a woman? An adult or a fellow student?"

Hero sucked her teeth, frustrated that she couldn't answer his questions and annoyed that he kept asking the same ones, and leaned back in her seat. She had positioned herself in the largest chair at the head of the table, a ridiculous, overstuffed monstrosity of mahogany leather with a high back and massive armrests. She felt like a queen even in her bloodstained clothing, stinking of Hell and demon dogs.

It wasn't lost on her that when she'd lived in Havenside, a place like this might as well have been on the moon to one such as her. A half-demon child, even one from a good family like hers, wasn't allowed anywhere near such venerated establishments like Clementine Prep. The stink of her presence seemed to permeate everything and everyone around her, and her very existence would have tainted the school like a rotten egg. She tried not to dwell on the unpleasant thought, to let memories of this town cloud her judgement. She was an inspector, a death speaker, despite all she'd endured, all the prejudice and abuse. She was *better* than them. All of them.

"As I explained, the shade gave me such a cascade of feelings and images. It was hard to sort them. We have names, however. A few. We'll still have to root out the truth the old-fashioned way."

Lips pursed, he jotted down a few more words. Like a good underling, DH Keen had taken the seat to her left, his back to the windows. Interrogees would sit opposite him, facing the only human in the room while she observed and absorbed their reactions. It was satisfying that she hadn't had to explain her plan for these interviews. Keen understood the assignment. Maybe he wasn't such a squirrel after all.

"You have good aim, DH Keen," she commented after the silence between them had stretched to a thread. Mother Francesca was taking her sweet time rounding up the first batch of suspects. "How fortuitous that you decided to deliver your report immediately rather than wait for me to return to the station."

It was the closest she would ever come to thanking him for saving her life. It was his job after all, to watch her back, just as she would watch his. They were partners for the duration of this case, however long or short that might be. Still, he deserved an attaboy for his quick actions. She'd have lost a lot more blood than the little on her sleeves if he hadn't shown up when he did.

"I had hoped to get a look inside Catarine's apartment, also," he said, flipping to a clean page in his notebook. He cleared his throat and pulled his chair closer to the table, glancing in her direction but unwilling to face her directly. The flaring of his nostrils amused her. Did she stink? Probably, to him at least.

"Not necessary," she said blithely. "The techs did their job and I've got what I needed, too. I don't want anyone else mucking about up there."

"I know how to process a scene, Inspector."

"I'm sure you do, but that's beside the point. What I needed from the scene has nothing to do with evidence and the more people are about, the more my senses get clouded. Can you understand that?"

His full lips flattened. She very nearly rolled her eyes, expecting further defensiveness. The prickly bastard. Instead, after a pause, he nodded, his face relaxing. "I can," he said. "As a demonhunter, sometimes all I can trust are my own senses."

Her mouth twitched. Even when he was agreeing with her, he had to bring up something unpleasant. She was really trying to forget he was her mortal enemy, after all. She had no idea what his upbringing had been like, but as he'd gone to Clementine, she could assume he'd been raised in wealth and privilege, like all those who'd bullied, mocked and outright shunned her. For him to go on to be a demonhunter, too – she had to suppress a shudder – he couldn't be anything but awful.

Hero kicked back in her massive chair and threw her heels on the table. "What's taking that blasted nun so long?"

Keen's cheeks darkened at her casual disrespect. Primly, he brushed away dust that had fallen from her sharp-toed lace-up boots. "We are in her house, Inspector. Show some respect."

"Respect." She drew out the word, making it sound as disdainful as possible. "She should be just as eager to uncover the truth as we are, so why be difficult? She's the one with a murderer running around her school. Unless, of course, she's involved."

"You think the mother ran her own student off the clock tower?' He scoffed. "You said the Communion was fraught, full of shadows and confusion. How can you be sure she was even murdered?"

"The violently departed are my purview, Keen. I know the difference between murder, suicide and accident. You stick to killing demons, all right?"

Keen fell silent. His eyes roved the room, taking in the polished wood, the leather and gilt. The look on his face did not reflect fond memories, she noted. He looked like he'd swallowed something bitter. She raised an eyebrow, intrigued.

"You know, I used to envy the kids who got to go here," she said casually. "I wasn't allowed, you see. Why, think of the scandal! I wasn't allowed to go to any school, actually. Not here in Havenside."

Finally, he met her gaze and held it. "Your envy is misplaced, Inspector. But," and this he added reluctantly, as if it pained him to admit, "you should have been sent to school. Every child in the Realm deserves an education. It is the law."

"The laws aren't written for people like me, Officer." She pushed her glasses higher on her narrow nose. "I did get an education, though. Eventually. Blackstone Abbey taught me in the ways of the Shield. A very thorough education."

"And you repaid them by burning down their home."

His sharp castigation made her grin. "Exactly," she said with a wink. "I'm glad you get it."

His mouth opened, but Mother Francesca chose that moment to enter the faculty room. Keen stood hastily and offered a bow. A very proper gentleman. Hero put her feet down and propped her elbows on the table. "About time," she said. "Did you bring the list like I asked? I need to keep track of my suspects."

The mother scowled. "Witnesses, Inspector, not suspects. You have no reason to suspect anyone at this school, no reason at all." She waved toward Keen to acknowledge his gallantry, allowing him to retake his seat, but gave him no further attention. Her bright eyes stayed on Hero, ripe with disgust. She approached the table, a sheaf of papers clutched in one plump hand.

"Except there's a dead girl on your quad," Hero countered pleasantly. "I feel that might be a good reason."

"A poor child who couldn't handle her grief. It's a shameful business, turning tragedy into something nefarious. After all, you were the one who called Hell onto our campus, not any of these *witnesses*." The nun dropped the papers beside Hero, gesturing toward them vaguely. "The list contains everyone at Clem Prep who had anything to do with Sister Catarine – her friends, her colleagues, her roommate, her sisters, her students. I've a dozen people waiting in the hallway as we speak, ready to be treated like common criminals."

"Good." Hero gathered up the papers and flipped from one page to the next, examining the names. She gave the nun a sharp look. "Where is your name, Mother?"

The nun sniffed disdainfully and smoothed the front of her scapular – proper black, red and solemn white with the three-sided battle shield emblazoned on its right breast, unlike Hero's blasphemous outfit of bright summer colors and golden thread. "We will speak when you've finished your questioning. I have a grieving family to deal with at the moment." She sighed, and for a moment looked genuinely distraught. "The second one I've comforted in a matter of days, by the way, so spare me some small grace."

Hero tapped her fingernails against the tabletop as if she was trying to decide. "I will. For now." She straightened the papers, keeping the nun in the corner of her eye. "But your name was on the lips of the dead girl's shade, Mother Francesca."

The woman's expression remained neutral, though her clasped hands tightened and the barest flicker of annoyance clouded her eyes. "I should hope so," she said. "I had tried comforting her mere moments before her suicidal plunge. My kindness toward her must have been foremost in her mind."

"A wasted effort, it seems." Hero waved a hand breezily. "You may go. Please send in the first *witness* on your way out."

"That was rather uncalled for," Keen admonished once the revered mother had exited, quite huffily in Hero's opinion. "Why make an enemy of the headmistress, of all people? Or is it just your particular way to antagonize everyone involved in an investigation?"

She scowled. "I don't like nuns."

"That much is obvious, Inspector Viridian. You wear your hatred on your sleeve."

Luckily for Keen, her sharp retort was interrupted by the entrance of the first of their interrogees. The young woman was Sister Catarine's roommate, the novice. Red-eyed and sniffling, she sank into the seat across from the demonhunter and wiped at her nose with a kerchief. Hero leaned back in her chair and let Keen do the talking. He had a pleasant manner and a broad, surprisingly charming smile considering his dour appearance in general. It put the girl at ease, and she spoke without hesitation.

"Cat was a good girl," she insisted when Keen pushed at her a little harder. Did that imply possibly sinful behavior? Had the sister enjoyed a drink now and then? Had she kept company with any men? Had she been led down a dark path?

Hero had to bite her tongue. She knew this line of questioning was necessary, yet she hated blaming a person for their own death. She'd seen Catarine's body. No one deserved that, no matter what she might have thought or done, no matter how "impure" or dangerous her activities. A few radical ideas shouldn't lead to murder. Unless she'd been Summoning demons in her spare time and one had turned on her, of course, but Hero couldn't bring herself to believe that. Even though she'd failed to find the sister's shade, she'd gotten a good sense of the woman from examining her room. Her mark remained on the world. Sister Catarine had been virtuous. If she'd been guilty of anything, it was spilling secrets. She'd had her tongue cut out, after all – *ripped* out. That was a clear message: a warning.

"She had questions," the girl admitted when Keen continued to press. She lowered her voice, leaning forward to speak in a whisper. "Doubts." The way she said the word made it seem absolutely scandalous.

Keen nodded sympathetically. "Even the most devote among us has doubts, Novice Eleanor. The real question is, did she act on those doubts? In a way that might have put her in danger?"

She shook her head, her lips pinched. "It wasn't like that. She… she just wondered if Clementine was the best place for her. Sometimes she mentioned changing schools. That's all."

"That's all?" Keen said, his disbelief coloring his question. "Teachers change districts all the time."

Eleanor squirmed in her seat, her cheeks bright. She seemed a simple sort, unable to articulate even the most basic thoughts, yet something had her flustered. A secret?

"She was considering a secular school, wasn't she?" Hero asked. When Eleanor's head whipped toward her, Hero licked her lips. The girl blanched. "Sister Catarine had more than doubts," Hero pressed, sensing weakness. "She was ready to leave the order."

Miserably, Eleanor nodded, turning her attention back to Keen, her eyes wide as if beseeching him to save her from the horrid demon nun. "It's true. She wanted to leave. Not just Clementine, but the Order of the Shield. But… how could that get her killed? No one even knew. Just me and–" Her lips snapped closed abruptly and she sank into her seat.

"You and who?" Hero demanded. "Who else knew her intentions?"

Keen threw her a stern look and leaned toward the girl, pouring on the empathy. "It's all right, my dear. You aren't in trouble. You've been very helpful. But please, for your friend's sake, tell us who else knew her plans. We aren't going to punish them or assume anything foul. We're merely trying to gather all the facts. Do you understand?"

It took a moment and a few more soft words, but the girl finally gave up the name. And it was a name Hero recognized, not from the list Francesca had given her but from the dead girl's spirit. The slip of a shade had whispered it, a man's name: Father Roger Kellan.

"Father Kellan knew," Eleanor said, growing more confident now that she could speak the truth. "He and Catarine were quite close. The very best of friends."

"I'm sure," Hero drawled, her heart thrumming It was always exciting to narrow in on a potential person of interest. She dismissed the girl, ushering her to the door personally, then leaned out into the hall to scan the line of waiting suspects. There were more than a few priests standing in the corridor outside, but she knew instantly the one she wanted. Her spectacled gaze arrowed to a man with dark hair and a fine, youthful face, now flushed and sweaty. His eyes met hers, bloodshot and red rimmed, and slid sharply aside.

The shade had held a memory of him in her mind, a memory she'd taken into death, all mixed up with memories of Catarine. His face contorted with anger.

"You," Hero said, pointing at him with a long, pale finger tipped with a nail that was very nearly a talon. "Father Kellan. You're next."

CHAPTER NINE

They grilled the priest for a good two hours, but he didn't crack, even when the demon nun turned her flaming eyes on him as she pretended to clean her spectacles. Despite his disheveled state and the liquor on his breath, the young man kept his story straight. He and Catarine had been close, yes. She'd confided to him on many occasions, over innocent lunches and teas with her and her roommate or with other faculty members – nothing illicit. Why would their relationship be so strange? Father Kellan was friends with lots of people, popular and kind and devoted to his calling, to his celibacy and to his Goddess.

The death speaker had tossed him a loaded question at one point, attacking out of the blue: "What was your relationship with the dead girl, Kellan? Did she have some reason to fear you?"

"Fear me?" he'd echoed, aghast. "Goddess, no! Not at all. She was a little slow, I suppose," he temporized, shifting uncomfortably. "I – I had to give her extra work to catch up with the others. Sometimes, she had to stay after class for help."

"And I'm sure you were delighted to help her, weren't you?" Hero purred, letting the implication lie heavy between them.

The priest turned a sickly shade of gray, but his jaw firmed. "I refuse to even entertain such a notion, Inspector. It's outrageous."

Oleander was inclined to believe him, and didn't understand Hero's suspicion and her vicious line of questioning. Why, she'd already practically accused the man of having an affair with the dead sister, a scandal of monstrous proportion in a place like Clementine Prep. Her sly inference of something indecent between them had made even Oleander blush, and he was no celibate priest or virgin nun. And now this? It was beyond disgusting. Whatever her goal might have been, she'd succeeded only in making Kellan seem even more sympathetic.

Finally, Hero had let Father Kellan go, and by then the other witnesses had left, which had thrown the death speaker into a rage. Mortified, DH Keen had kept behind the inspector as she'd berated the revered mother, tossing the holy woman apologetic looks he hoped Hero wouldn't catch.

"The children needed to go home, Inspector," Francesca had explained, unruffled by Hero's anger, standing firm against it, a powerhouse in her own right and hardly intimidated by the wrath of a half-demon, disgraced nun. The secular world had no authority over her, after all, an apostate even less so. "And my sisters and brothers are at their prayers – where I am going, as well. Be glad I paid you this last courtesy before you leave."

"Then we'll have to call everyone on that list into the station until we finish our interrogations," Hero said finally, still angry but obviously defeated by the older woman's obstinance. "And if you continue to obstruct this investigation, I'll have Chief Dewey put you in a cell. Do you understand me? You might think your holy robes protect you from the likes of me, but I assure you, you are mistaken. We have two murders on our hands, and possibly two murderers. The public good outweighs your daily devotionals!"

That got a rise out of the revered mother. She seemed to grow in stature at the insult and Keen groaned inwardly. She hadn't been his headmistress then, merely the head of her department, but she'd carried herself the same, as if she was indestructible, infallible. Not to be questioned.

"Leave. Now," she said stiffly. Her eyes flashed alarmingly, as if her irises might burst into flame to match Hero's incendiary gaze. "I will not be disrespected by you, a disgrace to the order. An arsonist. A criminal. They can clean you up and give you a badge, but I know what you are, demon child. I know what you've done, and I know what awaits you when you go to your eternal rest."

This last she said in a hiss. Shockingly, Hero recoiled, her skin as white as paste. She seemed to shrink, pulling in on herself, becoming child-sized. Keen was astounded. He'd thought nothing could ruffle his inhuman partner. A brutalized nun and a broken, dead girl hadn't. Hellhounds hadn't. What had her so horrified now?

"You think I don't know what awaits me?" The inspector spoke through clenched teeth, her lips drawn back like a rabid dog's. The revered mother looked down her nose at her – an impressive feat for such a petite woman, impossible but for Hero's cowering demeanor. "Pandemonium has been nipping at my heels my entire life, a punishment earned by nothing but the circumstances of my birth!"

Francesca uttered a disgusted huff. "You earned your place in Hell on your own. And whoever let you out of prison after you tried to murder a good man, a blessed man, deserves a place beside you, too."

"A blessed man?" Hero's scowl deepened and suddenly her demeanor shifted again. Keen blinked, wondering if he was imagining it, but, no, where she'd been shrinking before, now she was growing. Thin and pale and lithe, still, but decidedly bigger. Taller, wider, muscles straining against her blood-spattered sleeves. Small tears left by hellhound claws ripped wider. "Father Carmichael was more demon than half the creatures resigned to Pandemonium! His crimes were vicious, depraved. So many victims. Too many to count. And your precious order did nothing. Your battle nuns protected him when they were supposed to be shields against evil!"

"Bishop," Francesca snapped, unmoved by Hero's raging, scandalous accusations. "You will address him as Bishop Carmichael."

Hero jerked as if slapped. "Bishop? He was *raised*?"

"He was ordained ten years ago and given blessed authority over all the dioceses in greater Havenside. Clementine Preparatory falls under his guidance. I cannot believe he allowed you on the premises, but that just proves what a decent, just man he is!"

A tremor shook the air. Shimmers of heat. The demon ex-nun practically vibrated with barely contained rage. Oleander could feel it, taste it. Alarm rippled through him. His partner was about to do violence.

He acted on pure instinct, reaching into his sash for a vial of Serenity. It was a temporary potion, a quick-acting palliative to briefly subdue a powerful demon. He hoped and prayed it had a similar effect on a half-demon. Otherwise, he would have to fight her again – a perfectly disastrous option.

Luckily, Hero's entire focus was on Mother Francesca, who stood her ground with remarkable courage. Or perhaps she was too dense to recognize the danger swiftly looming higher and higher above her. But even she had to feel the heat radiating from Hero's alien frame, hear the low growl rising in her chest, see her hands twisting into claws, reaching for that plump throat–

Oleander crushed the vial in his hand and thrust his palm beneath the Inspector's nose. She started and reeled toward him, redirecting her rage at this sudden attack. But the potion was strong, as strong as anything he carried, only to be used in emergencies and difficult to create without a proper apothecarist's lab. He might regret this later, but for now it was a great relief to see her demon eyes glazing behind her tinted glasses. The whirling flames slowed, stilled. If he hadn't known better, he'd think her eyes were normal.

The air grew still around them, cool and calm. Hero staggered back a step, returning to normal proportions again – well, normal for her anyway: tall, angular, almost human. Her mouth grew slack, her jaw sagging, and she allowed him to take her by the arm. He cast the mother a dark glance, no longer feeling so apologetic for his partner. The wretched nun had deliberately antagonized the half-demon inspector. "We will leave as you insisted," he said stiffly, "but we'll expect your cooperation from here on out. Have the witnesses notified, Revered Mother, or you'll have to answer to the chief."

"What did you do to her?" Francesca demanded, voice colored with suspicion. There was a hint of inquisitiveness, too, as if she hoped to learn what he'd done so she could copy it. But a demonhunter never revealed the secrets of his order, any more than she would hers.

"I handled the situation, Mother. Now, I bid you good day." He steered Hero away from her, eager to leave, but paused when they'd moved only a few steps down the gleaming, empty hall, tossing a final glance at the diminutive nun. "I urge you to treat Inspector Hero with all due respect from now on, Headmistress. I cannot guarantee any intervention next time. Do you understand?"

Her back stiff, her hands clasped white-knuckled at her thick waist, Mother Francesca glared at him disdainfully but allowed him the smallest of nods. He took it for agreement and fled, his bootheels resoundingly sharp against the wooden floor. Hero let him lead her, stumbling along like a drunkard, docile and obedient – for now. It wouldn't do to worry about how she'd react once the potion wore off.

Hopefully, he'd be able to explain his reasoning and mollify her before it did, or he reckoned he'd have Hell to pay.

Keen took his demon partner to the sea – or close to it, anyway. Down by the docks, with their forests of tall masts rising above sleek, varnished hulls, crying birds wheeling avariciously overhead. Ships' bells tolling with the rhythm of the waves. The scent of brine on the breeze, the lapping of water against wood. A calm place. Definitely not a place for violence. He found a bench looking out over the harbor and the boats bringing in the afternoon catch. Not commercial boats; these were locals – potential witnesses – out for a fine day of fishing. Soon, their catches would stretch out along the boardwalk, fat and glistening, to be weighed and measured and exclaimed over.

He studied his soporific partner, watching for signs that she was coming out of the Serenity potion. She seemed quiescent, staring out at the glittering water, the sun behind them dipping fast toward the horizon. A chill breeze blew from the west, the false summer loosening its grip as evening approached.

"I know what you did back there," she said, her words slurred.

Keen grimaced. "You didn't leave me much choice. Was I supposed to let you attack the revered mother?"

She snorted softly, petulantly. "No great loss. She's probably our murderer."

"So that makes it right to execute her? We are officers of the law, Inspector."

"How very proper," she said, giving him a burning side-eye. "Your demonhunter compatriots weren't about to give me a trial, last time I dealt with them. No rights for the wicked, eh?"

It took some effort not to squirm with discomfort, though it shouldn't have bothered him. She had been an unrepentant arsonist, guilty of attempted murder, imbued with demonic power. There were no laws protecting someone like her. Yet somehow he knew she was right: The law had to be for everyone or for no one.

But he wasn't about to admit that to her.

"It's fortuitous that we're here," he said, changing the subject. "I believe Catarine's brothers work the docks. We should question them, yes?"

There was a beat before she answered – Serenity muddled the mind. "Chief Dewey spoke with them when Catarine's body was discovered. It's in the report."

Of course. "Shouldn't we speak with them, too?" he asked, unwilling to admit that he hadn't read the report yet. Not thoroughly, anyway. *Stupid.* "Perhaps they'll be more forthcoming with us than they would be with the local PKs?"

She made a dismissive noise. Then, brightly: "I have a better idea."

She stood abruptly and nearly tipped forward over the edge of the dock. A hiss slid from her and he rethought reaching out to grab her arm. "Your blasted potion better wear off soon," she warned him, recovering her balance with a little help from her ebony cane. She turned on him, fangs peeking from between her lips. "I could use a drink, DH Keen. And I know just the place."

Warily, he got to his feet. Havenside had many taverns and restaurants, but he knew she was going to suggest somewhere he wasn't going to like. The glee on her strange face hardly put him at ease as she spun her cane like she hadn't a care in the world and started down the boardwalk, though at a noticeable list, assuming quite rightly that he would follow.

When he realized where she meant to take them, he stopped dead in his tracks. "You can't mean…?"

She threw a look over her shoulder. "Come now, Keen. You are a demonhunter first rank, and I am a prestigious death speaker of some renown, and we are on official business. They won't be able to turn us away. I guarantee it."

He wanted to argue with her, but realized it was useless when she continued on toward the sprawling white clapboard building at the end of the docks. Maybe she was right. Maybe this time, he wouldn't be turned away at the door.

Built right over the water, its crisp blue shutters open to catch the sea air, Grantham House was an institution in Havenside, an exclusive club reserved for yachtsmen and the town's upper crust. It was a favorite haunt of men who could spend all day smoking cigars and lingering over brandies because their fortunes had been made a hundred years ago by ruthless opportunists no better than pirates, a place where the finest women sat in judgement over their peers, dictating who was in and who was out of their complex, albeit borderline incestuous, high society. This was a world so far from Otherside, it may as well have been across the vast ocean, and Keen had once been made brutally aware of this truth in a most humiliating fashion. The memory brought a tightness to his jaw.

For a brief moment, he'd thought graduating from the town's elite school might grant him access, and he'd dared to bring his mother to Grantham House for a celebratory dinner. As a chubby youth in his graduation robes, shabbily dressed mother on his arm beaming with pride, he hadn't made it very far. They'd been turned away on the steps by a scandalized maître d'. The humiliation had been complete when he'd slunk away sheepishly, his mother trying to laugh it off, right past a group of his classmates – Abigail Primm among them – and their smirking parents.

And now, here he was again, standing at the base of the broad, stone steps which led up to a wraparound deck of gloriously fine craftsmanship . There were tables on the grand porch with the best views of the harbor, all full on this fine day. The scandalized glances of the patrons burned like acid on his skin.

"Help me up the stairs," Hero ordered, looping her arm through his. "I wouldn't want to stumble in front of the looky-loos."

He did as she instructed, escorting her as if she were a proper maiden and he a real gentleman. No one stopped him on the steps this time and he felt a flush of confidence. Maybe Hero was right.

Inside, the foyer was dim and hushed. The murmur of conversation, the occasional hoot of laughter and the clink of glassware drifted in from behind another set of doors. Circular windows set at head height in the twin doors offered a view of the dining room. The sparkle of fine porcelain dishes, silver cutlery and exquisite cut-crystal goblets winked enticingly. Keen's heart sped; he was closer than he'd ever been to forbidden paradise. Hero slipped free of him and approached the hostess stand while he tugged his jacket straight and settled a hand on his saber hilt. His uniform was his armor this time, and his ticket. He was a demonhunter, first rank, accompanying an inspector, a death speaker.

A half-demon, disgraced ex-nun arsonist.

Currently harassing a white-faced hostess.

"No, I don't have a reservation, you silly twit," she said, not exactly yelling but not *not* yelling either. Hero pointed a long, sharp finger toward the doors. "You have space at the bar. I can see it from here. My partner and I will sit, have a drink, and no one needs to get hurt. Understand?"

"I – I don't – we don't allow, I mean…" the young woman gulped, the dark scattering of freckles across her nose and cheeks the only color remaining on her face. "PKs don't eat here," she said faintly. Then, gathering courage like a comforting blanket, she pulled herself together, lifting her chin, and added with great dignity, "This is Grantham House, sir, not a – a common tavern!"

"Well, today it's my house." Hero bypassed the hostess and her elegant podium of oak and gold leaf, ignoring the woman's sputtering outrage. Oleander, mortified yet emboldened, scrambled after her, not sure if he intended to stop her or join her.

Finally, the chance to rectify his past humiliation made his decision for him. Shadowing the towering inspector, he followed her through the doors.

CHAPTER TEN

The interior of the fabled Grantham House was bright and airy. Light poured in through the banks of windows along the east side of the dining room, floor-to-ceiling panels of sparkling cut glass splitting sunlight into rainbows. The tablecloths glowed, too white and crisp to be real.

A bevy of waiters circulated among the tables, unobtrusive in their understated black-and-white uniforms, moving like dancers in a secret ballet, filling empty glasses, whisking away dirty plates, replacing soiled napkins before the diners had to spare a thought or worry. Food arrived on delicate plates – works of art to rival any museum's – to jaded regulars who dug in thoughtlessly, ruining the carefully applied garnishes, the extensive efforts of a bustling kitchen sure in their skill and technique.

Into this secretive, insular, debauched world stumbled two PKs in uniforms rumpled from a day of murder and mayhem – the garb of people who worked for a living. All the tugging and straightening in the world wouldn't set their clothes right, not next to the fine tweeds, wool crepe and rich linens of the town's elite.

The lively conversations of the well-dressed patrons stuttered to a halt at their sudden appearance. Two of the waitstaff stumbled in their coordinated dance, colliding and dropping their trays in a clatter.

Mortification settled firmly in Keen's hot cheeks, and he nearly backpedaled the hell out of there. But Hero, in her voluminous pants and bloody sleeves, continued onward, unruffled, striding to the bar and alighting on a tall stool.

Swallowing his embarrassment, Keen joined her, his steps dragging like a man walking to his doom.

The bartender ignored them for as long as he could, washing glasses at a little sink station beneath the sweep of polished mahogany. A mirror of exceptional quality cast Keen's face back at him, and he was somewhat alarmed at the state of his appearance, washed of all color, hair poking from beneath his cap, bandolier askew and dotted with shimmering demon blood. He whisked off his hat and ran a hand over his hair, which had just enough pomade remaining to keep it smooth – mostly. He settled his military cap on the bar and cleared his throat pointedly, but it was the sharp rap of Hero's knuckles that finally got the barkeep's attention.

The man, old enough to be Keen's father, balding and trim in his neat black jacket, scowled in their direction before finally ambling closer.

"Bourbon," Hero said. She jabbed a thumb toward Keen. "I'll assume he wants something with fruit in it."

"I will have a gin, good sir." Oleander said, ignoring her rude remark. "With plenty of ice," he dared to add, letting a note of haughtiness enter his voice. Bars in Otherside rarely had ice.

The barkeep said nothing, merely scowled. His gaze connected with someone behind them – Oleander didn't turn to see who it was – and his scowl softened somewhat, became resigned. He began filling their order, noisily and resentfully.

Beside him, Hero groaned softly, deep in her chest. "You did a number on me, squirrel," she muttered. "I've got a bad taste in my mouth and a head full of cotton. Can't believe you managed to get the drop on me. Prison must have made me soft."

Soft as marble, maybe. "I told you: You left me no choice, Inspector."

"You won't be able to pull that trick again, fortunately – for your sake."

He stiffened. "Not all demonhunters carry the same stash," he said. "We each have our own unique formulas."

She huffed in amusement. "Please. You lot suffer from a failure of imagination. Your rigid adherence to your training may make you formidable, but it also makes you predictable."

She wasn't wrong. Keen said nothing. Where was that damnable gin anyway?

"Why did you bring us here?" he demanded testily, feeling the eyes of the other patrons upon them. He'd made it inside the fabled Grantham House, and it was clear he still wasn't welcome.

"Aren't these your people, DH Keen? All lofty and judgmental?"

"Hardly. This place is not... I don't belong here any more than you do."

She quirked an eyebrow, offering him a sidelong glance. "Really? I doubt that."

He ground his teeth a moment, considering. He wasn't after her sympathy or loyalty. Still, she should understand the situation, and his place in Havenside. "I grew up in Otherside."

"Otherside? Yet you went to Clem? Ah!" She shook her head. "One of the lucky ones, eh? A charity case. I presumed when I should have asked. No wonder you try so hard. Well, I must ask forgiveness, then."

"Forgiveness for what?" he demanded, suspicious of her sudden conciliatory tone. And being called a charity case was no better coming from her than from his classmates.

Hero grinned at him, showing off her bright white fangs. "My thoughts, DH Keen. I never realized how firmly I still hold on to my resentments. They are like rotten fruit – smelly, messy and useless."

He relaxed, softening toward a fellow outcast, even if she was a demon. "You have no need of my forgiveness. I had no idea how deep my own resentment lay. Not until I set foot back in my old school."

Their drinks arrived with a side of surly attitude before the barkeep made himself scarce. The two PKs shared a wry glance and lifted their glasses in an impromptu toast, not going so far as to clink the crystal tumblers together, but the implication was clear. As he sipped at his gin while his partner downed half her glass, Keen hoped this marked a new beginning, a much more auspicious one than him trying to take off her head.

"Father Kellan was in love with Sister Catarine," Hero said after a moment of silence. The dining room had resumed its normal rumblings, albeit somewhat subdued, though the amount of whispering had certainly increased. The glances thrown their way were hardly subtle, either. A few of the men glared with open hostility. Keen did his best to ignore them; he knew many of them by sight and reputation and he really didn't like attracting their attention.

"I think he loved her," he said carefully. "They were very close friends it seemed to me. Her murder devastated him."

"Only a man in love falls apart like that. I've seen it before." She turned her glass on the polished surface, her brow pinched above her long, narrow nose. "They had a sexual relationship or I'll put myself back in a cell."

Keen tried hard not to squirm in embarrassment. The idea of a nun and a priest fornicating did not sit well with him. They were supposed to be better than the rest of them. Holier. More righteous. More moral. It was preposterous.

Although if they *had* been lovers and Catarine had decided to end things, that was motive.

"You think a man in love would rip out her tongue like that? Leave her naked and exposed on a mountainside because she spurned him? It seems far too cold and calculating for a crime of passion." He shook his head. He was the rookie on this case, the damnable squirrel, and he was well aware of it, but he had instincts too and he had learned to trust them. "I don't see it, Inspector, even if you're right and they were in a – a *sexual* relationship." He spoke the word in a hissing whisper, as if a priest and a nun having sex was worse than a brutal murder.

"It would certainly throw people off your trail, now, wouldn't it? Half the PKs think it was a ritual killing, a sacrifice to an older, harsher version of the Goddess." She knocked a knuckle against the bar. "Human hands kidnapped her, tortured her, even if a demon was behind her demise ultimately. A spurned lover is a useful instrument."

"Nevertheless, it would take someone of such depravity and ruthlessness… No, I just don't see it. Maybe I didn't catch the depth of his feelings toward Catarine, I'll grant you that, but Father Kellan is a good man, I have no doubt."

Hero scoffed. She emptied her glass in a quick toss. "Always have doubt, my good demonhunter. Doubts keep you safe. Everyone is a suspect, you understand me? Everyone. And right now, Kellan is at the top of our list. There is no greater hate than love gone wrong. And hate leaves you wide open to Pandemonium."

Keen wanted to argue, but he knew better than to go against a superior, especially one who could literally talk to the dead. He buried his reaction in a slow sip of gin. Hero was waving down the barkeep for another bourbon, letting her glasses slip just enough to reveal a ruby haze of flame.

The barman showed a bit more alacrity in delivering her drink this time. "This one is on the house," he said as he settled the bourbon in front of Hero. "And you should find your way out the door when you've finished."

Keen stiffened. He'd been waiting for a confrontation beyond mere rudeness. It was stupid to think their status would shield them. He was a DH first rank, not a lieutenant or a captain or a commissioner. Those types were welcome at Grantham – PKs of high enough position to grant favors. The rank and file, no matter how good they were at their jobs, might as well be dockworkers or dirt-grubbed farmers to the city's aristocracy.

Hero smirked and tossed back her drink. It had to have burned going down but only a slight tightening of her lips revealed any discomfort. "This place stinks, anyway," she said. She spun her chair around to face the room and raised her voice. "Stinks of secrets and lies. Of death and dark magic." She sniffed dramatically. More than one patron was staring at her, transfixed. Horrified. A few men in tailored woolen slacks, cotton button-downs jauntily rolled back to the elbows and silk waistcoats paused in their game of cards to glare at her balefully. "You can only hide behind your fine clothes, your wealth and status for so long," she warned them. "Mark my words: there is a killer among you. And I will find him. Or her."

Mortified, Keen drained his glass of gin, nearly choking on the harsh liquor, eyes watering as he grabbed his hat. It was time to go, apparently. "Come on, Inspector," he wheezed, not daring to take her by the elbow and usher her out. Hopefully, the urgency in his voice would be enough. "Let's be on our way."

"Here now! You can't make accusations like that. How dare you?" One of the card players was on his feet, outraged, hands curled into fists. He was a big one, too, bulging at his sleeves yet trim at the waist. His thigh muscles were practically visible through the heavy crepe of his pants. Not a dandy like the rest of them. Inwardly, Keen groaned. Would he have to defend his partner against a violent man, or defend the man against a demon?

"I dare because I am the inspector on this case, and a death speaker," Hero said, stepping down from her stool, cane in hand, taking a few menacing steps in his direction. They were the same height, even if she was half his width. She leaned on her cane and peered at the other patrons. "I have Spoken to the dead, to Sister Catarine."

A scattering of gasps and soft exclamations. Murmurs. Whispers. Did there seem to be an undercurrent of fear running through the place, beneath the morbid curiosity? Was it just for Hero, or was it fear for themselves?

Fear of what the dead had to say?

Keen no longer cared what Hero was doing to antagonize these people. Instead, he kept a close watch on their reactions, looking for signs of guilt – a telltale grimace, a sweaty brow, a shaking hand, a too-loud laugh, a widening of the eyes. Observation caught criminals more than any other skill in a PK's repertoire.

"Then you already know what happened to her," a woman spoke up. Middle-aged and dressed in an elaborate frock of lace and silk and beads, she stared at Hero primly from beneath a wide-brimmed hat with a stuffed parrot pinned atop it, colorful wings open as if in flight but its black eyes dead and dull. Keen recognized her with a start. She was Abigail Primm's great aunt, Lady Sorsha Primm. Her family could trace its roots back to pre-colonial times, a family of impeccable reputation. "So, I am unsure as to why you are harassing good people in the middle of the day, Inspector Viridian."

"Good people." Hero scoffed. "You are a den of vipers."

The woman sniffed disdainfully. Her cold blue eyes landed on Oleander. "I know who you are, boy. Don't think for a moment that you have risen above your station. Your education was at our largesse. Remember your place."

Stunned, Oleander nearly stammered an apology. Abby's aunt was filthy rich and hugely influential. Abby's immediate family, as wealthy as they were, were the poor relations by comparison.

Beside him, the inspector tapped her cane against the floor imperiously. "I'll not have you disparage my partner, madam. And don't think you're above our authority, either. Your family has its claws in everything, I recall. I wouldn't put murder past you and yours. Scandals hover about you like flies on dead meat."

Gasps and angry growls answered her. Lady Primm paled, but her eyes were hard as diamonds. Her gloved hand clenched on the fine tablecloth, scrunching the cloth into a knot. A younger woman at the same table let out a soft cry and tumbled dramatically from her chair. The mood in the room shifted as the burly gentleman dashed to rescue the crumpled lady. Waitstaff swarmed around them, offering glasses of water, fanning the girl with unfurled napkins, creating more chaos than anything.

"Get out, you scum!" cried a man in a tuxedo, gesturing angrily toward the doors, handlebar mustache bristling with rage. "Get out before we toss you out!"

Oleander doffed his hat, apologizing profusely, and reached to drag Hero out by the arm, but the half-demon inspector had already slunk to the door – or so he perceived it. Actually, she had moved with oily swiftness, but with little urgency. The tinkle of her laughter echoed back into the dining room through the flapping doors.

CHAPTER ELEVEN

Someone was waiting for her when Hero returned to her rental flat in downtown Havenside. A few turns off the main square, it was a roomy place with a kitchenette, decent furniture and a working fireplace free of ash and soot. Comfortable enough for a short stay, though she was beginning to think this case wouldn't be as easy as she'd hoped. It had been a false hope, anyway. Nothing about Havenside could be called simple.

"Well, that was *fun*," she'd exclaimed once she and the scandalized demonhunter had exited Grantham House. "Tell me what you saw in there, Keen."

"A lot of angry people?" her partner had muttered, slapping his cap back on his head as he joined her on the sidewalk.

"Exactly. It was Chief Dewey who requested a death speaker, not any other town official," she continued. "The PKs might be desperate to solve this case, but many others not so much, eh?"

His lips thinned and he rubbed at his generous nose. "Your methods leave much to be desired, Inspector, but you certainly poked a few bears back there. Sister Catarine's death might be more complicated than we feared."

"Oh, my dear demonhunter, on the contrary. It is just as complicated as I'd feared."

After promising to meet her at the PK station first thing in the morning, he'd absconded. Maybe he didn't find her as offensive as he had upon their first meeting (though his nostrils still flared when she stood close), but he certainly hadn't come to like her much. Tolerance was probably all she could expect from him. Unfortunately, they were partners at the moment for better or worse, and trust was essential, especially when there was no one else in town they could trust at all. He needed to acquire it, and soon.

So finding a tall, dark figure lurking outside her door in the deep shadows of evening made her hackles rise. She nearly drew her sword before the person spoke.

"Helen," it said. *He* said.

A single gas lamp flickered above the entrance, casting the man's face in darkness. She didn't need to see his face to know who he was. Even after all this time, she recognized her brother's voice.

Half brother, she amended automatically. Unwillingly, she remembered the day she'd learned she had a different father than him – the day she'd nearly killed him. Accidentally, of course.

It was hard to forget that day. Her mother had tried to drown her in a rain barrel, shrieking and cursing like a madwoman while her brother lay crumpled on the grass after she'd dared him to jump off the roof. Only then did she understand that children shouldn't be able to leap off the roof of a two-story house and remain unharmed. It was the first time in her life she'd ever felt real fear, despite all the things her mother had done to her over the years. Seeing her brother so white and still…

Luckily, little Liam Franke had woken up and started crying, distracting their mother from her murderous task.

"Liam," she said, her voice carrying an unfortunate quaver. She cleared her throat and adjusted her glasses. "I didn't see you at the station. I assumed you wanted nothing to do with me."

"You assumed correctly," he replied. He moved closer to the light, and she could see him better. He looked haggard, the boyish face she remembered replaced by a hard jaw and sunken cheeks. His very normal brown eyes regarded her coolly. "You have no idea the shame you brought on our family, Helen, with your antics. I would just as well never lay eyes on you again, but here you are, working in my own PK unit, so that's impossible."

She backed up another step. The disappointment tightening her chest and clawing at her throat was unexpected. They had been close once. "What are you doing here? If it's about the case, you could have waited until tomorrow to speak to me. Unless you've found another body," she added, a little too eagerly.

Wrong move. His lip curled slightly, and his brown eyes filled with disgust. "This has nothing to do with the case. Mother sent me."

She jerked, unable to help herself. "Mother? That foul bitch is still alive?"

His sneer deepened. "Show some respect. She's our mother!"

"She was never a mother to me. Or don't you recall? Maybe you were too young to remember her gouging out my eyes?"

He winced. Well, at least it bothered him – that was something. She slipped by him to reach the door, the iron key in her hand shaking only slightly before she jammed it into the lock. His boots shuffled on the concrete stoop. He sighed, a sharp huff of a sound. "She's dying, Helen. That should make you happy."

"It's Hero now, or Inspector Viridian if you prefer." She paused, gripping the key and wishing she could escape inside. "I am not happy to hear it. Frankly, I don't care at all one way or the other. She means nothing to me."

It was a lie. She hated their mother with a bone-deep passion, and it warmed her heart – such as she had one – to hear of her impending death. She prayed to the Goddess that it would be a painful one.

"She's been asking for you, He– Hero," he said, stumbling over the unfamiliar name. She'd picked it for its strangeness, once given to a saint who'd been martyred long ago in a foreign land. It had been her chosen name as a novice, and she'd happily kept it. Viridian she'd made up out of whole cloth, deciding that Franke wasn't *her* surname. Her father was some disgusting incubus, not Collin Franke, esteemed barrister and landowner.

"She's desperate to see you," he went on softly. Their mother had always loved *him*. "I think she's hoping to make amends before she faces judgement."

Hero swallowed a sharp retort. She didn't hate her brother. What could he have done to help her? He'd been a child, too, only a couple years older than her. And he was here, reaching out – for their mother, yes, but he *was* here. "I'll think about it," she lied. "It's all I can give you right now."

He nodded, looking somewhat relieved. He even managed to smile at her. "Thank you. I won't tell her anything yet, not until you're certain. I wouldn't want to get her hopes up. Trust me, H– Hero, it's for your good, too." He put a hand over his heart. "Forgiveness heals the soul."

At that, Hero had to laugh bitterly. "Oh, dear brother, you forget. According to all of you, I don't have a soul."

Hero was in a foul mood as she made herself a coffee at the PK station the next morning. There was a reason for it. Instead of reading through Sister Catarine's correspondence and then dropping into bed for a good night's sleep as she'd planned, she'd spent the night polishing off a bottle of cheap whiskey and pacing like a lunatic. News of her mother's impending demise coupled with her sudden, inexplicable change of heart towards her only daughter kept Hero's mind racing. Bad enough she had the vision of a desperate dead girl in her brain, mouth gaping like a fish's while she tried to reveal her murderer but only managing hints and whispers. Vague visions of potential assailants, all wrapped up in terror and pain. And a dark presence behind it all, a looming shadow that gave Hero the willies.

Bad enough, yet somehow thoughts of her mother were worse. Being in Havenside had forced her to recall unpleasant events here and there, but she'd kept the worst of it at bay. Now, it was as if a floodgate had opened. She could almost feel the hot pokers searing into her eye sockets–

She took a slug of hot coffee, scalding her tongue. Grimacing, she nearly spit it out, but a hard swallow sent the fire down her throat. She sucked in a breath to soothe her burned tongue and settled her cup back on the table. The steam rising from it should have warned her, but she'd been too distracted by her whirling thoughts. Her demonic blood mended wounds quickly; she had only to wait for the pain to pass. It seemed interminable. Her mood plummeted, and it wasn't improved by Keen arriving at the samovar, practically tapping his toe as she added more sugar to her coffee.

"Officer Coates has the next witness ready. Are you finished with your break?"

All two minutes of it? She scowled. "Yes. Fine. Let's get back to it."

She returned with him to the interrogation room, blowing on her coffee as she went. "Have Coates send in the... who is it this time? Another nun?" she asked irritably as she took her seat again. "I'm sick to death of nuns."

"No, we've spoken to all the sisters who had contact with her on the last day she was seen alive."

"All but the revered mother," Hero snarled. It had infuriated her to learn Francesca refused to be questioned, sending a representative instead. Unfortunately, they had no legal recourse; the Church of the Goddess and the Branch was a powerful institution. She'd claimed being questioned violated the law of the Goddess, and Hero had no ready argument to counter that protection.

"We're starting with some of the lay staff, and then her students," Keen finished without acknowledging her interruption.

"Fine. Let's get on with it."

The interrogation room was small, devoid of windows and hope, with blank plaster walls, yellowing and water-stained. The air was slightly cold, the chairs hard and uncomfortable. Silent observers – Chief Dewey and her brother, Liam, his second-in-command watched from behind a small square of silvered glass. A clever new invention, this "transparent mirror"; Hero was impressed. Not even the much grander precinct in New Savage had one.

It didn't help to know Liam was watching her, judging her. She didn't want to care, but she did. For all she thought of herself as cold and heartless, apparently she was wrong. After all this time, did she even know herself at all?

Who really knows themselves?

Her gaze drifted to her partner. He sat trim and neat on the edge of his hard chair, taking prodigious notes with a fountain pen, brow scrunched as the pen flowed across the sheets of yellow paper.

Well, maybe Keen does. The simple ones always do.

The first staff member from Clementine was the school nurse, a Mrs Abigail Hollander, red-eyed and weepy like all the others, though maybe a tad more attractive than the average woman. Hero was a terrible judge of looks, but there was a certain appeal to her sleek black hair, held back by velvet ribbons, and the porcelain paleness of her skin which evoked fragility. Hero waited for Keen to begin the questioning. He put their witnesses at ease, leaving it to her to knock them off balance.

"Mrs Hollander," Keen said, rising when she entered and even going so far as to pull out her seat. Hero lifted an eyebrow. He hadn't done that for a single nun, no matter how pretty, and as he returned to his seat she noted a bit more color in his face and a sudden nervousness in his manner. Interesting.

"Are you comfortable?" he asked the witness. "Would you like some hot tea? I apologize for the temperature in here."

"I'm fine," she said with a hint of a smile. "I am here to help in any way I can. Catarine and I–" She seemed to choke for a moment. "We were very close."

"Of course. I understand this is difficult–"

"Everyone says you were best friends," Hero interjected. Now that she was focused again, she recalled a few mentions of this woman from the other witnesses. "The very best of friends, in fact. You must be quite devastated."

Mrs Hollander lifted a lace-edged handkerchief to her reddened nose, nodding. Too distraught to speak, apparently. Keen cast Hero a dark look. She ignored him, keeping her attention on the witness.

"Did you know anyone who might have wished to harm Sister Catarine?" Keen asked gently, starting with the obvious. "Perhaps she'd confided something to you that she wouldn't say to anyone else?"

She shook her head adamantly. "Everyone adored Cat. She was very popular."

"Even when she brought up the unfair discrimination against those with demon heritage?" Hero asked. Between interviews, during her so-called "breaks," she'd had a chance to skim through the letters she'd found in Catarine's apartment, missives from religious authorities concerning the treatment of certain individuals "cursed" with demon blood. Apparently, she'd been petitioning the Church to reconsider its stance on children of demonic heritage, to allow them some grace. Admirable. Hero would have appreciated such advocacy on her behalf all those years ago.

The pale woman blinked, barely glancing Hero's way. "Caring about the fate of the unfortunate is hardly a reason to dislike a person. It just proves Cat had a soft heart." She shrugged. "Some might have found it offensive, but they wouldn't have dared speak out against Sister Catarine. Like I said, she was very popular."

"Wouldn't have dared?" Hero echoed. "Sounds ominous."

"I didn't mean it like that." Her gaze remained on Keen, limpid and soft. "You know how schools can be – so many cliques. Even the teachers aren't immune to sorting themselves into groups. I merely meant Catarine's eccentricities were well known and accepted."

Keen's jaw had hardened at her words. "Still," he said, catching on to Hero's line of questioning. "It's a very controversial stance. Many believe all those cursed with demon blood should be culled."

He said it matter-of-factly. Coldly. Hero tried not to take it personally; she'd started them down this road.

"And many people don't think that way," Mrs Hollander countered, a bit sharply. "Catarine was one of them, that's all. Do you really think this has anything to do with her death?"

Hero pulled the stack of letters from the satchel sitting at her feet. She tossed them onto the table. "She went to great lengths to conceal these," she said. "It certainly leads one to believe she did it out of fear. Are you certain she never mentioned any concerns for her own safety?"

"Think carefully, Abigail," Keen urged. "She might have hinted at it, not said it outright. Or maybe she began behaving in a strange manner. Had she become withdrawn? Secretive?"

This gave Hollander pause. Her delicate brow grew pinched, and she sniffed a few times. "Maybe. She was very distant the last few days before... before she went missing. Distant and a little angry, almost." A look of pain creased her face. "I told her to stop acting so self-righteous. There must have been something very wrong. I wish I had paid better attention! Goddess save me, she needed me and I failed her."

The woman dissolved into tears. Keen jumped up to attend to her like a proper gentleman, throwing Hero a look of castigation as if she were responsible for the woman's hysterics. "Perhaps we should give Abby a moment, Inspector? This must be very upsetting for her."

So, it's Abby, is it? Hero adjusted her glasses, watching the woman to gauge the validity of her tears. They seemed genuine.

"No, no," Abby protested, giving Keen's hand on her shoulder a gentle pat. "I want to help. Please. Though I don't know if I have anything more to tell. Those last few days, Cat kept to herself, like I said." She sniffled, dabbing at her eyes with her kerchief. Keen lingered at her side, hovering. Her eyes grew wide all of a sudden and she met Hero's gaze, unflinching, evidently refusing to be put off by her swirling eyes. "You need to talk with Father Kellan. He spent more time with Cat than anyone, even me."

"Yes," Hero drawled. "We've spoken with Kellan. Did you know about the two of them? Their relationship?"

A deep blush infused her cheeks. "I did," she said faintly. "I warned Cat not to let herself be led astray, but she was a stubborn soul, and free-spirited." She leaned forward, lowering her voice. "They were planning to leave the order. *Together.*"

Keen exchanged a look of surprise with Hero. They'd been unable to drag that fact from either Kellan or Catarine's roommate.

Hero felt a swelling of satisfaction. "Thank you for being so forthcoming, Mrs Hollander. DH Keen will see you out. Have a good day."

CHAPTER TWELVE

After finishing with the lay staff – other than Abigail Hollander, most of the staff had little interaction with the sister – they moved on to Catarine's students, a string of wretched wide-eyed children still traumatized from the recent tragic losses. The death of their fellow student had many of them close to hysterics though none of them professed to have been friends with Cassie Graham when asked directly. Keen found it obnoxious and said as much to Hero.

He needn't have. Even Hero recognized the dramatics as a bit over the top. Perhaps they felt bad about how they'd treated the dead girl? She hadn't exactly been popular. Only a vanishingly few of the students seemed genuinely distraught over Cassie's death, and these she let Keen handle in his gentle way, observing in silence for the most part. Nothing any of these kids said opened new doors: Catarine was their favorite teacher. Everyone adored Sister Cat. Cassie Graham was weird, unpopular, always being dramatic. Her death was a shock, but a surprise? No. Catarine, on the other hand... well, she'd had everything to live for.

After an hour of questioning, the onslaught of fragile human emotions was making the inside of Hero's skin itch and she was about to suggest they break for lunch when the name of their next interrogee stopped her cold.

"Did you say Franke?" she blurted, sitting up straight in her chair as PK Coates, an officer so young he still had pimples, led in a girl with long, dark braids and a heart-shaped face. Hero stared at the newcomer. The pertness of her nose and her plain brown eyes were very familiar.

"Yes, Inspector Viridian," Coates said. "This is Molly Franke." He gave the girl a gentle push toward the chair facing Hero and Keen's table. Showing remarkable courage, Coates fixed them with a stern gaze, or at least as stern as a boy with a spotty face could get. "Be easy, please, DH Keen, Inspector Viridian. This is Lieutenant Liam's daughter."

Keen gave a slow nod. "Understood. But, Officer, we have a job to do. We don't play favorites for anyone."

Officer Coates ducked his head and exited, pulling the door closed behind him.

Hero leaned forward, arms on the table. The girl across from her couldn't have been more than fifteen or sixteen, so she must have been born before Hero had gone to prison but after she'd torched the abbey. Her eyes were red rimmed, cheeks puffy and nose swollen. Waves of fear and despair rolled off of her, more so than any other student Hero and Keen had interviewed so far. Genuine grief. Interesting.

Hero smiled, or gave as close a facsimile as she could manage. Basic human expressions didn't work quite right on her not-entirely-human face. The girl blinked and hiccupped and somehow managed to lose more color from her pasty cheeks.

Keen cleared his throat.

"Do you know who I am?" Hero asked before Keen could say a word.

The girl nodded, eyes wide. "You're my aunt," she said faintly, lips trembling. "I'm sorry. I don't know your name, ma'am."

"Ma'am?" Hero chuckled. "I honestly don't believe anyone has ever called me that."

"S-s-sorry!"

"No, don't be. It's amusing, that's all. What did your family tell you about me?"

"Is this pertinent, Inspector?" Keen interjected.

Hero silenced him with a raised hand then gestured for the girl to answer.

"Nothing," she said, a bit too quickly. "Really. I mean, just that you went to jail a long time ago, because you were cursed–" A look of horror crossed her face and she almost seemed to shrivel. Hero could hardly blame her, here in this cold room being questioned about dead nuns and dead friends. Who wouldn't want to shrivel up and disappear? Especially in front of a cursed aunt she didn't know at all except by reputation.

"Don't be afraid," she said, rather gently considering the roiling emotions in her belly. Cursed, was she? *Fucking assholes.* "I suppose it's nothing but the truth. Cursed with demon blood, aren't I? Not through any fault of mine. But. There it is. You can call me Auntie Hero, or Aunt Viridian if you want to be formal. The family pariah. The burned sheep." She laughed, a brittle sound.

A small, desolate moan slipped from the girl.

"Never mind." Hero waved a hand. "On second thought, call me ma'am. Shall we begin the questioning, DH Keen?"

Lips pinched with annoyance, Keen let out another aggrieved sigh and rearranged his notes. "I was about to make the same suggestion, Inspector. Now, young lady, you knew both victims, I understand? My condolences."

"Th-thank you."

"In fact," Keen continued mildly, "you were the last person to speak with Miss Cassie, weren't you? Other than the revered mother, of course."

The girl jerked like she'd sat on a pinecone. "I–"

"Was there anything she said to you in that final conversation? Anything that might have hinted at what she planned to do?"

"N-n-n-o! Nothing! She was... she was just sad. Like all of us. Distraught."

"Afraid?" Hero interjected. This child reeked of fear.

Molly nodded, looking both relieved and alarmed. Her mouth worked like she wanted nothing more than to speak. "She..." The word pulled from her reluctantly. Her plain brown eyes flicked toward the mirror. The child of a PK officer would no doubt understand what that mirror hid. Her father was watching, listening – as was his right, legally.

"I don't want to say the wrong thing," Molly said miserably, fixing Keen with a pleading gaze.

"Chief Dewey," Hero said, raising her voice. "Could you please ask Sergeant Franke to step away. Sometimes, it is hard for girls to speak of... uncomfortable things in front of their fathers."

There was a click and shuffle as someone opened the speaking tube, then a disembodied voice spoke into the room. "Is that absolutely necessary, Inspector?"

The girl scrunched her shoulders tight to her ears, but her look told Hero it was indeed necessary. "Send him away, Chief. That's an order from an inspector death speaker."

There was a muffled curse from Liam before the tube clicked closed.

Hero waited an appropriate amount of time, dead certain Dewey would do as she asked. He wanted this case solved more than he wanted his sergeant coddled, she suspected.

"Now, feel free to speak, Miss Franke," Keen urged gently, pouring on that useful charisma of his. Though not exactly handsome, there was something about the young man that seemed to put people at ease, a genuine kindness beneath his stiff professionalism. Hero was almost starting to like him, and he'd drugged her and tried to take her head off already. "It's just us, here in this room. Everything you say is confidential." *For now*, she added silently. *Unless it pertains to the case. Unless it points to the guilty party.*

PKs knew how to lie. Easy as breathing.

"She told me something horrible." Molly leaned forward in her seat, eyes wide and hands gripping the chair beneath her thighs. She crossed her feet at the ankles, maintaining propriety in her plaid skirt even in these difficult circumstances – a good girl through and through. "I – I didn't want to believe her."

"What did she tell you?" Keen nearly whispered, not wanting to break the fragile atmosphere. "Was it about Sister Catarine?"

She nodded miserably. "But it can't be true! Nothing she said made any sense. Cassie thought she was to blame for Catarine's death, for something Cassie told her about–"

Both Hero and Keen held their breath, waiting.

Molly glanced toward the mirror and leaned closer to the table. "About Bright Renewal Academy."

Hero exchanged a glance with Keen; he seemed flabbergasted, too. He shuffled through his notes as if maybe he'd missed something, but Hero was sure up until now no one had mentioned the place. "What is Bright Renewal Academy?" Keen asked.

Molly stared at him as if he'd lost his mind. "*The Academy*," she said with emphasis. "Where bad kids go to get reformed."

"Is this a new school?" Hero said. She'd been gone from Havenside for quite some time, after all. Things changed.

The girl blinked. "Maybe. I suppose, compared to Clementine Prep. But Bright Renewal has been a Havenside institution for as long as I can remember. But... I'm young. I might not be the best to ask about its history."

Another glance between Hero and her partner. Keen looked as confused as she felt. "You don't know the place, Keen? You left Havenside, what, six years ago?"

"I've never heard of it," he admitted, frowning. "You say this place is for bad kids?" he asked Molly. "What do you mean exactly?"

"Not bad, I guess, but kids who get in trouble, kids who need help so they don't go down the wrong path. It's a good place," she insisted with another glance toward the mirror as if it was unwise to claim anything differently. "But Cassie didn't think so. Her brother was sent there, and she was upset about it. She said she went to Sister Cat because she was worried about Cole. I don't know why she was worried. I really don't know much of anything." She was beginning to speak faster, words spilling out. "I don't understand why Cassie was so afraid, and I don't know what she said to Catarine. Not exactly. I swear I don't!"

"But she was afraid, is what you're telling us," Hero urged, trying to dredge up the truth. "Did she think this Bright Renewal Academy had something to do with Catarine's murder?"

"She didn't say that." Molly shook her head, hard enough to swing her braids. "She just said *they* had warned her about saying stuff she shouldn't say. Something like that." Her expression crumpled. "I thought she was being dramatic, lying for attention or something. Why would something she said get Sister Catarine killed? What could she know that would be so important? Or – or so evil? It can't be true, right?" She seemed on the verge of full-on panic.

"We aren't sure of much of anything right now," Keen said soothingly. "But what you are telling us is very helpful, Molly. Don't think otherwise. Here, have a drink of water."

White faced, Molly nodded and took the cup Keen pushed across the table toward her. Hero turned to her partner to give the girl a moment to compose herself. "The hellhounds," Keen murmured to her. "Someone wanted to keep the Graham girl quiet, even in death."

Hero nodded. Someone had certainly gone to great lengths to silence Sister Catarine, too. Her soul had been eaten.

Keen waited for the girl to grow calmer, then asked, "Did she tell you any names, Molly? Anyone she was afraid of specifically?"

Molly shook her head, toying with the cup in her hands. She glanced to the side, her expression pained.

"You didn't believe her," Hero said softly. "Is that why you feel so guilty about it?"

Molly started, then pulled herself together, wiping at her eyes with her sleeves. "I didn't, not at first. Then she said something so awful, I knew it couldn't be a lie." She spoke tiredly, fatalistically, as if she'd accepted that she couldn't avoid this any longer.

"What did she say?"

Molly hiccupped, then squared her shoulders with remarkable courage. "She said they took her to see Sister Catarine's body. High in a meadow, cold and still under a full moon."

Hero swallowed disappointment. Damn it, was this another bust? Everyone already knew the details of Catarine's death, that the body had been dumped on the mountainside.

"Molly..." she started to say, but then Molly met her eyes unflinchingly and blurted: "Cassie said she had no tongue. Someone had *ripped* it out."

Keen sat back in his chair, jaw slack. Hero had to snap her own mouth closed once she realized she was mirroring his expression. They exchanged another long glance, the unspoken hanging between them: No one knew *that*.

Molly caught their look. "So. She wasn't lying." Silent tears flowed down her cheeks. "Goddess forgive me..." She began to sob.

Hero's shriveled, half-demon heart felt a pang, sharp and undeniable. "Get Sergeant Liam," she said into the room, knowing the right ears would hear her. "Tell him his daughter needs him."

Sergeant Franke took his weeping daughter home for the day, leaving Hero and her partner alone to process their notes from the interviews. Her brother had given her a stiff nod as he escorted his child from the room, perhaps so she wouldn't think he blamed her for sending him out of the interview. She'd just been doing her job, after all. That's the way she chose to take the gesture, anyway.

Some progress had been made with their interviews. Molly Franke had been especially helpful. Now they knew for certain that Cassie Graham's death was connected to Catarine's murder. Perhaps no one had intended Cassie to die the way she had, but the girl was dead nonetheless, and silenced – except first she'd spilled her secrets, whatever they were, to Sister Catarine.

"We'll have to talk to the brother," Hero said. She and Keen were back at their shared desk – borrowed from a couple of uniform PKs who'd been relegated to a file room – with piles of paperwork between them. She'd given him some of Catarine's correspondence to read through while she went over his prodigious notes. He was observant, detailed, but he hadn't picked up on anything she'd missed. "And the Grahams, too. They might know what had their daughter so upset."

"If she'd talked to them, she wouldn't have needed to confide in Sister Catarine," Keen countered, opening another of Catarine's letters, brow furrowing as he scanned the page. "Who do you suppose this Mr B is? They seemed to have been exchanging letters. Quite recently, by the postmarks."

Hero shook her head. "I don't know. Not yet." He was probably right that the Grahams wouldn't know what had upset Cassie, but she still wanted to question the family, to get a sense of the girl's home life. Maybe her parents were part of this nightmare. They'd put her brother in a reform school, after all. Her twin brother. It had to have been hard on her.

"He mentions missing children in his letters. Kids this Bright Renewal Academy list as runaways. Apparently, he didn't believe them."

She'd read those letters, too. They were short, pleading, persuasive, playing on Catarine's sympathy. Yet none of the missing kids were from Clementine Prep. These were townie kids, the "bad" kids Molly had mentioned. "If Bright Renewal is a reform school, I'm not surprised kids run away from it. They can be hard places."

"We need to see this school," Keen said emphatically. He shook the letter in his hand. "Catarine seemed awfully concerned about what goes on there."

Hero frowned. It did seem important to their case, but she couldn't help feeling it might be a distraction. She wanted to focus on Clementine, on the revered mother and Father Kellan. The deaths, the *murders* – a teacher and her student – had originated there, not at this mysterious Academy. Was someone trying to steer them down a dead end?

"Some sort of summoning killed Catarine, according to Dr Virchow," she said, plucking the autopsy report from the pile. "The instruments for such powerful magic often leave residue..."

Thrown by the abrupt change in subject, Keen riffled through his own papers to find a copy of the same report. "They did," he said. "Around her neck."

She shook her head, skimming through the report again. "We have to visit the crime scene."

"But there was no evidence at the scene," he protested. "Just what was found on the body."

"No evidence that the PKs could see. I was foolish to leave it to them, especially after I failed to find Catarine's shade. Then that dead girl distracted me. Damn amateurs. Damn hellhounds. Damn nuns. Hidden letters and obfuscations." She adjusted her glasses and tossed the report back on the pile. "We need to go and see for ourselves."

He looked doubtful, but he followed her lead like a good PK. "I'll acquisition some horses, Inspector. First thing in the morning. It's a long ride and it's already getting dark."

"Oh." She looked out of the window and was surprised to see he was correct. They'd spent all day with their interviews. She ground her teeth. This was all taking so *long*. "Fine. Tomorrow, then."

CHAPTER THIRTEEN

Monstrous steel clouds hung low overhead. The skies reflected the mood of Clem Prep. The last few tumultuous days had left everyone on edge. Students hurried across the quad instead of lingering beneath the trees or gathering on benches, eyes slipping unwillingly to the patch of gravel still stained with Cassie Graham's blood. A hard rain might wash away the evidence of the tragedy, but despite the lowering sky, only a chill mist filled the air.

Molly moved through the morning isolated from the others. It was subtle, but obvious to everyone. Word had spread that somehow Cassie Graham was connected to Sister Catarine's murder. No one knew how, exactly, but speculation wasn't kind. Cassie hadn't been a particularly popular student. All the tears from a few days before had vanished, replaced by dark looks and whispers, all directed at the only target remaining: Molly Franke.

Everyone knew she had spoken to the peacekeepers, had told stories, maybe even implied something nasty about Sister Catarine. Plus, she'd been best friends with Cassie Graham, an unhinged liar with a thief of a brother. A lost soul. The whole family was bad news. Molly was the child of a PK, too. Those types always ended up bad. Rebellious.

Molly tried to ignore it all. She'd done the right thing, even though her father had been furious with her for withholding such important information from him.

"I didn't mean to, Papa!" she'd sobbed to him as they'd walked home from the station the night before, heartbroken that he was so angry with her.

"I just don't understand why you didn't come to me, Molly. I really don't."

"I don't know, either," she said miserably.

Lately, her father had been particularly prickly, always on the verge of a temper tantrum. Grandmama Franke was dying in their upstairs bedroom, the one with the big picture window, and he was taking it hard – not Molly; Grandmama had been a terror – but this was more than that. She felt bad for him, but even more sorry for herself. She'd had to tell the truth, to get it off her chest. The idea of him listening in on her confession had been too much. She should have told him immediately and was ashamed she hadn't. For whatever reason, it seemed easier for him to have heard it secondhand.

"To go to her, instead. I am flabbergasted."

Her. The family's great shame and terrible secret. That "cursed bitch," as Grandmama called her whenever she might be mentioned, which was exceedingly rare. Rare as a smile on Grandmama's shriveled face.

They began the uphill climb to their three-story walk-up off Briar Street, and Molly had to hurry to keep up with her father's long, angry stride. The Frankes were a well-respected family with a long history in Havenside, but they weren't exactly rich, merely well to do, thanks to Grandmama's pension. Grandpa Franke had made quite a fortune in lawyering, but he'd nearly drunk it all away later in life. Thank the Goddess for the runaway coal wagon that had crushed him when he left the pub one night.

"I'm sorry, Papa." Thoughts and regrets tumbled through her head. She wanted to try and explain, to talk about Cassie, about Sister Catarine, about her doubts and fears. Even about Auntie Hero! But her tongue was a knot.

"I only wish you'd felt safe enough to come to me first. I could have warned you off, left you out of the questioning." His perpetual scowl deepened. Their steps clipped along the brick sidewalk, momentarily synchronized. The air was crisp, the evening breeze rippling through the turning maples overhead, half green, half red or gold. Suddenly, he stopped and turned to her. "That girl was troubled. And she's left you with an impossible burden. But it's done now, do you understand me? Don't say another word to anyone else about any of it." There was an edge to his words, an insistence that was undeniable: *Forget all about this, Molly.* That's what he meant. And by the Goddess, she desperately wanted to forget all of it.

"Yes, Papa."

He nodded sharply, his scowl easing. It was settled – for him, anyway, but Molly had doubts.

By now they had reached home, a slim three-story residence sandwiched between other fine-looking walk-ups on Briar Avenue, with a brick-and-limestone exterior, cut-glass windows accented with stained-glass motifs, and a set of ornate double doors with brass knockers. The front steps were worn stone with iron railings, broad and welcoming. The porch was more of a stoop, but with enough room for a tiny wrought-iron table and matching chairs – the perfect place for morning tea. Except for Grandmama, dying in one of the upstairs rooms, it was a wonderful place, safe and welcoming. Home.

Father put a hand on her back, ushering her up the stairs ahead of him. Molly climbed slowly. Those doubts wouldn't leave, circling like crows around a pile of dried corn, pecking and swirling, black wings and beaks open. She shuddered. Nothing was settled. Nothing. Something dark was climbing up below her. Something terrible was coming.

The unsettling feeling had stayed with her the rest of that night and had only grown stronger by this morning. She'd hoped getting to school would be a distraction, but she hadn't expected the frosty reception from her classmates. As she crossed the quad, her cheeks burned from the stares and whispers. She clutched her books to her chest and hurried by the spot where Cassie had fallen, and when she reached the door to the west wing, someone ahead of her made sure to pull it shut behind them rather than leave it ajar for her. The unkind act brought a lump to her throat. Maybe she should have called in sick today…

Inside, the crowded hallways, once so familiar and comforting, now seemed threatening, as if monsters lurked in the shadows. She dismissed the feeling. Her mother – loud and cheerful no matter how she might feel inside, a bright and shiny foil to her dour father – always accused her of being too sensitive. Molly tried to live up to her expectations but failed more often than not. It was really hard to smile and be cheerful when she felt grim inside.

"Molly Franke."

She stopped, startled. She'd had her head down and had nearly run into two dour nuns. Grim-faced, they stared down their noses at her. She couldn't remember their names. All thoughts had flown out of her head.

"You are in serious trouble, young lady."

"What? Why?"

They flanked her and took her by the arms, fingers hard and unforgiving. She found herself being marched down the hallway. First bell rang as she stumbled along, the few students still lingering in the hall staring at her in fascinated horror. Her cheeks burned with humiliation as the nuns dragged her along, past classrooms with open doors and chattering students. Gasps and murmurs followed her. Even a few teachers peeked out to witness the unusual event.

Finally, the two nuns halted and spun with her toward a row of wooden lockers. One was open, the contents spilled out haphazardly. Molly stared in confusion. Books and notepads. A pair of spare stockings and a knit cap. *Her* cap. Her books. She was stunned to see her things handled so rudely. One item stood out from the others: a dark green bottle, its slender neck tilted against the open locker door, a cork worked almost loose. She stared at it uncomprehendingly for a moment, then she recognized it for what it was: a bottle of blessed wine. Used in the rituals. Only the highest priests and nuns were allowed to consume it. The non-ordained weren't even allowed to touch it.

"Stolen from the altar yesterday," the nun on her left said, voice heavy with loathing. She reached down to grasp the bottle, using a silken handkerchief to keep from touching it directly. She held it like it was a dead rat and thrust it in Molly's face. "What do you have to say for yourself?"

"That's not mine! I didn't take it!" It was the dead truth, but even to her own ears her words sounded false.

The other nun gripped her harder, glaring at her. "Confess, child, and things will go easier for you. Denial will only make it worse."

She began to cry, too stunned to control herself. This was crazy. She'd never stolen anything in her life! "I swear! Please, I didn't take it. I would never!"

They ignored her. "Recalcitrant," one said. "She is too far gone, I fear."

"Demon-touched?" the other speculated, making Molly weep all the harder.

"The mother will decide what to do with her."

There was no arguing with Revered Mother Francesca. The plump woman ignored every denial, scoffed at each appeal of innocence. Molly's crimes were laid bare: first, the stolen wine – expulsion-worthy! – then more accusations, one after the other. She was a disobedient child, always talking when she wasn't supposed to, fostering "unnatural" relationships with other students (she didn't really know what that was supposed to mean, but the implication made her stomach tighten and she wondered if she had), late with her work, refusing to adhere to the dress code, holding secret meetings in the woods for dark and sinister purposes...

Did they think foraging for mushrooms was "dark and sinister?" It would have made her laugh but for the terror crawling up from her stomach, choking her like a smog demon.

The mother herself signed Molly's death warrant, or at least that was how it felt. She was being sent to Bright Renewal Academy. Not tomorrow, not next week, but Right. Now.

That's how it happened, from the little she knew. Kids condemned to Bright Renewal, those "bad" children, vanished abruptly. Taken like a criminal from the streets. It was for their own good – everyone knew it.

But not me, surely?

"Can I talk to my father?" she asked, trying hard not to weep. "Please! This has to be a mistake!"

Mother Francesca, stern behind a massive desk raised up on a dais, stared down at her in contemptuous judgement. "I will only hear your confession, child," she said darkly. "Unburden yourself lest you let demons into your soul."

"There's nothing to tell, Mother!" she said. Too quickly. Too desperately. "I swear to the Goddess, I've done nothing wrong!"

"Ah, my poor wayward girl. I can sense the demons encroaching. Falsehoods fall from your lips like crumbs." Her head bent over the paper on her desk, a feathered quill in her hand, scratching furiously. "I have signed your admission into Bright Renewal Academy. You will find your time there enlightening, I hope. Be glad we care enough to save you, my child."

A surge of terror made her want to vomit. She swallowed bitter bile, her thoughts a mad riot, until a single realization popped in her head like a bursting bubble: *I'm being sent away because of Cassie.*

Her father had been right – she never should have said a word. Everyone knew she'd talked, including the people who'd taken Cassie to see Catarine's body.

Mother Francesca had taken Cassie down the hallway toward the nurse's office, yet somehow Cassie had ended up on the clock tower...

This was what Cassie had feared: being sent away. She'd run off the tower instead of facing it. And now Molly was going in her place. Fresh tears rolled down her cheeks.

The something terrible had come.

CHAPTER FOURTEEN

It was indeed a long ride to the crime scene high in a lonely meadow. Havenside lay in a valley flanking the broad estuary which gave it such rich fishing grounds and sheltered harbors, surrounded by picturesque hills covered in maples, elms and sweetgums. Usually, the autumn turning encouraged hordes of daytime hikers to seek the hills, but not today. This morning had brought colder weather and an unpleasant mist. Dreary and wet and cold as it was, Hero and Keen were the only two souls climbing the twisting path through the trees.

Their horses clopped along the steep pathway, hooves muffled by the hard-packed loam, ringing against the occasional stone. A murder of crows kept them company as they progressed, mocking them with shrieking caws, fluttering between the branches, in and out of the colorful leaves.

Hero lowered her glasses a few times to check on the infernal birds, making sure they didn't bear the silver glint of demonic energy. A few gleamed suspiciously, but the thick leaves kept her from being certain. There was a presence on the hill, one she felt as a mere glimmer but growing stronger as they climbed. She was on the right path. Finally. She could kick herself for not coming here right away, but she was so used to getting her information from shades. Her death speaking had never failed her so thoroughly before now.

They left their horses well outside the perimeter of the crime scene, which the PKs had marked out with twine and wooden stakes in a careful grid. Hero didn't like the onerous procedures of traditional police work, but she was a Goddess-damned professional. She wasn't about to contaminate a crime scene, unless it was absolutely necessary.

"I don't know what you hope to find up here," Keen grumbled as they made their way to the edge of the cordoned-off area. "I tested all the collected samples for demonic activity, hunted for any residue with every technique I could think of. Only Dr Virchow's findings had a demonic taint." Defensiveness oozed from him like an unpleasant odor, and it was Hero's turn to flare her nostrils.

"I'm not questioning your skills, DH Keen," she said. "Mine are merely superior. I meant no offense."

He rolled his eyes. "Why would I take offense?"

Hero sighed. Moving away from him, she stepped over the first line of string, no higher than her shin. The grass was half dead and had been thoroughly combed by PK technicians. That was fine; she wasn't here for physical traces. Off with the glasses – her shield against the world, a thin, transparent shield of green-tinted glass. The world sharpened.

She Saw the faint outline where the dead nun's body had lain. A vague shimmer across the grass, woman-shaped and shockingly small. No blood anywhere. No trace of any living person at the scene – no footprints, disturbed earth or broken plant stems – yet someone had carried her here, dumped her here. Someone had ripped out Catarine's tongue and left only a slight trickle of blood at the corner of her mouth. Dr Virchow had confirmed it had been removed peri-mortem, so by the time she was dumped here she'd stopped bleeding.

Catarine had been held somewhere else. Tortured, murdered, then dumped like garbage.

Hero's eyes landed on the sad, pale outline of Sister Catarine. An explosion of crows erupted from a nearby forest giant, an ancient oak standing proud among the showy maples. Startled, she spun toward the flurry of dark wings.

"Damnable birds," Keen exclaimed. "What's got them in a tizzy?"

Eyes aflame, Hero zeroed in on the oak. There it was, plain as day to her enhanced vision – a glimmering substance etched into the thick bark, faint and spectral but very real, as if something had scraped the tree as it passed. She focused on it and it became more solid, formed links. A chain. She felt a surge of triumph. The glimmer – the chain – arrowed down the hill, in and out of the trees, toward Havenside.

"Get the horses," she ordered, leaving her glasses tucked in the pocket of her long, brown oilskin duster. Keen recoiled when she turned to him, but she didn't have time for his sensitivities. She shed her jacket and tossed it to him. Her muscles were already bulging beneath her spare, cream-colored shirt, straining the seams. Her deep blue scapular and emerald trousers were loose enough to accommodate her modified form – they'd been designed that way, of course – but she liked a fitted shirt, even if she sacrificed far too many of them.

Keen stared up at her, eyes wide in horror, clutching her jacket to his chest. Her mouth opened in a snarl, revealing fangs as long as a wolf's. "And try and keep up," she growled. Then she turned, dropped to her clawed hands and bounded down the hillside.

Oleander scrambled for the horses, shaken to the core. He shouldn't have been, he castigated himself – he was a demonhunter, a sacred huntsman of hellspawn! He'd witnessed the transformation of human into demon firsthand many times before. His very presence drove most of them to reveal themselves, dropping the mortal masks they hid behind. And every time, he had attacked, not stared meekly in stunned horror. What had him so unnerved this time?

This demon is my partner.

Frantically, he bundled Hero's long jacket on the back of her horse, untied both beasts and flung himself on his mount. A jab of his heels and they were off. Thundering hooves kicked up soft earth and leaves, tore through the flimsy string and stakes marking off the crime scene – regrettable, but they'd found what they'd come for. Hadn't they?

Oleander didn't know. He didn't know anything! Except he had been ordered to follow. And one thing he was exceptionally good at was following orders.

Ordered around by hellspawn. Oleander's knees tightened on his horse, and he bent low over its neck. The Goddess was *laughing* at him.

Hero's path was easy to follow. In her beast-like state, far larger than her human one, she was barreling through the woods and leaving a trail of destruction in her wake. What was she chasing? He couldn't even speculate beyond the fleeting thought, focused as he was on staying atop his horse. Well trained, a fine hunter, the sturdy mare took the rough terrain in stride. Its partner followed – Oleander could hear its hoofbeats and the crashing of underbrush – not wanting to be left behind. He hoped the beast didn't break a leg.

The pommel of the saddle dug into his stomach after a particularly startling drop, and he lost a stirrup for a moment. It was a miracle he kept his seat at all, and he stopped worrying about the horses' legs and prayed fiercely he didn't break his own neck.

Coming down the hill took far less time than going up. They burst from the woods into cultivated land. Cornfields, stalks shriveled and dry and ready for harvest. Even more treacherous ground than the hillside. His horse jumped a split-rail fence, huffing and sweating but primed for the hunt and game for the chase. He glanced back to see Hero's horse balk at the fence. It didn't matter now. They were close enough to home for the steed to wander back to the PK stables. Its livery would deter anyone from absconding with it. Even the degenerates in Otherside would hesitate before stealing a police horse.

He winced. Technically, *he* was a degenerate from Otherside.

A slash of flattened cornstalks sent him toward the outskirts of town. The path led out of the cornfield and on to a road of crushed stone. A rural road, winding up another hill, this one mostly shorn of trees and brambles. Oleander had no idea where it led, yet felt he should have. He'd grown up here, and even though he'd been away at training, he'd come home every holiday. Last time he'd been home, this hilltop had been a wilderness. The strangeness was enough to break through his singular focus on staying astride his galloping horse. Then, shocked, he heaved back on the reins and slowed his horse to a swift trot.

How in all the great wide world had this hill been cleared and that been built?

That was nothing less than a mansion and its accompanying grounds. A brick wall encircled it, reminding him of the wall around Clementine Prep. It looked old, covered in ivy in some places, moss and lichen in others. Well beyond the wall, the mansion rose in ominous towers and cupolas. The iron arch spanning a gateway announced the place as "Bright Renewal Academy."

Stunned, he could only stare. *This* was the Academy Molly Franke had mentioned? It looked a hundred years old, but he swore, swore to the Goddess and the Branch, this place hadn't been here a year ago!

His gawping amazement ended when his eyes landed on a crumpled figure ahead of him on the road, a figure dressed in green and blue, cream-colored shirt torn and tattered around the sleeves and neck.

"Shit!" he muttered, yanking his horse to a stop. He jumped to the road and dashed to his partner. "Inspector!"

She had returned to her human aspect, skin whiter than normal, face slack and eyes closed. It looked like she'd been clobbered, but there was nothing and no one anywhere near her. Oleander took her by the shoulder and rolled her onto her back. A groan told him she was alive, at least. He called to her again and eased her up from the cold, hard ground to settle her against his knee. A few light slaps to her cheeks made her eyelids flutter.

Then he was staring into the flames of Hell.

Hero blinked, hiding those terrible fires for a brief second, and another groan erupted from her.

"Fuck me," she said. She struggled into a sitting position and Oleander scrambled to help her rise. Arms clasped, Hero swaying on trembling legs, they stood together and stared at the gateway to Bright Renewal Academy. Astonishment filled the air between them – for entirely different reasons, Oleander soon discovered.

"This – this shouldn't be here," he said, flabbergasted.

"I slammed right into a fucking shield!" she exclaimed at the exact same moment.

They looked at each other. "A shield?" Oleander repeated dumbly. "Against demons?"

She withdrew her hands from his grip and straightened her disheveled clothing, her eyes on the gateway. "I'm not entirely sure what it's meant to shield against, but it kept me out pretty fucking effectively." She looked around. "Where's my horse?"

He jolted at the abrupt change in subject. "Probably back in the stables by now. Oh, shit, sorry! Your jacket!"

"My glasses," she said, her lips pressed into a line. "And my cane. Never mind. I'll improvise."

She ripped at her voluminous trousers, tearing free a strip of the sparkly green cloth. He felt a sense of relief when she tied it around her head, shielding her eyes once more.

"It's overwhelming sometimes," she said, "seeing through things. And I can't look at that... place without some sort of shield. It's horrible." She waved her hand in the direction of the mansion. It didn't appear so horrible to him. Just a big, sprawling house...

...that had sprung up from nowhere.

"Let's see if this shield works on me," he suggested grimly. Hero nodded and he stepped forward gingerly, past the place where he'd peeled her off the road, then a little farther. He waved his hands in front of him but felt nothing. Another few steps – nothing. He took a breath. Maybe–

Ahead of him, the ornate gates of heavy wood and iron scrollwork split and began to swing inward. Oleander went for his blunderbuss, heart pounding, thinking of the potions he might need, cataloguing what was left of his inventory in a flash.

But it wasn't a demon opening the gates. Nothing supernatural at all, in fact. Merely men, dressed in uniforms of a similar cut to his own – similar, but not identical. The color was a dark gray, not navy, the jackets longer and boxier, trimmed in silver with a patch he didn't recognize on the breast – a rising sun in golden thread. His hand eased off his blunderbuss and he snapped straight. Behind him, Hero let out a low hiss.

He craned his head to look at her. She was frozen, unable to come any further. He, on the other hand, was unfettered. The shield only worked on her, apparently. Maybe it *was* set to guard against demons, in that case, or anyone with demon blood.

"Hallo," one of the men called. There were two of them that Oleander could see. One stayed back behind the gate, only peering out at them suspiciously. The one who spoke, short and ordinary-looking, stood in the gap, not quite as suspicious of them but not exactly friendly either. "Do you have business at the Academy?" he asked. "Or an appointment?"

"An appointment?" Oleander's gaze scanned the distant mansion. "We are peacekeepers of the Realm," he said, then added for good measure, "We demand entrance!"

"Oh, no, I'm afraid not." The man shook his head, sounding genuinely regretful. "Not without an appointment. Surely you must understand the necessity. We can't let just anyone in here – safety concerns and all that."

"Safety for what? For whom?"

"Why, our students, of course! They must be kept safe from outside influences. Such troubled souls need guidance and stability, not random gawkers."

"Random–? I am Demonhunter First Rank Oleander Keen," he declared, "and my partner is Inspector Death Speaker Hero Viridian. We are conducting an investigation, and our findings have led us here. You cannot deny us entry."

The man was unimpressed. He gave them a bland smile. "Return with a warrant, good sir. Only then will I grant you entry." His dark eyes shifted to Hero and narrowed in disgust. "And only you, DH Keen. Her kind isn't allowed inside."

Keen bristled, offended at his attitude toward the inspector. "She is an officer of the law, sir. Who do you think you are?"

"I am Mr Torrance, the gatekeeper of Bright Renewal Academy, and the students here are in my charge. I take my duty very seriously, sir." He began to back away, his hand rising to grasp the gate. "Return with a warrant, or don't return at all. Good day."

It took both men to push the gates shut, and the resounding boom echoed across the hill.

Frustrated, Oleander marched back to where his partner waited. She was still staring at the so-called "academy," as far as he could tell, her brow furrowed above the cloth over her eyes. "I guess we get a warrant," he muttered, glancing back toward the closed gates. "Although on what grounds, I have no clue."

"I saw the chain," Hero said. "At least, I saw the residue it left behind in our reality. Those marks on Catarine's neck, the strange substance on her skin, both came from a spectral chain. Surely you've seen the like before in all your demonhunting?"

"I know demonic chains are often used in summoning," he temporized. She sounded exasperated and he didn't want to contradict her, but he hadn't seen any residue left at the crime scene. "But until Dr Virchow completes his testing, we won't know–"

"*I* know," she insisted. Her blindfolded eyes turned toward the grand mansion, her body stiff with tension. "What is this dark and terrible place?"

"It doesn't look all that terrible, Inspector." He frowned. "I don't think I'm seeing what you are seeing."

Her face shifted toward him. There was a glimmer of fire bleeding through the green silk. "Very few people do, Keen. But look closely. Open your other senses, not just your eyes. Remember your training."

He did as she suggested, though his first instinct was to become defensive. He'd struggled so long to prove himself; he didn't need her reminding him to do his job correctly. *Take it with a grain of salt, Keen. She's not being insulting, just being… her.*

So, Demonhunter Oleander Keen *looked*. Looked hard. At the mansion sitting dark and silent atop a manicured hill. He opened his ears, his nose, breathed in the cold air. Felt the earth beneath his feet, vast and indifferent. His partner had found a chain, followed it here. He imagined it stretching toward the sprawling house. It flickered at the edge of his vision, and slowly the world around him began to change. The sky turned gray – heavy, crushing. The house on the hill seemed to darken, to grow ancient in a heartbeat, falling apart, splitting at the seams. Darkness spilled from it like smoke, creeping across the land, coming for him, reaching–

Keen gasped and stumbled backward. Only Hero's firm grip on his arm kept him from tumbling to the ground. He felt like he'd been kicked in the stomach, nauseated and sweating. His mouth was dry, his tongue thick. "What the *fuck*?"

"Now you see," Hero said with deep satisfaction. "Let's get our warrant."

CHAPTER FIFTEEN

"Bright Renewal Academy? You're writing a complaint against Bright Renewal?" Chief Dewey chuckled. "An actual search warrant! You know that's impossible, don't you? No judge would ever sign it."

Head pounding from her unfortunate collision with a spectral shield of almost unfathomable strength, Hero ground a fist against her forehead instead of punching her commanding officer with it. "And why is that, pray tell?"

Dewey sighed, then settled on the edge of her desk, tugging the complaint from beneath her pen. He read through it, less amused the more he perused the document. He crumpled it into a ball with a scowl.

"Is there a problem with my grammar?"

"Look." He crossed his arms. "I know you grew up here, but you've been gone a long time, and your childhood was... less than ideal."

She bit down on a sharp retort, wanting him to get to the point.

"So maybe your memories are fuzzy about how things work around here. But the people who fund Bright Renewal Academy are powerful. Important. They wouldn't be caught up in any of this mess, I promise you."

"*This mess* being murder?" she countered, frustrated and confused. "Honestly, Chief, you're right. My less-than-ideal childhood kept me out of the loop, and I honestly don't care who pulls the strings in this town. I'm after a murderer, and I go where the evidence takes me, no matter whose feathers I might ruffle."

"Yes, that was very obvious from your antics the other day at Grantham House." He scowled. "I need you to tread a little more lightly, Inspector. If you step on the wrong toes, this whole investigation will be shut down. If I give you free rein, I could be out of a job. Do you understand?"

No, she did not understand. "Why did you even bring me here, Chief?" she demanded. "Do you want this case solved, or do you want to maintain your position?"

"I would like to do both," he admitted. His eyes cut away from her, and he at least appeared somewhat embarrassed by her question. "And I called you because I believe there's a demon at work here – a *demon*, Inspector, not the Goddess-damned mayor or Madam Primm. Not the town's biggest benefactors. So focus on the supernatural aspects of this case, all right?"

"I *am*. And they are leading me to that creepy school on a hill, Chief. A place protected by a formidable shield, I might add. A place that didn't exist when I lived in Havenside – I don't care what you say. A place that looks older than Clementine, but by the halls of Hell, I don't think it was there before a year ago. And Keen agrees with me!"

There was a shadow of confusion in his eyes. "That's madness, Inspector. Bright Renewal Academy is an institution. It's been around as long as I can remember. It saves children from going down a bad path."

The words were rote. He sounded like Molly Franke had when she'd spoken of the place. It was as if everyone was reading off a script.

"It's a good place, right?" she said mockingly, suspicion turning in her belly.

Dewey's expression hardened. The confusion cleared from his eyes, replaced by absolute certainty. "It is," he said firmly.

There was a shift in the air between them. He didn't move, but Hero felt a chasm open wide. She pushed back in her chair and stared at him. "I feel like I'm losing my mind," she said, more to herself than to him. "What is happening here?"

"I don't know what you mean, Inspector."

Hero stood. The other PKs in the office had taken notice of their conversation by now and were side-eyeing them both, murmuring among themselves. She noticed a few scandalized expressions, some gleeful and some downright disgusted. She was used to the other PK officers giving her stares of disapproval – even after working in New Savage for three years, the looks never stopped, and not once did she think her rank and status made her one of them – but it still stung.

"Where's Liam?" she demanded, scanning the bullpen for his tall, rigid figure. Even if he hated her being here, he wouldn't lie just to fuck with her. Not like the rest of these bastards. "We grew up together. He'll back me up, I know it."

"Lieutenant Franke is taking a few days leave to deal with a family… situation."

Great. She seethed silently, but perked up just a bit at the idea her mother might have dropped dead. She glared at Dewey, who was glaring back, arms crossed tight across his chest. It made her irrationally angry. She'd thought he was one of the good ones, a real peacekeeper, but he was just like all the others. When push came to shove, he would protect the rich and powerful. Why did he even bring her here if he was going to stonewall her?

Unless it wasn't his choice.

The thought hit her like a physical blow. Could her enemy have the power to bespell an entire town? Was that why everyone had the same thing to say about this mysterious academy?

Billowing darkness oozing from a decrepit structure, spreading like ink across the hills, across the town…

She sat, stunned. Perhaps Dewey took it for capitulation, because he relaxed, his tone turning mild and reasonable.

"Listen, Inspector," he said. "Until you bring me real, solid evidence of foul play, I won't allow you to put in your complaint for a search warrant at Bright Renewal. Havenside is not like the city. People know each other here. Everyone has their fingers in everything. Start rocking the boat among a certain set and doors get slammed in our faces, understand? Please, Inspector Viridian, you must tread carefully."

For a moment, she considered staring him down with unshielded eyes – the sight of those swirling flames had cowed many a tough guy – but she refrained. It wouldn't do any good. She knew that now. "Understood, *Chief*." The words dropped bitter and hard. She swiped up the crumpled complaint. "I'll get that evidence, I promise you."

* * *

The old farmhouse at the end of Dewberry Lane was dark and empty, the paint peeling, nearly all the windows broken and the porch steps sagging. The faded front door stood ajar, hanging from rusty hinges. Once, it had been a bright and cheery blue, the steps leading to it solid and broad. The clapboards had gleamed white, freshly painted every spring. Shining windows had looked out upon the world. Now, all of that was a distant memory. This was a house of horrors.

It had always been a house of horrors.

When she'd stormed out of the PK station, her partner calling after her in confused frustration, Hero had not known where she was going. She'd just wanted to be away from Dewey and whatever was going on with him. She'd thought the chief a strong man, a good PK – he'd sent for her, hadn't he? At some point, he'd been clearheaded – but now, it was clear he'd been corrupted. The darkness underlying the town was growing stronger. And she didn't know what to do about it.

She'd briefly considered returning to the mysterious Bright Renewal Academy and taking a closer look at that shield, but her head still ached and she didn't want to tangle with it again. She'd expected to end up in a tavern, at the very least – a good, stiff drink was calling her name right now – but instead her steps had led her here, to the last place on earth she wanted to be. The one place she'd hoped never to see again.

Home.

The road in front of her old house had seen better days. It was a shame, really. This house, this farm, had been one of the nicest residences in North Havenside. Not a rich man's house, certainly, but one of a man who was up and coming. Her father, who was not her father, had overseen this place for a good decade before she'd come along to ruin it all.

Bad luck, having a demon child. Should have drowned the creature in the lake. Burned it alive. Staked it through the heart. Only a soft man would allow such a child to live.

Hero stared up at the dark and empty windows. They looked like eyes, watching her. Judging her. Blaming her. "It's not my fault you are wrecked and ruined," she muttered to it, her hands jammed into the pockets of her duster. "I didn't force Collin Franke to drink away his fortune. I was long gone by then, stashed away in that damnable convent."

The steps creaked under her boots. Dry rot had eaten into the wood and she had to jump over a hole in the porch to reach the front door, all the while cursing herself for being so stupid. Why was she doing this to herself? She hated this place. She'd known nothing but misery here.

Laughter in the halls. Two kids chasing each other, playing hide and seek. The boy could never hide from his sister. She could see through walls…

Red-hot pokers resting in the fireplace – the third set they'd purchased in as many weeks. Nothing would work. The eyes kept growing back. Finally, frustrated, Mother giving up, settling on daily beatings to keep the girl's demon half at bay.

The fireplace was cold, empty of even ash. No furniture remained, having been sold or scavenged over the years. Hero felt too big, standing in the old family room. The velvet wallpaper, white and rose, hung in strips, revealing horsehair plaster walls pockmarked and water stained. Images crashed in her brain, and she did her best to shake them loose. Her breath was coming a little quicker, the memories crowding her.

The climb to the second floor was treacherous. Hero glanced briefly into her old room, the one she'd shared with Liam until she'd been relegated to the attic. She paused at the door to her parents' room, the scene of the crime, where an incubus had seduced her mother. She hung on to the doorjamb, hissing in a breath through her bared teeth, her gaze fixed on the empty floor where her parents' bed had stood. All her life, she'd suffered and been blamed for something not her fault. The injustice of it took her breath away.

Her last stop was the attic. She really didn't want to go up there, but she'd come this far and figured she might as well see it all the way through.

Glutton for punishment, aren't I?

There was an actual room in the attic, not just a crawlspace, with finished walls she remembered sloping close to the head of a girl who grew too fast. Hero had to duck to get back to the eaves as she searched for signs of her younger self, but all evidence had been erased. Not even a scrap of blanket or paper remained from the many drawings she'd plastered on the slanted ceiling, pictures of flowers and birds and meadows, and of skeletons and dead squirrels and paths through the

Underworld – all the usual scribblings of a girl half human and half demon.

The round window letting light in from outside was still intact. Beyond lay the familiar view of the backyard and shed and fence – broken in places now. The roof of the shed was caved in and the walls leaned drunkenly. She remembered leaping from the roof overhead to the roof of the shed, landing lightly like a spider, limbs strong and flexible. She could jump back the other way, too, and there had been joy in the power of it even when it bought her an enraged beating.

A swirl of wind disturbed the fallen leaves in the yard, and she heard the distant lowing of cattle. All so peaceful and bucolic. Any child would have been lucky to have grown up in such a place.

Not this child.

The sun hung low in the sky, slanting through the window, painting the yard gold. She looked over the hills and the cropland and saw the creeping shadows. A sense of dread rose within her. To the left, nearly hidden by trees and distance, a hilltop stood drenched in darkness. She knew what it was, and a shudder rolled through her. She would crack it open. She swore it to herself, to Sister Catarine, to Cassie Graham.

"This town has always harbored evil," she said to the empty attic room. Her hand clenched into a fist, nails digging sharply into her palm. The pain gave her focus. "It reeks of Pandemonium."

A low, sultry laugh drifted to her ears. A sudden breeze whirled through the attic. Dust stirred and twirled behind her. She turned, unsurprised. It wouldn't be the first time her thoughts had summoned him, and her father had been foremost in her mind. Her *true* father.

A figure appeared, seemingly made of dust. A disembodied mouth grinned at her before a person formed around it – an exceedingly handsome person with skin like fresh cream and hair as black as soot, silky soft and hanging to puddle around his feet. He stood naked, of course. Even in front of his own daughter, he had no shame.

"You should not have come here, sweet child." He spoke in a lisping drawl, gently chastising.

"Nor you," she replied, hand tightening on her cane, ready to draw it if necessary. She couldn't kill him, or wouldn't, really. She despised him, but he was her father, and he had chains on her, invisible but as real and solid as her bones and blood. She wouldn't speak his name, Silvanus. It would only give him more power.

He grinned, playing with his hair, braiding it like a schoolgirl, all the while keeping his flaming eyes pinned on her. They had the same eyes, father and daughter. "This town is very dangerous for someone like you."

Traitor.

He didn't speak the word, but she heard it all the same, whispering from the empty air. A trickle of flame erupted from the edges of the floor, beneath the eaves. A heatless fire. A little taste of Hell. As a full demon, he brought Hell with him wherever he went, but his power was limited, unlike hers. He was a demon touching the human world, able to touch it, to influence it, but little else. She could squash him flat if she so chose.

"Whatever creature of Pandemonium resides here, Father, I will find it. And I will destroy it." She leaned on her cane and examined her long nails casually. "If you stand in my way, I'll happily send you back to the Spheres, too. Just for fun."

That brought a scowl to his gorgeous face. He didn't like it when she threatened him. She couldn't kill him, but she could weaken him enough to force him back to Pandemonium. That was the last place an incubus wanted to be stuck. Who was there to seduce in Hell?

"I am merely trying to warn you, daughter. You should heed my words instead of getting all prickly." He *tsk*ed chidingly. "You sound so... human."

She gave him a shrewd look. "Since when do you bring me warnings? You've never tried to protect me from anything. So. What's in it for you now, dear old Pop?"

In a flash, he was an inch from her, handsome face transformed into a hideous, fanged visage, red and bloody. She remained still, regarding him calmly. He always tried to startle her, the bastard.

"BECAUSE YOU ARE MINE!"

His shriek made the walls rattle and the floor shake, and Hero hoped the whole house wouldn't collapse at his outburst. He subsided almost immediately, returning to his pretty form several feet from her, working on his braid. "I'll not have you taken to Pandemonium as some other demon's prize."

Hero scoffed. "As if it would be so easy." Inside, however, she felt a small niggle of doubt. Was he telling her the truth? He wasn't one for honesty, her Pop. And he only ever appeared to make her life messy. However, there was no doubt that something very powerful was at work here, and she couldn't dismiss the possibility that he might be concerned for her – not that she would die, of course, but that she would escape him. He was a jealous incubus, after all. It was his dream to have her rule beside him in Hell, chained together for eternity.

I know what awaits you.

She fought the urge to scowl. That damnable nun thought she knew her fate. So did her accursed father. Let them both believe it. She refused to accept it. She just had to stay alive long enough to figure out how to avoid it. Easy.

"I appreciate the warning, Father," she said politely, smiling her own fanged smile. She reached beneath her scapular and retrieved the fancy lighter Culpepper had given her on her first anniversary as an inspector death speaker. The engraved device was pure silver and had never failed to light. She flicked open the top and ran her thumb over the striker wheel. A flame burst to life in the gathering gloom. With a hiss, her demon-father shrank away. It wasn't a normal lighter, after all, but one imbued with a righteous light, blessed of the Goddess. "But it's time for you to go."

Tucking her cane under her arm, she retrieved the crumpled complaint from her pocket and set it ablaze. No great loss – she could always write another one. It burned with an intense blue. Casually, she tossed it into a corner. The dry wood erupted beneath it and flames began to eat at the desiccated floor, creeping toward them like a living thing.

Unhurried, Hero strode toward her father then past him, slipping beyond his reaching fingers effortlessly. She'd had a lot of practice, after all. His enraged snarls followed her down the stairs before cutting off abruptly. *Good. Go back to Hell, monster.*

The crackle and snap of burning wood rose to a roar. Heat beat down on her head as she descended to the main floor, flames in her wake. A slight hop took her over the hole in the front porch and she leapt from the top step onto the ground rather than risk the rickety steps again. Whistling and swinging her cane jauntily, she began the trek back to town as her childhood home was consumed by a cleansing fire behind her.

Good riddance.

CHAPTER SIXTEEN

Inspector Viridian had abandoned him. Again. Not to run through the woods like some twisted, unnatural beast this time, of course, but gone just the same, along with half the station. Responding to some emergency at the edge of town – a fire, he thought someone had said. Apparently, many of the PKs of Havenside were also volunteer firefighters. It left him practically alone in the neat and tidy station, fixing a lonely cup of tea and feeling useless.

"Waste of my talents," he muttered to the steaming tea as he stirred in a lump of sugar. "Wouldn't even let me write up the complaint. As if I don't understand procedure!"

Well, he didn't. Not entirely. The law wasn't stringent when it came to demon rights. Usually, he did whatever he had to when pursuing supernatural subjects. Worrying about search warrants and the rights of minors never crossed his mind. Which, of course, was why Inspector Viridian chose to write the complaint herself, relegating him to the task of tending to their winded horses while she did it.

But when he'd returned to their shared desk, Hero had been on her way out the door, coat, cane, complaint and all. Chief Dewey had offered him only an infuriating shrug when he'd demanded to know where she'd gone. "I'm not her keeper," he'd muttered. "I'm sure she's gone somewhere where she can step on as many toes as possible."

Oleander had been taken aback at Dewey's change in attitude toward Inspector Viridian. Hadn't he asked for her personally? She wasn't exactly an unknown quantity. Had he expected she *wouldn't* step on toes in pursuit of the guilty?

Revealing the crimes of the powerful was SOP for this particular death speaker. Hadn't she exposed one of the most prominent railroad baron's serial-murder spree? There was the story of body parts dumped on a judge's doorstep...

"I'm sure she's following through on our lead," he said, feeling a strange compulsion to defend his partner. There was a certain code among peacekeepers of the Realm: You always had your partner's back. "Our interviews, and especially the events of this morning, have opened up our investigation considerably."

Dewey exhaled noisily. "Surely, you must understand how... fraught pursuing such a lead will be in this town?"

"Pardon, Chief, but I don't see the problem. A mysterious fortress appearing out of nowhere, connected spectrally to a victim – both victims! – surely warrants further inquiry?"

Exasperated confusion crumpled Dewey's face. He leaned back in his chair and stared at Keen like he had suddenly sprouted another head. "Have you both lost your minds? I thought it was merely Viridian being, well, Viridian. But you? Did you grow up in a cave, DH Keen? Bright Renewal Academy has been part of the fabric of Havenside for decades. That institution has done more for the good of the community than even the church, I dare say. Saving children is their calling! And you and Inspector Viridian dare to accuse them, to impugn their reputation? For what purpose? What reason other than a delusional hunch?"

Rendered speechless by Dewey's odd vehemence over the mysterious institution, Keen had returned to his desk wondering if perhaps he was the one who was mistaken. Perhaps he'd somehow missed the existence of Bright Renewal the entire time he'd lived in Havenside. It seemed utterly ridiculous, but he couldn't think of any other explanation.

Is Chief Dewey the crazy one, or is it me?

An hour later, after going over witness statements, searching for inconsistencies, clues and hints, Keen decided maybe Dewey was right after all. Many of their witnesses had mentioned Bright Renewal. There were several references to the place, scattered throughout the documents. All glowing remarks, too. He couldn't for the life of him understand why he didn't remember its existence.

"No, of course I remember." Keen caught the glance of a PK at the filing cabinet. He hadn't realized he'd spoken out loud. He shuffled the reports back into a neat stack, feeling utterly foolish to have forgotten such a venerated establishment in his own hometown. Why, half the children who'd grown up in Otherside had done a stint at Bright Renewal.

Goddess, his head hurt. Keen pinched the top of his nose and squeezed his tired eyes shut. He'd spent all afternoon going over the witness statements and nothing new had leapt out at him. Abigail had confirmed Sister Catarine's illicit relationship with Father Kellan. Inspector Viridian had already focused on him as a person of interest. Their only other lead was what Molly Franke had told them about the dead student, and that was hardly any lead at all – except it had dumped them on the doorstep of a respectable school which existed solely to save wayward children. Surely Bright Renewal Academy had nothing to do with a murder!

The shriek of a crow outside the station window startled him from his ruminations. Someone had left the window open, probably one of the peacekeepers who enjoyed smoking but didn't want to stand outside to do it. He stood up to close it, then spotted a cowled figure on the steps below. The person glanced up and met his gaze.

Pale-faced, unshaven, dark bruises around his eyes and a cut on his swollen lip, Father Kellan stared up at him like a drowning man spotting a life preserver.

With little fanfare, DH Keen ushered the priest into an interrogation room. The man kept his cowl on until they were behind closed doors, keeping his face hidden. He seemed to want to keep his presence low key, and luckily for him there were still only a few squad members at the station. That fire must have been a doozy for no one to have returned yet.

Where the hell is Viridian?

It didn't matter. He could handle this himself.

"Tea, Father?" he asked when the man had settled into the hard, wobbly chair they provided for suspects. This unexpected appearance had Keen's hackles up. Father Roger Kellan was already a person of interest. Appearing like this, disheveled and intoxicated... Sometimes killers inserted themselves into investigations, especially those who acted out of passion. They just couldn't help themselves. Guilt destroyed them. It was Keen's job to turn that guilt against them.

Kellan shook his head at the offer, then seemed to change his mind. "Yes, please. I think I need something…" He trailed off, his hands before him on the table open and trembling as if waiting for a gift to be dropped into them. "My head is a bit cloudy."

The tea arrived, hot and steaming. Keen took a cup himself and exchanged a glance with the aide who'd brought it, not a PK but an auxiliary clerk. She lifted her graying brows at him, seemingly unsurprised at the state the priest was in. She was older than Keen – a mother and a grandmother, or so he understood – and had no doubt seen it all before. Her glance toward Kellan on leaving the room was not a kind one.

Perhaps more people had suspected something scandalous between Father Kellan and Sister Catarine. After all, Havenside was a small town and gossip ran hot through her wide, manicured streets. He cursed himself for being so blind. Not until Abigail had said it out loud was he willing to believe it. Just because Kellan was a priest and their victim was a nun, it didn't mean they weren't a man and a woman. Young, attractive, always in each other's company. He sighed inwardly. He had a lot to learn about people.

Father Kellan held his cup of tea between his hands, letting the steam bathe his face. He seemed to be struggling to compose himself, tossing wretched glances at Keen every now and again. Keen waited. The man had come to confess – this he knew with deep certainty – but what was he going to confess to, exactly?

"I – I have to ask for your forgiveness, DH Keen," he began after a few long draughts of tea. It worked like magic, calming him. "I wasn't entirely truthful when you and that… your partner questioned me at Clementine. You were only doing your jobs, and it was foolish of me to try and hide anything. After all, Havenside is a small place. Everyone always knows everyone else's business, you see. Ah – you should know, you grew up here, didn't you?" A tremulous smile crossed his battered face, and the cut on his lip bled a little at the movement. He winced and touched it gingerly.

"What happened to you, Father, if I may inquire?"

Kellan waved a hand. "I'll get to that. First, I have to tell you. I mean, I have to get this off my chest. It's – it's scandalous. Which was why I found myself reluctant to say it out loud. The truth is, Sister Catarine – Cat..." He choked a moment on her name, his lips pressed tight, his throat working. Tears sprang into his eyes. "It's true. What... she suspected. The ex-nun. The demon nun. Cat and I were together. We... we were going to leave the order when Clem broke for winter break. We were going to leave Havenside. Not just because we were in love – and, yes, we loved each other dearly. We didn't mean to fall in love, mind you. But we did. We couldn't help it!" He stared at Keen beseechingly as if he might absolve him of this sin.

Keen said nothing, opting to let the priest unspool enough rope to hang himself. Already, he was beginning to feel his flesh crawl, knowing what was coming. The image of Catarine's body haunted him, tossed in the woods like trash, her tongue removed. What kind of monster sat before him?

And yet there was no stink of the demonic on him. Not a whiff. The one thing Keen knew about the sister's hideous death was that a demon was involved. Perhaps Kellan had been its unwitting tool?

"I loved her more than my own life," Kellan continued. His unshaven jowls shook with emotion, his eyes red-rimmed and wet. "I should have taken her away sooner, gotten her out of this horrid town, this hideous place. There is a darkness here, DH Keen, so subtle you might never even notice, but it is there beneath the surface – a rot. A stink."

Keen blinked. Was this a confession or not?

"She tried to tell me people were targeting her, making subtle threats. I brushed it off as a flight of fancy, just guilt talking. Leaving the order is no simple decision. Why, we could both be risking damnation. But when your calling fails you, what choice do you have? I swore everything would be all right, that I would protect her. I swore to take her away somewhere safe, but she said she couldn't leave yet because of her students."

"She didn't want to leave with you," Keen said flatly, feeling his anger rising. "Is that what happened between you?"

"No! She wanted to leave. She wanted to be with me."

"Or perhaps she changed her mind? You said she didn't want to leave her students. I can see how that might make you angry." Keen shook his head, forcing himself to sound sympathetic when all he wanted to do was throttle this miserable specimen of a man. "Women can be fickle, can't they? Promising us the world one day and spurning us the next. I understand what that does to men like us. Men of passion and daring."

Father Kellan stared at him, not looking passionate or particularly daring at all. "I – I think you misunderstand me. She hadn't changed her mind about anything. She only wanted to stay a little longer to make sure her students were safe. And I told her to forget about it, let others deal with it. We fought about it more than once, I'm ashamed to admit. But... why put herself in danger for those entitled brats?"

The bitterness in his voice was startling. He was a popular teacher, or so others had said. The students of Clementine considered him a friend of sorts, as much as any teacher could be. "She thought the students were in danger?" Keen said sharply. Perhaps Catarine had known something – something terrible. Cassie Graham had told the sister a terrible secret, and now both of them were dead.

"I'm sorry. I don't mean to blame them." He ran a shaking hand through his snarled hair. "I just wanted to be gone, so we could start a new life somewhere else. Somewhere far, far away from here. If I had convinced her to leave with me that night, the last night I saw her alive..."

He began to weep in earnest. Keen sighed, watching him dissolve into an absolute mess. Not exactly the cold-blooded killer he'd imagined. His "confession" had taken quite the turn. It wasn't unusual for a guilty man to weep crocodile tears for the person he'd killed, but Keen was beginning to soften. Kellan seemed so broken. How could he possibly have been capable of carrying out such a perfect murder, leaving no trace behind? No human trace, at least?

No, he no longer believed Kellan had killed the poor nun, tool of a demon or not. But still...

"You were the last person to see her alive," he said. "That puts you at the top of our suspect list, I'm afraid."

"I know," the priest answered miserably. "I know how it looks. Her brothers think I did it. They knew, you see, about the two of us, or were suspicious at the very least. They ambushed me, beat me up, tried to force a confession. I only got away by promising to turn myself in. But I am innocent of this crime! I would sooner slit my own throat than harm a hair on her head. I deserve no mercy, though. I deserve to pay for this, to pay dearly. I did not kill Cat, but I didn't save her, either. Throw me in the clink if you must, but don't stop hunting the real killers."

CHAPTER SEVENTEEN

With the smell of smoke still clinging to her, Hero ventured into town for supplies. She marched with purpose, leaves crinkling beneath her boots and dancing around her cane. She had a job to do, and she needed a few necessary tools. Downtown Havenside bustled with activity. The finer set were lunching and shopping as usual, but fear infected them. There were nervous glances, wide eyes and pale faces, and women huddled together outside boutiques, quietly whispering behind gloved hands. Murder was a stranger to quiet Havenside.

Not so to Hero Viridian. To her, murder was a close friend indeed.

She drew shocked stares and a few unpleasant scowls as she strode down the busy street. Did any of them remember the little white-haired girl she'd been, the perpetually blindfolded one? She was never allowed to go about the town alone, instead always trailing along behind her parents on the way to church – the only place she ever went in Havenside. Thoroughly unpleasant visits, every single one.

People had to know that this grown woman, this half-demon disgraced nun, was their very own Helen Franke, at least those who remembered her. The cursed child. The ill omen.

The constant scrutiny made her skin crawl. She was used to it, of course, yet somehow here it was different. Worse. This was the very first place she'd been an outcast, formed and nurtured.

Let them stare.

Hero moved carelessly, her long strides easy and sure. She was a death speaker, an inspector, respected and admired – well, tolerated anyway. As long as she solved cases.

The shop she wanted was at the corner of Grand and Wellington and sold nothing but art supplies – a frivolous indulgence only a town like Havenside could support, along with boutiques selling nothing but ribbons or hats. They even had an entire shop devoted to selling lampshades. Not lamps, just lampshades. Preposterous.

The door jingled merrily, announcing her entrance. The patrons – mostly young men dressed in drab colors with shaggy hair and a few girls in fine frocks pinned high on one side to show a scandalous stretch of hose – pretended not to notice her, but she felt the shift in the cluttered shop the minute she entered. It didn't matter. She had a job to do. This case, this damnable case, was going to require a board, a careful accounting of all their evidence so far. A painstaking process.

A lick of fire rose from her gloved finger, and she extinguished it against her scapular with an annoyed grimace. She had to get control of herself. This place contained mostly paper, after all.

"I need all of this," Hero said to the startled young clerk behind the front desk, laying down her list in front of him with what she hoped was a friendly smile. His narrow, foxy face went white at the kind gesture, so she assumed she'd done it wrong. She rearranged her face into an expressionless mask, quashing the urge to smirk. "Now, if you please. And charge it to the Havenside PKs."

"Y-y-yes, ma'am."

Hero rolled her eyes behind her tinted glasses. Her second ma'am this week. Good enough, she supposed.

Later, with her supplies tucked beneath one arm, she returned to her flat and set to work transforming one wall into a patchwork of documents, drawings and red string. Usually, she would have done this in the stationhouse, but after her confrontation with Dewey she was reluctant to show him any of her work. Her suspicions. He'd seemed like real police when she'd first met him, but something had happened. Somehow, since she'd found that spectral chain, the whole town had seemed to shift, just like the air in the Art Supplies Emporium. Her presence there, her discovery, had been noticed.

After she'd finished with her initial layout – the case was barely a few days old, after all; she had no doubt more clues would be unearthed – she left to find a meal. It had been a long day, and a bowl of something hot and a stiff drink would set her head straight. After changing out of her clothes, on which the smell of smoke still lingered, she stepped out into the night.

She found her partner waiting for her on the stoop, agitated and impatient. *Shit.* She'd completely forgotten about him. Keeping her teeth behind her lips, she gave him a smile.

"DH Keen," she said brightly. "Good evening. Will you join me for a drink?"

"A *drink*?" he said scathingly. His cheeks were bright, and his baby face bent in a grimace. "Where have you been? You just left me at the station like a forgotten toddler at the market!"

She tapped the brim of her hat with her cane. "Well, don't act like one now," she said. "I had some things to do, and I had to get out of there. Dewey has lost it. I'm afraid it puts our whole case at risk."

"*You're* putting our case at risk," he countered, catching up to her as she strode down the sidewalk, cane tapping a rhythm. "You put Dewey all in a lather going after Bright Renewal like that."

She stopped, turning on him, the butt of her cane coming down hard. "Not you too!" she cried, aghast. "I'd hoped you at least wouldn't have succumbed to whatever has befallen this town. Get yourself together, Demonhunter! You should smell an enchantment like a good dog smells a duck!"

He jerked back, blinking at her. They had stopped under a flickering gas lamp, and she could see the befuddlement in his gaze. He shook his head, his jaw firming up.

"Fight it," she hissed at him, getting in his face. "I need one ally here, Keen, and unfortunately you are all I have. So. Snap out of it!" She poked him hard in the chest, just above his bandolier of vile potions. Not all of them were designed to hurt demons – some were made to enhance a demonhunter's skills – but she didn't dare touch any of them.

"I – I don't know what you mean–"

"Oh, for Hell's sake, yes you do. *Think*, Oleander Keen. You grew up here. Had young Oleander ever heard of Bright Renewal Academy? Do you remember your friends talking about it? Do you *really* remember?"

He looked inward, his eyes bouncing, searching. The befuddlement, the confusion, grew more pronounced. Then with shocking suddenness, he grasped one of the vials at his bandolier and jerked it free, so terrifyingly quickly she nearly knocked it away with her cane, thinking he meant to use it against her. Instead, he swallowed the contents in a single gulp.

The empty vial shattered on the sidewalk at their feet. For a moment, they stared at one another, Keen breathing hard, blowing like a winded horse, Hero tensed, waiting for violence.

A grimace twisted his face. He bent at the middle, stricken, one arm clutched across his midsection. Passersby gave him looks but hurried on, leaving the two alone in the halo of the streetlamp. Hero took a step back, her cane at the ready. She'd club him, if necessary, but she felt a small hope it wouldn't be. Keen was a professional. He understood what she wanted from him, understood that things weren't quite right.

The potion took him to one knee.

"Pull yourself together, DH Keen," she ordered sharply. Men like him responded well to directives. She was his superior. That made a difference even if every instinct told him to distrust her. To kill her, even. She was risking a lot on his professionalism, but she hadn't been lying: she needed an ally. Damn the Goddess for this sick joke, but she needed him, now more than ever.

Whatever the foul concoction was, it was fast acting, at least. Keen suddenly relaxed, both fists dropping to the sidewalk to prop him up as he sagged. He took a few deep breaths, then staggered upright. She didn't help him, afraid to touch him lest he lash out at her. Instincts honed by experience were hard to suppress, especially when you were as vulnerable as Keen was now.

His face had turned sickly in the glow of the gas lamp, but his eyes were clear. The befuddlement was gone from his expression, replaced by hardness, an anger etched deep in the lines around his mouth and eyes. His lips screwed up and he spat as if he'd eaten something unpleasant. The potion or the broken enchantment?

"There now," she said quietly. "All better?"

He nodded. Another grimace and a hard swallow. He tugged at his uniform, setting it straight, took off his cap and ran a hand over his hair before replacing it. Shoulders squared, he clicked his heels together. "My apologies, Inspector Viridian. I – I was indisposed..."

"Yes, well, the important thing is you're better now, right?" She peered at him. He seemed clear-eyed and lucid. Could be a trick, though. Any enchantment that blanketed an entire town was a powerful one. But demonhunters were a special breed.

His attention stance wavered, and he looked about ten years old. "I should have known. I should have understood what was happening. The sudden shift with Dewey... Damn my blindness." He lifted a fist, but his anger was directed entirely at himself. "It won't happen again. I see what we're up against now. I'll be more vigilant."

Hero shrugged. She didn't want to belabor his failing. At least he'd managed to snap himself out of it. Most men, most humans, wouldn't have that fortitude; a demonhunter's Sight potions would kill an ordinary man. It hadn't been so difficult to break him free, though the pounding in her heart belied the thought. He could have just as easily responded with violence. Then she would have had to solve this whole thing alone.

"Right. All's well." She tugged at the brim of the ridiculously small top hat pinned to her hair – as was the fashion – and resumed her walk to town, strolling slowly to give him more of a chance to compose himself and follow. Soon, his shadow appeared beside hers, cast long and lean ahead of them. Their footsteps fell into synchronicity. "Let's get that drink."

Molly Franke was dry-eyed when her hulking guards escorted her into a chill, white-walled foyer with low ceilings and gas lamps. Her terror had receded on the ride to this terrible place and all she felt now was numb. Was this how Cole Graham had felt when they'd dragged him away at the beginning of the semester? Numb, hopeless?

In a fog of disbelief, she had been held in the revered mother's office until the end of the day and then taken from Clementine by men in strange uniforms. She'd protested vehemently, begging for her father, but nothing she'd said mattered; they'd lifted her off her feet with huge, hard hands and carried her to her doom, stinking of tobacco and sweat, deaf to her sobs and pleas. They didn't speak, didn't try and calm her, only tossed her like a sack of coal into the back of a wagon.

Upon arrival at Bright Renewal, the uniformed men handed her over to a woman in a plain gray dress covered by a white apron, her hair held back by a kerchief. Her eyes stayed dry even after she was led into a small room with only one high, barred window and a drain in the freezing concrete floor. Then she was ordered to strip.

Cheeks burning, she removed her clothes, fumbling at her buttons while the woman watched, face pinched with impatience. She tried to fold her garments, but the woman made a rude noise and swept them into a bundle, declaring they'd be "burned with the morning trash" and left her alone. Cold and naked, she wrapped her arms around herself and shivered violently.

The dour woman returned carrying a bucket of sudsy water in one hand and a scrub brush in the other. Molly's detachment broke as the woman came at her with the brush and bucket. Cold water splashed onto the floor, onto her feet, and she backed away, arms extended, palms forward in a warding gesture born from pure horror. "No, please, I – I can wash myself."

"Are you resisting?" the woman said, waving her sopping scrub brush. She seemed almost gleeful about it. "Girls like you are always trouble, I swear."

"I'm not! I don't mean to be–"

Scowling, the woman set down her bucket and grabbed Molly by the arm, yanking hard. The girl toppled, landing on her knees in a soapy puddle. "Settle down and let me get on with it."

The brush hit her skin, hard bristles digging and scraping across her back and shoulders. She couldn't help it – she screamed.

"Oh, so, that's the way of it, right?" The scrubbing stopped and a second later a wave of icy water crashed over her. She gasped, then found her breath for a shriek somewhere between outrage and horror.

"What's all the caterwauling about?" demanded a new voice, female. "Should I call the guards?"

Guards? Did she mean the men who'd brought her here? The idea threw Molly into a panic. She lashed out, kicked and fought, shaking her head wildly. Then suddenly the small room was full of people – all women, thankfully, she noted before her face was smashed against the concrete, multiple hands holding her down. Someone was practically sitting on her! It was all she could do to breathe. The scrubbing resumed, harder this time, and humiliatingly thorough. Crushed beneath this onslaught of cruelty, she gave in and went limp.

"There's a good girl," someone said soothingly. A hand stroked her wet and tangled hair. "You'll learn, child. You'll learn quick. I guarantee it."

"Or else," another added ominously, eliciting a slew of gleeful sniggers.

Scrubbed pink and raw, Molly stood trembling in a new room no bigger than a closet, this one containing a bench with folded clothes atop it. Her skin still damp, she was nonetheless ordered to dress by her escort, another woman in the nondescript "uniform" of plain dress, apron and head scarf. They looked like nurses but acted like prison guards, those hard men she'd seen her father interact with a time or two.

Once she was dressed in a scratchy, ill-fitting outfit that was a washed-out facsimile of her Clem Prep uniform, with a spare set clutched in her arms – shirt, skirt, two pairs of underwear, two pairs of socks, two bandeaus: all the clothes she was to be provided with here at Bright Renewal, apparently – she was taken to yet another small room. This one had a window, at least, though it was covered by thick curtains. The walls were raw brick, the floors sanded wood, cold and bare like all the other rooms she'd been in so far. Here, she learned the rules of Bright Renewal Academy:

There was no talking – *none*. (This was emphasized sharply.) Not with other students, not to teachers or faculty (unless they ordered it first.) Laughter was prohibited. Smiling, too. Frivolity led to sin.

Letters to parents were allowed but would be carefully scrutinized for "falsehoods" and "nonsense." Uniforms were to be kept neat and clean (she would be doing her own laundry; this was not a place that coddled disobedient children!). Chores would be assigned daily: scrubbing the common areas, cleaning the lavatories, kitchen duty, laundry, etc. Demerits would earn additional chores and other punishments (these were not explained in detail, but Molly did not want to find out.)

Every day, the students rose at dawn for prayers and "reconditioning," then spent the day at their studies, curated into a "specially designed curriculum," whatever that meant. Healthy, nutritious meals would be provided. Anyone found to be hoarding food would be punished. Good attitudes and adherence to the rules would earn a student points toward graduation. The faster one obeyed and learned correct behavior, the faster one would earn their reward. Points would be lost for every violation of the rules.

"Your time here can go swiftly, Ms Franke," one of her new (teachers? guards? handlers?) said to her as she stood at the center of the cold, empty room, stiff and stinging from her scrubbing, stunned into submission, "or it can be interminable. Do you understand?"

Terror kept her from answering. Was she supposed to speak now, or would it earn her punishment? She stared at the woman, older than her mother with thick jowls and hard eyes. "Well?" she demanded, scowling. "Answer me!"

"Y-y-yes," she blurted, clutching her new clothes to her chest. "I understand."

"I understand, *Mistress Blume*," the woman said, speaking slowly and clearly, as if to an idiot.

"I understand, Mistress Blume."

A smile cracked her granite face. "Very good. Now, it's been a long day and it's time for bed. Tomorrow, everything will be better. The Goddess only gives us as much as we can endure."

Meekly, Molly followed Mistress Blume down a long, grim hallway, up two flights of iron stairs which led to another long, grim hallway, this one lined with doorways – not doors; there were no doors anywhere. As they passed rooms, Molly could see into all of them. Cots and bunk beds filled each room, four to six children crammed in together, all girls. None of them looked back at her as she passed. Outside each room sat a woman on a chair wearing trousers and a thick jacket – the place was frigid. Each one eyed her sharply as she walked by.

So even when she slept, she would be guarded. A wild despair made her stomach drop.

There was a lavatory on this floor, which Mistress Blume took her into so she could perform her nightly ablutions. There was a wooden toothbrush among her clothes and a small tub of baking soda beside the sink, along with a sliver of soap. She brushed her teeth and washed her face quickly in the ice-cold water, then turned toward the row of stalls. The bathroom wasn't so different from those at Clem Prep, she reflected, but for the utter bleakness and the fact that these stalls had no doors.

"Do your business," Mistress Blume ordered when Molly hesitated. "You have lost the privilege of privacy through your reckless actions, missy. Being treated like a normal girl again must be *earned.*"

A hard cot with a thin blanket awaited her in a room near the end of the hall. Three other girls were already huddled in their beds in the same small space. She caught the glint of one pair of eyes as she made her way to her new bed. Slowly, they blinked – once, deliberately – and then the girl flipped over to put her face to the wall.

Shivering, Molly crept into her cot. Despair filled her throat in a hard, sore knot, but she held in any tears, distinctly aware of the guard outside her door. Instead, she focused on the memory of those eyes, the slow blink. A smile of solidarity where smiles were forbidden. She felt a small spark of hope and held it close. All she had to do was obey – obey and endure.

How long could this nightmare last?

CHAPTER EIGHTEEN

"So, you have Kellan in the holding pen?"

Keen nodded, taking a sip of his pint. Froth clung to his upper lip, and he wiped it away on his sleeve. "Seemed best. I'm afraid Catarine's brothers might have another go at him if they see him walking free."

"No doubt." Hero swirled her bourbon, enjoying the sparkle of it in the tavern's lanterns. This place wasn't as hoity-toity as Grantham House, but it was still rather upscale, all fine-grained wood and brass fittings, stuffed leather banquettes and heavy tables. The clientele were mostly professionals – litigators, doctors, merchants, teachers. Not a soiled cuff, dirt-scuffed boot or worn pair of dungarees in sight. She and Keen weren't the only uniforms in the place, either.

"You were right about the two of them," Keen added.

"They were fucking?"

"Good Goddess, Inspector, there's no need to be vulgar. But... yes."

"So, a crime of passion, was it?" For some reason, she was vaguely disappointed. For all her suspicions, she didn't think this murder would prove so simple. It didn't mean a demon wasn't involved – they often used weak humans as their tools – but a truly powerful demon had no need to resort to such mundane measures.

Keen shook his head. "He's not our man. I'm certain of it."

She wasn't, despite everything. It *could* be as simple as a crime of passion; she wouldn't know until she questioned him herself. At least he was being cooperative – supposedly – and at least now he was being truthful about his relationship with the sister – again, supposedly.

"So her brothers thought they'd take care of things themselves," she mused. "I'm surprised they didn't kill him."

"I think Kellan managed to talk them out of it, thankfully. Justice at the end of a rope will satisfy them and leave no blood on their hands to boot."

"Good thing for our case that they didn't kill him." She took a quick drink, enjoying the burn of the liquor – warm like the fires of Hell. "It never ceases to amaze me how people withhold information in an investigation." She shook her head mournfully, then gave a one-shouldered shrug. "Although frankly, I've never had to deal with it much. The dead don't lie."

Keen shifted in his seat, leaning closer. "He also confirmed what we learned from Cat's letters and from Abigail Hollander. She'd been working to erase the stigma attached to those of demonic heritage." This he said quickly, keeping his eyes on his pint. "A very unpopular stance. I also questioned him about the mysterious Mr B and the missing children from those same letters, but Kellan had no idea about any of that."

"Of course not," she murmured. Kellan hadn't added much to the investigation, except to propel himself to the top of the suspect list. Unless he was lying about not knowing about this Mr B, a man, presumably, with whom his lover had been communicating. She tapped a long fingernail against the tabletop. "She was about to take her concerns to Mother Francesca when she disappeared, or so he told you," she said pointedly. "Or perhaps she did take her concerns to the mother, and that's why she disappeared."

He grimaced, but didn't deny the theory. "Someone wanted her silenced. The missing tongue was a warning to Cassie, yes? Or maybe to any number of people in on this scheme, whatever it is. Why was she held for six days first?" he wondered. "What happened to her during those six days?"

"She was collared. Chained." Hero rubbed her pointed chin. "Forced to kneel on hard, rocky ground. The evidence supports it. That spectral chain confirms our suspicions. What is it connected to? What sort of demon does it feed?"

"We are dependent on Dr Virchow for those answers. Hopefully, he'll be able to determine what sort of demon were dealing with, at least."

Hero sighed. Time. It would take time and effort. "We also need to find out who runs the Academy. Look into its finances and root out who pays the bills."

"And who has the most to lose if the Academy is shuttered," he added. "We'll need help for this. I'll see if Dewey can lend us some uniforms or junior inspectors. This is the biggest case Havenside has seen in decades. He'll have to give us help, right?"

"Maybe." She leaned across the table and lowered her voice. They had taken a booth in the back of the tavern, like secret lovers on a tryst. "I don't know how deep or strong this enchantment is. Perhaps it merely inserted the memory of Bright Renewal, or perhaps it has turned the town against us. Against the truth."

He frowned. "That would be an awfully powerful enchantment. As it stands, most Havensiders still want to know who killed Sister Catarine. They're afraid a murderer is on the loose; that fear is palpable. This spell, whatever it is, has limits."

"True." She relaxed against the smooth leather, appraising him. "You're pretty sharp for a squirrel, Oleander Keen."

He lifted his pint to her. "This squirrel has been around the block a few times, Viridian."

Something darkened the corner of her vision, a great, looming bulk. Startled, she nearly called the fires of Hell, but it wasn't some demon or nightmare come to life, just a man – a giant of a man who reeked of liquor. Across from her, Keen's expression had hardened.

"Did I hear right?" the man said, unleashing a cloud of fumes. "Is that Ollie Keen, the great demonhunter?"

Keen's upper lip curled ever so slightly before he hid it with a polite smile. "It is," he said brightly. "Do I know you?"

Any fool could have read the recognition on his face a moment earlier. The man chuckled knowingly. "Oh, don't be sore, Charity. Let bygones be bygones, right? Things turned out pretty well for you, didn't they? I mean, look at that fancy uniform and shiny sword. You've made Clem Prep proud, I'd say."

Keen relaxed a bit, turning the pint glass in front of him in a little circle. "I suppose we can, Dirk," he said. He stopped fiddling with his glass and threw a sharp look at this Dirk fellow. "If you stop calling me Charity then perhaps we can let all those bygones stay gone, right?"

A subtle tension filled the air. The big man – more muscle than fat, Hero noted as she readied an escape plan – snickered nastily. "And what if I can't manage it? That name just fits you so perfectly." He leaned over, keeping one hand on the back of the booth behind Hero and getting right in Keen's face. "When Abby told me how insulted you were when she called you Charity, I could hardly believe it. She had to be mistaken, I thought. Good old Charity would never–"

Keen's pint glass smashed against the side of Dirk's head, showering Hero with ale. She was astonished by how fast he'd whipped the impromptu weapon at his target. But the big man, Dirk, was no slouch. He shook off the attack and lunged at the demonhunter.

"I warned you!" Keen shouted, grappling with the much larger man. He got his foot up and into Dirk's ample gut and managed to shove him back, then stood, snarling, inadvertently knocking the heavy table into Hero's midsection. She winced and barely managed to save her drink as the table tipped dangerously. It was hard to decide whether to be amused or annoyed. She loved a good fight, after all.

"You were always a cowardly little shit," Dirk growled, squaring off with him with meaty fists. He was unarmed, and Keen wisely didn't go for his own weapons; even PKs couldn't run someone through without cause, and barroom brawls were hardly a good enough reason to skewer someone, even an asshole like Dirk.

"Not cowardly," Keen countered, his own fists up as he danced lightly on his toes. Good – always keep moving. Tire out a bigger opponent if you couldn't match strength for strength. "Just a kid. You were twice my size!"

Dirk snorted contemptuously. "You were a fat, lazy fuck!"

Snapping out with brutal swiftness, Keen's fist caught him on the nose. Blood spurted spectacularly and Hero burst out laughing. Maybe Keen was more fun than he'd let on? She crawled out of the booth, drink in hand, ready to back up her partner if necessary. Others were beginning to form a ring around the combatants, and judging by their shouts of encouragement, Dirk was the obvious favorite. Hero was beginning to understand the dynamics – a person never forgot their first bully.

Snarling, Dirk swiped away the blood, barely fazed by the punch. He launched a laggardly roundhouse that Keen easily evaded, ducking and swaying, then the DH came up under the bigger man's guard and pummeled his midsection. Hero approved. This was pugilism, pure and simple. Keen could easily kill the man, but that wasn't the goal here. She took a last gulp of bourbon and gestured to a passing server for another. The girl shot her an aggrieved look but went to fetch the drink, skirting the boxers like they were a spill on the floor.

"Show him what's what, Hollander!" someone shouted. "Put the stuck-up bastard in his place."

Good old Hollander wasn't going to be putting anyone in their place; that much was obvious. Keen was keeping out of reach, striking strategically. Hero eyed the ardent fan lest he give Keen trouble, letting her glasses slide down her narrow nose a bit. The man, trim and balding and wearing a vest, caught her stare and went pale, whatever he was going to say next lodging in his throat. She smiled. He sank into the crowd, letting braver men take his place.

The two men circled each other, the fight resolving into a stalemate. Dirk seemed reluctant to engage Keen, and Hero could hardly blame him. So far, he hadn't managed to lay a hand on the spry demonhunter. For his part, Keen looked savagely gleeful. How long had he been waiting for this chance to turn the tables on an old tormentor?

She understood. Visions of flames eating through a convent warmed her heart. A righteous fire...

Her bourbon appeared on a silver tray, and she took it without a glance at the server. The girl vanished, though she left a whisper of a sigh behind her. A world-weary sort for one so young. Hero grinned again. She rather liked this place.

Dirk made a move at last, closing with Keen, burly arms spread wide. The pressing crowd prevented Keen from dancing out of reach and Dirk caught him in a bear hug. Grappling, the two men crashed into a table and chairs, scattering the occupants and sending glasses shattering.

Now the bartender intervened. "Here, now! Take it outside!"

No one paid him any heed. Cheers rose as Dirk seemed to gain the upper hand, and Hero tensed. She didn't really want to jump in – how would that look for Keen? – but she couldn't let her partner get hurt. Not badly, anyway.

Somehow, Keen slithered free and managed to trip his opponent as he did so, sending him to his hands and knees. Ah, so he knew how to wrestle, too – a man of many talents. He landed a good kick on Dirk, right in his ample midsection, before resuming his boxing stance. Dirk stayed down, gathering himself. One hand snuck into his coat as he snarled up at Keen. "You always were a cheater!"

"Get up, Dirk." Keen crooked two fingers at him. "You've caught your breath by now, I imagine."

A few guffaws followed, making Dirk's face burn red. His muscles bunched under his coat. He seemed ready to charge, but Keen remained unflappable, on his toes, supremely confident.

A little too confident.

He didn't see the gun, a little snub-nosed affair one would expect a lady to carry, palmed in Dirk's meaty paw. From his angle, it would have been impossible, but not from Hero's broadside vantage. She *tsk*ed. Talk about cheating! The gun looked laughably puny, but lethal just the same.

"Now, now," she said briskly, her cane whipping forward and striking his hand as it rose toward Keen. Dirk's fingers spasmed open and the pistol clattered to the floor, its ivory handle catching the lamplight. Gasps were followed by disapproving groans. The hero had suddenly lost his adoring fans.

Some of the PKs in attendance, until now unbothered by the brawl, grew alert at the sight of the gun. They didn't know Keen from a tree stump, but he wore the uniform and that was all that mattered.

"How dare you draw on a peacekeeper!" cried one of them, incensed.

"You'll spend the night in the tank for this, Hollander," added another.

The two PKs shouldered their way through the crowd, one going for his cuffs.

Out of nowhere, a woman dashed forward. She was wrapped in a cloak and wearing a fur hat over her jet-black hair. A nightdress peeked out from the bottom of her coat, as if she'd leapt straight from her bed. She blocked the peacekeepers on their way to Dirk, still crouched on the floor and cradling his hand.

"Abby?" Keen said, sounding horrorstruck.

Abigail Hollander stared at him, shamefaced, a trembling hand lifting to her mouth. "DH Keen, please, he's just drunk. Don't let them arrest him."

All Keen's confidence and swagger vanished. He ran a hand through his hair, sending it awry, flustered. Abigail had managed to quell Keen's righteous anger without raising a hand against him.

"He pulled a gun on a PK officer," he said, clearly torn.

"It wasn't loaded," she said quickly. She stooped to pick up the weapon, opening the cylinder with a practiced hand. It was indeed empty.

Hero stared, wondering if the woman had managed some sleight of hand. Why would the man carry an unloaded weapon?

"Please …"

At Abigail's soft plea, Keen looked at the other PKs, as if hoping they would take the burden from him, but they were waiting for his go-ahead – a demonhunter outranked them.

"Why don't we find another pub, Keen?" Hero said into the awkward standoff. "I'm sure your friend there learned his lesson, right?"

Abby swung toward her and gave her a grateful look, unflinching as she looked into Hero's flaming eyes. A smile lit her face. Grudgingly, Hero understood Keen's reaction. The woman was radiant.

After a moment, his eyes narrowed at the cowering Dirk, Keen relented. "Quite right, Inspector. We should go elsewhere."

"Why don't you all go elsewhere?" the aggrieved bartender suggested sharply. "I don't want any more trouble here!" He gave Abby a hard look. "Take him home, Mrs Hollander. And tell him to find a new drinking hole."

She nodded hastily and started to help her husband to his feet. "Thank you, Inspector Viridian," she said, giving Hero an appreciative look. "I'm forever in your debt." Her blue eyes were wide, guileless, and she seemed to Hero nothing more than an embarrassed wife, far too used to a drunken husband's antics. Her hands fluttered and trembled, her cheeks aflame.

On his feet, Dirk hung his head, completely cowed. His eyes shot toward his wife and away again. He seemed to shrink into himself as he stood beside her. It was blazingly obvious who was in charge between the two of them. Hero frowned, forced to reassess the situation.

"Are you certain you don't want to press charges, DH?" the PK sergeant asked Keen. His gaze flicked to Hero, and she caught his slight grimace of distaste. "Inspector?"

Keen shook his head, his lips pressed tight. He was shooting daggers at Dirk, oblivious to the man's sudden meekness. Every line of his body told Hero he wanted to rescue the woman like some knight in a tale.

"Come on, Keen," Hero said, starting for the door and giving the brim of her hat a jaunty tap with her ebony cane. "We've worn out our welcome."

CHAPTER NINETEEN

"What in the world was that all about back there?" Inspector Viridian asked once they were well down the street, heading for Otherside. Keen was flustered and mortified to the core at his actions and wanted to get as far away from the more privileged part of town as fast as possible. What had gotten into him? It was as if some other hand had thrown that pint glass.

A child's hand.

He was too keyed up to go home, too angry and ashamed and embarrassed. Viridian was a tall, odd presence beside him, so alien and strange it was almost comforting. Another outcast, just as he had been. As he still was.

"I'll explain over another pint," he said stiffly. "I am not nearly drunk enough."

She eyed him, her tinted glasses firmly in place, thankfully. He could just make out the swirl of her damned irises. "This is a good night to drink," she said, nodding, then twirled her cane, matching his long strides. "I assume you have a better place in mind?"

"Yes. I want to go to my side of town."

Otherside. The name said it all: the other side of Havenside. The wrong side. Separated by iron rails from the more well-heeled districts with their broad avenues and tree-lined streets, their neat brick sidewalks, their beautifully painted houses with stained-glass windows and wide porches. The tracks cut through town, leaving beauty and privilege on one side and ugliness and want – rundown houses in dire need of fresh paint, tattered brick streets full of weeds and potholes, stringy trees struggling through broken concrete – on the other. The kids living in Otherside didn't attend Clementine Prep, they went to the Realm-sponsored school by the train yard with its overcrowded classrooms, tired and disillusioned teachers, books with missing pages, pencils sharpened down to nubs. Oleander had started there, but his stellar coursework, discipline and determination had led him to Clem. The neighborhood church had raised the money for him, given it to him as a scholarship. He'd been their chosen charity.

Charity.

As soon as they crossed the tracks, he felt personally to blame for the state of Otherside. He gave Hero a surreptitious look. Would she judge him for where he'd grown up? Her pale, narrow face was hard to read. He steeled himself, telling himself it didn't matter. This was his home; he belonged here. He almost steered them toward his house, guilt taking hold of him. His mother would be up until he was safely home, waiting, worrying. He blew out a breath. He wasn't ready to go home yet. The night was young, and it had been a long, strange day.

"There are a few taverns in Otherside," he said, leading Hero down a narrow street once they'd cleared the tracks and a ramble of empty lots. Apartments lined the street, small flats occupied mostly by longshoremen and brakemen, a transient lot who followed their work up and down the coast. They were vital workers to the Realm, but not exactly welcomed in wealthier areas.

He took Hero to a tavern on the corner of East and Hawthorn, the Jenny Wren. His father had gone there often, even took his little boy a time or two, put him up on a tall stool and let him eat peanuts and throw the shells on the floor. While the elder Keen enjoyed a freshly drawn pint, little Ollie would suck the foam from his root beer and kick his feet, feeling grown up and decidedly special. His ma hadn't been too thrilled with their visits there, but Oleander had loved them. It was one of his best memories of his father.

The door was weatherbeaten, a window made to look like a porthole adorning it. The establishment had been named either for a ship or a woman, or both; Keen wasn't sure and had never bothered to find out. He hadn't set foot in the place for over a decade, but memories flooded back the minute he stepped inside, the inspector on his heels. A narrow place with a tin ceiling painted red, a few tables in the back, a couple of wooden booths and dark alcoves. Bones and simple stars adorned the walls, along with images of the Goddess naked and drenched in blood (forbidden by the Church, but common among less-educated worshippers.) A long bar dominated the narrow space, a tarnished mirror behind it, with liquor bottles lined up in front in an array of shapes and colors that had captivated him as a boy. Now, he knew they were cheap and common brands and felt a strange sort of embarrassment at the display, as if he were the cheap and common one just by entering the front door.

The bar itself was stained and cracked, the edge wrapped in maroon leather worn rough by myriad elbows and spilled drinks. The barstools, rickety and backless, appeared to be the same ones from his childhood. The floor, sticky and badly in need of a sanding and a fresh coat of varnish, creaked as they made their way to the bar.

If Viridian felt the place was beneath her, or unappealing, she gave no sign of it. She tipped her hat to the rough-looking patrons and gave them her best smile, which sent not a few of them further into their dark corners. They must have recognized her. How many other half-demon women dressed like a parody of a nun were wandering about town? And he, of course, was a dead giveaway in his uniform. He cursed himself for his shortsightedness. PKs weren't exactly popular in Otherside, even rare demonhunters. He took off his cap and loosened his jacket, hoping they understood he was here as a patron.

Humming to herself, Hero perched on a barstool and rapped the bar top to get the barkeep's attention, though not quite as rudely as she had at Grantham House. The barkeep, a surprisingly young man with a well-groomed beard and neat haircut, sauntered over while cleaning a mug with a bar rag. His brow was furrowed and his dark eyes bounced between the two of them. Oleander took a seat next to his partner, nodding to him, trying to seem as unthreatening as possible. He'd wanted to come home, to a place he knew, but he'd forgotten that he was an outsider now. And this had never been his place. Not really.

Suddenly those dark eyes widened and a smile spread across the man's bearded face. "Ander?" he said. "Is that you?"

Oleander stared at the barkeep, trying to place him. They were of a similar age, he realized, and that smile and the bright twinkle in the man's brown eyes tweaked his memory. He recalled a much younger face, smooth-cheeked, mouth sticky from candy, eyes sparkling with mischief.

"*Braun?*" he exclaimed, inordinately pleased to see a face he recognized from somewhere other than Clementine Prep. He thrust out his hand and his friend tucked his rag away to grasp it. "Jerry Braun, you old devil! I haven't seen you in a lifetime. By the Goddess, how have you been?"

Jerry grinned, pumping his hand. "Good as you could expect." He shook his head. "Ander fucking Keen, as I live and breathe. Never expected you to set foot on our side of the tracks again, I have to say. Thought you shook the dust off your heels back in school, never to be seen again." His smile faded and the friendly clasp of his hand became rougher. "Goddess knows I haven't seen you since then, right?"

Keen retrieved his hand from Jerry's grip, uncomfortable at the sudden turn. It had been a long time since he'd been back home, other than brief, obligatory visits to his mother. Even when he'd lived at home, once he'd started at Clem, he'd kept himself separate from his old chums. He could have blamed his mother for it – she'd encouraged him to find new friends among his "betters" – but that wasn't entirely fair. He'd thought the same himself.

"Yes, I know." He smiled sheepishly, his cheeks warm. "I was so busy back then, but… it's not an excuse. I was…" There was no explanation to give. Not a worthy one. Keen faced his old friend. "I was an ass. A complete and utter ass. I'm sorry, Jerry, truly I am."

His old friend, the boy he'd chased through the woods, daring him to jump off stone walls, climb trees and dive into deep, cool ponds, relaxed, his face softening with good humor. "Ah, it's the past, Ander. The distant past. I was a little shit back then, too. Used to lob rocks at you when you wore your fancy uniform."

Keen jerked. He'd forgotten all about that. "I suppose so."

"Here, have a pint on me, all right? You and your… friend."

"Oh, excuse my rudeness. Jerry Braun, this is Inspector Hero Viridian. Sent all the way from New Savage to help on a case."

Jerry eyed her as they shook hands, looking only somewhat unsettled. "Nice to meet you."

"Likewise," she said, showing her teeth. "Always nice to meet my partner's old friends. You seem a better lot than the last one we encountered."

Jerry's brows dipped toward his nose.

"Hollander," Keen offered as explanation – which was enough, given Jerry's expression. The barkeep moved away and began pulling two pints for them.

"Looks like no one likes the Hollanders," Hero observed blandly.

"No one likes him," Keen said. "He's been a jackass since birth, far as I can tell. Biggest bully on campus, and I was his biggest target. Adding alcohol to his personality has done nothing to improve it, either."

"Is it going to be a problem?" she asked, turning to him, leaning an elbow on the cracked leather curb. "This case is getting to be a mess. I don't want personal issues gumming it up even more."

Keen ground his teeth. "I promise not to let my personal issues get in the way of our investigation. If you can promise the same."

She grinned. Snarled, really. "Oh, I can't promise that at all. Everything in this town, I take personally. Every look and whisper, every secret and lie. They've been waiting for me all these years, ready to fuck up my entire life."

What life? he wondered. She'd been in prison for ten years and out for only a few. What kind of a life did she even have, this half-demon, disgraced ex-nun?

"Let's just be professional, then," he temporized. "Keep our focus." He shifted on the wobbly stool, hooking a heel on a rung, still embarrassed by his earlier lapse. That he hadn't recognized such a powerful enchantment left him with a bad taste in his mouth. A fucking demon had helped him break it. He was an embarrassment to his profession.

And here he was lecturing her about being professional.

"Listen, Keen, older, more experienced PKs are working under that enchantment without a clue. You managed to break it, didn't you? I couldn't get through to Dewey at all."

There she went, reading his mind again. "My potions won't work on Dewey," he said quietly, aware of nearby listeners. "I don't know how we break them out of this."

She grimaced. "We can't. Not until we find the source and tear it out at the root."

"It starts at Bright Renewal Academy, doesn't it?"

Their pints appeared before she could answer, golden and sparkling with a healthy head of foam. Jerry Braun was scowling. "Did I hear you mention Bright Renewal?" he demanded. "Black Lilith take that place!"

Keen exchanged a glance with Hero. "You have an issue with that esteemed institution?" she asked carefully.

"Esteemed?" He snorted. "It's a pit of darkness, that place. All the kids that go in there never come out the same. Most of them *our* kids."

"*Your* kids?"

He shook his head, arms crossed over his chest, muscular forearms bulging. "Not my kids, personally. I mean ours, the neighborhood's. Those are the kids that get sent to Bright Renewal. So-called troubled kids. Kids whose parents can't pay their bills so they might steal a piece of bread from the grocery store, kids who talk back or maybe drink a fifth in the alleys. Stupid stuff. Kid stuff. They get swooped up and taken away. To be *reformed*."

"I take it you don't think very highly of their reformation," Hero said dryly.

Jerry scoffed. "They make a big deal of it – the graduates of Bright Renewal. Bunch of automaton little fascist brats. They come out preaching the Academy's screed, all righteous, upstanding, soulless citizens. I suppose they seem like the lucky ones, if you ignore the dead look in their eyes."

"And what happens to the unlucky ones?" Hero pressed. She looked at Keen, and he saw she was thinking the same thing he was. Catarine had been investigating missing children.

Suddenly, Jerry became very interested in wiping down the bar. "There's always a report," he muttered, leaning toward them subtly and keeping his voice low. "A condemnation. Unable to handle the curriculum, too violent, too drug-addled, too demon-touched, or some other nonsense. The PKs mark them down as runaways, no matter what the parents might say. No matter how much they beg for help."

"The PKs do nothing about missing children?" Keen asked, aghast at the idea.

"The ones who disappear are always the most troubled, the least likely to be reformed, anyway, so no one cares enough to investigate." He hesitated, throwing Hero a nervous glance. "A lot of them are rumored to have bad blood, if you know what I mean."

Keen understood all too well. It was all he could do not to look at Hero, too.

"Whenever parents make complaints, half the time the PKs blame *them* for the kid's disappearance," Jerry continued, grimacing. "No one in Havenside believes there's even a problem. Half of them are either funding the Academy or profiting off of it."

"Profiting?"

"Tuition," he said flatly. "Some of the kids sent there do need help, I'll admit it, and their parents are desperate. They will pay almost anything to save their children from going down the wrong path. The ones too poor to pay petition the Realm for help. Either way, Bright Renewal's benefactors get their gold."

Finally, Keen looked at his partner. Could this whole thing be about greed? A profit-making scheme targeting desperate parents and their wayward children? Horrible, unethical, perhaps even evil, but worth murdering someone over? It seemed the whole town was already fully on board with the scheme, anyway. There had to be more to it. He raised a brow, watching Hero's expression grow smooth.

"This can't be all about money," he said. "We have missing children, spectral chains, that shield…"

"They're sacrificing children for a few pieces of gold," Hero said flatly. She wrapped her long fingers around her pint glass, squeezing hard enough to whiten her knuckles. "Subtly, I suspect, only a few here and there. Kids that won't be missed, at least not by anyone important. Right?"

This she directed at Jerry, who nodded, his lips pressed hard together.

Hero lifted her glass, her long face still smooth, but Keen could see flames licking at the edges of her glasses. He didn't know her very well, but he recognized cold rage when he saw it.

"I believe you," she said after a long gulp of ale. She settled her glass carefully on the bar, those flames tickling the air. "Whatever is going on behind those gates, I will stop it, I swear to the Goddess."

Jerry's rigid shoulders relaxed at her vow and a look of relief crossed his face. He nodded gratefully. "Thank you, Inspector. You're the first person of authority who actually seems to give a damn. Everyone else who's tried to help–" He stopped abruptly, lips tight, and shook his head.

Keen blinked, staring hard at his old friend. "Do you mean Sister Catarine? Do you know something about her case, Jerry?"

"No!" he blurted, a little too quickly with a look of panic. Keen could hardly blame him – no one wanted to be connected to such a brutal murder – but he couldn't ignore the stirring in his gut. Jerry definitely knew something.

Was he the mysterious Mr B?

"I mean," Braun tried again, "I knew her. Everyone did! Half of Otherside attends services at Clementine's chapel. She's very popular." He grimaced. "Was. She was popular."

"Hey, Braun! We need another, you slacker."

Laughter and jeers erupted from the other end of the bar. A man in a thick sweater and rubber boots was waving his empty pint glass in the air. The two men with him set up a rhythmic pounding on the top of the bar with their empty glasses. "Jer-ree! Jer-ree!"

Jerry scowled. "Hold your horses, you lousy drunkards," he said and gave Hero and Keen an apologetic look before moving away to deal with his rowdy customers. Keen thought he looked more relieved to be escaping their questions than annoyed by the men's demands.

"We might have to bring him in," he murmured. It bothered him to think his friend might be involved in all of this, but they couldn't ignore any lead.

Hero twisted on her stool to face him. "Sister Catarine was starting to investigate Bright Renewal Academy," she said.

He frowned. "Possibly, but we have no proof. Just speculation and rumor."

"We have missing children. We have spectral chains. We have a powerful shield and a spell of Fog." She ticked off each item on her impossibly long fingers, flickers of flame running along each digit. "You said as much a moment ago. This isn't about mere greed. Something far darker is happening here and it's affecting the entire town. Cassie must have told Sister Catarine something truly terrible, what with the two of them whispering together and having private meetings – Molly said as much. It got her killed, and Cassie Graham, too."

"We need to talk to Catarine's brothers," Keen said. "Maybe the family can give us permission. It would get us into the Academy without having to wait for a warrant."

Hero was silent for a moment, her face unlined porcelain but for a tiny grimace at the corner of her red, red lips. "Not without Dewey's cooperation, and I don't think he's going to give it. Besides which, I'll never get past that shield if we go in through the front door. We'll have to find some other way inside. We might have to get... creative."

She cracked a smile, and he winced at the ghoulishness of it. "Anything we do outside of legal avenues will be inadmissible when, or if, we go to trial," he pointed out.

"That's a problem for the barristers," she said breezily, but seemed to reassess the statement a moment later. "I suppose it will end up our problem, too. Okay. So. We can't do anything rash. Not until we run out of options, anyway."

He blew out a breath. "We can expand our investigation in the meantime, include the locals here in Otherside – the parents of missing kids, especially. They'll appreciate the effort, I imagine. Be eager to talk."

Hero's eyes slanted to him, flame-red irises peeking out from the sides of her tinted glasses. "We'll start with the Grahams. Both their children are caught up in this. Why?"

Keen nodded, giving his old friend another glance. Jerry Braun was suddenly very busy with his other customers. "Fine. We start with the Grahams."

CHAPTER TWENTY

Life at Bright Renewal took on a miserable monotony that did more to break Molly's spirit than anything else. Up before dawn, the light gray outside the few, high frosted windows. Then a cold shower – in front of the ever-present Guardians, of course – with a hard scrub brush and harsh, lye soap, and a scrap of thin, scratchy cloth for drying.

"Hang it up, girls. Always in the same place. Don't lose it! You get one, and one only. You will learn to appreciate all the Goddess provides."

Shivering, half wet, they pulled on their "uniforms" – drab wool skirts and shapeless cotton tunics, stockings and cheap canvas shoes. Molly's uniform was a size too big and hung from her. No one seemed to care as long as she was covered adequately.

"Modesty is vital for a proper young lady."

Once dressed, bleary-eyed veterans and terrified newcomers like her marched in a single line to the cafeteria to break their fast with warm tea and cold porridge, laid out on long, narrow tables in the cafeteria, a vast room that would look less out of place in a factory than a school. (She'd only ever seen glimpses of Bright Renewal Academy from the outside, but it had always seemed a grand mansion. The inside left much to be desired.) The girls ate on one side and the boys on the other. Fraternization was not allowed.

On her first day, still stunned by her sudden change in circumstances, Molly had nevertheless scanned the tables of boys as she came in, seeking a familiar face. Not many kids from Clementine ended up at Bright Renewal. She'd heard tales of some Clem students going down a bad path but knew of only one personally: Cassie's brother, Cole Graham. So she'd dragged her feet, hoping to spot his curly red hair – so like Cassie's – not knowing exactly what she was going to do if she did find him. Cassie had been afraid for him; part of her just wanted to see if he was still alive.

"Stop dawdling!"

The blow caught her across her upper back and she gasped and whipped her head around, outraged, her skin stinging. A short, thickset woman in trousers and a shirt buttoned up to her chin stood there scowling, a leather strap dangling in her grip – one of the many so-called "guardians" who kept the students in line. "Take your place," she hissed, "or you get another."

Molly swallowed a retort – she'd never been hit in her life and still could hardly fathom this casual violence – and clambered over the benches next to the girl she'd been following and stood at the table. She took her cues from the others and didn't sit, not until she was instructed. It wasn't until after a long, droning prayer, led by a layman in the same trousers and shirt as the strap lady, that they were ordered to sit. By then, her back had stopped stinging and her stomach was gnawing at her spine.

They'd eaten in silence that first day and every day since, the only sounds the clatter of spoons and soft slurping. Molly didn't even think about trying to find Cole again that first day, just eating her food and keeping her head down. The girl beside her, the same one who'd slow-blinked at her – girls from the same rooms were grouped together – managed to touch her leg at one point: a quick, furtive pat. Molly's throat had tightened and it was all she could do to choke down the bland porridge.

That first day bled into the next, and the next.

After breakfast there were lessons – long, boring lectures. The students were then required to recite back scripture and pray to the Goddess. There was no science, no literature, no poetry or art, though occasionally they studied rudimentary mathematics.

Molly was baffled. Even the basic curriculum at Clementine was far beyond this claptrap. It made no sense. She'd heard more than one adult, even her instructors at Clem, insist that Bright

Renewal had a rigorous academic focus with an emphasis on discipline and obedience in order to prepare young, troubled minds for the world. Bright Renewal was supposed to be reforming students, not merely punishing them. It cost a mint to send children here, after all.

Frustrated, she wondered at first if she would be placed in a more challenging class once they assessed her work – but no, each day was the same: basic, boring, pointless. She was terrified she was going to fall behind. What would she do when she got back to Clementine Preparatory? How could she make up all she was missing?

Soon, she realized all her lessons and other activities at Bright Renewal were designed to wear her down rather than lift her up, the afternoon assemblies in particular. After a simple lunch of sandwiches and juice, barely enough for growing teenagers, they were divided into groups in a vast fieldhouse. Led by no-nonsense instructors, they knelt in circles and slapped hands on the ground repetitively, clapped and snapped their fingers, over and over in a simple, synchronized rhythm. It was one of the few places where they could speak outside of prayers – well, chant, anyway, emitting meaningless, guttural sounds to match their hand movements. They did this for hours, leather straps encouraging anyone who faltered. Molly kept up as best she could, but no one avoided correction. Those that lasted the longest and managed to maintain their rhythm and form received praise at the end of the session. While others wept silently, wrung sore hands and nursed bruises, these lucky ones were allowed to partake of a refreshment table.

Some lorded it over the rest of them, smirking and making a big to do about their bit of cake and juice. Others merely looked blank-faced. Yes, they were good at the "rounds," as they were called, but their spirits were broken. Molly wondered how long she would last before her own was broken and she too stared blankly at the walls.

Day after day for a week (she thought) the pattern repeated. It felt eternal. She was exhausted yet restless, bored yet terrified. She understood the faster she complied with every rule and circumstance thrown at her, the faster she would be set free, but somehow she was always getting marks against her, no matter how hard she tried. Some students seemed preternaturally able to excel in this miserable place and rose in the levels, earning merits which allowed them to speak if they wished (only to others of the same level or those beneath them, and in that instance only to order them around), to read books from the library, to eat better food in the private lounges reserved for them – the upperclassmen. Their elevation had nothing to do with age or schooling, merely compliance.

Try as she might, Molly couldn't keep from smiling or giggling at someone's antics (carefully hidden behind their instructors' backs) or rolling her eyes at some new stupidity thrown at them in the classroom (yes, she knew long division already, dear Goddess!). She even dared to whisper to her new friend, Rebecca, the two of them growing closer and closer each day, brought together through their mutual misery. Somehow, Rebecca – one of those angelic-looking students whom the instructors loved – avoided the black marks, but even proximity to a favorite couldn't keep Molly from losing points every single day.

At night, Rebecca snuck into Molly's bunk so they could talk. Not even the threat of dire punishment daunted Rebecca, who had assured Molly that their particular guard was a lazy sack who couldn't help but fall asleep as soon as her charges were in their beds. Molly had lain frozen in fear, at first, until she heard the heavy snores of their guardian. After that, she felt no more than a quickening of her heart when they dared to snuggle close and gossip like regular girls.

Rebecca was from one town over, Plainfield, and she'd been sent to Bright Renewal by parents who thought she might benefit from its much-vaunted "rigorous academic training." She'd done nothing wrong at all. It astounded Molly, but Rebecca seemed resigned to her situation.

"They want their daughter to be morally upstanding," she'd told Molly one night as they shared Rebecca's cot, whispering in the dark, the snoring of their guardian drifting in from outside the doorless doorway. Molly thought she sounded far too understanding about it. "I've almost earned enough points to be raised to an upperclassmen. If I stay the course, I could even graduate early." She sighed, her warm breath bathing Molly's cheek. "I've tried so hard to be good."

Molly squirmed deeper beneath the thin cover, glad for Rebecca's warmth. "You *are* good," she replied, feeling strangely protective of her new friend. Rebecca never caused trouble, never misstepped – not where she could be caught, anyway. Molly couldn't believe she'd earned her friendship, but she appreciated it nonetheless, and the thought that she might be leaving her soon sent a sliver of cold fear through her belly. What would she do if Rebecca moved into another room? "Not like me," she whispered mournfully. "I can't even control my face. I get marks for looking impertinent, and I don't even know how I'm doing it."

Suppressed laughter shook the cot. "You do have a very expressive face. It's all I can do not to burst out laughing when you give Mistress Blume such scathing looks."

Molly stifled her own giggles. "I can't help it. She's so *stupid*."

It was easy to be bold late at night, knowing your guardian was dead asleep outside your room. For that moment, before she went back to her own bed, Molly felt almost normal again, almost happy. She'd never had a sister, never even had a friend like Rebecca. They were in this together. Allies.

Rebecca had become a source of light in this dark, dismal place.

After a week of the same dull routine, Molly found herself waiting impatiently all day until nightfall when she could creep into Rebecca's bed for their illicit chats. Despite her terror and fear, her boredom and despair, she found herself daydreaming about her friend, about her shining auburn hair and milky skin, her quirky smile and the bright freckles scattered across her nose. Rebecca was beautiful and kind and funny, and thinking about her brought a queer feeling into Molly's belly that felt like longing.

But that was ridiculous. Rebecca was just a friend. Just a girl who was keeping her from losing her mind. Maybe even a girl willing to help her...

"Do we ever mix with the boys?" Molly dared to ask one night. She thought it might be her seventh night at Bright Renewal, but they had no calendars and there were no breaks in their routine. The days bled one into the other. "Like, do you think I could talk to one of them?"

Rebecca made a moue. "Do you fancy one of the boys?"

Her question prompted sputtered denials. Molly wanted to make it very clear she had no interest in a boy, any boy. "No, no, of course not. It's not like that. I just... I know one of the boys here. I need to tell him something important." She grew serious, grim. "I don't think he knows yet."

Evidently mollified by her vehement denial, Rebecca had snuggled closer. Her hair brushed Molly's face. "Knows what?" she asked breathlessly, eager for gossip. Anything to break the boredom.

"That his sister is dead."

"Oh, my, that's awful. He should *know*. What a terrible thing to have to tell someone." She sighed, stroking Molly's arm in sympathy. Molly fought back tears, overwhelmed suddenly, and Rebecca murmured soothing noises, settling her.

"What's his name?" she asked after a moment.

"Cole Graham."

Rebecca was silent for a moment, and Molly sensed her brow furrowing in the darkness. "Cole Graham. I know him. Everyone does. He's a troublemaker. Keeps getting tossed into solitary."

Molly shuddered. Kids sent to solitary returned vacant-eyed and blindly obedient. It didn't surprise her to learn that Cole was constantly in trouble. Had he managed to tell Cassie about the abuse here at Bright Renewal? Had Cassie gone to Sister Catarine for help?

Is that what had gotten them both killed?

But... why? None of the kids who had graduated from the Academy ever had a bad word to say. Those who'd failed out or been expelled had all kinds of complaints, but of course no one ever listened to them, and then some ran away for good, too ashamed to face their failure. It hardly seemed a reason to kill anyone, let alone a nun. And yet Sister Catarine was dead and a mysterious *they* had shown Cassie the body as a warning.

A warning she'd ignored by speaking to Molly about it.

And look where it landed me.

"I need to talk to him," she said more forcefully. "Or... or get him a message, at least."

"A message?" Rebecca's lips pursed. "Let me see what I can do."

* * *

The only time the boys and girls of the Academy were allowed to interact was during Circle, a brutal session of reconditioning. These took place every other day, wherein students were subjected to personal abuse and condemnation by their fellow classmates, listing all their flaws, sins and failures. It accomplished little except to further break the wills and minds of Academy students, just in case anyone was developing self-confidence or self-esteem,.

Nevertheless, Rebecca insisted Circle would be her best opportunity to pass a note to Cole. This would require her to pocket a strip of paper filched during their lessons, an act of brazen thievery that left Molly sick to her stomach and terrified it would be discovered. But with Rebecca's help – the girl had swift fingers and folded the paper into a tight square easily concealed in the seam of Molly's shapeless skirt – the theft went unnoticed. A stick pin and a bloody finger provided the ink. The note was short by necessity and horribly to the point: *I'm sorry. Cassie killed. A fall. Why?*

She'd wanted to write more, to offer some explanation, but she lacked the ink, the paper and the will to do it. Maybe Cole would find a way to message her back, to tell her what he might have communicated to Cassie. Maybe he knew why Sister Catarine had been killed.

Maybe it was all his fault.

The Circle sessions were particularly disturbing events in a place rife with them. Each student took their turn at the center, being called out on their faults, their sins, their failings. The sessions started reasonably enough but always dissolved into chaos. Everyone hated Circle, though some relished the chance to scream and curse at their classmates, enjoying some semblance of control, a little taste of power, no matter how bitter and grotesque.

On the day she planned to give Cole the note, a thin, pale-haired girl was the first in the Circle. All her crimes were listed – for her own good, of course. She was a slut. Wanton and despicable. The teachers and her fellow students screamed, "Whore!" into her face until she broke down sobbing and begged for absolution.

Next, a pimply faced boy, shaggy-haired and thick-limbed, was excoriated for his lack of hygiene, his former drug use, his violent tendencies. Like many other subjects, he initially scowled back as he was subjected to a torrent of abuse, refusing to relent or beg for forgiveness, no doubt trying to maintain a sense of self, of dignity. But eventually, like everyone else, he broke, weeping inconsolably as his own roommates turned on him and exposed his most intimate habits.

Molly waited impatiently for her turn in the center of Circle, her second. Her first experience had broken her quite thoroughly – everyone knew she'd "stolen" sacramental wine – and she trembled at the prospect of undergoing another, but her ulterior motive kept her from giving into that dread and despair. This time, she had a mission.

The Circle was well and truly riled up, swaying and moaning in religious fervor, beseeching the Goddess and the Branch and rebuking Black Lilith, the queen of the Underworld. The wooden floor of the fieldhouse rang with stamping feet. Boys and girls intermingled, weaving back and forth, lunging at the victims at the center, then retreating. Molly noticed not a few of the others managed to touch, to stroke arms and clasp hands quickly, furtively. Fraternization was forbidden but impossible to quash entirely.

A hand on her back sent her stumbling forward. Thrust into the center of the writhing mass of excited children, Molly caught herself and stood up straight, clutching the illicit note in her fist. Her eyes darted to find Cole Graham in the throng.

Her peers turned on her immediately. The instructors had listed her crimes the first session, and now they were gleefully reiterated – drunkard, laggard, slut (of course), unnatural girl full of unnatural desires, damned–

"Demonkin!"

Molly spun at this new curse, searching for whoever had spat it at her. Her mouth gaped and she felt her cheeks grow even hotter. Why did it bother her so much? She didn't know, but she couldn't deny that it did. You might think you'd grow immune to insults shrieked at you over and over, but you never did. You tried, oh yes, you tried...

"Who said that?" she cried, knowing she'd get a black mark for it but not caring in the least. Fury made her dig for a forbidden word, one she'd heard time and again from the mouths of tough PKs lounging in her father's study. "Who *fucking* said that?"

Her profanity was met with howls of disbelief and approbation. She wasn't the first kid at Bright Renewal to curse back at her tormentors, but it was the first time *she* had shown any backbone. Even the instructors looked startled, though her least favorite teacher, Miss Blume, wore an expression that was nothing short of pleasure.

The students had seen how the word had struck home.

"Demonkin! Demonkin!"

"Cursed one!"

"Repent, hellspawn! Beg the Goddess for mercy!"

The Circle closed on her, egged on by the instructors: "She must be saved! Do not let up, else she may be damned forever!"

Faces and bodies pressed in on her from every direction, suffocating, drowning under the onslaught of words, flung at her on a barrage of spittle and hot breath. She shrank back, seeking someone familiar, someone safe. She spotted Rebecca in the back and threw her a beseeching look. Then another familiar face thrust into view, nose to nose, hissing words beneath the chaos.

"Give in, Franke," Cole Graham said to her. He lifted fists, shaking them at her. "Cry, dummy, just cry!"

It was easy to let the tears spill. She reached out a hand, the note tucked between her thumb and forefinger. "Absolution! I seek absolution!"

He took her hand – the only time contact was allowed between boys and girls – and clasped it to his chest. "Our sister repents! Praise the Goddess!"

The tone shifted dramatically. The hateful screaming ceased, ecstatic moans and cries replacing the cruel frenzy. Hands touched Molly, some kind and gentle, others stinging and painful, the fingernails like claws.

"Praise! Praise!"

"Praise the Goddess," Cole said. He slipped the note from her hand before melting back into the swarm, and for an eternity all Molly could do was stand and weep.

CHAPTER TWENTY-ONE

It was never fun, dealing with the bereaved. One never knew how a person would react to losing a loved one. Would there be tears? Screams? Curses? Violence? Hero had seen them all, which was why she usually left the task to someone else. Anyone else. Getting emotional was a waste of time, and watching someone get emotional was a waste of her time. Thankfully, the Grahams had had over a week to come to grips with the loss of their daughter. She expected them to be reasonable by now.

What she hadn't expected, when she and Keen met with the parents of Cole and Cassie Graham, was utter indifference.

"She was always a weak child," the mother, Shelly Graham, intoned blandly from where she sat on her floral-patterned couch while Hero and Keen stood in the center of her living room. She'd offered neither of them a seat. "Prone to flights of fancies and hysterics. She was never the same after her brother went into the Academy."

"She was very close with her brother, I imagine," Keen said sympathetically.

The mother held a small oval picture frame containing the solemn visage of a young, red-headed boy, and she clutched it now to her heart. Her indifference evidently did not extend to her baby boy. "Cole doted on her, protected her. She was always dragging him into her problems."

The father, Mr Richard Graham, owner and operator of a small religious trinket shop in downtown Havenside, sat in a chair by the hearth, packing a pipe with utmost concentration. Neither had been terribly surprised to find the two PKs at their door; it wasn't the first time they'd been questioned. "We told all this to the chief," he said with a slight scowl. "What more do you want from us?"

"We're only trying to better understand what happened to your daughter," Keen said, "to make sure we haven't missed anything. We know Cassie was distraught for her brother. Were they in communication at all? Surely the Academy lets him write to his family?"

"They do," Richard said grudgingly, focusing on his pipe. "But Cole didn't write to us. He only ever wrote letters to Cassie."

"Was he angry at you for sending him there?"

"Of course not!" Shelly Graham snapped, finally showing some spirit. At Hero's sharp look, she subsided a bit. "Well, not really. Not more than any child who needs a little guidance. That's why we enrolled him at the Academy at Mother Francesca's urging, to get his head straight. He'll be back on a righteous path in no time." This she said more to herself, nodding.

"I'm sure, ma'am," Keen murmured. He cleared his throat and turned his cap in his hands. "Did either of you happen to read his letters to Cassie? I mean, you had to want to know if he was well, didn't you? I'd understand perfectly if you read their correspondence. Good parents look after their children."

They had both looked a little uncomfortable at his first question, but his comments seemed to mollify them. *Very nice work.* Hero held back, a tall, silent ghoul, and let him do the talking, though she kept her eye on the Grahams, assessing them. The mother wasn't exactly slovenly, but she was dressed in a housecoat and her hair was tied into a loose bun like she'd just risen from bed even though it was past noon. The father wore tweed trousers with suspenders over a plain white shirt with ink-stained cuffs – not the clothes of a wealthy man, but not those of a poor man, either. They had a house in Havenside, right on the edge of the tracks – the right side of the tracks. They had no servants, no staff. A working family.

How had they sent two children to Clementine Preparatory?

"We both read all the letters Cole sent," Shelly Graham admitted, throwing Keen a pleading glance. He responded with a kind smile and an encouraging nod. "But they were mostly gibberish. Those two, twins and all, they have their own language."

There was a hint of jealousy in her voice that Hero recognized all too well. Hadn't her mother hated the way Liam had chosen Hero's company over her own? She'd always been trying to get her son to hate Hero too, but back then Liam had refused to turn on his little sister.

Ah, how times have changed.

"Perhaps he told her something important about his situation?" Keen prompted.

"His situation?" demanded Richard, whose indifference was beginning to swing toward anger. "My son got himself into his *situation* by his own reckless actions. Lost his scholarship and embarrassed the family!"

"It wasn't his fault!" his wife wailed. "The other boys made him break into the chapel. Those entitled brats! They weren't kicked out, were they? No, just our boy!"

Hero exchanged a look with her partner. Spots of color stood high on his cheeks. So, the Graham children were charity cases, too.

"I didn't mean to bring up a touchy subject," Keen said. "Trust me, I know what it's like, going to Clem when you aren't wealthy as a bishop. Everything is harder for us."

Both parents stared at him, their demeanors softening. "They were always so jealous of him – of Cole," Shelly said eagerly, proudly. "He's…" And here she hesitated, giving her husband a look as if waiting for him to shut her down, but Richard Graham kept his eyes carefully averted. She put her back to him. "Cole is special, DH Keen. He always has been. Goddess-blessed, some say."

Hero's interest was piqued. "Goddess-blessed?"

The Grahams reacted as if a ghost had appeared. Shelly gasped, clutching at the arm of her couch as if she might fall off it, while Richard stood abruptly, his pipe falling from his hands to clatter on the stones of the hearth. Hero knocked her cane against her hat in greeting, trying not to grin; the last thing they needed to see were her fangs. "Pardon," she said. "I didn't mean to startle you."

"S-s-sorry, Inspector. No, you didn't. Goddess bless me. I just… I forgot you were there." Shelly sagged against the back of the couch, fanning herself with one hand.

"I'd wondered if maybe you were a figment of my imagination," the father muttered, stooping to grab his pipe.

Hero smiled. "You wouldn't be the first to wonder such a thing. Now, you were saying."

Shelly swallowed, her skin the shade of milk, and began to explain.

"So," Hero said when they were finally free of the unpleasant couple. Shelly Graham's explanation for her son's specialness had gone on for some time. Goddess-blessed, indeed.

"So," Keen echoed, slapping on his cap. "I suppose now we know why that shield is set against demons."

"Or anyone with demon blood," she amended, taking the lead as they marched down the sidewalk. Back to her flat, for now. She'd set up an impromptu situation room in her rental, keeping all their more delicate work out of the stationhouse. One entire wall of her living room was dedicated to mapping out their case, complete with a detailed sketch Keen had drawn – as well as he could while perched in a tree near the venerable Academy – of Bright Renewal along with maps of the town and surrounding countryside. All the art supplies she'd purchased on the Havenside peacekeepers' coin were being put to good use.

"I wonder if that's why Sister Catarine had taken such an interest in children with demon heritage? For Cassie's sake? Maybe her brother's, too?"

"Possibly," Hero granted. "However, her concern seemed to predate those two. She might have merely recognized the signs. We Goddess-blessed are a peculiar lot." She let out a sarcastic grunt and shook her head. "Goddess-blessed. What a joke. That mother might as well have pinned a target on her boy, calling him that."

"Someone at Bright Renewal seems to have a particular interest in children with 'bad blood,'" he said, the quotation marks clear by his tone. He fell silent, rubbing at his chin, his long strides matching hers. Finally, he spoke, albeit hesitantly: "Do you have any idea why that might be?"

Because of my bad blood? She tapped her cane along the sidewalk. "My kind attracts Pandemonium. We can't help it. Put enough of us in one place and something huge and hungry will take notice. A talented summoner could feed any number of powerful entities with a stable of demonkin." It had been done before. Many a fortune had been built with demonic help.

"But... children?" Keen's shock was delightfully naïve. "Who would countenance such depravity?"

"Humans think all demonkin are inherently evil." She said it breezily, but inside her stomach clenched. It made sense – so much sense. In the end, who would care about the sacrifice of a few "cursed" children? The Grahams might have convinced themselves their children were blessed of the Goddess, but no one else would see them that way.

The end of her cane came down hard. "They are the perfect victims," she said, and suddenly all she could see was fire.

After their night at the Jenny Wren, they had expanded their investigation. The complaint against Bright Renewal Academy was tabled – officially – for the foreseeable future, but that didn't stopped them from pursuing the lead discreetly. Under the guise of their murder case, they began questioning the residents of Otherside whose children had supposedly run away, though in their official reports they were careful not to mention Bright Renewal by name, referring to it obliquely only as "the school," which could just as easily have meant Clementine or the public school. The subterfuge kept Dewey off their backs for the most part, though he did grumble about them wasting time on useless hunches, saying that the link between Sister Catarine and the missing children – who were most likely runaways – was tenuous at best. But Hero had argued that every avenue needed to be explored, every thread tugged to see what might unravel.

So far, they had learned depressingly little. Some of the kids turned out to be actual runaways, now returned home with little good to say about Bright Renewal but nothing truly nefarious to report outside of unusual methods of discipline and instruction. Most seemed to have only vague memories of the time they'd spent behind those walls. None of the children they'd spoken to – the ones who'd run away and returned home eventually, and those who'd graduated from the Academy – were of demonic heritage either.

Hero had finally had a chance to question Kellan too. Despite her initial suspicion of the priest, she had to admit that Keen was right: he wasn't their man. She'd left him sobbing in his lonely cell more than once, to no avail – his story didn't change. She couldn't break him, even with the threat of Hell. Perhaps he wasn't the white knight Sister Catarine might have believed he was, but he wasn't a brutal killer who'd handed his girlfriend over to a demon-summoning cabal either. He was just a grieving man, racked with guilt for failing to save his lover.

Handling all the new interviews as well as researching the money side of Bright Renewal Academy was more than she and Keen could manage alone, so they'd asked for help from the rank-and-file PKs. Dewey had agreed immediately, offering up a half dozen or so underlings eager to advance in rank. The murder of Sister Catarine was still the top priority of the entire squad, thankfully. Keen had been right – the enchantment was a strong one, but it had limits.

Dewey was much more amenable to their needs when they kept the focus on finding the murderer. Even so, after several days of endless questioning, they'd arrived at the consensus that Bright Renewal Academy was a venerated institution whose sole mission was saving wayward children, but also a dark stain on Havenside which preyed on desperate parents and their troubled children for financial gain – depending on who you asked, of course. But everyone agreed it had been up there on its high hill for as long as they could remember.

What became clear after talking to dozens of individuals was that all knowledge of Bright Renewal was surface-level only, hearsay and gossip. Even the parents with children enrolled there, paying exorbitant tuition fees in the hopes of getting their kids on the right path, had no clue about the actual day-to-day operations of the Academy. They received letters from their children, of course, but these were consistently vague missives extolling the virtues of their new school or filled with complaints about scratchy uniforms and lack of freedom – hardly damning.

All this information led Hero to the certainty that Bright Renewal Academy sat hunched at the center of their investigation like a fat spider in its web. Its influence touched everything in Havenside. Even the glowing compliments carried an undercurrent of fear. The more effusive the praise, the more obvious the anxiety. The wealthiest of its donors refused to meet with the PKs outright, further reinforcing Hero's increasing suspicions. Many were profiting off of Bright Renewal, including the esteemed Madam Primm and half the Grantham House set. They had no desire to see it exposed as a fraud or, worse, as a looming threat.

Hero didn't lay out her concerns at the squad house, especially about wealthy benefactors. Grumblings from the town elite would end their investigation faster than anything.

"We need to bring in the headmistress," she murmured as she surveyed the array of pictures and notes and red string she and Keen had put together in her apartment. A crackling blaze sat in the hearth, warming the small living room – perhaps a bit too much, as Keen had taken off his jacket and rolled up his shirt sleeves. But Hero liked the warmth, basking in it like a satisfied lizard. "She is of the Shield Order. She would know demon blood when she saw it, no matter how buried or well hidden."

"To the station?" Keen said, eyebrows lifting.

"Of course to the station. We've already interviewed her twice, but always on school grounds, on her turf. She controlled every conversation, steered and directed us like a fucking pro."

Memories of her time at the Abbey stuck in her mind, stirred up by her encounter with the revered mother. Having to sit in seats made for children, the miserable woman looking down at them from behind her raised desk like a queen. Being disciplined by the abbess was a regular occurrence for Hero, who couldn't seem to avoid committing infractions – failing to keep her eyes covered properly, to recite the daily devotions. Such a stubborn, obstinate, devious child.

"I don't think the mother knows anything," Keen said distractedly, standing in front of the wall with their case splattered across it. Hero was sprawled on the rug, her bare feet propped on a velvet-wrapped settee. Keen threw her naked appendages looks now and again, perhaps disturbed by the nails which so resembled stubby claws. She would wiggle them enticingly when she noticed his glances. Some men fancied her toes.

"I think she lies like she breathes," Hero muttered, but she didn't press the point. This was one area where they vehemently disagreed. Her partner really had to get over his worship of nuns. They were people, just like the rest of them.

Well, except her.

Suddenly, Keen straightened. "I knew it! Look. The chapel at Clementine, the one connected to the convent. You can draw a straight line from the apse to Bright Renewal. I mean, straight as an arrow."

She didn't appreciate the change in subject but went to take a look for herself, rolling catlike to her feet and sauntering over. The detailed schematics they'd requested from city hall showed a network of streets and the underlying sewer system, as well as several catacombs located beneath area churches. A place like Havenside had a dozen or so churches dedicated to the Goddess or to the Branch. They were a saintly lot, this den of murderers.

It wasn't the proximity or location of the chapel to Bright Renewal that suddenly caught her eye – although Keen was right: the two points aligned as if they had been planned that way.

"The catacombs," she murmured, tapping a finger on the rendering. The lines demarcating the underground crypts were faint and faded away at the edges. From what she knew about catacombs, most were built atop each other, graves on top of graves, stretching out from beneath the home church in meandering corridors. Each generation added more and more tunnels and crypts as needed for their dead. This made it very difficult to map them accurately, and very few city officials cared to spend the time doing it. These days, following a shift to green-space cemeteries, the catacombs were mainly defunct. Too grim, most had decided.

Personally, Hero liked them: silent and dismal, pitch black without a lantern, cramped and labyrinthine – the perfect hiding place for a half demon. She'd made her home in plenty of them over the years, so she knew how far they tended to stretch beyond the church above them, and how easy it was to traverse them in complete concealment.

"Right. The catacombs." Keen sounded exceedingly satisfied, as if that was what he'd wanted her to see all along. "Look closely, Inspector. And keep in mind, the map only shows a fraction of the corridors. The spot where Bright Renewal currently resides once held a church. See the outline on the city map? It's long gone, of course – it's just a pile of bricks now – but beneath it, like all area churches, are its catacombs. Ancient, vast, perhaps extending into newer crypts."

"What if they've been excavated by now?"

He scoffed. "A church may fall to disrepair, but no one would dare desecrate graves. They would have been left intact, leading... well, who knows where?"

She gave him a raised eyebrow, recalling how horrified he'd been when she'd suggested using more creative means to enter the school. "Are you suggesting we try and get into Bright Renewal Academy through Clementine Prep's catacombs, DH Keen? Because that would be decidedly illegal."

"Yes, well, I didn't think you'd have a problem with that," he admitted with obvious embarrassment, "considering–"

"Considering I burned down an entire convent?" His silence made her grin. "I'm just messing with you, Keen. I already told you we had to get creative. Sometimes it's necessary to work outside the law to bring criminals to justice. Wouldn't you agree?"

He went for his gin, left warming above the hearth, and turned to her, lifting the glass in a salute. "I am a demonhunter. It's sometimes necessary to work outside the law."

"Yes, I'm well aware," she replied flatly. He at least looked somewhat abashed by her comment, but he didn't try and stammer out an apology. She wouldn't have believed him anyway. Turning back to the board, she studied it a moment longer. "We might be able to go under their shield," she mused, "but we wouldn't be able to use any evidence we find."

"If there is a demon at work, Inspector, we won't need evidence. We'll just deal with it ourselves, yes?"

She nodded, her mood lifting as Keen tossed back the rest of his gin, and settled her empty glass on the coffee table. They had gotten into the habit of sharing an evening drink while they perused their evidence. She'd had to buy gin especially for him as she preferred whiskey or bourbon. The alcohol softened his edges a bit, which was a decided benefit, but their evening ritual, as nascent as it was, accomplished much more.

As far as they were aware, they were the only two people in the entire town not under some sort of demonic influence, and it had helped to form a tenuous bond between them – a good thing for a couple of detectives trying to solve a life-and-death case. If there came a time when they were forced into danger together, they would be able to put their lives in each other's hands without hesitation. Of course, encountering that kind of situation grew more likely the further they proceeded.

Hero dropped to the sofa and reached for her rolled-up stockings on the end table. It was time to get to work.

CHAPTER TWENTY-TWO

Clementine Preparatory was shuttered for the night, but gas lamps still lit the paths and quadrangle. The clock tower chimed out eighth bell as she and Keen made their way to the cloisters. There was no trace of poor Cassie Graham but for a marked-off section near the base of the tower. Hero could smell her blood, and the blood of the hellhounds she and Keen had battled here. Her partner seemed oblivious to any odors, but his eyes did slip toward the crime scene as they slipped across the quad, following a disgruntled nun with a torch – not a lantern but an actual torch, with flames licking toward the dark sky, a billow of smoke following them. The nun wore her bedclothes beneath a thick cloak, her habit tossed haphazardly on her head, stray strands of hair poking loose here and there. She'd let them in after a mild protest, Keen giving her his best smile and apologetic grimaces, blaming Hero for the late hour.

"We quite appreciate this, Sister Agnes," he said to the nun when she glanced back at them nervously. She was just young enough to be charmed by his politeness and his disarming humility. "You are helping our case immensely, I promise you."

She slowed enough for him to catch up to her. Hero hung back, keeping a sufficiently neutral expression on her face, and let Keen lead. "I don't know why this couldn't wait until morning," Agnes huffed, but there was no real hostility in her complaining. She gave Keen a pout. "I was nearly ready for bed. But I suppose you can tell that, being a detective and all." Then she giggled – tittered, actually – and Hero was glad for her tinted glasses, which reflected the light of the torch enough to conceal her eyeroll.

"I'm afraid it couldn't wait," said Keen, and made a slight gesture toward Hero. "The inspector feared we might lose evidence."

Sister Agnes glanced at Hero and away again, lifting her chin. "No one's been in her room since... since she was found." Her voice hitched and Keen murmured sympathy, laying a quick hand on her elbow. The woman practically melted, and Hero smirked. Keen might have been an outcast as a child, bullied and ostracized, but he'd certainly gained confidence since then.

Sister Catarine's apartment was sealed by a red cord and a dollop of wax. The roommate had been moved to new quarters and been forced to leave behind most of her belongings while the investigation was ongoing. Hero had no suspicions regarding the roommate, but she hadn't entirely ruled out the possibility that a jealous rival had been involved in the murder. Someone remaining at Clem Prep had chased young Cassie Graham to her death, after all.

"I'm breaking the seal," she announced formally. The nun blinked at her, the torchlight casting shadows across her face. "Bear witness, Sister."

"I – yes, of course. I – I bear witness."

The red wax snapped in her grip and she let the ends of the cord fall free. There was a soft sizzle as the ward was broken and the door tipped open of its own accord – only a crack, but the sister gasped in shock and backpedaled. What they could see within was only blackness.

"Do you need the torch?" Sister Agnes asked, her voice shaking, glancing back down the hall of the cloister and its rows of closed doors, deathly silent at this time of night. Hero doubted she would be willing to venture back to her room in the vestibule without a light. It would be a long walk alone and in the dark.

"Take it," Hero said, slipping off her glasses. Her flaming eyes rivaled the torch. "We won't need it."

With a little shriek, Sister Agnes turned and hastened to the stairs.

"That was just mean," Keen said as they entered the apartment, though the demonhunter sounded more amused than upset.

Hero shrugged. "I can't help how people react to my oh-so-special eyes." She turned to him. "At least you seem to have gotten used to them."

Except for a slight wince, he held her gaze. "I suppose I have. Out of necessity."

Good enough.

Inside the small apartment, Hero stood behind Keen as he kept a watch through the cracked door, sweeping her fiery gaze over the simple furnishings. The place felt decidedly empty to her now. Whatever had remained of Catarine was gone.

Finally, after a tense moment of silence, Keen said, "All clear."

"Right," she said, feeling a grim excitement. "Let's go."

The catacombs lay beneath the convent's chapel but were accessible via a stone mausoleum in the adjoining cemetery. The former revered mothers of Clementine were interred there, ten of them, stacked atop each other in stone crypts. At the back of the mausoleum, a steep, narrow stairwell led down into inky blackness.

"Now you probably wish you had that torch," Keen said to his partner as he stared pensively into the abyss. His hands went to his bandoliers, taking inventory of his potions and vials before he adjusted his saber and loosened the strap around his blunderbuss. If they ran into trouble, he would be ready.

Viridian stood motionless. She wore her long coat over her usual garb, her green harem pants peeking out beneath its hem. Her cane was in her fist, and she'd left her fashionable hat back at her rental. Flames dripped from her unshielded eyes. Keen blinked. Again, the half-demon inspector seemed to grow in size, until her presence filled the mausoleum. Light and heat poured from her, fire dancing across her skin and skimming across her clothes.

"Or not," he said faintly.

"A torch might be a good idea," she countered. "In case we get separated."

And why in Hell would we get separated? Keen wanted to ask. Instead, he fetched a torch from an iron sconce just outside the bronze doors. His partner lit it for him with a touch of a long, slim finger, corpse-white beneath the dancing flames.

"I'll take the lead," she said in a voice as deep as the ocean. "I memorized the map, but it was sketchy." She tapped the side of her nose. "This will lead us better."

The narrow steps took them down to a paved corridor wide enough for both of them to walk side by side. A low ceiling arched overhead. The brickwork was ancient. Archways opened on to more pathways, some broad and well kept like the one they traveled, others narrow and worn, unpaved, little more than dirt paths leading who knew where. Crypts lined every avenue, some merely pits filled with bones, others better built and maintained, stacked like berths on a ship. Words carved into stone plinths were so worn they were unreadable.

Hero's fiery outline illuminated the way but made the shadows beyond even darker. The air was chill and dusty. Every breath was full of someone's bones. Keen shuddered, his palms growing slick as they ventured deeper into the labyrinth, the light from his meager torch swallowed by Hero's radiance. The corridor seemed to stay relatively true, leading due west. Would they be able to breach the walls of Bright Renewal? Were the catacombs deep enough to take them under that impenetrable shield?

They descended. The crypts and vaults seemed endless. By now, they had to be outside the limits of Havenside itself. A few quick calculations placed them under the cropland on the northwest side of town – empty fields, mostly, with a few farmhouses scattered here and there. If they had stayed their course through the dark and the twisting tunnels, they would be nearing the academy grounds.

The catacombs became more cramped and decrepit, the mortar crumbling from between narrow, broken clay bricks, the ceiling hanging closer and closer to their heads. They made their way down some more worn steps to a passage where rows of skulls and the knobby ends of long bones replaced the stone walls, a macabre architecture of hundreds of dead souls. Empty eye sockets stared in silent recrimination, teeth bared in final grimaces.

He'd been right, Keen realized; the tunnels of the dead went far beyond what the map had shown. Despite the wall of bones, the tombs, the deathly silence, the foulness in the air growing ever stronger, he felt his excitement rise. This had been the right call. Finally, he felt useful, like he was carrying his own weight again.

Ahead of him, Hero stopped abruptly. They had entered another broad corridor, though not nearly as neatly put together as the ones they'd previously passed through. Here, the stone pavers sat under layers of dirt and the bone walls were crumbling in places. It reeked of ages long vanished. And of demons.

"I can go no further," she announced. The flames lighting her skin flared. "This damnable shield!"

Her fist flew and hit an invisible barrier, rebounding in a shower of spectral sparks. Lurid red ripples of light extended outward from the point of impact.

Keen's spirits sank. Was this another dead end? "There's no way through it?"

"Not for me." She eyed him, flames dribbling disconcertingly down her cheeks. "You'll have to go on alone, DH Keen."

Of course. The shield wouldn't stop him. The realization should have brought back his excitement, but instead he was filled with unreasoning dread. The way ahead was a passage through the dead in total darkness with only a flickering torch to guide him.

Ah, well. I've been through worse.

But had he? Really? When had he ever gone up against the forces of Hell without other demonhunters to watch his back? Dear Goddess, he *was* a squirrel.

Maybe Viridian sensed his prevaricating. Her lips twisted into a scowl. "That's an order, Keen!"

Her sharp voice brought him to attention. His heels snapped together, and his spine stiffened. His fear remained, but he had a job to do. "Right," he muttered, and tightened his grip on the torch. "Onward."

He stepped forward, passing through the area which had gleamed so fiercely a moment ago. No reaction from the shield.

"Looks like my blood is pure," he joked nervously.

Hero's crimson eyes were unreadable wells. "If there's any trouble..."

"What?" he asked, voice quavering.

"Run."

Hero paced on the ancient flagstones, kicking up bone dust and wishing she had a tail to lash like some of her demonic kin. A fine, forked tail of reptilian nature would add to her mystique.

It would give those damnable nuns a fright, too. She whirled, giving a flick of her imaginary appendage, a nice whip crack. Nasty creatures, nuns. Always looking down their noses at her – when they weren't trying to vaporize her with Goddess-blessed water, that was. Why she even cared about a dead nun at all was the greatest mystery of this entire investigation.

In this wretched underground crypt, the overwhelming stink of malevolent power surrounded her, mocked her. She was insignificant in comparison, a helpless bug. She'd called her flames for more than just a handy torch. They were her armor, her protection against a foe she was only beginning to understand. What had she gotten herself into? Her own miserable sire seemed worried for her. So. Why was she still here? For what? A dead nun?

My past. My brother. My niece. My sanity.

She shouldn't have sent Keen ahead without her.

Turn. Pace. Turn. Pace. The fires dripping from her clothes lit the floor in incandescent shimmers.

Not because she and Keen were particularly close – quite the contrary, but it wasn't right for him to be taking all the risk. He was good with his weapons, yes, but he was young, inexperienced. What did he know about the true power of demonic enemies? He hadn't even been able to best her with a surprise attack. And what sat at the heart of these catacombs? What defensive traps might be in place for unwary trespassers?

She spun, facing the invisible shield and the black depths beyond. The light of Keen's torch had vanished by now, swallowed by the dark and the distance. How far was he going? Too far, if she couldn't see his torch anymore. "Keen!" She held her breath, listening to her voice echo in the empty corridors, ears pricked for any response. Dogs had nothing on her hearing, nor her sense of smell – which she regretted right now, her gorge rising as a sudden stench, like that of a thousand corpses rotting in the sun, wafted along the corridor. It wasn't the smell that clutched at her stomach – she'd lived in a sewer for a year, after all – but the fear crawling up her throat, strange and unfamiliar. "Keen! If you can hear me, come back!"

Silence, except for the beating of her own heart. *Thud. Thud. Thud.*

"Keen!"

Goddess, she was starting to sound shrill. She gritted her teeth, put a hand against the shield – ignoring the pain – and pushed, palm out, fingers splayed. A low hum made her jaw ache, but she didn't let up. Could she break it? Crackling energy erupted across the surface of the shield, and it reached out and snapped at her, sizzling across her skin. Her power flared, flames roaring in response, and she pushed harder. Knives lanced her palm, sliced through her fingers. Her lips pulled back from her teeth, the pain igniting anger in her belly, almost enough to override her terror.

In the dark beyond, she heard howling, like violent winds whipped to a frenzy. Distant, but growing closer. Somehow savage *and* gleeful.

"Keen!"

Her cane hit the floor with a dull clatter and she pressed both hands hard against the shield. It burst into a raging lightning storm, engulfing her even as she pushed with all her might. Her partner was in deep trouble, and she'd let him walk into it all alone!

Fuck me to the end of time. I never should have let–

The thunder and rattle of Keen's blunderbuss echoed up the tunnel. The howling turned vicious. Beneath it, she could hear a voice shouting defiance. Then a second blast, different in timbre – a potion exploding. Shrieks followed it, close to human-sounding but not quite.

It's guarded.

The random thought shot in and out of her head and she clawed at the shield with renewed desperation, cursing herself vehemently. Of course it was guarded! And not just by a spectral shield. Whatever "it" was – the Academy, or the thing which had created it. A demon? Demons? What?

Her hands were bleeding and burning. The power in the shield was like acid against her skin. She didn't care. She fought through the pain. She'd rip this damnable thing open if it killed her.

There. A glimmer in the dark. A swirl of red and gold, reflecting off the rock walls of a twisting tunnel. Fire demons. On *this* plane! Not like the hellhounds waiting to ambush her in the realms of Chaos. These beasts had been summoned.

More flashes. A streak of silver. An explosion. Another. Good. Keen was fighting, deploying his noxious potions. The tinkle of breaking vials reached her ears, a bright note in all the chaos.

"Use the phosphammite!" she screamed. "Vials of Extinguish!"

The bedlam roared closer. Her partner appeared around a bend, a whirling figure at the center of the storm, fighting back with saber and potions as he ran for safety. He'd lost his torch, but the passageway glowed with elemental demons – there were glimmers of sylphs among the fire creatures, bright blue alongside their crimson cousins. They had him surrounded. Silver fangs took their toll in flesh. A mist of blood hung like a nimbus, caught in a tornado of swirling demons, but the wounds didn't seem to be slowing him down.

Adrenaline. It wouldn't last.

Snarling, desperate, she pushed against the shield, paying her own toll. She managed to move a few feet closer to the yawning tunnel entrance just as Keen burst through–

–and stumbled, going hard to his knees. The fall knocked his saber from his hand and the demons pounced, tearing at his uniform with their claws, catching at his hair and skin. He fought wildly, trying to knock them back with his blunderbuss. His wide eyes found her as he struggled, beseeching. He would have been close enough to touch if not for the damnable shield!

Hero roared and her hands, red and burning, skin peeling loose, plunged through the shield and grasped his shoulders. She had him! She pulled–

Power shivered through the invisible shield – a repulsive force. Together, they were flung back, landing in a heap outside the protective barrier. The shield re-formed, oozing closed like disturbed scum on the surface of a lake. Trapped on the other side, the elemental demons could only howl with rage.

CHAPTER TWENTY-THREE

The unending monotony of life at Bright Renewal took a subtle turn the day after Molly slipped her illicit note to Cole Graham. The routines stayed the same, every second of every day planned and monitored by staff with only a moment here and there for an exchanged look, a subtle smirk, a whisper in the night. Marks were handed out liberally to the intractable, no matter how minor their crimes. Molly watched her own black tally grow with a sinking heart; she would never earn her way out of the Academy.

Contrarily, her best friend, Rebecca – her only friend, really – was rising in the ranks as swift as a sparrow. Held as a perfect paragon of a Bright Renewal student, she could do no wrong, and Molly watched her earn praise and accolades with both jealousy and awe. She understood why she was so beloved, always well groomed, always obedient, always pious, her beautiful hair in perfect auburn braids, her frumpy, misshapen uniform somehow trim and flattering.

As a reward, Rebecca had been given special duties by Mrs H, the school nurse, and was her helper in the infirmary. This spared her from the worst of the menial work – scrubbing floors and toilets, doing the laundry, grueling yard work. Molly wasn't nearly so lucky, of course. If anything, she was burdened with extra work on a regular basis.

Even so, she had no envy of Rebecca, only a nagging worry. Mrs H's interest in Rebecca was unseemly. No teacher, no matter how young looking or pretty, should be consorting with a student, calling her into her office for private, unsupervised meetings. Rebecca would grow flustered when Molly pointed out how inappropriate it was and accuse her of being jealous, so Molly stopped bringing it up, despite her worry.

Molly had liked Mrs H before all this. Clementine's head nurse had been as popular as Sister Catarine with all the students – a kindly confidante, a sweet laywoman any Clem student could trust – yet here she was, volunteering at Bright Renewal. It wiped away every good feeling she'd ever had toward her. Now, Molly wondered if she could trust any adult in her life. Not the Celestial nuns, certainly. Not the adults in charge of Bright Renewal. Not even her father.

A parent could withdraw their student from Bright Renewal anytime they wished. When she'd learned this fact, she'd nearly thrown up from weeping so hard.

But it wasn't Mrs H and her inappropriate behavior that caused the tension in the air. Since Molly had handed Cole Graham the note telling him his sister was dead, the mood in the entire academy had become fraught, and Cole was at the center of it. He was a tall, burly boy possessed of a singular rage. Anger shivered in the air around him. He said nothing and did nothing out of turn – for once – obeying all rules and direct orders, yet his anger was palpable, his entire being screaming resistance. There was no other way to describe it. He went through the motions, acting the model student, but he was a tower of pent-up rage. It sat in the rigidity of his jaw, the stiffness of his back, the quivering of his formidable muscles. He was big enough to be the match of any staff or teacher, a boy in a man's body. He was a time bomb that everyone was waiting to explode.

It eventually happened one lunchtime. At first, no one was even sure what was happening, it started so simply. When all the students took their seats, in meek silence but for the scraping of bench legs on the floor and the hushed rumble of a hundred children moving at once, heads hung in preparation for the blessing, one head remained held high: Cole's. He stood, shoulders squared, gaze sweeping the cafeteria, piercing, judgmental. Eyes began to go to him, the prayer forgotten. The braver of the students lifted their heads and stared back at him openly. Encouragingly. Molly found herself craning her neck to watch him, wondering – dreading – what he was going to do. Disobedience was dealt with rapidly at Bright Renewal, and violently.

"Take your seat, Mr Graham," the boys' head guardian said sharply, uncoiling a short whip from his belt and taking a few menacing steps toward him. "You get one warning."

A few of the other guardians had also taken notice of Cole's behavior. They began to thread their way to him, some faces creased with outrage, savage glee in others. Molly watched one man crack his knuckles, grinning eagerly.

"You killed her," Cole said, his voice nearly a shout. Slowly, he turned, marking each teacher, guard and staff member with a cold, steely glare. "She knew. Knew your secrets, your lies. I told her. I told her the awful truth about this place! I told her what happens in solitary! And you killed her for it."

"You're talking nonsense," Guardian Lafferty said. He had his whip in one hand, but he made a placating gesture as he neared Cole and his voice became cajoling. "It's all right, Mr Graham. We understand you are grieving." He shook his head, grimacing. "A terrible business, suicide. I know how hurt–"

"*She did not kill herself!*" Cole's voice boomed out, filling the cafeteria, demanding attention. He spun on Lafferty, beefy hands clenched into fists. "One of you got to her! She knew too much, and you killed her for it!" He pointed an accusing finger. "You did this, and I am done playing your game. Done!"

By now, the other staff had surrounded Cole, keeping him at the center. They pulled the students from his table, ordering them out of the way, leaving Cole on his own. They scrambled to obey. No one wanted to get hit by the fallout of what was coming.

"You're out of control, Graham," Lafferty said. His beady eyes made contact with a few of the other teachers behind Cole and he gestured with his whip. "Leave the cafeteria. You need a few days of solitary, I think, until you're right in the head."

Cole didn't move. He stared straight ahead, evidently waiting for them to make the first move. Molly found herself drawn into his gaze. Somehow, she was on her feet, too. Not a few other students were standing, watching the events unfold. Excitement and trepidation boiled through the onlookers. She wanted to shout, to tell him to capitulate. What good would this do him, or any of them? There was no winning here. Not by resistance.

"Sit down," Molly whispered, her own hands bunching into fists. Their eyes locked. For a moment, no one else seemed to exist. Cole stared back at her, his gaze softening. He blinked, slowly, deliberately, conveying some sort of message, though she didn't understand what it was. Was he letting her know he didn't blame her for Cassie's death? She'd been so worried he would hate her for bringing him the news. It was strange – they'd never been friends, barely acquaintances, yet somehow, in this instance, they were allies.

"You all know where they take us for solitary. You all know about the crypts," Cole said, his eyes finding his fellow students this time. "You all know what happens there. The chains! The pit. They drain us of–"

The teachers and guardians pounced on him and dragged him to the floor. A ripple of discontent went through the student body, an angry murmur. Benches scraped loudly against the floor. Other staff waded into the fray, ordering the students back to their places, deploying whips and hands and wooden rulers freely. For once, the rigid obedience so ruthlessly beaten into the students of Bright Renewal Academy failed. The students howled their displeasure, ignored the ruthless punishment and urged their friend to fight.

Cole obliged, growling and bucking against the men trying to hold him down. It was all they could do to keep him restrained, and they weren't being gentle. The head guardian had abandoned his whip and had Cole in a chokehold. The boy's face was red, his mouth open and gasping. Grown men lay across his body, crushing him with their full weight.

"Stop! Stop it!" Molly cried, her protest drowned among many others. "You're killing him!"

A surge of kids pushed toward the combatants, spurred by nothing more than emotion, and Molly found herself swept along with them. She stumbled over someone's feet and fell, her knees scraping hard against the wooden floorboards. Some of the staff wrestling with Cole disengaged to push back this new threat, but Molly stayed crouched on her hands and knees and they ignored her. A new tussle began behind her, another knot of violence, while in front of her Cole lay pinned beneath three men. He wasn't moving and his lips were blue.

"He's not breathing!" she shrieked, panicked. She rounded on the adults crushing him, the teachers and guardians who were meant to keep them safe. "Help him!" she begged, clasping her hands beneath her chin. "By the Goddess, please!"

Mr Lafferty stared back at her, then looked down at the boy beneath his hands. His face went slack and he sprang back as if Cole had burned him. He urged the others to do the same. "Come on, come on. He's learned his lesson."

But Cole didn't move, even when one of his tormentors shook his shoulder. He was limp, unresponsive. His face had no color.

"No," Molly breathed, and Lafferty glared at her. The disturbance had extended throughout much of the cafeteria, but suddenly she, the head guardian, his two henchman and the unmoving boy were surrounded by a pool of stillness. Outrage wiped away all her fear. "You killed him."

Lafferty shook his head, scowling. "He's not dead. Don't be hysterical." He gestured to one of his henchmen. "Here, help me lift him. We'll get him to the infirmary and he'll be right as rain."

The floor beneath her began to vibrate. All around, kids were screaming and crying and fighting their so-called guardians, but these sounds were eclipsed by the pounding of booted feet marching in unison. Resistance faded abruptly as the dreaded campus security entered the cafeteria. Anger turned to fear, to compliance. No one wanted a club to the head. Molly dragged herself to her feet as the gray-clad guards took control of the situation. A couple of them came for Cole, helping Lafferty's staff carry his limp body between the four of them. A stunned silence fell over the students, but for a few muffled sobs and gasps, as they watched their fellow classmate hoisted along like a sack of meal.

"You killed him," Molly said, louder this time. Horror gripped her. Had she caused this, with an innocent note?

"You killed him!"

She screamed it over and over, lost in the horror of it.

"You killed him! You killed him!"

She couldn't stop, couldn't think; she could only shriek… until something hard and heavy cracked against the back of her skull and the world went black.

* * *

"This one is an unrepentant troublemaker."

"You were right to send her here. She's unredeemable. Doesn't listen, doesn't conform, doesn't bend."

"What do we do with her?"

A small scoff. "What we do with everyone like her at Bright Renewal."

"But this one is complicated. She isn't cursed. Her father is a PK sergeant, too. And her aunt – well, we all know what *she* is."

"All the more reason to keep her in solitary until the Ascension. Keep her out of sight in case anyone important comes calling."

"Out of sight and out of mind." A thoughtful pause. "Her family will expect a letter soon."

"Easy enough to fake."

"Right. I'll get started on it."

"Send in Miss Reilly on your way out, will you? I need her."

"Yes, ma'am."

Then quiet. Molly lay lost in a drowning darkness. The disembodied voices had pulled her close to the surface, but she couldn't open her eyes. She wasn't asleep, exactly. Her head floated, feeling disconnected from her body, but she was aware of her surroundings: the smell of antiseptic, the soft murmur of swishing cloth and padding footsteps, the clink of vials against metal trays. The infirmary! Had she been injured?

"You killed him! You killed him!"

She found light and struggled toward it. Her eyelids dragged open and she winced. An overhead lamp was aimed right at her face. "Cole," she said, the name scraping past her lips. Was he really dead? Had she gotten him killed?

"Molly," someone said brightly, sounding relieved and glad. "You're awake. Thank the Goddess!"

She knew the voice. "Rebecca?"

Someone took her hand, squeezing tightly. "It's me. Stay still." A hand on her shoulder. "Mrs H! She's awake!"

"Ah, it's a miracle!"

Molly stiffened. She recognized that voice, too. It belonged to one of the specters contemplating her fate moments ago when she'd been struggling to regain sense. There was a clicking of heels against a tile floor and someone hove into view. Molly's eyes slid toward the newcomer, her heart racing. A woman in a head scarf, gray frock and apron leaned over her, smiling kindly. Her black braids gleamed in the harsh light, tied with red velvet ribbons. Molly knew her: Mrs Hollander, the sweet, caring, compassionate school nurse of Clementine Prep.

She wants to put me in chains.

"How are you feeling, Miss Franke?" Mrs H asked, a delicate line appearing between her brows. So concerned. So sympathetic. "You took quite a blow to the head."

Took...? "Someone bludgeoned me," she croaked.

The kindly expression cracked. A gleam entered her cornflower eyes and her perfect lips pinched unpleasantly. She blinked and the mask returned. Molly wondered if she'd imagined the dark look, the pure disdain.

"It was so crazy in the cafeteria," Rebecca said, speaking quickly. Her hand was tight around Molly's. "A lot of kids got hurt. By accident."

"Yes, a terribly unfortunate event," Mrs H agreed. She sighed, bustled away and returned with a tray, then settled it on the table beside her bed and smiled down at Molly. This time, she wasn't fooled. Mrs H's expression was empty. "Be glad you got a private room, Miss Franke. The infirmary is full to capacity!" She shot Rebecca a grateful smile. "Luckily I have Miss Reilly to help me. Such a good girl. You know, you could learn a thing or two from her."

Rebecca beamed at the compliment, giving Molly's hand a hearty squeeze at the same time. An insane giggle threatened to bubble up from Molly's gut. It was a joke. Rebecca managed to break every rule possible, yet somehow she had them all fooled. She gave Molly a look while Mrs H busied herself with the tray, waggling her brows and sticking out her tongue. Silent laughter shook Molly. She was grateful for her friend and reflected that she did need to learn to be more like her. It might make things here easier.

She sobered abruptly. What was she thinking? She wasn't going to get the chance. Mrs H had other plans for her.

Solitary. Crypts. Chains.

"Cole Graham was always a troublemaker," Mrs H said. She had a syringe in her hand and was flicking it to free an air bubble.

Molly shrank into the stiff sheets of her hospital bed. "Is Cole...?" She couldn't say the word.

"He's fine," Mrs H. said flatly. Her eyes cut down at her, cruel and hard, any pretense of kindness gone. "Worry about yourself, young lady."

The woman took her by the arm, the needle poised above her pale skin. Horrified, Molly struggled – or tried to. A lightning flash erupted in her head and she slumped.

"Calm down, Molly," Rebecca urged. "It's for the pain."

"No," she protested weakly. Her thrashing did nothing but ruffle her blanket. Mrs H had her arm firmly in her grip. The needle pricked her skin and slid deep. With a sneer just for her, Mrs H pressed the plunger. A rush of warmth followed, filling her veins. The pounding in her head faded and the room grew dim.

"I'll be here when you wake up," Rebecca said. "I promise."

Molly felt a flutter against the back of her hand. The gentle touch of her friend's lips. She wanted to scream, but she was frozen. Rebecca wouldn't be able to keep her promise. Molly knew it. And then she knew nothing.

CHAPTER TWENTY-FOUR

"This is beyond egregious! Blatantly unlawful. Disrespectful. Blasphemous!"

Hero picked at the bandages on her hands while Chief Dewey listed her crimes one by one, wanting to be anywhere else but in his office getting a dressing-down. He was red faced and practically shouting at her. She sighed. This was not her idea of a good time.

"You opened the Gate to the Underworld on *sanctified ground!* You endangered your partner and threatened the integrity of our entire case!"

Especially with Liam Franke observing from the corner, grim and stiff-backed, his arms crossed over his chest, staring down his nose at her. Judging her. At least he didn't look smug. That was something. Apparently his leave had ended and he was back to full-time duty. Maybe her mother had died? The thought perked her up and she straightened from her insolent slouch, letting her hands fall to her sides. They would heal better without her picking at them, anyway. But the bandages itched.

The bandages were unnecessary, but she'd let the young medic who'd responded to the scene put them on her, more for his comfort than for any accelerated healing effect. His older partner had been busy seeing to DH Keen. Her hands might have looked horrific – blistered, raw, bleeding – but they would be fine in a day or so. Keen, on the other hand, had real wounds, and human flesh didn't heal like half-demon flesh. The teeth marks and gashes on his arms and back and one lean thigh – his uniform was in absolute tatters, too – were deep and bloody. The elder medic had her hands full tending to them.

For Keen's part, he sat in stoic silence as she worked, an occasional grimace the only sign of his distress. The medic had wanted to load him into the ambulance right away, but Keen had refused, wanting to give his report first.

Selfishly, Hero was glad he'd stayed. Their report would sound half mad as it stood. Coming from her alone, the PKs might dismiss it as demonic folly.

Sister Agnes had called the authorities when Hero and Keen had crawled up from the catacombs, singed and bloody. Keen's wounds had been so obviously of demonic nature, the poor nun had woken up several of her sisters with her shrieking.

Now, a gaggle of half-dressed sisters stood watching beyond the PK lines, fervently praying and extolling the grace of the Goddess, armed with blessed water and silver prayer beads – the weapons of their order. The revered mother herself appeared almost immediately and insisted she accompany the PK officers who entered the catacombs to investigate Hero and Keen's story.

"I'm not surprised to find you at the center of this travesty," the mother said, stopping by Hero's side before descending with the other officers. Her sparrow eyes landed on Hero's ragged hands and narrowed. "You'll heal," she said dismissively. But then a moment later, to Hero's great shock, she made a sign of blessing over the wounds. Those bright eyes of hers met Hero's burning gaze. "As you tread through the shadows, may the Goddess light your way." And with that, she spun away and stalked to the mausoleum and the waiting PKs, leaving Hero to wonder if she'd read the odious nun as wrong as Keen thought.

Unfortunately, neither the mother nor the PKs found anything below but Keen's discarded saber surrounded by burned and bloody brickwork. None of them, all fully human, could sense the shield, and if the revered mother scented the elemental demons, she certainly didn't speak up about it.

So now the PKs were throwing Hero suspicious looks while the medic bandaged her hands, as if they thought she might be responsible for Keen's wounds and all the talk of demon protection spells and dark power lurking beneath Bright Renewal Academy was a farce. Keen did his best to back her up during the subsequent interrogation by the responding officers –

Hero wasn't insulted by their questions; she would have done the same if the situation were reversed – but the interview came to an abrupt end when he inconveniently fainted.

Promptly thereafter, she was escorted back to the station in a PK meat wagon like a Goddess-damned criminal. They didn't go so far as to make an accusation, though they stuck her on a back bench with shackles on the floor beside her, claiming there was no room for her to ride up front – an intimidation tactic, no doubt. It hadn't bothered her much. She'd busted out of meat wagons a time or two in the past, even while chained. Shackles on her were like the bandages: simple window dressing.

Instead, she'd spent the ride considering their discovery, such as it was. Keen's recollection of what he'd seen beneath Bright Renewal was sketchy at best. A vast cavern. A deep pit. A dark presence. Then the elemental demons had attacked him.

The best part, the only shining light she could pinpoint, was her battle with that despicable shield. It had bent beneath her onslaught. If she had more time, more preparation, more tools, she might be able to–

"Well? What do you have to say for yourself?"

Hero blinked, coming back to the present. Ah yes, she was being torn a new one "I followed a hunch, Chief," she said simply. "And I was right. That so-called academy is a hotbed of demon activity. It isn't my fault your PKs are too blind to see the evidence. Surely someone at this station must have the slightest sensitivity?" She cast a glance at her brother. "You were particularly sensitive as a child, Liam. I recall that much. Or did Mother beat it out of you after she got rid of me?"

Liam jerked, coming to life at last. He turned bloodshot eyes on her, his mouth hard with anger. His cheeks were unshaven and sunken and his uniform was askew, very unlike his usual professional appearance. Grief? Her spirits lifted.

"You know nothing about me, Inspector," he said sharply. "You'll not drag me into your madness. Not this time. You made your bed, now lie in it."

"Better than lying in a fog, Lieutenant," she countered. She faced Chief Dewey, exasperated. "How can you not feel the hex you all are under? Don't you have protocols? I know this is a small town, but you are peacekeepers – professionals, supposedly. Why, a half-grown demonhunter has you all outclassed. At least he broke himself free of the spell."

"Spell?" Dewey echoed, his face screwed with confusion. "What are you on about now?"

She scowled. "Find your center, man," she admonished.

Suddenly, he seemed to deflate, his jowls sagging. He ran a shaking hand through his dark hair, his brow furrowing. His eyes stared at nothing for a moment and his mouth worked as if he was trying to speak and couldn't.

Eagerly, Hero stepped forward. "Chief," she said. "I need your help, sir. This case is far bigger than I knew, far more dangerous. I need your PKs. I need to get into Bright Renewal Academy!"

"Enough about Bright Renewal!" Liam snapped. "There's nothing wrong with the Academy. It's a grand place, a place of hope for desperate parents. You wouldn't understand how important their work is for the community. What would you know about community?"

She turned on her brother. "Oh, you're right, Liam. I know nothing about community except how to be excluded from one. But I do know this so-called Academy didn't exist until maybe a year ago." At his furious glare, she struggled to change her tone, to try a softer approach. Her brother looked on the verge of something – of what, she had no idea, but it wasn't good. "We grew up together, at least for a while. I – I know you remember our childhood. We share the same history. This place, this Academy – it is something new, something dangerous. Hidden in plain sight."

"You cannot target Bright Renewal Academy," Dewey interjected, but his voice was a monotone. The words held no conviction. "It is an esteemed institution." He blinked, looking startled, as if he couldn't believe he'd just spoken. His hands lay on the desk before him, shaking like those of a drunkard coming off a bender.

But Liam nodded along, oblivious to the chief's strange behavior. "That's right," he declared with a sneer, a most uncharacteristic expression for him; he was usually so dour and serious. *What's going on here?* "Would I have sent my own daughter there if I thought it was dangerous?"

The air left the room. "You... you sent Molly to Bright Renewal Academy?" Hero said, stunned, her mind whirling. She barely knew the girl, hadn't even known she'd existed until a few weeks ago, yet horror gripped her. That girl, that little girl, had no idea what true evil could do. And she was in the belly of the beast. Why? To what end? Who had sent her there, really?

The air seemed to go out of Liam too. His bloodshot eyes grew wide and agony painted his face. "She was getting into trouble. All the time. Something had to be done before it was too late. Before she was lost to us entirely."

"Getting into trouble?" Hero thought back to the interview, remembering a girl who comported herself with modesty. So meek and frightened. Of course, looks could be deceiving sometimes, and Molly wouldn't have been the first child to fake an air of innocence, but Hero trusted her instincts. She was sure she'd read the girl correctly: Molly was an innocent, just a girl caught up in something awful.

Like so many others I've known. Like me.

She fixed her brother with a hard glare. "Do you really believe that, Liam?" she asked, wincing inwardly as she heard her own voice rising, growing mocking and shrill. "Did she give you any trouble at home? Was she talking back, staying out past curfew? Was she out drinking in an alley with hoodlums? Did she curse at you, disrespect her mother? Any of those things?"

She advanced on him and he shrank back, putting Dewey's desk between them. Doubt and guilt played across his features, a wincing struggle. "Mother Francesca told me—"

"What? What did that shriveled goat tell you?"

Liam's eyes pinned her, defiant. "Molly stole sacrificial wine! A blatant theft! And she's been doing other things, evil things. Out in the woods."

Hero scoffed. "So a nun says." She turned on Dewey, giving her brother a dismissive wave. "Did you know about this?" she demanded. "One of our main witnesses gets shipped off to prison, essentially, and it doesn't strike you as suspicious?"

"Bright Renewal Academy is an esteemed—"

"Enough!" She slammed her fists on his desk. He jerked back, blinking furiously, and Hero got in his face, almost screaming, "Snap out of it! Do your damned job, Chief!"

If she'd thought that trying the same tactic that had worked with Keen would work on Dewey, that she might shout the spell out of him, she was proved wrong when his eyes cleared, hardened. She saw sense returning to him – no more shaking hands or vague stares. "I have been doing my job, Inspector," he countered with immense calm. "While you were desecrating tombs and getting your partner very nearly killed, I was following a lead."

Well, this was unexpected news. "A lead? From where? From whom?"

He shook his head. "Doesn't matter. It was legitimate. A witness saw the perpetrator exit Sister Catarine's apartment on the night of her disappearance, sneaking down the back stairs of the cloisters. With the sister."

Stunned, Hero rocked back on her heels. "What witness? Another sister? Surely, you know you can't trust a single one of them!"

"But we're supposed to trust you implicitly?" Liam said. "A disgraced half-demon nun fresh from prison?"

She scowled. "I've been out three years. And I'm no longer a fucking nun. You should trust me because I'm a death speaker, an inspector! I know what I'm doing."

Dewey and her brother exchanged glances, sharing expressions of disdain. Then Dewey smiled at her smugly. "Nevertheless, Inspector, we managed to make headway without your help. Despite your help, really. The witness feared coming forward, given your obvious hatred of the sisterhood."

This was a trick. A lie. Hero looked from one to the other, flabbergasted, but a sliver of doubt lodged in her heart. Could it be true? Could fear have kept a witness away? Had she only felt comfortable coming to *human* police?

Was Hero an impediment to her own investigation?

"We have the suspect in custody, if you'd like to peek in on his interrogation," Dewey continued.

"Who's running the interview?" she asked, meekly now, all her righteous anger having left her, giving way to doubt. It was an uncomfortable and unfamiliar sensation. She was very rarely caught flat-footed on a case – *she* was the one who brought in suspects. Nevertheless, she had to determine for herself whether the suspect was a person of interest, even if it meant watching from the sidelines. For now, she had to play the good PK.

"Inspector Smith and Officer Coates," said Dewey.

"Coates? That fetus?"

The chief frowned. "He's a trained officer, Inspector, and he was one of the uniforms assigned to help you. He's more than qualified to interview a suspect. Besides, Smith is a murder PK, trained in New Savage."

She struggled not to launch into a tirade. This was unbelievable. "I'll take your word for it," she said, as calmly and as reasonably as she could in the circumstances. She didn't know Smith from a hole in the ground. "I would like a crack at our suspect too, if you please. After the initial interrogation."

"Fine. I'll allow it." Dewey gave her an indulgent smile that sliced through her like a knife. So, he was throwing her a bone, was he? "He's in Interrogation Room One right now. You can watch through the glass."

She adjusted her clothes needlessly – there was no putting back together her ruined outfit with a few tugs – and gave him a respectful nod. *I'm going along with this like a good PK.* "I'd like to have DH Keen observe as well," she said. *The only one I can trust.* "We've built a good rapport."

"That's up to him," Dewey said sternly. "If he's recovered enough. Last I saw of him, he was drugged to his eyeballs. Do you want to wait for him that badly? You know time is of the essence."

Hero ticked off the hours in her head and ground her teeth. Keen would probably be out for another day probably, maybe longer.

"I'll watch alone for now." She shrugged. "If they get a confession, I won't interfere, but if our suspect is recalcitrant, I'll have to involve myself in his interrogation. In the meantime, I'll need the file and all the evidence you've gathered on..." She raised her brows.

"Braun," Dewey said. "Our suspect is Jerry Braun. And the evidence against him is damning. He was the last person seen with the victim, and there's an entire trove of communication between the two of them. Looks like they had a relationship of some sort." His frown returned. "No one is going to like it, but we're pretty sure Catarine got mixed up with some religious nutjobs. You know the type – all into the gory worship of the past, blood sacrifices and rituals. It all makes sense when you think about it. Braun and his heretical accomplices probably murdered her to appease their primitive version of the Goddess. So barbaric."

Hero barely heard a word he said. It was all bullshit. Braun wasn't their man; she'd stake her life on it. "I need to speak to the suspect," she blurted. *"Now."*

Dewey eyed her. "You'll get your chance. Right now, you observe. Understood?" He tapped a finger on his desk. "You are on very thin ice at the moment, Inspector. Tread carefully. I don't want to have to send you back to Savage."

She ground her teeth, tempted to open the Gates of Hell right there in his office. "Yes. Chief. Whatever you say."

CHAPTER TWENTY-FIVE

The sun woke him, bright through his eyelids. His mother had drawn his curtains but not all the way, leaving a spear of light in the exact wrong place. Keen groaned and did what he always did: he rolled over. Except this time, shooting pain froze him in place. Blinding sun or not, he couldn't move. His arms ached and one leg was... The muscles felt shredded. Dear Goddess, what had happened to him?

Then it came back in a flood: the catacombs. The bone dust and skulls. The foul oiliness of demonic energy. The trek alone down a long, echoing tunnel with only a flickering flame to guide him. And at the end of the tunnel–

A shudder racked him, bringing him fully awake – awake to pain and confusion. He was lying on his back, a slash of sunlight falling over his eyes. He blinked and managed to turn his head. Where was he? Blue curtains, white walls, crooked shelves heavy with books, a worn desk and chair in the corner. *Right. I'm home.* He vaguely remembered the ambulance ride, the specially designed wagon smooth as silk despite the bumpy roads in Otherside, a female medic hovering over him, dark face scrunched with concern. Memories of his mother weeping and demanding answers, and he trying to reassure her – uselessly, since he could barely speak or move without help. Somehow, the two medics and his frantic mother got him up the stairs and into his bed. Oblivion soon followed, thank the Goddess.

Suddenly, his breath came hard and fast. A tightness squeezed his chest. He sat up, too quickly; agony roared through him and he hunched over, teeth clenched. The pain eased and left him panting. His heart galloped. He touched the bandages on his forearms with trembling fingers. A thick swath swaddled his thigh beneath his blankets. Gingerly, he stretched. A tug across his back told him he'd caught an injury there, too.

For a moment, he could almost feel demonic claws tearing through his skin. Sweat coated his upper lip, sprang from his armpits and forehead. He felt dizzy. At the time, in the thick of it, he'd acted instinctively, his training taking over, quashing his fear, but now, in the quiet of his childhood room, the terror roared up. Not because of those shrieking, swirling elemental demons, but from what they'd been protecting.

A deep darkness. A bottomless pit. A presence. Pure malevolence.

Rising...

Moving stiffly, he threw back the covers and flung his legs to the side. The wooden floor was cold beneath his bare feet, but he was sweating by the time he managed to lever himself out of bed. A clean uniform waited for him in his closet, freshly pressed, neat as a pin. He assumed the uniform he'd worn last night was in rags somewhere. Aches and stinging pain racked each movement as he struggled into his clothes. He had to stop and catch his breath with his pants still at his knees, but he finally prevailed and finished dressing. His sash and bandolier of potions were on his desk, laid out for him with special care. He noted with surprise that his array of vials had been fully replenished, and his heart warmed at his mother's attentiveness and quiet efficiency.

The delightful aroma of sizzling pork tickled his nose once he had his weapons securely in place and his stomach growled noisily. There came a gentle tap on his door and he smiled. "Come in, Mama," he said in a voice cracked and raw. He cleared his throat as the door swung inward and turned to greet her. But it wasn't his mother standing in the doorway holding a tray of food.

"Your mother sent me up with lunch," Abigail Hollander said with a tentative smile.

Keen's knees gave out and he sat on his rumpled bed, the old springs creaking embarrassingly loudly. He felt his cheeks and ears grow warm and hoped the dim lighting would hide his furious blushing. Abigail Primm was *in his room*. Young Oleander Keen, good ole Charity-case, was beside himself. It was a dream come true, even under such strange circumstances. Nevertheless, the investigator inside him had to ask, *why* was she here?

Abigail flowed into his room and settled the tray on his desk. She gave him a look, her cheeks apple red, as if to apologize for her intrusion, and moved closer, her steps a whisper against the smooth floorboards, a simple smile on her lips. She stood tantalizingly close, almost close enough for him to touch her. This time, she wore a satin frock in a demure midnight blue with a touch of lace at the collar and cuffs rather than her nightclothes. The dress hugged her curves intriguingly and the rich color brought out tones of blue in her black hair. Her beauty took his breath away and he was fifteen again, awkward, shy and vulnerable.

The sweet smile turned to a look of deep concern, her smooth forehead wrinkling prettily. "I heard about your troubles, Officer Keen, and felt I must come pay a visit." A tremor shook her lower lip. Was she that upset for him? "After what you did for me the other night... I couldn't–" Tears glimmered at her eyes and she bit her lower lip, evidently overwhelmed.

Keen stood, swallowing a hiss of pain and fighting to keep from grimacing – he didn't want her to worry – and closed the distance between them. Brazenly, he took her by the arms – a kindly gesture, a friend comforting another. "I'm fine," he said, squeezing gently. "It's all part of the job. Really."

Her smile lit the room and his heart swelled. Who needed the sun with Abigail Primm around?

It's Hollander now.

He let go of her and stepped back. Her smile dimmed somewhat, and she seemed to lean toward him... or was he imagining it?

"Your job is so dangerous," she exclaimed breathlessly, "though I blame the PKs for putting you in such peril. Who knew that inspector was a madwoman? I suppose I didn't understand the risk of having a half-demon partner. She seemed so *nice* the other evening, so helpful and kind." She shook her head ruefully. "I'm not always the best judge of character, apparently."

Was she referring to Dirk? He felt a surge of hope, forgetting that the woman standing in front of him was married in the eyes of the Realm and the Goddess. If her own husband was a threat to her–

"Wait, what?" He blinked rapidly, forcing himself back to reality. "What did you say about my partner?"

Now she did lean toward him, resting a slim, pale hand on his arm. A slight wince creased her face at the touch; she must have felt the bandages underneath his uniform. "The rumors have been flying. The sisters are saying Inspector Viridian attacked you after forcing you into the catacombs on some wild-goose chase!"

Aghast, he shook his head. "That isn't what happened! My partner saved my life. *Demons* attacked me, not Viridian. And it wasn't a goose chase, for the love of the Goddess. We found... *I* found something, something evil. I fear it threatens the entire town. It lurks beneath Bright Renewal Academy, a – a presence of demonic origin!"

Her hand snapped back, like his arm had burned her. "Bright Renewal? You must be mistaken. Nothing evil could come from that place. They do the Goddess's work. Why, I should know; I volunteer at the Academy twice a week."

"You work there? At Bright Renewal?" Something cold crawled through his belly. He took her by the arms again, grabbing her roughly, worry and fear making him bold. "It's dangerous, Abby. You shouldn't go there."

She laughed, a bright peal. "It's hardly dangerous," she scoffed. She didn't pull out of his grip. If anything, she moved closer to him. Her hands rose to rest on his chest, and she looked up at him, blue eyes limpid. "Thank you for being concerned, but I have nothing to fear at the Academy. No one does. I think someone might be playing a trick on you, Officer Keen. Or... can I call you Oleander?"

For another long moment he forgot himself, swept up in the moment, his name on her lips a wish fulfilled. Only his worry made him push past the sweet fluttering in his belly. "Abby, please listen to me. I saw it. I *felt* it. That... *thing* is ancient, and it's like nothing I've ever come across as a demonhunter. Powerful doesn't begin to describe it."

Her smile vanished and a line appeared between her brows. "Oh, Oleander, I cannot take these wild flights of fancy seriously. A demonic entity? Wild fights in the catacombs? I know your job forces you to confront terrible dangers, hideous darkness, but none of that is here in Havenside. This town is peaceful. Good. Why, the only thing I fear–" Again, she bit her lower lip. A trembling lip. Her eyes cut away from him and her cheeks turned apple red once more.

Concerned, he pulled her ever so slightly closer, longing to kiss those rose-bright cheeks. But beneath his desire was smoldering anger. He knew what she feared. *Who* she feared. "If he's hurt you…" he said in a low, intense voice. "You have to tell me. I can keep you safe, Abby."

Her eyes returned to him, blinking furiously as if keeping back her tears. Her lashes were long and as dark as her hair. Keen swallowed. He'd kiss those soft eyelids, too, when he got the chance.

"Don't trouble yourself with my little problems," she whispered, forcing him even closer. He could feel her warm breath on his skin. "Keep safe, Oleander. For me. Watch your back. I – I think your partner is not to be trusted. The rumors surrounding her frighten me. And who's to know she didn't do something to you down in the catacombs, something to muddle your mind? Demons possess strange and awful magic – the scriptures warn us! Even half demons are dangerous. They look like us, but they are *not* us."

Despite everything he knew so far, everything he and Viridian had been through, her words caused a sliver of doubt to enter his heart. He remembered how he'd felt when he'd first met Hero Viridian, when his first instinct had been to attack her – because Abigail was right: she was dangerous. They'd managed to build a working relationship these past weeks, but could he really trust her? Could anyone with demonic ancestry be trusted? Was he overcoming his training regarding the inspector, or ignoring his training because she liked a drink at the end of the day?

Had he really found a malevolent darkness beneath the Academy, or had Hero tricked him somehow? Everyone seemed to believe she'd attacked him. In fact, no one seemed particularly shocked by the idea, either.

"I trust her," he said, the words grinding from him. Did he? No. Yes, he did. "She saved my life."

Her expression softened. "Of course," she said gently. "I'm sorry, Oleander. I didn't mean to cause you distress. I came to make you feel better." Another peal of soft laughter. It shook her petite frame and sent waves of sensation through him. He nearly yanked her into a passionate kiss, but then she patted his chest, smiled and disengaged. He lowered hands still curled in grasping claws, empty of her. He swayed, bereft and off balance.

"Why don't you come to Bright Renewal Academy?" she said suddenly, brightly, as if it was the best idea in the world. "You can see the good work we're doing and put all your fears to rest."

He blinked. An invitation to Bright Renewal? How could he pass up the opportunity? Hero would gut him if he refused. At least one of them would finally get inside the place!

"I would–"

A shriek from below startled them both. Abigail's eyes went wide and she pressed into his arms. He caught her but nearly pushed her away. That had been his mother! The patter of rapid steps up the stairway made him sag with relief. He would know her tread anywhere, anytime. A moment later, Mrs Keen burst through his bedroom door, her face white and her eyes wide.

"They arrested him!" she cried. "For murder! It can't be, Ollie! Something's gone terribly wrong. It cannot be possible. Nellie's son wouldn't do this."

"What are you talking about?" And as much as it hurt, he released Abby to go to his mother. "Who's been arrested?"

"Jerry Braun." A sob burst from her. "You have to help him, Ollie! This is a mistake, I know it. He couldn't have killed that nun! It's impossible!"

Oleander learned the whole story on the way to the station. The entire neighborhood was buzzing. The PKs had come for Jerry while he and Viridian had been in the catacombs, ransacking his apartment and uncovering presumably damning evidence. Apparently, the junior inspectors they'd enlisted to help with questioning had found the eyewitness, pursued the lead and discovered a trove of letters and other evidence in Jerry's room above his bar. He found it hard to believe. Many of their helpers had next to no experience. How had they dug up this key witness and convinced her to talk? He and Viridian had questioned every single nun with even the slightest connection to Catarine, but somehow they'd missed the lone nun who'd witnessed Jerry Braun leaving with Catarine the very night she disappeared? Extremely unlikely, if not impossible to believe.

But he'd wanted to bring Jerry in himself, to find out if he was the mysterious Mr B in Catarine's letters. And it turned out he was. This was very bad.

Still, the man who'd been concerned about missing children at Bright Renewal Academy was suddenly the prime suspect in Catarine's murder? Why, a more cynical man might think Braun was being framed. He wouldn't decide anything until he talked to Jerry directly, with Viridian. They would be able to tell immediately if Jerry was guilty. Of that, he was certain.

Except...

Abigail's words came back to haunt him: *Who's to know she didn't do something to you? Half demons are dangerous.*

The stationhouse was as abuzz as Otherside had been. The PKs seemed certain they'd found their man and an air of jubilation suffused the place, along with a sense of palpable relief, as if the entire station had been spared a reckoning. And it had, in some ways. The town of Havenside had been living in fear for too long. Tensions were high, the situation fraught. Now, perhaps peace could return for its citizens.

Not fucking likely.

Keen found Hero observing the interrogation. For once, she looked a mess. Stained, tattered bandages covered her hands, her scapular – burned and bloody – lay across a chair in the observation room, and her cream-colored shirt had seen better days, untucked and singed. Her billowing harem pants bore the marks of their adventure, and he could see patches of pale, scratched skin through the rents. She'd shed her boots, too, though had kept on her stockings, the floor being cold and unforgiving. Her hair was loose, a lank silver tangle down her back.

She didn't even turn to greet him when he entered. Her entire focus was on the window into Interview Room One. He joined her, eyes roving briefly to the vicious wounds on her thighs – healing, he was happy to see. She'd been hurt while dragging him from the grasp of ravaging demons. Nothing any good partner wouldn't have done, but he still felt gratitude toward her.

Two officers were conducting the interview, and by their appearance – collars open, hair mussed – they'd been at it for some time. Jerry looked miserable, eyes sunken, hands shaking, hair awry. He sat hunched over the desk, his elbows propped on the table and his head drooping. His knee was bouncing beneath the table, a nervous tic he'd had since childhood.

Coates sat across from him, speaking in a low, cajoling voice: "This can all be over if you just tell us the truth, Jerry. Make us understand what happened, why you lost your temper with the sister."

"He doesn't need to talk," Smith interjected harshly, looming over Jerry and speaking right into his ear. "We have everything we need. Let the hangman have him. No one will shed a tear for this one."

"Easy, Inspector Smith," Coates chided. "I'm sure Jerry would rather unburden himself. Right, Jerry? The judge always goes easier on the ones who confess. The ones who show genuine remorse."

"I've done nothing wrong," Jerry said, his voice raw and cracking. His tone was monotonous, as if he'd already said the words a thousand times already. He hid his face in his hands, his shoulders trembling. "Please, this is all a mistake."

Smith slammed a fist on the table. "Liar!"

Jerry started to weep. The two officers exchanged a look as if they'd finally made some progress, and Keen wondered if his friend was close to breaking. Coates jumped in again with his cajoling while Smith leaned over Jerry and whispered threats in his ear, but no confession seemed forthcoming.

Watching through the transparent mirror, Inspector Viridian made a rude noise. "Amateurs," she said. "They've been at this same routine for hours."

Keen cleared his throat. "Is there a file on Braun?" His heart hurt to see his old friend in such a state, but he couldn't be influenced by feelings. He had to remain objective, to look at the evidence and make his own judgement. Still, maybe he'd been right to be suspicious of Jerry. Somehow, his old friend had avoided coming into the station to answer their questions for over a week now. Was his guilt the reason why?

His partner jerked her chin. "On the table." She turned to watch him as he went to the file. "It's all bullshit. But I think you already know that."

"I don't know anything yet, Inspector."

The file was bigger than he'd expected and contained an eyewitness statement from Sister Agnes that looked legitimate and read plausibly. He remembered Agnes from their previous visit to Clementine Prep. She was the convent's unofficial night watchman and so had a handle on the comings and goings in her own house. She had no doubt that the man she'd seen leaving with Sister Catarine had been Jerry Braun. Her description of him was spot on, and in fact she'd recognized him. He'd been making quite a stink lately about the kids in Otherside who'd supposedly "run away."

Along with the statement were descriptions of Jerry's room above his tavern – apparently, he'd had quite the shrine built for Sister Catarine along with evidence linking him to her. Letters from him to her, undelivered and dripping with mawkish sentiment, and a few from her to him, addressed to "Mr B." A few mementos...

"Dear Goddess, he had her cincture in his possession?"

"He had *a* cincture," Hero countered stubbornly. "And a few pictures and mementos of a girl isn't exactly a shrine to her. He's admitted to having contact with her, in regard to the missing children only. But," and here she hesitated, adding reluctantly, "he did also confess to having feelings toward her beyond friendship. Unrequited feelings."

"Fuck."

She grimaced and joined him at the table, dropping wearily into the chair holding her scapular. "It's bad, I know. But is it damning?"

"It's motive." He flipped through the papers, reading all the reports from the crime-scene investigators, stunned that this entire operation had been happening without their involvement. "It's the same motive you pinned on Father Kellan when you thought he was our prime suspect. So it's entirely plausible, right, and we just missed it?"

She scoffed. "Maybe. But I just don't buy it. I mean, how many jealous lovers could one nun have?" She snagged the witness statement. "All this subterfuge and secret assignations. When did she have time to teach?"

Keen sighed and reshuffled the remaining pages into a neat pile. "Are we just angry that this happened without us? That somehow we misread the entire situation?"

"Do you really believe that, Keen?" She crumpled the witness statement into a ball, her eyes smoldering behind her tinted glasses. Shockingly, the paper didn't burst into flames. "This sudden resolution seems just a bit too convenient for me to stomach. I feel like someone is manipulating the situation, handing us a suitable patsy to appease the town and the peacekeepers, to keep us off the real target."

"What if he doesn't confess?" he asked. "Will they shut down the investigation anyway? Is everyone so sure that Braun is guilty?"

Her lips pressed into a hard line. "Dewey seems elated, and he's not the only one. They want a suspect. They want a murderer, someone handy and human who can be tossed in a cell forever or dangled at the end of a noose. Our suspicions are too complicated for them. If we're right, then something quite hideous and dangerous is afoot and that would send all of Havenside into a tizzy, now, wouldn't it?"

The voices from the other room rose suddenly, roaring through the speaking tube: "Yes! I took her into the woods, but it's not what you think. We were just talking–"

"What went wrong? What made you snap? Just admit it, Braun! Admit what you've done!"

"She needed my help! Someone was harassing her–"

"*You* were harassing her, Braun! And when she refused you, you raped her, held her captive, then cut out her tongue to appease your bloodlust! You're nothing but a depraved monster and I'll see you hanged."

"No! No! I'm not – I'm not a killer!"

Jerry's denials dissolved into bitter weeping. Hero stood and returned to the window, arms crossed tightly to her chest. "Another round of the same shit," she muttered, her back stiff with displeasure. "He's not going to confess."

"Because he didn't do it, or because he's a cold-blooded killer?" Keen picked up one of the letters Jerry had addressed to Sister Catarine, one that hadn't been delivered yet. It was innocent enough, a discussion about the missing children, Jerry confessing his deep worry and pleading for help. He frowned, re-reading the letter. Why was he asking Sister Catarine for help? Was she even in a position to give any assistance, or was Jerry's plea a ploy to get her attention, the act of a stalker?

"It's because he didn't do it," Hero replied with a certainty he envied. "I read all of those letters. Twice. They were subtle in broaching the true subject, avoiding naming anyone or anyplace directly, but it is clear to me that Catarine was starting to investigate Bright Renewal, as we already suspected, and needed Jerry's help."

Unfortunately, it wasn't quite as clear to Keen. He wasn't seeing the subtext his partner was, but it made sense given all they'd learned. Catarine had been sniffing around, asking questions, and someone had wanted her silenced. If Jerry had been helping her, what better way to rid oneself of another nuisance than to make him the prime suspect in her murder?

The voices from the other room rose once more, the ebb and flow following a pattern, highs and lows, cajoling and threatening, though Smith and Coates seemed to be veering increasingly toward threatening. After so many hours, they had to be getting desperate for results. Sometimes it worked and the suspect spilled, but the unrelenting pressure didn't seem to be working with Jerry. Despite his broken demeanor, he remained steadfast in proclaiming his innocence.

"They won't ask him the right questions," Hero complained, her words a low growl. "Who was harassing her? Why would she go into the woods with someone she hardly knew? A man, no less. What had her so worried? And how in Hell do they think Jerry drained her very essence? How did he hold her for six days and no one noticed? Have they even looked at Virchow's forensic report?"

"Can we take over the questioning?" he asked, eager to be able to talk with Jerry himself. Hero was right: his friend was being railroaded. He was a convenient dupe from the wrong side of town, and people would accept his guilt without a murmur – quite happily, in fact. But he refused to believe Jerry was guilty. True, he'd lost touch with him over the years, but they'd been close once, and the boy he'd known would have been incapable of such a vicious crime.

It's been years. I knew the boy, but what about the man?

"I said I'd give them a chance," she said. She turned to him and started to wrap her hair into a tidy bun. "Now let's run those idiots out of there."

CHAPTER TWENTY-SIX

It was as good a time as any to take a break, and neither Coates nor Smith argued when Keen appeared with a tray of hot tea and biscuits. The demonhunter used his easy charm to convince the two officers to vacate the interview room. Let the suspect stew a bit, eh? Give him a moment to reflect on the seriousness of the situation. A little time in a cold, uncomfortable room, hungry and tired, might be the final straw. Men sometimes broke for just a blanket or a sip of hot coffee.

But Hero wasn't trying to break Jerry Braun; she just wanted the truth, and every peacekeeper in town was currently trying to prevent her from finding it. Best to get them out of the way, then.

She and Keen made sure the observation room was empty and then locked the door behind them. Coates and Smith had taken their tea to the bullpen, eager to brag about their progress, never mind that they hadn't made any. The other PKs were happy to listen and share tips, and no one even noticed when Hero and Keen locked themselves in with the suspect.

"Jerry," Keen said softly, offering his friend the first sincerely kind voice he'd probably heard in hours. Hero approved; they weren't here to force him into a confession.

Braun jerked at his name, cowering as if he expected violence – sensible, given the tirades of abuse and threats he'd endured. He pulled himself up, blinking dazedly. "Ander?" he said. Hope trembled in his voice. "Is it really you?"

"It's me. We need to talk, Jerry, and we need to talk fast. You have to tell us everything."

His face collapsed, red eyes filling with tears. "I've told you *everything*. I swear to the Goddess, I didn't kill anyone!"

"Of course not," Hero said briskly, coming to stand beside Keen. Slowly, she unwound the tattered and stained bandages from her hands. The burns were half healed, but the wraps were driving her crazy. "We know this is all nonsense. Nevertheless, we need to know what you've been up to with Sister Catarine. Do you understand me?"

He stared at her, face pale beneath his full, dark beard. She kept her glasses firmly in place, not wishing to distress him any further. It wasn't lost on her how her presence alone affected people, but Jerry Braun knew her – sort of. He blinked rapidly, his eyes dropping. With a shudder, he pulled himself together. "I tried to explain to – to those officers," he began, voice raw from weeping. "They wouldn't hear me, just kept accusing me of…" He blanched, swaying slightly. "But it wasn't like that between us. We – we were working together."

Hero didn't want to lead him, but she did give him a little push. "This is about Bright Renewal Academy, isn't it?"

He nodded, looking wretched. "Everything leads back to that place," he whispered. "Cat – the sister – came to *me*. She'd seen my flyers plastered outside Clem Prep and wanted to ask me questions. About the kids gone missing."

"What did she want to know, exactly?" Keen prompted when Jerry grew quiet.

"Their ages, how many were missing and for how long. She wanted to talk to some of the families, to see if any of them were willing to share their concerns. I didn't see the harm in it." He looked up at them pleadingly. "She was a Celestial nun! She was someone important, here to help us. Finally."

"Did she talk to any of the families?" Hero asked.

"She tried the Grahams first. They have a son inside – Cole. He was writing his sister letters; he was too angry with his parents for sending him away to bother writing to them. Catarine had one of his letters, all marked up with deciphering because the boy wrote in code, apparently. She wanted to tell the parents he was in danger and force them to remove him from the Academy. At first, they refused – they didn't believe her – but I think they were starting to wonder, to worry. They finally agreed to meet with Catarine, at least."

Hero grimaced. "She never got to that meeting, did she?"

Miserably, Braun shook his head. "She disappeared soon after. The letter vanished with her."

"Did you know what the letter said?" Keen asked.

Braun swallowed. "There is a pit beneath Bright Renewal Academy," he said, speaking slowly as if he were trying to picture words in his head. "Deep and dark. It stinks of brimstone and rot. There are chains in the rocks. Chains with collars. Chains made of pale stone. Unnatural. Full of pale light. A sickly light. Except when the collar is placed around someone's neck. Then the links glow with an unholy brilliance. The victims are drained of energy. Milked of their essence. Only the strongest withstand it for long." He blinked rapidly as if coming out of a trance and stared up at them, eyes wide. "That's what Cole had written to his sister, but it was all laid out in nonsense words and backward talk."

"Cassie Graham decoded it for her," Hero interjected, starting to see the pattern. Cole went to his sister for help, Cassie went to Catarine, and Catarine went to Braun because of his criticism of Bright Renewal. It made sense.

Jerry nodded. "Cassie was desperate, according to Catarine. She was going to go to her superiors if the Grahams wouldn't cooperate. But I warned her not to tell anyone about the letter. She was already being harassed in her own school for speaking up about unpopular things, and now she was criticizing Bright Renewal. People were leaving her little warning notes and other... unsavory things. Dead rodents. Rotten meat. I begged her to wait, to speak only to the Grahams. That's why I asked her to come with me to the woods that night: I told her I'd bring the Grahams."

"But you didn't bring them, did you?"

"I had no choice but to lie. She was in grave danger, don't you see? I only wanted to talk her out of going to her superiors."

"She disappeared that night," Hero pointed out sharply. If Jerry had lured her there to convince her of the danger, he might have led her right into it. "Did you leave her out there alone?"

"No!" He shook his head wildly, his trembling hands clutched into fists. "I'd never let anyone face such danger alone, much less Cat! She was the best of us. So very kind–" His words choked off.

Hero watched him fight off tears and her ire with him deepened. Dear Goddess, he'd been in love with her too. A very popular nun was Sister Catarine. "You escorted her home, then?"

His face turned red and he looked guilty. Some internal struggle had him suddenly squirming like a hooked fish.

"Tell us, Jerry," Keen said softly. "Let us help you. Please."

Braun looked at his old friend, finding a sympathetic soul in Keen's kind expression. Hero was impressed; Keen had a knack for this.

"She – she came home with me, to my apartment," he said at last in a rush, full of shame. "I'd convinced her not to go to her superiors, but it took half the night. By then, it was pitch dark and Catarine worried about returning to the convent so late at night with a strange man escorting her. It seemed best for her to stay with me until morning, when she could return without being noticed."

"She spent the night with you?" Keen's voice was remarkably even, considering how appalled he'd been by the idea of Catarine and Kellan carrying on together.

"Not like that! She stayed on the couch and left well before I woke up. I'm so sorry I lied about it, but you can see how it looks."

Hero sighed and stepped back. It did look very, very bad. No wonder he hadn't spilled this part. A beautiful young woman – a woman he'd been clearly attracted to, judging by his letters – had slept on his couch, then subsequently disappeared. But the letters had never been delivered, so Catarine had probably had no clue about his feelings. Why else would she have dared stay in his apartment?

"So," she said, drawing out the word as she pieced together a timeline. "She left your place sometime between midnight and...?"

"Dawn," Jerry said immediately. "I woke up as the sky was just beginning to lighten. I went to check on her, and she was gone."

"And you heard nothing? Saw nothing? Anything odd or out of place?"

He shook his head. "Everything was in order. She'd even folded the blankets I gave her."

She shared another meaningful glance with Keen. "She was taken somewhere between the Jenny Wren and Clem Prep," she said. "No wonder we found nothing incriminating in her apartment."

Keen hesitated, seemingly torn. He stared at his friend, his brow wrinkled. "Did you rape her, Jerry?" His words were flat, emotionless.

Jerry didn't seem particularly shocked by the question. "No," he said steadily. "I would never harm Cat, in any way. Never. But" – his calm shattered – "I got her killed! It's my fault she was there! It's all my fault! *I killed her!*" He buried his head in his arms, his hunched shoulders shaking with sobs.

Keen reached out to comfort him, laying a hand on his back. "Well," he said to Hero, his expression grim. "What do we think?"

She opened her mouth and there was a click from the wall, a soft shuffling, then a muted voice came through the speaking tube. "Thank you, Inspector, DH. That's just what we needed to hear," said the disembodied voice of Officer Smith triumphantly.

"Wait, that wasn't a confession!" Hero protested, taking a step toward the mirror. "Weren't you listening? We have new information. Vital information!"

The door burst open and two uniforms crowded into the interrogation room, one of them carrying a pair of shackles. Hero spun, her heart thundering, and tore off her glasses, letting her eyes whirl. One of the uniforms backpedaled, but the other, undeterred, hauled Jerry to his feet and shackled his wrists together, giving Hero a sharp, warning look. "Don't interfere, Inspector. This one is going in a cell."

Hero seethed. "This is a mistake!"

"No," Keen interjected, rising to pull her back – gently. *Smart boy*. "It's all right, Inspector Viridian. Jerry will be safe enough in a cell. Right, Jerry? You'll be okay for now, won't you?"

Too stunned to speak, Jerry just stared at Keen. Terror lurked in his dark eyes. He managed a shaky nod, and in the next instant he was stumbling out between the two PKs.

When the door closed behind them, Hero turned to Keen. "We need to search the area near the Jenny Wren," she said. "And we need to go into the woods behind it. That's our crime scene."

Keen grimaced. "That's a lot of territory to cover for only two of us."

"We have no choice, and we have no time. Once they draft a confession, they'll force his signature, by trickery if necessary. We're racing the hangman's noose, DH Keen."

CHAPTER TWENTY-SEVEN

Jerry Braun was placed in the one remaining empty cell at the PK station, the others containing drunks and rowdies and pickpockets – all relatively harmless; Havenside peacekeepers didn't deal with dangerous criminals every day. The station's holding cells would have to do for now, at least until they got a signed confession out of him. Then they could ship him off to the penitentiary in New Savage, Hero's old stomping ground. She had to do everything to stop that from happening, having no doubt that he wouldn't last a second there. No one would spare the killer of a nun any mercy. If the other prisoners didn't get him, the guards would.

The adjoining cell held a despondent Father Kellan. The priest had deteriorated considerably since coming to the station for protection. Even though it was for his own safety, being locked in a cell wasn't exactly a trip to the country. The PKs treated him decently enough, providing the standard meals they'd give to any prisoner, but there was an undercurrent of disgust running through those tasked with his upkeep. To them he was a fallen priest, a disgrace to his order and collar. A fornicator and a liar.

Hero spared Kellan a glance while the PKs opened the cage next to his. The priest barely lifted his eyes while the female officer removed Jerry's shackles and tossed Braun into the cell. Only when they slammed the iron door closed did he react, jerking at the sound and pulling his knees up onto his cot to huddle like a child awaiting punishment. Looking at him now, it was hard to believe she'd ever considered him a suspect.

"There, he's all safe and sound," the female officer said, giving Hero a grimace of distaste. "Just like we promised."

"You're dismissed, Officers," Hero snarled, her lips pulling back from her teeth like a rabid dog's. The woman's skin paled a shade or two and hustled her partner back down the hall, leaving them at the cages. She and Keen had insisted on supervising Jerry's transport, even though it was literally down the hallway. This case was too volatile to take any chances on his safety, and he wouldn't have been the first suspect to have had an "accident" on the way to his cell. Neither PK could object; an inspector outranked any uniformed officer, even a lieutenant like Liam.

"Hang in there, Jerry," Keen told his friend, now standing at the center of his cell, a stunned and pathetic-looking figure. "We'll work this all out."

Hero wasn't so sure, but she said nothing. Why make him feel any worse? She gave Kellan another glance before she and Keen headed back to the bullpen. The priest was still huddled on his cot, knees up and his head down, looking no less pathetic than Jerry Braun. She sighed. Love had gotten them into this, nothing more. Tragic, or tragically stupid?

Out front, Coates and Smith sat at their desk, all pleased smirks and puffed chests. Coates was writing a report by hand, his pen scribbling furiously, and Smith lounged above him, supervising, perched on the edge of the desk, murmuring the occasional correction. They were evidently crafting a confession for Braun to sign. *Fast work*, thought Hero, a prickle in her spine tingling all the way to the top of her head.

"I don't know why you took it upon yourselves to interview our witness, but job well done," Smith said when they appeared. He was a short, stocky man with years of service under his belt and an attitude to match. Unlike Coates, in his PK uniform, he wore civvies: tailored tweed pants, blue broadcloth shirt and natty suspenders – a professional. Hero didn't know him well, or at all really, but she already didn't like him. He played the bully PK all too easily.

"We had our reasons," Keen said stiffly. Apparently, he didn't like Smith much either. Who would have guessed she would see eye to eye so often with a Goddess-cursed demonhunter?

"Did you really buy all of his nonsense, or were you just steering him into a trap?"

"We steered him into nothing," Hero snapped, feeling decidedly uncharitable toward the two officers. "You are taking his words out of context and you know it. The only nonsense here is that confession you're fabricating."

Smith scowled and slid off the edge of the desk, bristling like an angry bulldog. "What are you saying, Inspector? Are you calling us liars? You heard it out of his own Goddess-cursed mouth – it was his fault. He did it! It's plain as day."

"That's not a confession, you incompetent lackwit."

"How dare you say that to me, you demon-spawned harridan!" Smith growled, lifting his hands like a pugilist.

She hissed and showed her fangs. It would feel good to knock this bastard around a bit, but she had to let him throw the first punch. Self-defense was hard to justify when you struck first. "It was the nicest thing I could think to call you," she spat back.

He sneered. "No one wants you here, hellspawn. We only tolerated you for your so-called *skills*, yet you've proven useless from the start. I will suggest they put you back where you belong when I file the final report. PKs don't need demons in their ranks." His eyes flicked to her partner. "You're a demonhunter, Keen. Surely you understand how little this one can be trusted? She deserves to rot in a cell. Or better yet, tossed in a river with a concrete block around her neck."

His insults weren't anything she hadn't heard before, and Hero laughed them off inwardly, no matter how much she wanted to eviscerate this fool. She knew he was goading her into an attack and she wasn't going to fall for it.

Unfortunately, her partner didn't have her self-control. Keen's saber screeched from its sheath, the bare blade drawing every eye in the precinct. The sharp point leapt to Smith's chin, hovering a hair's breadth from his skin. He jerked back, eyes crossing to stare at the sword, eyes as wide as coins.

"Touch my partner and we'll see who's expendable here, Inspector Smith!" Keen growled, his face red with fury and his gaze dark with menace. No one witnessing the exchange doubted for a moment that he wouldn't follow through on the threat. There was a scrabble and general kerfuffle as every officer grabbed for their weapons. The PK station had suddenly become a powder keg of impending violence.

And Hero and Keen were at the center of it, every hand there against them.

"How dare you draw on a fellow officer!" Coates cried, rising from the desk to defend the other man, papers scattering in his haste. "Stand down, DH Keen!"

Smith wasn't nearly as formal. "Are you fucking mental?" he shrieked. "What kind of demonhunter are you, anyway?"

"The very successful kind," Keen said, growing calmer. His blade didn't waver, nor did his threatening posture, and his voice was even. "Apologize to Inspector Viridian. Threatening a superior officer is a serious offense."

Smith grew apoplectic. No apology seemed forthcoming, so Hero stepped forward, raising her hands placatingly. "Here now," she said, pitching her voice so everyone in the bullpen could hear her. "It was merely a joke, wasn't it, Smith? You didn't mean to threaten a superior, I'm sure."

He glared at her, nostrils flared and brow furrowed, hands balled into angry fists. Keen, for his part, was a carved statue.

"You wouldn't want anyone filing a report about this little incident, now would you?" Hero prompted. She narrowed her eyes. "I may be demon spawn, but I have friends in high places, PK Smith."

That brought him around finally. He eased off, hands dropping, fists loosening. "Right," he said, nodding. "Just a joke, Inspector. No harm meant."

The tension broke. Sabers, pistols and bludgeons went away and relief rippled through the ranks. No officer had any real desire to tussle with a demonhunter – or her, more likely. They all had to know the stories of her capture. No one wanted to fuck with Inspector Death Speaker Hero Viridian.

"Why don't we all go to our corners?" she suggested mildly. She didn't smile; that would have just set everyone off again. "Keen? Sheathe your weapon, please. We have some work to do, remember?"

Her partner didn't look at her, his eyes remaining locked on Smith, sharply suspicious. Finally, he returned his saber to its home. "Yes, Inspector. We're done here, it seems."

"That's right, you're done," Smith muttered, returning to the desk with Coates, the two of them scowling and exchanging pointed looks.

"Let's go," Keen said. Glaring straight ahead, he stalked regally to the exit, his long legs eating the distance in a few strides. Hero gave the room of PKs a mocking salute and followed after him, catching up to him on the street.

"They don't want to hear the truth," he said. "Bright Renewal Academy is at the center of this and no one wants to admit it. They'd rather an innocent man die than besmirch that place. The entire town of Havenside seems complicit. Nothing happens in this town without the approval of the council, the mayor and the PKs. They *must* know!"

Normally, Hero would have agreed. "Unless, of course, the entire town is under a spell," she said. "We'll know who's actually complicit once we break it, and we can't break it until we get inside that place."

A heavy silence followed. She pulled at Keen's arm, forcing him to face her. "What?"

"I've been offered an invitation," he admitted, his eyes cutting away in embarrassment.

Her skin crawled. "By whom?" But she knew, even before he said it, by the way his ears turned pink and he wouldn't meet her gaze.

"Abigail Hollander." He spoke her name almost defensively, as if he knew she would disapprove. Very perceptive of him.

She pressed her lips into a thin line. "You know her husband is afraid of her, don't you? It was obvious to anyone paying attention the other night."

He flushed and yanked his arm from her grasp. "That's preposterous. She's the one in danger from *him*. She as much as admitted it to me. How could you think any differently after he pulled that stunt with the pistol? Dirk is the threat, not Abby!"

"She controls him, I'm certain of it. And now she's using your feelings toward her to draw you into a trap. I already had my suspicions, but now I wonder if she's part of this conspiracy too. Do you even really know her, Keen? You two obviously ran in different circles at Clementine. What'd they call you there? Charity, right?"

His mouth gaped as he struggled to find a response. "You've got it all wrong," he managed to say, shaking his head angrily. "Abby is good and decent. She was kind to me at Clem when everyone else treated me like something dragged in on their shoes. She thinks Bright Renewal is a good and decent place too, because that's her nature. It's why she's invited me inside to take a look and put my suspicions at ease. There's no way she knows what's going on there. She's not involved. I don't believe it."

"You *won't* believe it. There's a difference." Hero sighed, suddenly exhausted after the events of the previous night and that afternoon. She couldn't handle arguing with her partner on top of everything else. "Look, Keen," she said wearily, "I want to make this abundantly clear: We are the only two people in Havenside who aren't under this Fog spell. And that means we must be careful who we trust. I trust you, Oleander Keen, when every experience I've had tells me I cannot trust demonhunters. Nevertheless, I trust *you*." She paused, holding his gaze, almost afraid to ask the question. "Do you trust me?"

His eyes cut away, but she caught the guilt within them, and the doubt. His hesitation made her stomach curl. When had she ever cared what someone thought of her? No one trusted a demon, and the fact she was only half demon made no difference.

She made a small sound, a weak attempt to laugh off his reaction. "I guess I have my answer," she said wryly.

"No, don't think that, really!" His denials came fast and furious, and were altogether empty. "I don't *not* trust you. It's just, I – I – it's hard to overcome my training."

"Training. Got it." She turned away from him, a feeling of overwhelming loneliness engulfing her. Once again, she stood on the streets of Havenside completely and utterly on her own. She couldn't even count on her own partner–

A deafening shriek split her eardrums. She clapped her hands over her ears, mouth open in agony. What the–?

Fearfearfearfear–
Painpainpainpain–
A blast. An ending. Darkness.
Silence.

"Viridian? What's the matter? Hero!"

Keen. He had her by the arms, shaking her. Her ears rang thunderously and her heart felt like it was trying to shatter her chest. She blinked, trying to clear away the dark spots speckling her vision and focus on her partner's face, hovering just inches from hers – a blur, slowly resolving into familiar features creased with concern.

"Souls!" she gasped. "Crying out in agony."

"Someone murdered?" His hands were tight on her arms. "You felt it?"

She nodded, her senses returning, at least enough to figure out where those soul-shrieks had originated. Behind them. Her gaze settled on the stationhouse and the blood drained from her face. "Shit." She turned to Keen.

"Jerry," he whispered, his eyes wide. He released her and tore down the sidewalk.

CHAPTER TWENTY-EIGHT

The station was in chaos when Keen burst through the door, the PKs on high alert yet shocked and grim. He shoved his way past stunned uniforms by the tea kettles and dashed down the hall to the detention cells, his heart thudding violently, as keyed up as he was before facing the worst of demons.

The copper stink of blood flooded his nostrils and he slowed his pace as he rounded the corner to the holding pens.

The cell doors were open and the cages full of PKs. Smith stood in the hall, grim faced and angry, smoking a thin cigar. Beside him, Coates was running a hand through his hair, eyes wide and trained on the sprawled figure in one cell. Blood painted the prone man. His head was propped up against the bars to the next cell, his body stretched along the blood-soaked floor. He stared at nothing, his mouth slack, chin on his chest, a limp ragdoll of a man, so obviously dead no one had even tried to help him.

Bile rose up Keen's throat. He swallowed it down and entered the cell, careful to avoid the blood splattered across the dirty floor. His drumming heart slowed as his training asserted itself and he separated his feelings from his intellect. He gazed at the scene with analytical objectivity. There was a jagged wound across Jerry's neck and blood fanned down his shirt. A fork lay incongruously beside him, a bloodstained rag covering its tines.

Keen's gaze kept returning to the makeshift weapon. The handle of the fork had been honed to an edge, sharp but not enough for a clean cut. The attacker would have had to saw at Jerry's flesh while holding him flush to the bars. It would have taken phenomenal strength.

His eyes flicked toward the other cell. There lay another body – the attacker, Father Kellan. Someone had put a bullet through his brain and he'd fallen beside the bars of Jerry's cell, one arm still stretched through the bars. The sharpened fork lay close to his limp hand.

Immediately, he dismissed the conclusion his brain leapt to. It was impossible. How could this weak, broken man have managed to seize Jerry and slice open his throat? This had to have been planned, premeditated. The fork was a weapon that would have taken days to prepare, yet Jerry hadn't even been arrested until a day ago! But every scrap of evidence – the blood, the wound, the weapon, the dead men sprawled so near the bars – led to the unavoidable conclusion that one had killed the other, then been killed himself when the PKs intervened.

Jealousy, passion, rage, despair. It was all so clear.

Bullshit. This is bullshit.

A presence entered the detention area, cold and darkly furious. The PKs ceased their investigation, their careful marking of bloodstains and the handling of the weapon. The fork clattered to the floor from a uniform's numb grip. Everyone turned to the source of this leashed anger: Inspector Death Speaker Hero Viridian.

"Out," she spat, tall, imperious and uncompromising even with her torn and dirty clothes, mussed hair and reddened hands. "Everyone out. Now. Do *not* touch the bodies!" She screamed this last at an overeager PK who had been reaching to pull Kellan's arm from between the bars. The woman froze, wide-eyed as a rabbit in a hunter's sights. Hero removed her tinted glasses, letting Hell roar from her gaze. "Out," she repeated in a voice as deep as eternity. "I must Speak with the dead."

The PKs scattered hastily, all but Keen. He squatted beside his friend's body, feeling a strange elation. Now, they would learn the truth. The dead could not hide from his partner. They could not lie to her. Hero would root out the truth; she'd chase it right into Hell.

"How did this happen?" he asked raggedly, turning to look at her. "Please, Hero, tell me this isn't as simple as it appears."

Eyes swirling pools of magma, Hero entered the cell.

Bonelessly, she settled on the floor, careful to avoid the blood spatter, legs pretzeled. "Do not disturb me," she warned, "no matter what, lest–"

"The fires of Hell consume me, yes, I know. I won't interfere, and I won't let anyone else interfere. On my life."

"Yes. It is."

And with that ominous statement, she opened the Gate to the Underworld.

A stillness settled. A deep calm. Keen froze, still crouched, watching his partner speak to the dead. Her red tongue flicked across her lips, disturbingly lizard-like, but otherwise she didn't move. He held his breath until his chest ached, then hauled in a wheeze as quietly as possible. The flames in her eyes grew torpid, hypnotic. They drew him in, and for an eternal moment he was lost in the flames, burning–

A violent cramping in one of his calves brought him back to himself with a hiss. He flopped onto his ass and stretched out a leg to relieve the sharp ache. How long had he been squatting beside Jerry's cooling corpse?

A wretched moan drew his attention. His partner was bent over her lap, groaning as if in horrible pain. Her pale hands were locked into fists on her knees and her lips were drawn back from her teeth.

"Dear Goddess," she gasped. She rose to her feet and turned a baleful glare on poor Jerry. Her face was whiter than usual, her lips pale and pinched as if she might throw up. "Fuck me. Fuck us all. He did it, Keen. He fucking did it!"

"Did what? What do you mean? What did you see?"

She had her glasses in one hand and slapped them back on her face, hooking the wires over her elongated ears as if they offended her. "Jerry killed her. He raped her. Tortured her for days. His pleasure…it tasted like tar." She grimaced as if she might spit. "Jerry bragged about it to Kellan. The priest went mad and attacked him."

Keen couldn't believe what he was hearing. She had to be wrong. "That's impossible. It doesn't match the forensics. And – and – come on, Viridian, ask yourself: How did Kellan have a weapon at the ready like that?"

"It was in his cell, left behind by some other prisoner. I watched it happen; the attack was spontaneous."

He pressed, sensing her wavering. "A little convenient, don't you think? Hero, *please*."

"The dead can't lie," she said, no longer furious but deeply, deeply weary, shoulders sagging and cheeks sunken. She wiped her mouth. "How did I get this so wrong?" She heaved a wretched sigh. "I have to write my report before I forget anything."

Finally, she looked at him. Guilt and shame played across her sharp features, confusion drawing a line between her brows. "Goddess damn me. I'm sorry, Keen. For everything. Perhaps I let my personal feelings get in our way. I don't know; I can't explain it. I've never been so–" Her lips thinned. "Nevertheless, this case is over."

There was no arguing with her. Viridian seemed lost in a fog of furious self-doubt, scribbling out her report with a manic hand. Keen caught details that made his stomach shrivel: Jerry had held Catarine, using her cincture as a collar. It hadn't been a complex summoning, merely an offering to his demon overlord, an Aerial named Maelwind. It had taken days to drain her essence, and in those days of captivity…

Keen thought he might vomit.

His mind jumped to those elemental demons that had chased him in the catacombs. Guards of a powerful entity? Or slaves of Maelwind?

Jerry had torn out her tongue in a fit of demonic fervor and fed it to a pack of feral dogs roaming the streets of Otherside. Appalling. Horrifying.

He reeled away and somehow found his side of their shared desk before his knees gave out. How could he have misread a man so completely? How could he have been so blind?

No. He didn't believe it. He *wouldn't* believe it.

A dark presence. Powerful, ageless, rising…

"What about the dead girl?" he said, trying hard to keep his voice low – difficult, as his emotions were running high. The energy in the station was subdued now. The coroner and his technicians were dealing with the dead, leaving the PKs to process their shock. The righteous satisfaction of a job well done had been replaced by general horror at the resolution of this case. With the murderer dead, there would be no trial, no justice for the families, no chance to confront the killer. Even Smith's supercilious pomposity had faded while he attempted to comfort his traumatized partner: Coates had fired the shot that killed Kellan and no PK suffered through the fallout of their first kill in a breezy manner.

His question made her pause. The scratch of the pen ceased and she held herself very still.

"What about the spectral chain?" he pushed. "The pit beneath the Academy? The Fog spell? Your ravaged hands, for the Goddess's sake. You pulled me through that shield. It was real!"

"Yes. It was." Her forehead wrinkled then cleared abruptly. The scratching of her pen resumed. "But…one might have nothing to do with the other. I was sent here to solve a murder, Keen. Not investigate a school. I did my job."

Exasperated, he yanked his chair closer to the desk, dropping his elbows hard on its surface, which sent spears of pain up his injured arms. "Catarine's chain led to that school. And we have two murders, Viridian. What about Cassie Graham?"

Another pause. Ink spread from her pen tip, pressed hard against the paper. "I wanted evidence that the girl was murdered even though everything pointed to suicide. I let my own personal demons" – she grimaced at the unfortunate word choice – "cloud my judgement."

"Bull*shit*. Something is terribly wrong here. More distraction, more obfuscation!"

The tip of Hero's pen snapped off and he found himself pinned by her flaming gaze, rendered only mildly less terrifying by the tinted glasses. "The dead can't lie," she said flatly.

He didn't flinch. "And souls aren't eaten, either."

Finally, his words seemed to reach her, but not in the way he'd hoped. She looked aside. "Perhaps this has all been a delusion I brought to life. Maybe my gifts failed me when I tried to commune with Catarine's soul and I merely refused to admit it. How else could I have gotten everything so wrong? What I saw, what those two shades revealed… Curse me, Keen, it matches our evidence. I – I must come to the conclusion that *I was wrong.*"

Her doubt in herself was disheartening to witness, especially when Keen didn't think her gifts had failed. He refused to believe his old friend had committed such a brutal crime, and he refused to believe that everything they had uncovered meant nothing.

"Children are in danger," he said, reaching for something to hold on to. "That isn't a lie or a distraction. Children who committed no sin except to be born with demon blood. Right now, they are locked behind a powerful spectral shield. For whatever nefarious reason. Do we forget about them now that we *presumably* have our murderer?"

Hero pulled a handkerchief from her scapular and blotted at the ink splotch her broken pen nib had left on the report, her face smooth. Keen held his breath, and at last her eyes flicked up to him, slow-burning pools of flame muted behind cool green glass. "They have my niece at Bright Renewal Academy," she said.

Shit. Keen let out a shaky breath. "I'm sorry," was all he could think to say, but he couldn't help the swelling of excitement in his gut. Their case wasn't over. Not by a long shot. "I'll go to the Academy, Inspector. I'll get inside and try and find her. Just promise me you won't sign your report yet."

She looked at her broken pen and then tossed it aside. "I suppose I can't right now, can I?"

He ran his hands down his face. "Thank you–"

"Inspector Viridian."

They both turned to find the diener approaching their desk wearing her medical whites, looking out of place in the room full of uniformed PKs. Keen raised a hand in greeting. He'd watched her prepare Catarine's body and had been impressed with her stoic efficiency. Fresh-faced and freckled, she appeared barely old enough to be out of braids and knee socks, but she was a good five years older than he was and a consummate professional. She and Dr Virchow made a good match, sharing a rather macabre obsession with unlocking the secrets of dead bodies.

"What is it, Miss Grace?" Hero asked tiredly.

"The doctor wants you down in the morgue, Inspector," she said. "To discuss his findings."

Hero sighed. " I don't know if it matters anymore."

Miss Grace was unperturbed. She tipped her head like a curious crow and regarded Hero. "Now, please, Inspector." Without waiting for a reply, she turned and began to thread her way back through the grim PKs.

Hero sighed again, then stood to follow her. "I'll see what he found," she said. "Most likely, the substance we collected from Catarine's skin will link to the Aerial demon Braun was in cahoots with. If it does, I don't see how I can justify holding back on my report."

"I'll go to Clementine and find Mrs Hollander in the meantime," he said briskly, hoping she was wrong about Virchow's findings. "I'll take her up on her invitation. Don't sign anything until I return," he added firmly, daring to give her an order for a change.

Hero wavered. "You should proceed carefully, DH Keen," she said, keeping her voice low. "If you are right, and I can no longer trust what the dead have to tell me, then we are in grave danger." She lifted her lip, flashing a fang. "Distrust is your greatest asset right now."

He swallowed the urge to defend Abby and instead gave her a stiff nod. "I'm always careful, Inspector Viridian. Always."

CHAPTER TWENTY-NINE

The last thing Hero wanted to do was visit the morgue. Especially a morgue containing two bodies which represented her utter failure as an inspector and death speaker.

They were laid out on tables, side by side, rather than stuffed discreetly inside coolers. Sheets covered the still forms, tucked up to their necks to offer some semblance of dignity but leaving their faces bare, slack and silent with reproach. She entered the examination room with a heavy tread, feeling distinctly uncomfortable to be near these particular dead. An odd and unpleasant sensation. When had she ever felt uncomfortable with the dead? They had always been with her, for as long as she could remember, telling their tales, begging for her to Speak to them – to Speak *for* them.

What if I can never trust my abilities again? she wondered, a sharp spike of fear piercing her heart. Even Culpepper might give up on her then and send her back to her cell.

A shudder rippled through her. She hid it with a tug at her scapular.

"Doctor," she said in greeting, spinning her ebony cane as if she hadn't a care in the world. Virchow was hunched over a table near the bodies, one with trays and vials and an impressive-looking microscope gleaming under the bright lights. He turned to her and lifted the magnifying goggles he had strapped to his face. Tufts of white hair stuck out from the sides of his head, but his crown was as smooth as an egg. A short man with spidery limbs and a long face, he was nevertheless a giant in his field.

"Ah. You're here. Very good," he said brusquely, not bothering with pleasantries. Like her, he had little patience for the niceties of human behavior, preferring to get right to the point. "I've narrowed down the source of your spectral chain. I couldn't pinpoint the breed, unfortunately, but it is most definitely of Pandemonium."

"Let me guess, an Aerial demon?" she said, trying not to sound annoyed. What a boring development. A puny little demon she could snuff in her sleep had had her chasing her own tail for days. She scowled. The murder was solved. The investigation was over. The damnable demon was probably long gone by now, too. She fought the urge to break that shiny microscope.

"An Aerial demon?" he echoed, then laughed as if she'd made a joke. He gestured toward the microscope with a gloved hand. "Look through the scope and tell me what you see. Without your glasses, if you please."

She did as he asked and settled her glasses on the table while the doctor watched her expectantly. His gaze on her was disconcertingly bright. There was an eagerness in his manner, a snapping energy barely contained, and even a sharp glance with her flaming eyes didn't deter his staring. She pressed an eye close to the aperture. It took her a moment to focus, and then an entire world opened to her.

And it was a bad, bad world. A swirling nightmare in miniature. Pure evil on the head of a pin. A yawning chasm immense enough to swallow existence but no larger than a single cell.

And it was old. She felt like a newborn staring into infinity, helpless, new and shiny against a filthy, decrepit, eldritch authority.

Master...

With a ragged gasp, Hero backpedaled. Her hand moved in an automatic sign of warding, something she hadn't done since she was a novice. "By the Goddess, the Branch and all the roots of the world! That's no Aerial demon. It's not a demon at all!"

"Hence my inability to determine either breed or class," Virchow said. "The signature upon the chain which held our victim is something new, I believe. It's something I've never encountered, at least."

Hero focused on catching her breath, keeping her eyes on the microscope and the innocuous sample slide resting beneath the brass tube. She half expected a void to open up and swallow the entire morgue. But the substance they'd collected was merely residue. It couldn't harm them. Not in this form. Whatever spawned it was the true threat.

"Not new," she said, her lips numb. She didn't want to say more, didn't want to give it any more power.

"Do you recognize the signature?" Virchow demanded. "I cross-referenced every source I could think of and found nothing."

She shook her head. She didn't know the creature behind these samples, only that it wasn't a demon she knew, that in fact it wasn't any true demon at all. No, this was something far older. Far more dangerous.

Devourer.

The word whispered through her head and she gripped her cane as if an enemy might appear from thin air.

"Gather all the samples, Dr Virchow," she said, getting a hold of herself with some effort. "Put them all in a consecrated coffer. You have one, don't you?"

"Of course. All peacekeeper stations possess one. Why, Inspector? What beast lays claim to this chain?" His beady eyes slid toward the microscope. "Should we be concerned?"

"Yes," she said. "Very concerned. And, no, I can't tell you any more. Words have power. You understand me?"

"I do, Inspector. I'll do as you ask."

She retrieved her glasses while Virchow started to gather up all the samples he'd collected from Catarine's body. "Keep your results quiet for now, Doctor. I have some further investigating to do. I want to make sure there's something there before I bring anyone else into this."

Virchow was slipping his vials into a small wooden rack, readying them to be placed in the coffer. He paused and lifted a brow in her direction. "Where are you taking your investigation, if I may ask?"

"To Hell, Doctor. Straight to Hell."

It was dark where they'd sent her, and the walls were made of bones, brown with age and covered with a thin film of moisture, as if the long-dead still sweated. Or wept.

She huddled at the center of her "room" – a crypt, in fact, empty of any desiccated corpses, but no less welcoming for it; she tried not to dwell on the fact – keeping as far from the walls as she could. Her head ached from the blow she'd received, but it was just one more discomfort to add to her misery.

During the first few hours of her incarceration, she'd been in hysterics, laughing and weeping simultaneously, uncontrollably, until someone came and doused her with a bucket of ice cold water. Now, huddled on the floor, hunched over her knees, palms pressed flat to the damp earth, face smashed against the back of her hands, Molly felt hysteria rising again. Giggles bubbled up from her empty belly, bursting from between her lips no matter how tightly she held them closed. She didn't want another bucket, but she couldn't help it. The situation was hysterical. Hysterical, hysterical, HYSTERICAL!

A shrill keen leaked from between her teeth. This was it; she'd finally lost it completely–

"*Franke!*"

A whisper. Molly froze, her rising scream lodging in her throat. She strained to listen, holding her breath along with the screams and mad giggles. It wouldn't do to move, not yet, not until she was sure. Movement brought pain. Punishment. This could be another trick.

"Can you hear me?"

Yes. She mouthed the word, still too afraid to speak. No speaking allowed!

There was movement somewhere outside her cell, a shifting, and she heard her name again, spoken with a desperate urgency. Slowly, carefully, she lifted her head. Light from unseen fires flickered on the walls outside her crypt. This prison was an ancient catacomb and hers wasn't the only crypt within it. Someone was talking to her from another of the tombs. A fellow prisoner?

"You can't give in to the despair, Franke," the voice continued. "That's how they get you."

"Cole?" Her voice wavered, certain she was speaking to the dead. "They killed you."

A grunt of laughter. "They tried," he said. He *sounded* very much alive.

"What is this place?" she asked.

"Solitary."

The word held layers, all grim. "What's going to happen to us?"

There was a silence, stretching uncomfortably. "This time? I don't know." He sighed. "I don't think I'm leaving here again. But if you can keep yourself together, you might have a chance."

A chance. Molly crawled closer to the bars sealing her inside the crypt, her knees scraping across ancient brickwork. She grasped the bars and looked out – the first time she'd ever dared to see beyond her crypt. With her face pressed hard against the cold iron, she could see a vast cavern down a short length of tunnel. There, the fiery light was strongest, limning dripping stalactites and rough, rocky walls. "Do you... do you think they'll really let me out of here?"

"I don't know."

"We aren't supposed to be talking!"

A new voice, shrill, farther away than Cole's. A girl's voice.

"Who's there?" Molly demanded in a loud whisper. There were crypts lining the dark tunnel on either side, all barred like cells. So "solitary" wasn't so solitary after all. She waited for an answer, holding her breath.

Finally: "I'm Katy. Katy Bell."

The name was familiar, and Molly realized she knew her. A thin, dark-haired girl from Otherside. The Guardians had accused Katy of wanton behavior, a common accusation against the girls sent to Bright Renewal. "I'm Molly Franke."

"You went to Clem Prep," Katy said, sounding almost resentful. "Your dad is a PK, right?" The resentment turned to eagerness. "Can he help us?"

Bitterness welled up in Molly. "He sent me here."

A low moan echoed down the tunnel. Molly gripped the bars. "Who else is down here?" she demanded of the darkness.

"Jonathan Dell," said another of the prisoners. "I know you from Circle, Molly. You too, Katy, and Cole." He huffed a laugh. "Everyone knows Cole!"

"I know you, Jonny," Cole said. "You're tough."

"Thanks. Lot of good it did me."

"George Quinn," said a new voice, another boy. "This is my second trip to solitary. I tried hard to stay straight, but... well, I just can't manage to avoid pissing off my guardians."

There was a smattering of laughter. Then more voices joined the mix, offering their names and various offenses. At least a dozen kids were locked up in this so-called "solitary."

"Cole, do you know what's going to happen to us?" Molly dared to ask after everyone settled, all a little less lonely and frightened.

A heavy silence answered her. Then Cole spoke: "We'll be chained. Soon, I imagine. Around the pit. You can see it, can't you?"

She nodded – stupidly, since no one could see her. It didn't matter; they all knew he meant the vast flame-lit cavern at the end of the tunnel. That was where the pit awaited them. "Why?" she wondered, her throat thick with fear. "Why chain us down there? We're already prisoners."

"It's... the chains are not... normal chains." He seemed to struggle to find the right words. "They glow. I – I feel weak afterwards. As if I've been drained of all my energy."

"You live, though," Molly said, desperate to find a ray of hope. The fear and dread in his voice was infectious.

"Others don't," he said softly. "Only the strongest walk away from those chains." There was a pause. "I watched them chain Sister Catarine." His voice was small. "They made me... made me watch when... her tongue..." His words choked off. Only Molly knew what he meant about Sister Catarine's tongue, but shocked silence filled the tunnel anyway. Even those who hadn't gone to Clem Prep knew Sister Catarine. Her good works were legendary.

An unbidden image of her favorite teacher blossomed in Molly's head: chained, her mouth gaping, filled with nothing but blood. Gooseflesh shivered across her skin. She squeezed her eyes shut, but it didn't help to erase the picture her mind had conjured.

A few soft sobs broke the stillness, then a low moan of horror.

"She was here," Molly whispered, not even caring if anyone heard her. "All that time. Six days..."

"When I sent C-C-Cassie that letter, I didn't know it would... I didn't want anyone to get hurt. I just wanted out of here."

Cole's despair broke Molly's heart. Her hands tightened on the bars of her cell. "It's not your fault," she said fiercely. "None of this is your fault! Or ours. We – we didn't do anything to deserve this!"

"But why?" Katy Bell asked, her voice quavering. "Why are they doing this? Why *us*?"

Cole's low, bitter laughter drifted down the corridor. "We are all cursed," he said. "My parents called me Goddess-blessed to hide the fact that the Grahams are cursed with demon blood. Have been for generations, probably. It manifests sometimes. A person might stand out, be a little… different. That was me. Mrs H, back at Clem, she targeted me. She told me my blood made me special. But she was the one who said I broke into the school. But I didn't!"

"I believe you," Molly said quickly. "Everything they accused me of was a lie, too."

There was a soft grunt from someone. "Not me," Jonny said, sounding almost proud. "I stole my dad's liquor all the time. His smokes, too. Still, I don't think I deserve all *this!*"

"You don't," said Molly. "*We* don't. I don't care if our blood is cursed. We aren't evil because of it." Sudden outrage filled her. She couldn't help but think of her aunt, ostracized, outcast, abandoned. For what? Her incubus father had been the villain, not Hero. "I *am* demonkin," she declared. "My aunt is half demon, and she brings murderers to justice!" She clung to a desperate hope. Auntie Hero was investigating Sister Catarine's murder; she knew about Cassie's connection to Bright Renewal Academy. The truth would lead her here. "She's an inspector death speaker, the greatest in all the Realm." She wasn't sure about that, but it didn't matter. It sounded impressive. "If anyone can save us, she can."

The whispers resumed, skeptical.

"The demon nun?" A scoff. Was that Jonathan or someone else? "No one's coming to save us. No one cares."

More soft sobs filtered into her crypt. Molly grimaced. "*She* cares."

How do you even know? You don't know her at all!

It didn't matter. Molly shoved her doubts aside. *Aunt Viridian is coming.* She knew this with a sudden, bone-deep conviction. She spoke louder, no longer afraid of reprisals. Let them beat her. Let them freeze her or starve her. She didn't care anymore. She wouldn't stay their helpless pawn.

"My Aunt Hero is powerful, and smart. She'll discover the truth, I know it. They want to paint her as a fiend, but she isn't. She does what's right, no matter what. We just have to hold on until she finds us. I swear to the Goddess and the Branch, she'll come for us!"

The others fell silent, but the undercurrent of despair had lessened. This silence was more contemplative than resigned. Did they believe her? Did she even believe herself? Was she offering them anything but a false hope?

Better than no hope at all.

"Molly's right," Cole said. "We have to stay strong. When they come for us, we have to fight back. Make it as difficult as possible. If we can hold out long enough..."

"She'll come!" Molly said. "I swear it!"

"Then we fight."

CHAPTER THIRTY

The halls of Clementine Preparatory seemed far more ebullient than the last time he'd entered them. Students chatted and laughed, risking punishment for a little heady horseplay. The cloud that had overlain the place before had lifted, replaced by giddy relief. Even the instructors, nuns, priests and the few laymen on the staff smiled easily and shook their heads at the students' liveliness, granting them unusual indulgence.

Keen could hardly believe how quickly the news of Jerry Braun's arrest had traveled, but it really shouldn't have surprised him. Nothing happened in Havenside without everyone knowing about it immediately. Still, it annoyed him. It meant someone among the peacekeepers had leaked the information, most likely hours before Kellan had attacked Jerry in his cell – well before they had even confirmed his guilt.

I still don't believe it. I won't believe it. Ever.

Nevertheless, Jerry Braun was now condemned by the court of public opinion. There was an undercurrent of smug satisfaction beneath the relief, as if finding out the murderer was from notorious Otherside was only to be expected. This fact had restored the order of things. No one from the *good* side of town would ever commit such an atrocious crime.

He caught a few looks as he navigated the halls, broad smiles dissolving when they met his gaze, heads turning, kids scurrying away. His uniform seemed to draw the glances and the smiles, but something changed the moment eyes landed on his face. It wasn't until he passed a trophy case and caught a glimpse of himself did he understand why. His features were screwed into an expression of pure rage, head sunk between hunched shoulders. He didn't walk down the hall; he stalked like a lion hunting prey.

It took effort to lose the scowl from his lips and loosen his posture, but somehow he managed before he arrived at the office of the revered mother. He had with him a list of names he'd discovered among the papers taken from Jerry Braun's apartment. He recognized some of the surnames, families he had known from his time at Clem, all of them donors to Bright Renewal, although they gave freely to Clementine too. All of them had children enrolled at Clem Prep.

He was here to find Abby, but he also wanted to confront Mother Francesca. Was she complicit in what was going on at Bright Renewal? Did she know but didn't care? Was she being deliberately blind or was she truly unaware? He'd argued with Hero about the revered mother so many times. Was he the one who'd been blind?

He rapped sharply on the door and a nun answered after a moment: Sister Agnes. She smiled brightly.

"Oh, DH Keen, how wonderful to see you well," she said, ushering him into the reception room, which was mostly empty but for Agnes's small desk in the corner and a line of chairs against the wall for visitors. "We were all so worried after... well, after the other night."

Keen started; it felt like an eternity had passed since he'd emerged from the catacombs, and her words sent him right back down there. That presence – it had been real, not a figment of his imagination, not some trick Hero had played on him, no matter what Abby or anyone else might think. Looking down at Agnes's sympathetic moue, certainty clicked into place with the sharpness of a stone and he knew that his and Hero's suspicions were accurate. Everything led back to the Academy, and to that malevolent presence.

And everyone was in on it.

But Keen had come prepared. He was full to the brim with every potion of Reveal he could swallow. Nothing from Hell would be able to hide from him. Not this time.

"Yes, well, what we discovered is rather worrying, I would think."

His flat tone made her expression dim. She blinked rapidly

for a moment, then resumed her vapid smiling. "If you could have a seat, DH, I will let the mother know you're here."

He took a seat while she went to the massive oak door separating the waiting room from the mother's sanctum. It wouldn't be the first time Francesca had allowed him inside – she'd even let Hero into her office – but it would be the first time he'd entered armed, so to say.

Agnes tapped the door lightly and was summoned within by a muffled command. She threw him a nervous glance before slipping into the next room, the door closing behind her, a soft click telling him he was locked out. He waited, knee jiggling, hat in one hand, the list in the other.

Finally, after a few endless moments, Agnes emerged from the mother's office looking chastened. She had no smiles for him this time.

"The mother is not to be disturbed," she said, pulling the door shut behind her with marked finality. "Please tell me any business you wish to and I will relay the message to her."

Keen stood up, unsurprised, the list crumpled in his grip. "You should have told us about Jerry Braun," he said. "You cost our investigation days."

She blanched. "Yes, I know. I'm sorry. I – I was afraid."

He frowned and slapped his cap back on his head. "We're not the ones you should fear, Sister. Here, give this to the mother. I want to know if she knows what her generous benefactors have been up to concerning Bright Renewal Academy. Or does the Church only care about missing children from the *good* side of town?"

Tentatively, she reached out to take the list from him. Her eyes roved down it, widening. She had to recognize most of the names. "I – I don't know anything about this," she said, the denial falling a bit flat.

"Yes, but the mother does, doesn't she?"

Her eyes cut to the side. "I'll give her the list, but don't expect her to welcome you back anytime soon. She'll hear no ill words about Bright Renewal Academy. They've saved many a wayward soul, and that's all you need to know." She met his gaze again, her chin trembling only slightly. Darkness swirled in her gaze, a film of oil over her hazel eyes. Keen nearly gasped, but his training helped him conceal his shock.

By now, the potions he'd downed before stepping into Clementine had reached full strength. He could See clearly now, even better than Hero could when she unshielded her eyes, and what he Saw filled him with dread. He cursed his stupidity. Why had it taken him so long to believe Hero, to take her warnings seriously? But... these nuns were part of a sacred order established to fight Pandemonium! The power it would take to corrupt them was mind-boggling.

He looked around the room, shocked and dismayed. Shadows bled down the wall, great gobbets of darkness dripping like thick paint. His breaths grew quicker, but he gave no other sign of his distress. The room was a hotbed of demonic activity, centered on the heavy, closed door leading into the next room. It was a veritable vortex of evil, which reminded him eerily of the dark presence beneath Bright Renewal Academy.

The mother had been avoiding them, obfuscating and refusing to cooperate from day one. No wonder Hero had suspected her so fiercely! They were all under a dark spell, one even more powerful and direct than the Fog blanketing the town. It couldn't have been at full strength until now or Hero would have caught it. While they'd been focused on Bright Renewal, it had sunk its claws deep into Clementine.

Dear Goddess, the power needed for a spell of this magnitude!

The shadows began to move toward him, as if sensing his presence. Demonhunters were often targets of Chaos; he and his kind were their biggest threat.

No, Hero Viridian is. It's why they've targeted her and disrupted her power.

"Don't bother the mother," Keen said, keeping one eye on the encroaching shadows as he backed toward the exit. "I've learned all I need to know. Good day, Sister Agnes."

Her expression turned vicious. Something else stared at him using her eyes. "You cannot win, Oleander Keen, little charity case. You were born a loser, and you will stay a loser. Go back to your precious Citadel. You are done here."

Her lip lifted into an actual snarl and Keen nearly reached for a repellant potion. Instead, he clutched the hilt of his saber and lunged for the door behind him, trying at the same time to keep the black-eyed woman in his sight. Scrabbling at the doorknob, he managed to turn it and pull. He had to look away from her briefly to slip out the doorway, and when he glanced back a final time she was looking at him placidly, as vapid as ever.

With a shudder, Keen slammed the door closed and retreated down the bright hallway. He wanted to flee the place entirely, but now he was even more desperate to see Abigail. His gut screamed at him that she was in great danger. There was no way he would leave her in this place with darkness encroaching on all sides, and he could not let her return to Bright Renewal Academy.

But when Keen found his way to the nurse's office, Abigail was absent.

"Oh, she's been called to Bright Renewal today," the woman who'd replaced her told him brightly, completely oblivious to his ragged emotional state. "Some sort of medical emergency." She lowered her voice to a conspiratorial whisper. "Probably an outbreak of some sort. Most of those children come from terrible homes, you know. Bad hygiene."

He gritted his teeth and held in a sharp retort, although he did manage to mutter, "How compassionate of you," before turning and storming out. Dodging the hordes of students moving from class to class between bells, he made his way out of Clementine, his heart in his throat, expecting to be stopped at any moment, to be attacked. But he was allowed to leave unmolested.

Once outside, he stood in the bright sun, unsure of his next move. He still didn't have an official invitation to Bright Renewal. Would they turn him away at the gate if he showed up unannounced?

His jaw firmed and he fingered the hilt of his saber.

Let them try.

He went home first, to replenish his potion supplies and grab the extra ammunition for his blunderbuss. His mother was in the kitchen when he arrived home with a cup of tea in front of her that she wasn't drinking, just staring at nothing, stiff-backed in her chair. She hadn't even gotten dressed yet from when he'd left that morning.

"Mother," he said rather loudly as he stepped in through the screen door and let it slam shut behind him, just like when he'd been a thoughtless kid.

Her head whipped toward him, a hand flying to her chest. "Oh, Mother Mercy, you frightened me to death, Ollie!"

"Sorry, Mama," he said sheepishly.

His mother dismissed her fright and got down to business, rising from the table to fix more tea. "What's wrong? What's happened now? Do you need anything to eat?"

"I don't have time for tea, Mother. I have an appointment to keep. I was just coming home to grab a few things."

Settling a kettle on the stove, she looked back at him, her brow furrowed, and he noticed how much older she was looking all of a sudden, the weight of years taking a toll out of nowhere. It was hardly surprising given all the recent events. Havenside, and to a lesser extent Otherside, really didn't experience violent crimes. Nothing really bad, anyway. Nothing this shocking. "A letter came this morning," she said softly. "After you left for the stationhouse."

His heart pounded as he looked around for the missive. Usually, his mother kept the mail on the kitchen counter, along with everything else in the free world. It served as a convenient dumping ground. Her haphazard organizing used to drive his father crazy, but his mother insisted the system worked.

By now, Keen knew how to navigate the piles of paperwork and he spotted a crisp, clean envelope – fine stationery reserved for the upper class. He grabbed it up with a sweaty hand and licked his lips. The flowing letters across the front spelled out his name and address in sweeping loops. The paper smelled faintly of lavender.

Maybe I do have my official invitation...

He managed to open it carefully, using the letter opener rather than tearing it. The note inside was a single page, and the handwriting matched the writing on the envelope – Abigail's. Her penmanship had changed very little from their schooldays.

My dearest Oleander,

I am so sorry. Events have transpired and I am forced to seek safety within Bright Renewal Academy. I would give anything to see you, my dear old friend, but I fear it is not safe. The invitation to Bright Renewal stands; I want nothing more than for you to witness firsthand our Good Work here. Unfortunately, the wheels of Fate turn against us. There are People who wish you gone from Havenside. Gone Forever, I fear. You should not try and contact me, not now. I worry it may put you in Danger. I cannot say more, just know I care about you and wish you the greatest Happiness in this world. My dear Oleander, may the Goddess Bless you.

Yours truly,
Abigail

He read the note again. And again. His hands shook and fear rose up from his belly to choke him. Abigail was afraid, seeking asylum within the walls of a nightmare – and the reason why she'd sought safety was far too obvious: Dirk. He had threatened her. Probably for coming to see *him*. The bastard!

He folded the letter and jammed it into his jacket.

"What's it all about, Ollie?" his mother asked quietly. She didn't sound frightened or upset, more resigned than anything. "What does she want?"

"It's nothing," he said. "Just demonhunter business. I – I need to go. I'm sorry I interrupted your tea."

"Oleander." She laid a hand on his arm, her expression more serious than he could ever recall, even when she'd told him his father had died. "Whatever she's told you, don't believe it."

"What? What are you talking about? You don't even know who it's from."

She gave him a look only a mother could manage. "That girl played with your heart when you were a boy like it was some sort of shiny bauble. She started back up without missing a beat, didn't she?"

He blinked. Had she known all along how he had pined for Abigail? He truly thought he'd kept it completely hidden. Now, he felt like a fool. Of course she knew. His mother knew everything about him.

"It's not like that, Mother. She isn't a girl anymore. Maybe she was a bit shallow back in the day, but she was always kind to me."

"Oh, yes, she was a cunning one. Always with that smarmy sweetness, that treacly smile and wide-eyed innocence. 'Who, me? Why, I'd never hurt a fly!'" She spoke in a falsetto and batted her eyelashes at him. "I don't trust her. And you shouldn't either."

"Mother!" he cried and pulled away from her. "You are wrong. Dead wrong. And I don't have time to explain why. Abigail is in danger. I only hope I'm not too late to help her."

His mother's eyes widened, disdain replaced by terror. "What does she want from you, Ollie?"

"She's asked for nothing, Mother," he said coldly. He had to leave. Now. He couldn't waste any more time indulging his mother's suspicions. He bent and gave her a swift, dry kiss on the check. Her skin was icy cold. "I'll be home later. Don't wait up for me."

"Oleander, please..."

He couldn't listen without losing his temper and he had no wish to fight with his mother. "Good day, Mother."

He closed the door on her, feeling guilty but determined. She'd see he was right and would understand eventually.

Later, he would reflect on that moment and wish he'd stayed and listened to her. But he hadn't been ready to admit he was wrong about Abigail Primm, that he'd always been wrong about her.

By the time he did, it was far too late.

CHAPTER THIRTY-ONE

In the end, Hero didn't go straight to Hell. First, she returned to her rental flat for a quick bath and a change of clothes. Once the stink of blood and ash and terror was washed from her skin, she felt more grounded, more able to look at the world again with some objectivity. She was a renowned death speaker, after all, an inspector peacekeeper in service to the Realm. A consummate professional in a fresh cobalt scapular, glittering emerald pants and fitted cream shirt – her chosen uniform, her shield against the world as much as her green-tinted glasses.

Dressed, clean and put together, she went to Jerry Braun's apartment. It wasn't easy; she feared what echoes would remain from Catarine's imprisonment. Ever since she'd communed with Jerry's shade, she'd been reeling. Rarely had a session with the dead left her so off kilter. It was baffling. She'd seen the truth, watched it play out against the flaming backdrop of the Underworld: in the woods where Braun played on her worry and compassion for the missing children; him luring Catarine back to his apartment after he'd kept her far too late for her to return to the convent; Catarine being distraught enough to agree to spend the night on his couch. Despite seeing the scene play out from Braun's perspective, Hero had *felt* Catarine's distress, her fear and worry – and yet she'd also sensed her profound trust in Jerry Braun, her absolute certainty that he was a good and decent man. That trust, of course, had been her downfall.

Experiencing rape and murder from the attacker's perspective was unusual for Hero. Normally, the victim Spoke to her. Bad enough to feel the pain and horror of the murdered;

absolutely intolerable to feel the lust and excitement of the murderer. She'd fled the halls of Hell feeling tainted with a foul stink on her skin, an oiliness she'd never experienced before and feared she would carry with her always.

The worst thing about all of it, besides the details of the actual murder, was that she'd liked Jerry Braun and had thought he was an innocent man being framed. How could she have been so wrong? All her experience, her instincts, her professionalism had utterly failed her.

I didn't see Kellan's potential for violence, either. I saw only a broken man.

In the holding pens, the assault on Jerry Braun had been the first thing she'd seen once she'd opened the Gate. An ambush. A crime of opportunity and passion. The weapon had been in Kellan's cell already, tucked between the springs of his cot – some previous occupant's unfinished project. The priest had made the handle with part of his cassock just in case. Then along came Jerry.

It had taken a deeper dive to discover the truth about Catarine, and Hero almost wished she'd let it lie, had let the shade and its memories be lost in Hell forever. But that wasn't how she operated. Once she caught the whiff of truth, she had to follow it.

But was it the truth? Could Keen be right? Was her ability compromised?

"I would know," she muttered to herself as she climbed the stairs to Jerry's apartment. "I would know!"

And yet here she was. Jerry's place above the Jenny Wren was small and sparsely furnished, a bachelor's flat. He had a small collection of books on a set of pine shelves, but she didn't bother examining the titles. She wasn't here to get to know Jerry Braun; she was here for the truth. She had to know if the crime she'd witnessed had actually happened.

Of course it did. The dead can't lie.

They can't be eaten, either.

Keen's comment echoed in her head. He was right, damn him. Something very powerful had embedded itself in Havenside; she couldn't be sure of anything, even her own vaunted skills.

Doubt. It tasted like ashes, and she fucking *hated* it.

Hero left her ebony cane propped beside the door and stepped into the center of the apartment. A rag rug, rustic and homey, cushioned her booted feet. Two windows looked out on the street and light filtered through them, slanting low from the west. It would be dark soon. The report had mentioned some blood spatter, and she wanted to see it for herself. Ripping out someone's tongue would be a messy business.

With a deep breath, she removed her glasses, tucking them into her pants pocket. From the other, she pulled out a long, braided belt of golden silk: Catarine's cincture, the murder weapon, the device by which Jerry had allegedly held her and drained her of her essence. Despite what she'd seen in the Communion, Hero felt nothing from the simple belt, yet it was a link to Catarine – the only one she had.

The world sharpened in her unfettered vision and she Saw beneath the layers. Flames licked at the corners of the room. Hell beckoned. She opened the Gate, the barest crack. Holding tight to the cincture, she whispered, "Catarine Cisco. I'm here for you."

Visions flashed through her mind. Once again, she was caught in the crime, and once again, she witnessed it from Jerry's perspective. Her skin crawled, but she refused to shy away from the horrific details. The memory of it – as seen through his eyes – was crystal clear. In the woods behind the Jenny Wren, she watched him plead with Catarine, the sister wrapped in a cloak, her habit concealed. She wasn't wearing a veil, either. Her blond hair gleamed even in the darkness. There was no fear on her face, only concern, along with a touch of righteous anger revealed in the spots of color high on her cheeks.

Hero blinked and suddenly the two were climbing the stairs to Jerry's apartment, just as she had done a moment ago. He ambushed her the moment they entered his flat. A flash of struggling figures, the pale length of a knotted cincture. Her heart thudded. Catarine went down hard, and then he was on her, one hand going for her throat, the other covering her mouth, smothering her screams. His body pinning hers to the floor, knees knocking her thighs apart effortlessly. Each move meant to control her, to dominate her. Like he raped and murdered women all the time.

A shudder racked Hero and bile rose in her throat, but she didn't turn away from the memories. She had to See everything.

After he'd sated his lust, he'd bound her using her own cincture, imbued with demonic power from the Aerial demon he'd supposedly worshipped. It had left marks around Sister Catarine's neck like the links of a chain.

Time sped up and days passed, Catarine growing weaker and weaker, slumped over her knees on the dirty floor. Jerry tormented her, taking delight in her suffering. He'd ripped out her tongue in an orgiastic moment of pure evil. Blood fanned down her bare breasts, splattered on the floor.

Hero stared at the spot on the floor, Seeing the blood spray in her memory. She stared until her eyes ached, calling as much of Hell to her aid as she dared.

No blood marked the varnished floorboards. Not a shadow or a trace was embedded in the wood. She felt a surge of emotion. The Goddess Herself couldn't hide blood spatter from Hero Viridian. The knowledge erupted in her head, drawing her sharply back to reality. A gasp broke from her lips. How could she have been so stupid? Even after Speaking with the dead, the evidence had to match. It *always* matched.

Except this time.

"Fuck me," she muttered, drawing up those visions again but this time with a more calculating eye. She forced herself to replay the events, watching every excruciating moment, registering every hideous detail. It made her skin crawl, made her want to vomit, but she forced herself to focus, to be detached as Jerry Braun raped the helpless sister, collared her with her own cincture, tortured and drained her, ripped out her tongue. Again and again and again.

The visions began to shimmer, to grow frayed at the edges. She clutched the cincture to ground herself in reality. The feel of it, the silken softness, belied what evil it had wrought. She could see it digging into Catarine's neck. It was knotted in places; it could have left marks like chain links...

No. The word growled through her head and she stumbled back to reality. Her gaze swept the room. She Saw traces of Jerry, going about his life, eating and sleeping and entertaining friends. He'd had a lot of friends.

None of them had noticed a kidnapped nun in the corner of his living room?

She saw nothing of Catarine but the barest echo of her sleeping on his couch. That was real. All the other memories – the visions of Jerry's terrible crime – were as fake as a smile on a Celestial nun.

Outrage made her breathless. Keen had been right. Something had muddled her mind, blocked her abilities, planted a lie! Her rage rivaled the fires of Hell and flames erupted around her, silent and heatless. If there was anything of the truth left behind here, she would find it. A feeling, a vibe, a–

A glimmer.

A thread of gold in the corner of her eye.

Hero didn't move, yet she focused all her senses on that glimmer. Her heart leapt. Could it be a shade, still lingering between the Spheres?

No. It was more like the shade of a shade. A residue left behind. Vaguely human-shaped. Woman-shaped.

Hero held her breath, not wanting to disrupt any potential Communion. The golden thread solidified, became real for a breath, became Sister Catarine tiptoeing through Jerry's apartment in the dark, the windows starting to gray with dawn, gathering her slippers and cloak before slipping out the door.

"She left sometime before dawn."

Jerry had been telling the truth. Relief washed through Hero. She kept the cincture tight in one hand, her feet grounded on that homey rag rug, and pursued the elusive glimmer through the paths of the Underworld, traveling the realm between the living and the dead. This was her domain and she trod it easily.

The sky grew lighter, heading toward morning, yet the sun also rolled toward the horizon, a fat, bright ball mellowing into late afternoon. She kept an awareness of the true time; she didn't know what Keen was up to, but she feared he might go to Bright Renewal without her. She pushed those worries aside. She couldn't lose this pale shadow of their victim. Obviously, Sister Catarine had not been kept or killed in Jerry Braun's apartment.

Then where? And who had done the killing?

The shade slipped through the woods behind the Jenny Wren, flickering in and out of the trees. Catarine had known the way.

Soon, the trees thinned and Hero found herself on the outskirts of a vast green expanse which she recognized as Our Lady of the Meadows Cemetery, where her "father" had been buried, along with all her human ancestors. Beyond the carefully manicured grass dotted with shining white tombstones shaded by majestic oaks stood the walls of Clementine Preparatory.

As the sun broke the horizon – and also shone brightly from the west – Hero spotted the glimmer of Catarine slip through a small gate set in the tall brick wall: a secret entrance. Hero cursed herself; she should have guessed. She'd lived in an abbey for several years and knew that the novices always found a way to sneak in and out unnoticed.

With a careful shifting of her steps and a deeper dip into the Underworld, she found herself within the walls of the cloisters. Catarine was on the back steps leading up to her apartment on the second floor. It made no sense; she'd come back to her apartment that last night? Her roommate had to have seen her!

But no. Catarine paused on the bottom step. Her head turned to look over her shoulder, then the shade of a shade hurried across the grounds, through the small cemetery attached to the cloister's chapel. She went straight to the mausoleum where Hero and Keen had entered the catacombs a lifetime ago.

And all at once, Hero knew. She remembered that stench of demons and evil permeating those tunnels. This was where Catarine had been lured: the catacombs.

She raced toward the mausoleum. This was the scene of the crime. She was sure of it! This time, she would plumb the catacombs at full power and crack that damnable shield if it killed her.

Hero jerked and the world snapped back in place around her, and she found herself swaying on Jerry's rug, the windows blazing with afternoon sun. The Gate to the Underworld had slammed shut abruptly – not by accident; someone had broken her hold on it. Something brushed her neck with a silky caress that sent a shiver down to her toes and back again.

Leave, sweet child...

She spun round. There was no one behind her. Certainly not Silvanus, her wayward father. Still, she had recognized his voice. Another warning.

"Not yet, Father," she murmured, her lips lifting from her teeth. "I still have a job to do."

For the first time in days, she felt a savage hope. She knew where to hunt now. And her powers hadn't failed her; she'd found a way to see through the planted Communion. Whatever eldritch power lurked beneath Havenside, it would have to do better than that to stop her.

Hero grabbed up her cane, tapped the brim of her cap with it and set off to find her partner.

CHAPTER THIRTY-TWO

It had taken Keen longer than he'd liked to requisition a horse from the station's stables, and by the time he'd mounted up he'd been champing at the bit as badly as the animal. The quick-stepping roan gelding was responsive to his commands and carried him swiftly from the brick streets of Havenside, over the iron rails into Otherside and along the country road to Bright Renewal Academy. This time, there was an actual sign marking the distance to the mysterious school – innocuous, perfectly ordinary, yet it made his hackles rise and he kept his saber loose in its scabbard. His mother's warning rang in his head, along with the image of Hero's face pinched with suspicion and doubt.

Neither of them know Abigail like I do. They're wrong about her, I swear to the Goddess.

But Demonhunter First Rank Oleander Keen was no fool. He eased his horse into a ground-eating trot between the rows of towering pines, planted as windbreaks along the road, keeping one eye on the rutted track and the other on the trees. Cropland stretched away beyond the pines, open land providing little cover to potential assailants.

It was only when he reached the tangled woods at the base of the knoll upon which Bright Renewal perched, the sun dipping behind the looming hill and casting the road in deep shadow, that he slowed his horse to a walk, every sense alert. His heart thudded in his chest as he scanned the dark woods. If anyone was going to ambush him, it would be here.

His anxiety spiked, sensing danger lurking near, though he had no fear for himself; it was for Abigail that his heart pounded so fiercely. She'd taken refuge within Bright Renewal. Had her husband threatened her? Had he hurt her? The possibilities whirled in his head, each more disturbing than the last. If Dirk had laid a single finger on her, he would kill the man and be justified in doing so. It was his duty as a peacekeeper!

As keyed up as he was, and as afraid as he was for Abby, it didn't stop his mind from conjuring the sweetest scenario: him, the hero, sweeping the grateful damsel into his arms, her tears of relief and joy falling upon his shoulder, her arms leaping about his neck. Finally, she would be free to confess her true feelings for him, feelings she'd hidden all these years due to the difference in their stations, their upbringing. None of it would matter anymore. Not after he saved her from a brutish husband–

An explosion of black wings erupted from a tangle of oak trees, rust-colored leaves twirling through the air as a murder of crows took flight. His horse startled, dipping and prancing into a sidestep, forcing him to focus on his seat. The roan whinnied and snorted, tossing its head, and he soothed it as best he could, cursing his inattentiveness. So much for the conquering hero. He couldn't even keep his own horse on a steady path. The birds wheeled overhead, shrieking, wings flapping. What had them so riled?

He'd lifted his eyes to the crows for only a moment, but when he returned his attention to the road, there were men blocking his path – only four of them. He could handle four. He reined to a halt, not making a move for his weapon. Not yet.

The men wore cloaks, their faces shadowed by deep hoods, but he felt their eyes on him, full of malevolence. All of them carried clubs, long and knobbed at one end. He caught the glitter of glass embedded in the weapons. They all had knives in their belts, too. Highwaymen?

He dismissed the idea. These were not mere robbers. Not even the most despicable highwayman would accost a peacekeeper. Keen kept his horse's nose pointed forward, prepared to charge through them if need be.

"For your own good, you will let me pass," he said calmly, his hand drifting toward his blunderbuss. "I have business at Bright Renewal Academy. Do not prove a hindrance."

Silence answered him. A breeze picked up, sending swirling leaves across the road, tugging at their cloaks. He gripped the pommel of his weapon, prepared to draw. The figure standing just in front of the others seemed familiar to him, and he peered at the shadowed face of the apparent leader.

"I see you, Hollander!" His calm vanished and anger sizzled through him. "You won't stop me!"

Dirk threw back his hood. His expression was pained. "Turn back, Keen," he said, and there was a shocking tremble in his voice. "For the Goddess's sake, turn back now!"

"Not until I know she's safe. Stand aside!"

Dirk grimaced. "I cannot. Go back the way you came, Keen!"

A deep anger filled him, along with a delicious satisfaction. He'd waited so long for this chance. Punching Dirk in the nose the other night had only given him a taste. "Very well, Hollander. You asked for it!"

Keen's heels dug into his horse's flanks as he went for his saber, ignoring his blunderbuss – he'd give Dirk a fighting chance, at least. He brandished the gleaming blade as the beast leapt forward, expecting the men to scramble out of the way, hoping Dirk would be stupid enough to engage him–

The men scattered – no, they *flowed*, with unearthly speed, parting like water before his charge.

He swung his sword through shadows and reined in hard, putting his horse on its heels. The well-trained roan spun in a tight circle, lashing out with its forelegs, meeting nothing but empty air. He searched for his opponents wildly, trying to keep sight of all four men, now at the edges of the road, he at their center. How had they moved so fast?

They are not men.

Something landed on the rump of his horse. Shockingly, it was one of the shadow-men, dropping on him like a spider. The roan squealed and shivered, attempting to buck the man off. Keen swung an elbow, twisting wildly to knock away his assailant, and the others swarmed him in a blur and he was dragged from his saddle. He landed hard on the packed-earth road, breath slammed from him, the reins still in his fist. His horse reared, whinnying in terror, and jerked the leather from his grip. He rolled, hitting a tangle of legs while the thunder of his horse's hooves juddered through the ground as it ran away.

Fists pummeled him. A club rose above him, shards of glass catching the evening light. He managed to meet the weapon with his saber, saving his head from being staved in. The men closed on him, surrounding him, only Dirk showing his face. The others remained concealed in their hoods, but strange light gleamed from where their eyes should be, pinpoints of eerie red.

Keen threw the club back and slashed at his attackers to drive them away, at least enough to gain his feet again. His sword met resistance, slicing deep, but it didn't slow the rain of blows or cause the men to back away. A club smashed against his shoulder and his sword arm went numb. He barely managed to keep a grip on the basket hilt. He scrambled for a potion with his other hand, but someone grabbed his arm and wrenched it to the side.

"You should have run," Dirk said in a forlorn voice, his fist driving into Keen's belly. The air left him in a rush. Someone stepped on his saber, pinning it to the ground. Knees landed hard on his arms and Dirk's bulk crushed his legs, trapping him on his back like a bug.

They raised their clubs, moving as if one mind controlled them, eerily silent. Keen braced himself for the blows, struggling uselessly. How had the tide turned so quickly? How had he fallen for such an obvious trap? He'd ridden into a nest of demons!

Abigail, I'm sorry.

He expected that to be his last thought, but then a hideous howling erupted from the woods and his attackers paused, heads turning as a pale figure streaked from the trees, lightning quick. He saw fangs, silver in the shadows, hooked claws and long, sinewy limbs – a nightmare beast, its eyes lit by fire.

And then it was ripping through the gang of cloaked men as if they were paper dolls, tearing through bellies and throats. For all their inhuman speed, their shadowy quickness, Keen's attackers seemed as defenseless as babes before this onslaught.

Suddenly he was free, the weight on his arms vanishing in a wash of black blood. He rolled, sending Dirk tumbling. Somehow, his nemesis had avoided the absolute destruction meted out to his accomplices, scrambling back and rising, club in hand, face pale. Keen grabbed up his saber and advanced furiously. Dirk parried his first vicious slashes, moving with remarkable speed, but Keen gritted his teeth, keeping Dirk's mournful visage in his sight. Something was enhancing his skills; the Dirk he knew had never moved with such grace or swiftness.

Sounds floated to his ears as he fought with his childhood bully: growls, hideous crunches, shrill, inhuman screaming... then silence, but for the thud of steel against wooden club.

"Please," his opponent said, eyes wide, sweat coating his pale face even as he fended off Keen's saber with preternatural ease. "Please... help me."

"*Help* you?" Keen gasped, trying again to get past his guard, to no avail. "I'll kill you!"

"Keen! Stop!"

The voice was an inhuman growl, low and rough and almost at his ear. He didn't dare turn around, but he knew it was Hero standing behind him. Was she *mad*? She'd torn those men to shreds! Why should he stop? Dirk deserved to die, deserved to pay for everything he'd ever done to him! Hatred flooded him and he went at Dirk in a wild flurry of blows. Finally, the man wavered, the club dipping at just the wrong moment. With a cry of triumph, Keen ran him through.

"Keen!" Hero's angry shriek echoed down the empty road, but it was too late. Panting, muscles trembling with fatigue, Keen stepped back from his opponent, letting the man slide off his saber to land face down on the road.

Finally, he dared to face his partner. Whatever beastly aspect she'd used to destroy his attackers had vanished and she stood on the road, a tall, silver-crowned figure in a scapular and harem pants. Her swirling eyes of flame met his. "What have you done?" she said.

"He attacked me! What else was I to do?" Her approbation seemed wildly hypocritical considering the body parts strewn about her and the blood dripping from her hands. Scowling, he waved his saber at the evidence. "You just slaughtered three men!"

She didn't spare the dead even a glance. "They were demons," she said. "If you hadn't been so distracted by your *alleged* damsel in distress, you would have known that. Instead, you rode right into a trap and failed to properly assess your danger. He–" she stabbed a long finger at Dirk "–was human. A human under a powerful spell. Didn't you hear him begging for help? Goddess damn you, Keen!"

Shock turned his belly to ice. "I – he–" The words wouldn't form. He glanced back at Dirk's body, lying in the dirt, and felt a rising nausea. Was she right? Had he just murdered a bespelled human? Had his jealousy and hatred and need for revenge prevented him from seeing it?

Hero strode toward him, tall and indomitable. "There's only one way to find out for sure," she said angrily, and took him by the arm with fingers made of steel. "Prepare yourself."

"For what?"

Her swirling eyes pinned him and a roaring filled his ears. "For Hell, Demonhunter."

The halls of the Underworld spun away from them in rippling corridors, appearing and disappearing seemingly at random amidst great walls of flame. Shades flickered in and out of existence, going about their business, seeking the proper Sphere. Keen thought they were moving, but it was hard to be sure; nothing made sense. Hell *was* Chaos. He could feel his pounding heart and Hero's hand clamped on his arm but little else. Did he even exist anymore? Could a living person, a human man, delve the worlds of the dead and survive?

"As long as we maintain contact, you will be fine," Hero assured him, which did little to put him at ease. She faced him with eyes no longer aflame. Here, they were normal, if crimson irises could be called normal. Somehow, it was comforting to look into them. In this insane place, she seemed the least insane thing. Her grip on his arm suddenly felt like a lifeline.

"Don't let go," he said, an embarrassing quaver in his voice.

She smiled a very human smile. "You aren't really here, Keen. Not physically, just spiritually. Nevertheless," she went on, her smile turning less human, "don't try and wander off or you might get lost for all eternity."

He had no intention of wandering anywhere in this place. "Why did you bring me here?"

"To find the truth before it can be meddled with," she said cryptically. The rippling flames became streams, giving a sense of movement. "I will Commune with Hollander's shade before anything can get to him. You were right, Keen: Jerry's shade lied to me. I think the whole thing was planned – Jerry's arrest, forcing a confession, having him murdered in his cell – all to plant those visions in my head. The dead can't lie to me. Why would I ever question the Communion? But I was wrong. And now I know Catarine wasn't held in Braun's apartment or killed there."

He clung to the sound of her voice, going limp in her grasp as he was led along like a toddler. "Where was she killed?" His voice was faint, echoing, but she heard him.

"In the catacombs," she said grimly. "Someone lured her there after she'd returned from Jerry's. She went willingly, which tells me she knew who it was. I believe she was taken through the tunnels to where that presence lurks beneath Bright Renewal."

Keen would have shuddered if he'd been able to feel his body. "How did you discover this?"

"I went to Braun's place after Dr Virchow confirmed the substance left behind on Catarine's skin wasn't the residue of some common demon of Pandemonium. I had to see for myself whether *any* of those visions made sense. Lo and behold, there wasn't a trace of blood at the supposed crime scene, but I did find something of Catarine Cisco: a shade of a shade, barely a glimmer. It's all that's left of her, the poor thing. I chased it to the catacombs."

"She must have had a strong spirit," Keen pointed out. It was unbearably tragic. All Sister Catarine had wanted to do was protect her students.

"There he is," Hero announced, and they slowed to a stop, the flames re-forming around them again in dense, impenetrable walls. He felt dizzy even though he couldn't really feel his head. His vision dimmed and then sharpened. A dark form stood in front of them, man-shaped, big and broad-shouldered.

"Dirk Hollander," she said, an undeniable authority in her voice.

The shade turned or morphed or... something, and then Keen was looking into the eyes of his dead tormentor. Dirk's eyes were soft and full of confusion. Did he even know he was dead? Keen had no idea how any of this worked.

"Watch," Hero whispered to him, "and learn. I will begin the Communion."

Images flooded his vision as Dirk's life played out on the walls of flame. His death came first, his fear and panic overwhelming as he fought for his life. Silent screams for help echoed in his thoughts even as he parried and sought to kill his opponent – Oleander Keen. His desperation was an oily stink. Then there was pain, shock and an upwelling of relief as his torment finally ended.

Then came visions of that torment. Dirk stretched on a rack, hot pokers searing his skin. Laughter mixed with his screams, high and feminine and oddly familiar. Dirk on his knees, begging for forgiveness, groveling, weeping. A slim hand settling on his head, patting him as if he were a good dog.

Keen wanted to look away but couldn't. He couldn't even close his eyes since he had no eyes in this place.

The images changed, became distorted. He was seeing the world from Dirk's perspective now. The man was in a vast cavern with flame-lit rock walls and dripping stalactites above a deep, dark pit carved from solid stone. A woman knelt at the edge of the pit, nude body white against the darkness. Around her slim neck was a pale, gleaming collar of something like stone. A translucent chain led from it, dropping over the edge of the pit into nothingness. Energy pulsed through the bright links. A second woman, dressed in a long, white robe edged in crimson lace, approached the kneeling victim.

Again, Keen desperately wanted to look away, but Hero had him in a ruthless hold, controlling what he was seeing. So he had to watch as Abigail Hollander wrenched open Catarine's mouth, fingers digging cruelly into her chin, and took hold of her tongue. Catarine didn't even struggle as Abby's hand worked deeper, twisting and wrenching, until with a fierce jerk she yanked the tongue loose in a spray of blood. A wash of crimson poured from the nun's mouth, sluicing down her bare chest, only to rise in a sparkling wave and stick to the chain like metal filings against a magnet, then vanish. Consumed.

Devourer.

Keen would have thrown up if he'd been physically present. As it stood, all he could feel was a psychic pain so awful he thought he might die.

Abigail stepped back, leaving Catarine slumped over her knees, then turned and handed the raw bit of flesh to her husband. Keen now watched from Dirk's perspective, his beefy hand accepting the gift and tucking it into a jacket pocket – a damning piece of evidence, to keep the man in line.

Keen's attention returned to the motionless nun. Was Catarine dead now, or dying? The pulse of energy flowing down the spectral chains began to slow, a final heartbeat slowing... slowing...

"Here is where her shade was eaten," Hero whispered in his mind. "It took six days to drain her life, but only a moment to consume her soul. A Celestial nun is a tasty snack for whatever Abigail is summoning here. Although why she sacrificed her best friend, I do not know."

"This – this cannot be," he said. Could Hero's power even be trusted anymore? "How do you know this isn't another trick?"

"I don't," she admitted, her spectral voice making the flames around them shimmer. The vast cavern vanished, along with the horrible images of Abigail and the dead nun. Only the fiery walls of Hell remained and a single shade – a sad, slumped, diminished essence of a once-living man. "But enough of me believes it. Believes him."

Dirk stared back at them mournfully. Sorrow and regret radiated from the spirit. His mouth didn't open, but suddenly Keen heard his voice: "I always hated you, Keen. I didn't like how Abby treated you like her little pet. I thought you were beneath her attention, you know? A shitty little kid from Otherside." The shade's head turned to glance behind it as if sensing something they could not. A ripple shivered through it. "But I was wrong. I was blind to her faults, her manipulations. She wanted me to hate you; she encouraged it. I was so twisted up, so angry and jealous all the time, I didn't even care when she revealed that she and her family were beholden to a creature beyond nightmare. By then, I was under her complete control. I did what she asked. Always." The shade began to thin, to grow transparent, but Keen felt Dirk's gaze upon him. "I see so clearly now, but it's too late for me. Don't make the same mistake I did. She has sold her soul for immortality, wealth and influence. She and her cabal would rather see the entire world consumed than give up a hair of their power. They think they can control this Devourer, give it scraps and offerings in exchange for wealth and influence. But it is evil. It is pure destruction. And it will come for us all."

The shade wavered again, more strongly this time, rippling like a flag caught in a strong wind. "Catarine knew Abby's secret, so... she had to die."

In a sudden upwelling of darkness, the shade vanished, only the echo of a scream remaining. Whatever was left of Dirk Hollander was gone, sucked into a void. Keen felt himself being drawn in as well, but Hero let out a hiss of defiance, tightened her grip on his arm and dragged him from the grasp of oblivion.

The next instant, he was on his knees on the dirt road, the sky dark above them, the trees rustling in a stiff breeze. The chilly air wrapped around him, making him shiver. He replayed the final thrust of his saber through Dirk, felt the resistance of flesh against the sharp blade, heard the sickening scrape of metal upon bone. Bile rose in his throat. Dirk had been begging for his help–

Keen bent forward and vomited, his partner silent above him. But he felt her judgment, as unforgiving as the Goddess Herself.

CHAPTER THIRTY-THREE

It took a few hours to sort out the incident on the road to the Academy. By the time the PKs arrived, along with Chief Dewey, in a towering rage that she and Keen were anywhere near the vaunted institution, the dead demon-men had faded into dust, leaving only one human body at the scene. Luckily, the case for self-defense seemed clear cut, especially when coupled with the testimony of Hero – an unimpeachable witness, at least in this regard.

"Someone will have to tell his wife," one of the PK's muttered as he collected Dirk's weapon and other evidence scattered about his corpse.

His partner – the uniform who'd shown Jerry Braun to his cell – smirked at his comment. "I don't think she'll be crying many tears over this one," she said, circling the body and taking notes. "Hollander's always been a useless sack."

Hero caught Keen's wince at the woman's callous remark and bit back a sigh. This one was going to stick with him for a long time. He'd killed an innocent man, blinded by his hatred and his longing for the dream girl from his past. She'd known Abigail was going to be trouble for Keen and fiercely regretted not pushing the point. But feelings were a messy business. Every peacekeeper thought they knew how to be objective, that they were better at it than any civilian, but every person was driven by their biases, their emotions. Even PKs. Even demonhunters.

Even death speakers.

"You two are *off* this case," Dewey hissed at her. His dark eyes were sunken, his hair spiky and unwashed. She had no doubt the Fog spell was taking a toll on him. He was a good PK, after all. Deep inside, in some corner of his mind, he had to know he was being manipulated. And there wasn't a damn thing he could do to stop it.

I will stop it.

Hero gave Dewey a casual shrug. "Understood, Chief. I could use a little break after all of this. A real mess, am I right?"

Dewey grimaced, his anger easing at her words. Maybe he'd expected another fight? Well, she was done fighting him.

"It is a mess, but Dirk has been a troublemaker for a while now," Dewey said. "No one will be too shocked. How many people watched him try and pull a gun on Keen? It'll blow over, I've no doubt." He peered at her in the light of a dozen torches as his people processed the scene. "I do appreciate your help, Inspector, but we can handle things from here. The train to New Savage leaves tomorrow afternoon. I suggest you be on it."

She nodded, struggling to keep her face neutral. "What about my partner?" she wondered. "Will you send him back to the Citadel?"

"After this? Count on it." He scowled at the stunned demonhunter sitting at the side of the road, Hero's jacket around his shoulders, before turning back to her. "Take him home, Inspector. I'll tell him tomorrow that his services are no longer needed here." He grunted. "Weren't any demons for him to hunt here after all, were there?"

Hero grinned, a most disconcerting expression given Dewey's wan reaction. "Only me, Chief. Only me."

After that, she and Keen went to his mother's house at the end of Sycamore street, arriving in the dead of night, dirty and exhausted. Keen's mother had been waiting up, of course – a good mother, not like hers at all. She took one look at them and ushered them inside, produced basins of steaming water, soap and towels, and allowed them the chance to wash before she planted them at her kitchen table for hot soup and tea. The tea was sweet and creamy with milk, just the way she liked it. Hero drank it down gratefully and didn't even need to ask before Ma Keen refilled her cup. The soup was delicious, too, if a bit on the thin side. Nevertheless, after the events on the road, Hero needed sustenance. She felt her strength return with every slurp of the salty broth. Good – she was going to need it.

A bit of shriveled flesh sat in one of her jacket pockets, a great weight for such a small thing. There was a fine piece of crimson-and-cream ribbon around it, as if it were some souvenir, and Hero recognized that it matched the ribbons Abigail Hollander preferred to use to hold back her shiny black hair.

"Thank you, Mama," Keen said again, the only words he'd managed to put together in the last few hours. He sat wrapped in a quilt, his hair tousled and a shadow of stubble on his cheeks, sipping at his tea but ignoring the soup, eyes wide and staring. Lost. She wanted to shake him. This was not the time to fall apart, not with what they still had to do.

"It's no trouble, Boo," his mother replied. She was bustling about the kitchen, but stopped long enough to kiss the top of his head and give his shoulder a gentle squeeze. The simple gesture made Hero scowl. It was hard to watch these two together sometimes. The love they showed was an agonizing display of all she'd missed.

No hugs for me. Just fists and hot pokers.

The older woman must have noticed her expression for she stopped and looked at Hero, whose eyes were now once again safely shielded behind her tinted glasses. "Do you need more soup, Inspector?" She smiled kindly. She had never shown fear towards her, not for a minute. "No one goes hungry in this house."

That drew a soft snort from her son. Hero's lips quirked, glad that he wasn't entirely catatonic. "Yes, Mrs Keen. Please and thank you."

"Here now, none of that. Anyone who breaks bread at my table can call me by my given name. I'm Ruth to you, dear."

"Then you may call me Hero, Ruth." It felt odd to speak her name. It was so ordinary, whereas *Mother* held such power.

"All right. Hero. What a nice name. Have more soup."

Another steaming ladleful appeared in her bowl. Ruth hummed as she returned the pot to the stove, a soothing backdrop to Hero's slurping. Across from her, finally, Keen reached for his own spoon. His hand was steady, at least, though that stunned look in his eyes hadn't faded. There was a creaking of iron hinges behind her as Ruth checked the firebox.

"This will stay hot for a while," she said, latching it closed once more. She straightened and turned to them, drawing her robe a little tighter. "Could you keep an eye on it? I don't mean to be rude, but it's well past time I sought my bed."

"We can manage, Mama," Keen told her, summoning a small smile for her. It would have been reassuring but for his washed-out appearance. "I'll see you in the morning."

She nodded, face placid as she placed a hand on his head, but her eyes were sharp with worry. "Everything will be all right, my sweet."

He looked up at her, a little boy in a man's body. "I should have listened to you. About–"

"Shh. It doesn't matter." She patted him affectionately, then crossed her arms against an imaginary chill and gave Hero a final glance, pointed and knowing, communicating all her fear and worry for Keen and all her trust in Hero – a vast, undeserved faith that a half-demon disgraced nun would take care of her only son. Hero returned her nod, a rock lodged in her throat. Ruth left them alone.

"What do we do now?" Keen asked after a long moment of silence. The stillness of night had settled around them, the creaking of the house and the rattle of wind against the windows the only disturbances.

It was a deceptive peace, Hero knew. An eldritch presence lurked beneath Havenside, a demon of no known class or breed, a foe older than bones, strong enough to eat the dead. The town lay in its influence, the fog of its existence muddling minds and hearts. She and Keen had to assume every lever of power was turned against them now. They were on their own.

She turned her teacup on the tabletop, deep in thought. She'd been considering their next move since she'd discovered the truth about Catarine's disappearance – the catacombs, the shield, the pit. She had to destroy the shield before they could get to the pit. Hopefully that would break the hold that thing had over the town. Maybe they would even get some help from their fellow peacekeepers.

We can't expect that. We have to assume we're alone here.

"We return to the catacombs," Hero replied at last. "And this time, we break that fucking shield."

Keen's face scrunched up, his spoon clutched in one hand like he might wield it as a weapon. "How can we fight that… that thing? We don't even know what it is, only that it's ancient and powerful."

"I didn't say it would be easy."

He looked aside. "Is there any chance she could she be under a spell? Like Dirk was?"

She gritted her teeth, biting back harsh words. "You heard him. This didn't just happen. She's been involved from the start, for years. This is the work of generations, Demonhunter. The entire family is most likely involved. Corrupted. Humans making deals with demons is nothing new."

He blanched, his lips bent in a tight grimace.

"You have to let her go, Keen."

A shudder racked him, but then his expression cleared and he threw the quilt back from his shoulders. "I never had her to begin with," he said sharply, rising from the table. He rifled through a cabinet and returned with a bottle of gin, setting it on the table between them. "Ma always keeps it on hand," he said. "It was my pop's favorite too, apparently, so I guess I inherited something from him after all. Besides my ears, of course."

The bitterness in his voice surprised her. So Keen had his own dysfunctional parent, too? Good to know. She tossed back the last of her tea and extended her cup expectantly. He filled it, then his own.

"We could take our findings to Dewey," he suggested. "The… evidence." The tongue. "Your word means something, right? You said so yourself. So write a new report, sign it as an official death speaker."

She shook her head. "What good would it do? It would only lead to more prevarication, more delay, and my reputation would be in tatters if I contradicted myself yet again. Besides, we're running out of time. I believe those missing children are being used to raise this Devourer. Their demon blood is a source of great energy, even more than a battle nun of the Shield." She sipped her gin, grimacing at the sharp taste of juniper. It definitely wasn't her drink of choice, but the burn felt good, the heat dissolving into her weary muscles. Dear Goddess, this fight was going to take everything she had.

But she had no choice. *They* had no choice.

"They have my niece, Keen," she said quietly, staring into her cup. "And all she did to deserve it was try and help us."

He said nothing, merely drank down his gin and refilled his cup. Then: "Can we do it alone? We have no idea what awaits us behind the doors of that Academy, or who. How many people are willing acolytes of this Devourer?"

She shrugged. "Half the town? Who knows? Humans are paper dolls strung in my way."

"Paper." He scoffed. "Flesh and blood and bone and will. They could have an army in there, demons and humans and only the Goddess knows what."

She tapped her empty cup and he poured her another drink. "*We* are an army, Demonhunter." She lifted an eyebrow and let her glasses slip down her narrow nose. "I have fought darkness my entire life. And you? You are trained for precisely this. I know what demonhunters can do firsthand."

"Even squirrels?" A hint of a smile.

She kicked back in her chair, balancing on two legs. "You've gotten better."

His cheeks grew bright and he gave her a rueful smile. "So. An army of two. I guess that'll have to be enough."

"Right." The gin was starting to go down easy – a little too easy. She put a hand over her cup when he went to refill it. "I need to return to my flat and pack up, make it look like I'm catching that train tomorrow. Dewey is sending you back to the Citadel, too, by the way. Very soon, I suspect."

He frowned but didn't seem particularly surprised. "With Jerry dead and the two of us gone, the whole town will think this case is tied up in a neat little bow. Nothing will convince them otherwise, and this place will be doomed."

"Unless we break the spell," she countered. "Look, I think I can crack the shield." She made a stabbing gesture. "With a needle to the dragon's heart. I believe the fog will be lifted when we destroy it. We have no other option, either way. I have to get inside, and I can't as long as the shield exists." She tossed back the last of her gin and gestured at him with the empty teacup. "Get some sleep, Oleander. I'll be back as soon as I can."

He stood when she rose from her seat, polishing off his drink in a careless toss down his gullet. "I can't let you go alone," he said, voice a little strangled by the hasty slug of booze.

"We should stick together from now on. Our enemies might think we've given up, but we can't be certain of it. We're safer together."

Hero blinked. Depending on someone was an alien concept for a lone wolf like her. She'd been alone her entire life, even when surrounded by people. Even those other unfortunates cursed with demon blood avoided her.

"I'm only going to my flat," she protested, but he was already snatching up his blunderbuss and saber – laid out on the kitchen counter, carefully cleaned and oiled by his mother.

"I'll help you pack," he said sternly, his voice brooking no argument. When she raised a brow pointedly, he added, "I have to make sure you organize all our files correctly. You are abysmal at paperwork, Inspector."

She almost tapped the brim of her hat, but then remembered she'd lost it saving him. "All right. Just try and keep up, DH Keen."

"Ah, Viridian, I do hate it when you say that."

CHAPTER THIRTY-FOUR

It took longer than expected to pack up their files, though a lot less time to gather Hero's possessions; her diminished wardrobe was easily stuffed into a duffel along with a spare cane and jaunty hat. Still, dawn was a good two hours away when they took to the alleys on the return trip to Otherside. Somehow, today had bled into tomorrow with no end in sight. Keen felt exhaustion creeping into his limbs beneath the adrenaline still coursing through him. He was keyed up for a fight and so far all they'd done was sneak around town.

They put the tongue in a small box – it was their best piece of evidence, after all, and the remains of a Celestial nun – and added it to the files detailing Virchow's findings, the location of the substances locked in the consecrated coffer at the precinct, and an accusation of murder against Abigail Hollander. All this they gathered into a fat satchel Keen looped over his shoulder. Hero had a plan for what to do with it, but she hadn't filled him in on it yet, merely given him a sly grin when he asked for details.

"Trust me, Keen, it's a good idea," she said. "And I'm sure she'll go along with it."

"Who?" he'd demanded, and had gotten only another sly look for his trouble.

They'd skirted Clementine Prep on the way back to Otherside, so Keen could show her the growing shadows engulfing the place. Hero had been unsurprised, and not a little gratified at the sight.

"Clementine is under the See of the Celestial Order of the Shield. Traditionally, they are a battle order in the fight against

Pandemonium. If I were planning to summon an ancient demon from the depths of Hell, I'd compromise my biggest threat, too. Either they allowed the corruption inside this place – called it, even – or they are innocent victims. We will know once the shield is gone."

"How will we know?"

"By seeing which side they choose."

That hadn't exactly soothed Keen. "How do we know they'll even pick a side? Why not stay safe inside their walls?"

"Oh, you poor, naive demonhunter. When we kick this particular hornets' nest, only the dead will be able to avoid choosing sides."

With that pleasant thought, they'd slunk through the silent town like a pair of alley cats, avoiding any possible witnesses, until they finally crossed the tracks into Otherside. All appeared peaceful in the autumn chill. Shivering, Keen readjusted the satchel over his shoulder and hurried to stay abreast of his partner. It probably hadn't been necessary to go with her, but he'd take anything to keep himself distracted, to keep him from feeling the shudder of his saber against his palm as he stabbed it into Dirk, from hearing the sickening scrape of metal against bone and from seeing Abigail's ecstatic expression as she ripped out Catarine's tongue–

Keen shuddered, his mind shying away from the memory – Dirk's memory, a vision of the past.

Or a lie. Like Jerry's false memories. How can Hero even know the difference anymore? We don't even understand what we're up against.

Devourer. Darkness manifested. Rising...

He couldn't believe Abigail was a willing participant in this evil, regardless of what he'd made Hero think. As long as he had even an inkling of doubt, he couldn't completely condemn Abigail Primm, the girl he'd loved with a hopeless devotion.

But even his own mother didn't trust her. Was he a blind fool? Or was he the only one who saw clearly?

Keep your focus. His hand tightened on the strap of the satchel as a stiff wind kicked down the street and tugged at his clothes. *No matter what you may face.*

"I'm ready," he murmured softly, too low for even Hero's sharp ears.

And he really, truly believed that he – Demonhunter First Rank Oleander Keen – was ready for anything. He'd gone up against entire nests of demons, sent the denizens of Pandemonium back into that terrible place broken and denied.

Certainly, he'd made a few mistakes here and there, but didn't everyone in his line of work? Every good peacekeeper in the Realm made missteps, false assumptions and slip-ups. Even the famed death speaker Hero Viridian made mistakes. Keen wasn't any different, any better, but he was confident, self-assured – even now, with an innocent man's death on his hands. Even with the doubt about Abigail wriggling in his heart, he was ready to face anything.

But DH Keen was not ready for what came next: the smell of smoke as they crossed into Otherside, or the flames leaping skyward over the shingled roofs. He wasn't ready for the wild stab of fear through his gut, the sudden certainty that it was *his* house on fire. A paralyzing terror stopped him dead in the street.

"No," was the only word he could summon – a horrified, hollow sound – before he cast aside the satchel and broke into a run.

By the time he reached the end of Sycamore Street, there were flames shooting from the bedroom windows on the second floor. He lunged up the front steps, barely noticing the searing heat as he grasped the brass door handle and hauled open the door–

–only to be driven back by a wall of flame. He flung an arm across his face and stumbled back down the steps.

"Mama!" he screamed. He inhaled for another scream and choked on burning air. Someone grabbed his arm, dragging him away from the conflagration. "No," he tried to say, but it was a croak. "My mother – my mother is in there."

"I know."

Viridian. Keen blinked ash and tears from his eyes, trying to focus on his partner. She was blurred, and not only from the smoke; cold blue flames surrounded her, a nimbus of rippling light. She turned her eyes on him, the crimson flames unshielded, now swirling with cobalt streaks. "Stay. Here."

Then she was gone, bounding up the stairs and through the flames without hesitation. Keen tried to follow, ignoring her order, but again the heat drove him back. He wheezed, any exposed skin stinging, the tears on his cheeks evaporating as fast as they fell. His heart felt lodged in his throat and his chest was tight. It hurt to breathe yet he wanted to scream. His Mama. She couldn't... She had to be all right!

The sound of shattering glass and cracking wood drifted from the house. Somewhere inside, something heavy crashed to the ground. The roar of the flames peaked. Another crash – this time from above – and a dark, misshapen figure burst from an upper-story window, dragging glass and splinters with them as they leapt in a graceful arc to the ground. A blanket-wrapped bundle was clutched huddled in its arms, smoke rising from the patched cloth.

Keen dashed to his partner, his mind blank with panic. He grabbed at the quilt, taking the burden from Hero. A weak cough emerged from the blanket, along with his mother, soot-stained and disheveled. He clasped her to him, too thankful to form words, shaky with relief. His mother could only cough helplessly, though she did manage to pat his back.

Behind her, Hero had returned to normal, the strange blue flames having dissipated. Her narrow face was streaked with ash and soot had darkened her silver hair. A hard frown bent her face and rage sparkled in her fiery eyes. She spun back around to stare at the burning house, shoulders quivering.

"No fair," she said, voice harsh. "That's my trick! They go too far!"

The clanging of alarm bells sounded in the distance. *Finally, the bastards.* Keen grimaced, drawing his mother into the crook of his arm, and stared at their burning house, now fully engulfed at this point. Whoever had done this had waited until they were certain the fire was out of control before sounding an alarm. They'd thought to catch him asleep in his bed. Maybe they'd even expected Inspector Viridian to be inside the house, too. He snorted. Imagine, trying to kill a demon with fire!

"We have to get out of here," he said, counting the seconds in his head, imagining PK fire volunteers loading into their wagons. "They'll take us in for questioning. Maybe even blame us for this, somehow."

Hero didn't argue. She turned to them and reached out. "Give her to me," she ordered.

"I'm strong enough to carry my own mother, Viridian!"

"I don't need carrying," his mother said, watching her home of thirty years burn with a blank face. "My friend Vera's out of town," she said, sounding a bit vague, but her words made Hero smile.

"Very good, Ruth. Very good. Lead the way, if you please…"

CHAPTER THIRTY-FIVE

News of the fire at Demonhunter Keen's childhood home spread through Havenside as rapidly as the flames which had devoured the old clapboard house on Sycamore Street. The wreckage was too hot to comb through after the flames were doused, but the conclusion that both mother and son were lost was easily reached. Speculation on the cause of the tragedy ran the usual route: a terrible accident, a stove left unattended, a lamp kicked over in the night.

Or *had* it been an accident? Maybe that half-demon partner of his had snapped and set the fire? For fun or malice, who knew? It wouldn't have been the first fire she'd started...

But there would be no chance to question the dead man's partner. Witnesses observed the half-demon inspector – her usual blasphemous get-up covered by a heavy cloak against the cold – getting on the afternoon train out of Havenside, carrying her ever-present cane and a heavy leather satchel with an official seal, no doubt containing the report from her successfully solved case. No one cared enough to follow up on the sighting, glad to see the demon spawn's backside. Every soul in Havenside breathed a sigh of relief knowing she was gone from their good town. If she had started the fire that killed Oleander Keen, well, then let New Savage City deal with her.

It took Keen going undercover to hear all the rumors. He'd refused to let his mother go to the train station alone, so he'd tailed her while dressed as a laborer, face dirty with coal dust, knit cap pulled over his distinctive ears and his broad shoulders hunched inside a ratty jacket. None of the other travelers on the platform – most dressed in fine traveling clothes with valets tending to their luggage – looked twice at him, or lowered their voices while they spread gossip, or hid their curious glances at the tall, cloaked figure in harem pants striding to the first-class car. He learned everything they'd needed to know in a matter of moments.

"She's safely on her way to your captain," Keen reported to his partner once he'd returned to his mother's friend Vera's house, now serving as their temporary base of operations. It was remarkably similar to the house they'd just watched burn to the ground but for the furniture, wall coverings and other personal touches, and the constant stream of cats slipping in and out of a small flap cut into the kitchen door. Hero didn't mind them; cats had a good instinct for supernatural threats and these were particularly calm and relaxed. The house was truly safe – for now, at least – but they wouldn't be staying for long.

Keen, on the other hand, looked at the cats askance, keeping a good distance from them while he nursed a swollen nose and red eyes.

"If we're lucky, Culpepper will send the calvary, but we can't count on it," Hero said, stroking a friendly tuxedo lying belly-up on the kitchen table. "He's a stickler for procedure. By the time he collects the necessary paperwork, it might be too late. With the two of us out of the picture, I imagine our enemies will be confident enough to make their move and complete the ritual."

Keen shooed a hissing gray tabby from a kitchen chair before taking a seat across from her. "With *you* out of the picture," he clarified bitterly.

"Don't sell yourself short, Demonhunter. They did burn down your house."

That drew a rueful snort from him, followed by a spectacular sneeze. "What are we waiting for?" he asked, wiping at his nose with his handkerchief and eyeballing the tuxedo as Hero gave the cat's belly another vigorous rub, releasing great puffs of fur. He frowned, staring as the bits of fluff danced in the sunlight streaming through the window above the porcelain sink. Suddenly, his face contorted and he looked like a true demon with the dirt on his cheeks and the fire in his eyes. "They burned my *fucking* house down!"

Hero understood his rage. A similar anger burned in her belly. She liked Ruth Keen.

"Use it as motivation," she told him, giving her new best friend a boop on his pink nose. His purrs became deafening, and he peered at her with clear green eyes, pupils mere slits in the bright light. Caught by their beauty, she couldn't look away...

Suddenly, every cat in the house began to yowl but for the beast beneath her hand. His black-and-white fur took on a strange sheen, an inner light which captivated Hero. The other cats fled, bolting for the little door-within-a-door in a panic, knocking objects off shelves, tipping over a plant stand and sending a vase of wilted flowers crashing to the floor. Keen cursed and leapt to his feet, his chair skidding back. "What the *devil?*" he cried, his saber appearing in his hand.

Hero blinked. She hadn't even realized Keen was carrying his weapon; he was still in his laborer's clothing. The saber wouldn't do him any good, anyway, not against this particular "devil" uncurling on the tabletop. She hoped Keen had a few potions handy, preferably some sort of powerful repellant, for this creature was a vile pest she'd love to be rid of once and for all.

The air grew thick. Keen's movements slowed, his eyebrows comically high as his saber swung toward the apparition as unhurried as cold molasses. Hero shook herself, knocking away the spell of Sloth like the shedding of a coat.

"Hi, Pop," Hero said to the naked demon sprawled belly-up on the kitchen table. She tossed a checkered napkin over his exposed genitals, sending a silent apology to Vera. "Who let you out of your hellhole?"

"I go where I please, sweet child of mine." Her father gathered himself and jumped off the table, landing gracefully on his clawed feet. The napkin fluttered gently to the floor, and he kicked it away before turning to face her with a fanged smile – disturbingly similar to her own. She didn't react, merely kicked back in her chair, feigning disinterest, yet her heart was racing. What was he doing here? Why now, when she was about to face untold evil? Did he think this might be her last day on earth? Was he slavering in anticipation?

She narrowed her eyes and brought her nerves under control. Let him think it. It made no difference to her. The bastard was just here to rattle her; she was sure of it. How was he mixed up in all of this?

Silvanus sauntered over to Keen, circling the frozen demonhunter, a long finger with an even longer nail tapping at his pointed chin. "Interesting allies, daughter. A demonhunter and an old woman."

She bristled. He knew about Ruth Keen. Had he hurt her? "I don't know what you mean."

He cast her a chiding look. "You might have fooled a few blind humans, but I know you like I know myself. You cannot fool a demon with a human in disguise. Such pointless subterfuge. Take one step toward the Devourer's lair and evil will descend upon you like a swarm of wasps." Now, he stabbed his long finger at her, hissing, "Sting, sting, sting, little spawn. Not all the demonhunters in the Realm will be able to save you then." He flicked Keen's earlobe. "Least of all this scrawny specimen."

It was hard to jump to her partner's defense while he stood frozen by her father's foul magic. Never mind that she'd been caught unawares, too; she could still move, at least. "I'm not worried," she said blithely. "Let them come. I'll be ready. It won't be the first summoning I've disrupted, after all. An angry demon and its silly human worshippers are child's play."

"Oh, you stupid, silly girl. You'd be correct, I suppose, if this were merely a demon Rising from Pandemonium. Even your pet demonhunter could handle it. But this is far beyond anything you've dealt with before, ignorant daughter." His tresses, black as tar, brushed the floor as he wandered the room. "I'm giving you a warning. A chance. All you have to do is take it and leave." He frowned at her. "Why should you care what happens to Havenside?"

She shrugged. "There's the simple matter of a few dozen children being drained of their life force to attend to, actually. Havenside can go to Hell, for all I care, but I won't let those kids be sacrificed to... what did you call it? The Devourer?" She instantly regretted speaking its name, but she gave another dismissive shrug to hide the fact. "A demon with an outsized ego, no doubt, to pick such a grandiose moniker. It's embarrassing."

Her father shook his head, no longer smiling. "Such an arrogant fool. And a sucker. Look what happened the last time you took it upon yourself to rescue human children – on the run, hiding in sewers and catacombs, ten years in a deep, cold pit – and for what? Did you get a single thank-you from any of those girls?"

"Not a one," she admitted, grinning. "More like ear-shattering screams and witness statements against me."

"And what do you expect this time? A death sentence, perhaps? Or *decades* on the run, hiding?" In a blink, he was back beside Keen, nearly engulfing him with his twisting, oozing figure. "Maybe you'll be hunted by your little friend here? If he survives, of course."

Reluctantly, Hero's gaze settled on Keen. His eyes were blank, trapped in time. What was he seeing? Just her, sitting in her chair, most likely. Or nothing at all. Could he hear their conversation?

"It's so nice of you to worry about me," she said. "I suppose there's a first time for everything."

"I worry about losing my prize, nothing more. I have no wish to see my favorite progeny consumed by the Devourer of Souls." He scoffed, waving a long, elegant hand tipped with black talons.

Devourer of Souls. An ominous name. Sudden doubt filled her. What awaited her beneath Bright Renewal Academy? Something older than demons, and far stronger.

"Even I know to keep my distance when *it* emerges," Silvanus went on. "How could someone of my own blood not understand the danger? The Devourer consumes *everything* once it achieves Ascension, human and demon alike. If you dare get close to it, enter its sphere, you may gladly dance to your own destruction. The humans stupid and arrogant enough to think they could harness its power will be devoured as well. This town and the great enclave of humanity to the north will be consumed before its hunger is satisfied. And then it will sit like a great fat spider and rule over the ashes for eons."

His tone had grown more and more portentous while his form had taken on a hideous aspect, all bulging muscle, claws and fangs, his silky raven black hair writhing snakelike about his narrow skull. He loomed over her threateningly, as he had done so many other times in her life. She had stopped fearing him after his initial visit when she was still a child, quickly coming to realize that her father was all bark and no bite.

Abruptly, Silvanus clapped his hands and returned to his usual beautiful self. One didn't seduce hundreds of human women by appearing ugly. "So," he announced brightly. "You merely have to travel a few hundred miles, hmm, west, preferably, before the beast breaks its bonds and rises. Leave these humans to their fate and save yourself, daughter."

Hero's mind raced. A few hundred miles? So it wasn't the unstoppable force he was intimating. He'd been warning her off since the start. Why? She could come to only one conclusion: her father wanted her away from it – which meant she had a chance to kill it, or at least stop it.

It hasn't yet reached Ascension. There's still time to keep it locked in Pandemonium.

The one thing any good demon loved was chaos, and unleashing such a powerful creature on this plane would provide it in spades. Her father's lust for women was only outshone by his lust for destruction – which begged the question: What did he have to gain from the Devourer's Ascension?

"What comes in the wake of this Devourer, dear old Dad?" she asked. "I have a feeling you're leaving out something important, yes?"

He shrugged. "Death. Destruction. A little Hell on Earth perhaps." A disingenuous grin split his face. "It won't matter to you, though. You'll be free and halfway across the Realm with no one left to chase after you."

No one left ...

The Citadel in New Savage. Goddess. He hoped to see the source of all the demonhunters of the Realm sucked into oblivion. As much as she was loath to admit it, without demonhunters, there would be no one left to stand against Pandemonium. The Realm would become a demonic playground.

And she would be free.

Free to do as she pleased. Free to watch humanity suffer.

He took her silence to mean she was considering his proposal. Joy practically radiated from him, his skin shimmering with excitement. "Think of it, daughter! This could be *our* Realm – here on Earth, not in the halls of Chaos! Demonkin would rule unopposed. Humans would be our slaves!"

She stood, snatching up her cane from where it leaned against the table. It was time to end this farce. "Tempting, Father." Slowly, she drew her blade and watched his grin turn to a frown. He didn't step back – she couldn't really hurt him; he was too smart to appear before her in his corporeal form, no matter how it might look from the outside. "But you forgot one thing."

His frown deepened and his eyes blazed. "What have I *forgotten*?"

"I am not just an inspector death speaker disgraced ex-nun arsonist half-demon." She struck her sword, blade flat, against the table and it leapt back up, the steel vibrating in her hand. A metallic ringing filled the room, rippling the very air, the ripples striking Keen's frozen form, stuck in mid-swing. It broke her father's spell and her partner stumbled forward, his saber cutting through empty air. He grabbed at the table, nearly losing his balance, but he was shaking his head, coming around.

Her father hissed in alarm, backpedaling. Hero pointed her blade at him, filled with righteous fury. "I am half HUMAN!"

The next instant, a vial landed at Silvanus' feet and exploded with a pop. Yellow smoke billowed up from the faded linoleum, engulfing the wide-eyed incubus. His shriek was music to her ears. He vanished in an ear-breaking *clap*–

–just as Keen's saber split the air where he'd been standing.

"Mother Mercy, what the fuck was that?" Keen spun on her, panting, eyes wild. How much had he seen or heard? Anything at all? "It was a cat a moment ago!"

Hero returned her sword to its ebony sheath. Irritatingly, her hands were shaking. "*That* was a liar and a rapist and a trickster. *That* was my father."

Keen seemed at a loss for words, staring at her wide-eyed. Finally, he shook himself. "Well?" he demanded, a bit shrilly. "What did he want?"

"To warn me off, to try and get me to run." Filled with a sudden surge of energy, she went to grab her jacket from the coat rack in the corner. "He wants the Devourer to win. He wants Pandemonium to get a toehold on *this* plane. He wants to see all the men and women like you destroyed."

"Like me? You mean demonhunters?" he asked, looking shocked. "Is that really a possibility?"

"I don't know, not for certain, but we can't ignore the chance that it might be." She threw on her coat and fixed him with a hard stare. "Gird yourself, Keen. We're going into the belly of the beast, and we're going *now.*"

CHAPTER THIRTY-SIX

Waiting was interminable in solitary. The gray-coated guards tending to them made conversation difficult, but they tried to keep each other's hopes up when they could manage to talk. Molly had no idea how long she'd been in her cell. Time dragged, the constant fear draining her of strength, but she clung to the fierce hope that her aunt was coming. It was all she had in this dark, grim place.

And then, something changed. There was a shift in the mood. An excitement. It bubbled up through the ground, through the bone walls. It drove Molly to her feet in a panic. Nothing that brought joy to the guards of this place could be a good thing. Murmurs drifted to her from the other cells and she pressed her face against the bars of her own. Her fellows were doing the same, staring out at each other in trepidation.

"What's happening?" asked Katy in a trembling voice.

The bars were cold on Molly's face as she tried to look down the tunnel. She could hear voices, indistinct but high with excitement. Foreboding gripped her. The moment she'd been dreading had come. Why else would there be such excitement animating this terrible place? They were going to be fed to the pit, drained of their life force until nothing remained.

The flames illuminating the rocks beyond the end of the hallway surged suddenly and silhouetted several shadowy figures. Not their guards this time, but people in long, dark robes. They moved with purpose, going to the cell doors one at a time. She heard the clank of metal against metal, the click of turning keys and squeak of hinges. A clamor rose among the prisoners. Fear shivered through her at the cries of fear and panic as her fellow captives were pulled from their cells.

"No! NO!"

"Where are you taking me? Let me go!"

"Please, please, let me go…"

The voices blended, overlapped. Screeches drowned out words. Her heart slamming, Molly watched as her friends were dragged down the hall toward the flames by these new, implacable tormentors as they fought and struggled. For a moment, she feared they would be tossed into the great pit, but then they disappeared from view, pulled in different directions once they left the tunnel.

The robed figures moved down the line of cells. Were they going to take everyone? It certainly seemed like it. She backed away when one of them reached her cell, ready to fight. Cole's angry voice reached her, and then the thud of clubs against flesh. She steeled herself; she couldn't be less brave than him, though she winced at the sounds of violence.

The cloaked person unlocking her cell was Mrs Hollander. Molly was not glad to see her; Clementine's beloved head nurse had put her here, after all. The woman's bright eyes peered from beneath her cowl, her lips set in a hard line. "You weren't to be included in this sacrifice," she said bitterly, as if it was all Molly's fault for being in a cell. "I feel a… kinship to you, after all. But I know Cassie told you things she shouldn't have. So. I just wanted you somewhere out of the way, until that witch was gone."

"That witch?" Auntie Hero?

"But you backed me into a corner with your antics," she continued. "No one could understand why I was protecting you."

"Protecting me?" Molly dared to exclaim, outraged. "By sending me to Bright Renewal? You may as well have thrown me to a pack of wolves!"

Mrs Hollander made a face. "See? That mouth again. I see her in you, and I don't like it. But family is family. I would have spared you." She swung open the cell door. "If you'd only submitted like a good girl then this wouldn't have been necessary. But you had to resist, you had to fight me, just like Cassie. And now you pay the consequences."

Cassie had *fought* her? "You chased her off the tower," she said faintly.

Mrs Hollander sniffed contemptuously and entered the cell. Molly stood with her hands locked into fists, feet spread for balance. Abigail gave her a withering glance. "None of that," she cautioned. "Cole Graham learned the hard way, and he'll be unconscious for most of the ceremony, I can guarantee. Do you want to be knocked senseless too?" She kept her distance, lifting a slim hand to gesture for one of the guards down the hall.

Molly gritted her teeth, crouching, ready to fight, but the man who entered her cell was tall and burly with hands big enough to crush her skull. Still, she backed up and lifted her elbows.

"Is this the last sight you wish to see in this world, Miss Franke?" Abigail asked blithely, studying her nails as she leaned against the bars. "Because you can join the Ascension with open eyes and bear witness to glory, or you can go to the Underworld now without ceremony." Her eyes were sharp and cold. "Your choice."

Her words did what weeks of Bright Renewal Academy's special brand of discipline and brainwashing had failed to do. Finally, after holding fast for so long, Molly Franke broke. The surge of strength brought about by fear left her in a rush. She dropped her fists and let the giant guard take her by the arm and drag her from her cell.

As she was led down the tunnel toward that vast pit of flames and darkness, she lost all hope. If her aunt was coming to save her, then where was she? Molly was all alone.

She submitted to her guard, obeying his instructions to kneel on the hard ground at the rim of the vast pit. Not far from her, Cole Graham knelt as well, not unconscious as Abigail had claimed, but dazed and swaying. The others were staked out around the pit's edge. Chains made of a strange, translucent material lay coiled on the ground, gleaming eerily. One end of each coiled chain disappeared over the edge of the pit, the other end attached to a collar made of the same strange material. Her friends already had collars around their necks, she noticed as the guard snapped one around hers, too. Immediately, a soft glow erupted from the links and rings and she felt a rush of weakness. The chains pulsed to match the beating of her heart, rapid and fraught. Soon, she knew with a terrible certainty, the pulse would grow slower and slower.

And, eventually, cease.

They braved the drowning shadows at Clementine Preparatory to reach the entrance to the catacombs. Despite the darkness – perhaps visible only to him and Hero – the school was on high alert. Nuns of the Shield patrolled the grounds in their battle habits – similar to Hero's ensemble of choice, though their black-linen scapulars were covered by hauberks that fell to their knees. Leather bandoliers of blessed water hung across their chests and short, curved swords were tucked into golden cinctures. They looked ready for a fight.

Unfortunately, Oleander suspected they were prepared to fight him and his partner, not supernatural foes. Perhaps the human PKs had been fooled by their subterfuge, but Hero's father appeared to have given them accurate information: Their demonic enemy knew she was still in Havenside.

There were nuns stationed outside the mausoleum armed with staves – one of the Order's preferred weapons – though Keen was encouraged to see how awkwardly the women held their weapons. The Shield Order here at Clementine Prep didn't see much action, tucked as they were within peaceful Havenside.

The perfect target for hungry demons, Keen decided as he watched the women stalk like testy housecats through their domain. Who would suspect an entire order of battle nuns to be under the influence of Pandemonium?

"How do we deal with them?" Keen whispered to his partner as they crouched at the gate into the cemetery behind the cloisters, the same gate through which Catarine had passed undetected on the last night she was seen alive. No one could have guessed that she'd been abducted while on consecrated ground, steps from her own door.

Keen pressed back into the shadows as a pair of nuns strolled past them, thinking that they made terrible guards; he could have tapped one with his saber if he so chose. It was an unfair thought. Most of the patrolling women were novitiates, barely older than the oldest students at Clem and half trained at best.

"I can't kill a nun," he said fiercely, trying to imagine running one of them through and failing.

Hero made a little sound of disagreement.

"They're bespelled, remember?" he said.

"Some of them." She grimaced. "Most of them, I suppose. Fine. No killing." She removed her glasses and tucked them into a pocket. With a firm grip on her cane, she turned to him, smiling tightly. "We might have to knock a few heads, though."

Keen adjusted his bandolier and sash – thoroughly replenished with every last potion in his possession. Fortunately, he'd lost very few of them thanks to his mother's foresight. He'd changed back into his uniform, still reeking of smoke and stained with ash, but he was a demonhunter and this was official demonhunter business. His saber was sharp and ready along with his blunderbuss and extra ammunition. The two weapons would serve well when they reached their main target, but neither would help him right now. Queasily, he supposed his fists would have to serve in this instance.

As for Hero, she had her sword cane and that was all. Her demon blood was her best weapon. She wore a long duster over her scapular and billowing pants, but she'd given her last remaining hat to Keen's mother. Her eyes spun hypnotically in the deepening dusk. "Are you ready, Demonhunter? Surprise is our best weapon."

"Ready, Inspector."

They waited for another patrol to pass, then rushed the mausoleum, Hero in the lead, surrounded by a nimbus of flame, a raw red-and-orange conflagration. She bounded over tombstones and crashed through a line of low boxwood hedges while Keen followed in her wake, hoping he wouldn't have to engage at all. The two women guarding the entrance met the attack gamely, eyes wide but bodies moving confidently as they lifted their staves in a defensive posture. One opened her mouth to scream for help, and Hero laid her out with a tap of her ebony cane even as she blocked the other's staff with a raised forearm. With impossible speed, Hero shifted her stance and tore the weapon from the stunned nun's grip. A quick conk on the head, and the erstwhile guard joined her companion on the crushed-stone pathway.

"Two down," Hero said, leaping over the two unconscious women to mount the steps into the mausoleum. Keen followed, feeling somewhat useless if relieved not to have had to punch a nun. Yet.

By now, the alarm had been raised and bells rang out across the campus – a call to arms. Inside the mausoleum, Keen helped Hero drag the great bronze doors shut behind them, regretting that there was no way to seal it from the inside – but then, who would need to lock themselves *inside* a crypt? Keen glanced toward the inky stairwell leading down into the catacombs. Maybe they could block it? Knock down the walls at the entrance or something?

A wave of heat made him stumble backward toward the stairwell. He lifted an arm to shield his face against a sudden swelling of flame as, before his astonished eyes, Hero seemed to grow. Fire swirled around her, through her, in and out of her like a twisting serpent. Each time the flames passed through her flesh, she seemed a little larger, a little more terrifying. His mouth grew dry and his eyes hurt from staring, but inside his heart swelled and his confidence soared. What could stand against *this*?

Hero had drawn her slim sword from its ebony sheath and flames now rode the length of it. With careful deliberation, she set the tip against the seam where the doors joined and sparks flew as she drew the sword slowly downward. Where it moved, the bronze glowed red and started to soften and melt.

Keen swallowed. Sweat stood out on his forehead and he backed as far away from his partner as he could.

When she stepped back from the doors, the flames died to a flicker, yet the door still glowed. "There," she said. "Now we're sealed inside. No more nuns to worry us."

Fantastic. The dark well of the catacombs drew Keen's gaze. Only one way out now...

He turned to his partner. "After you, Inspector."

Their journey through the catacombs passed in a blur of endless bones, the darkness broken only by Hero's bright nimbus. Keen kept on her heels; he had no torch this time, but he knew where they were going. They both did.

Keen had hoped never to return to this dreary underground abode of the dead, but he should have known better. Ever since he'd stumbled upon the eldritch evil lurking beneath Bright Renewal Academy, this confrontation had been inevitable. One thing he knew for certain, however: this time, he would not face it alone. There was no way in the whole of the Underworld he would go ahead without Hero Viridian at his side. Not if he hoped to survive.

"We're here," his partner announced when they found themselves at the end of a wide, decrepit corridor, standing at the threshold of another stairwell leading down into blackness. Keen recognized the place and shivered as he remembered fighting for his life on the broken clay bricks, strong hands yanking him from the jaws of doom, a whirlwind of fire and claws and howling monsters. How had he ever let Abigail seed doubt in his mind about his own partner? Shame filled him.

Beside him, Hero dragged her sword across the air, leaving a trail of sparks behind it. She hissed, sounding somehow both eager and appalled. The shield remained, but she had gotten through it once. She would do so again.

"I'm about to stir up some trouble," she said, shedding her long duster and tucking the ebony half of her cane through the golden braided cincture around her waist. She looked of her order more than she ever had – girded for battle – but he wasn't about to tell her that. She was an *ex*-nun, after all.

"You have to watch my back." She said it like she wasn't quite sure if he would, and he was struck by deep shame once more. She'd saved his life that night and a few times since. Saved his mother's life, too.

"Inspector. Hero." He spoke softly but earnestly. This might be his last chance to make things right. "I will watch your back. I swear it. You can trust me with your life, Hero Viridian. As I trust you with mine."

Hero blinked, her flaming eyes spinning languidly. She'd been shaking out her arms, preparing herself for whatever she was going to attempt, but she paused to stare at him. "Are we giving speeches, DH Keen?" she asked, sounding amused. "Should I say something inspiring?"

"I – uh – if you want." This wasn't the reaction he'd expected. Flustered, he adjusted his saber and stared at his feet. He deserved her disdain.

"Eh, maybe later." She raised her sword. Again, flames wreathed it – wreathed her – and one of her flaming eyes darkened in a wink. "I trust you, too. Oleander Keen." Her voice deepened, grew hard. "Are you ready, Demonhunter?"

He snapped to attention. "Ready, Inspector Death Speaker!"

She pressed the tip of her burning sword against the invisible shield. A needle to a dragon's heart.

CHAPTER THIRTY-SEVEN

A low hum rattled the rocky ground beneath Molly's knees and rose through her with a palpable force she felt in her bones. Beyond the edge of the pit, a lurid light appeared, pierced by shadowy tentacles emerging from below, seeking. Her heart galloped and as fear flooded her she forgot her stiff limbs, her cuts and bruises. She pulled back as far as her chain would allow, her head twisting to the side. Not far from her, Cole struggled against his own bonds, clutching at the chain as if he thought to yank it loose. Useless.

"What's happening?" she cried, voice shrill with terror.

Cole's gaze rolled toward her, white-edged. The chain-leash holding him gleamed and pulsed. His bruises were dark against his white face. He shook his head and muttered, "Devourer."

Molly's attention shifted back to the pit, to the rising tentacles. The hum deepened and turned to a staccato huffing – a low, alien laughter. Sudden weakness made her limbs shake. Her arms dropped to her sides and she sagged on her numb knees. The fear remained, but it grew distant. A strange, fatalistic calm settled over her. She observed her approaching doom dispassionately.

"Our lord comes," said a sweet, familiar voice full of religious fervor. "At long last."

Molly roused herself, blinking. The voice had seemed to speak right into her ear, but there was no one near her but Cole to her left and a weeping Katy to her right, and neither of them had spoken. She peered across the vast pit and saw figures emerging from the dark mouth of the tunnel leading from the crypts, gathering at the edge of the pit. They wore gossamer robes, pale in the garish glow, that did little to conceal the bodies of the men and women wearing them. She recognized the squat outline of her most hated teacher and the burly build of a particularly vicious guardian. At the center of the group, standing a little apart, her robe edged in scarlet lace, was Abigail Hollander.

"Our wait has been a long one," Abigail said, her voice soft and intense. It filled the cavern, echoing from the rocks. "Generations have prepared the way to our ultimate triumph. Countless of my blood have sacrificed to bring us here. Rejoice, faithful! The Ascension is at hand."

The robed figures stepped forward to the very edge of the pit, faces aglow with fervor.

"Yours is a necessary sacrifice." Abigail's voice slithered in Molly's ears, and nearby Cole jerked and let out a strangled howl. Abigail was speaking to them all directly. "You have fed our great lord, you and many others like you – a greater destiny than any of you deserve." Her tone turned wicked and cruel. "The wayward, the broken, the useless. Your blood is cursed in the world above, but here it is blessed. It feeds our master well. In death, you will serve a higher purpose. Take pride in that!"

The robed figures began to move, a solemn procession along the edge of the pit, leaving Abigail alone. Each of them stopped beside a chained child, and each held a long, curved blade in their hands, the metal glinting in the rippling light. Molly's breath quickened. Panic broke through her catatonia. She huddled on the hard rocks, on her hands and knees, watching a guardian approach her with an ecstatic smile on his lips. He gazed at her with something close to kindness.

All she could see was the gleaming knife in his hand. She knew what he and his associates intended to do. Drained of life, and then of blood...

Dear Goddess, save me!

A strange, low shriek reverberated throughout the cavern. The shadows heaved, tentacles lashing wildly. The guardian looming over her suddenly stiffened, along with all the others, their attention drawn to the tunnel mouth. As one, they swarmed toward it just as a tall figure emerged, wielding some kind of long-barreled weapon.

There was a deafening blast and one of the guardians dropped to lie writhing on the rocks. The newcomer, dressed in a peacekeeper's uniform, did something to his weapon with his free hand and fired again, taking out two more guardians with one shot, all in the span of a few seconds.

The remaining guardians ran full tilt against the shooter, blades raised, but he held his ground, plucking small vials from the bandolier across his chest and throwing one after the other at them. Explosions and smoke rose from the rocks, enveloping his attackers. They fell, screaming, skin peeling and blackening. Molly wanted to look away, but she couldn't move.

It was over as soon as it had begun, leaving only the man and Abigail Hollander alone on the ledge. The black-haired woman had remained close to the pit, her back to her "great lord." The man took a step toward her, his gun pointed at the ground, his free hand held high. A small blue bottle glinted in his grasp. Molly held her breath. Would the potion ruin Mrs Hollander as it had the others? She prayed to the Goddess it would!

But the man hesitated, his raised hand wavering. He seemed oblivious to the danger, his eyes pinned on the seemingly helpless woman in her long, diaphanous robe.

Molly saw the knife before the man did. He never saw it coming at all.

It had taken more effort than she'd expected to break through the damnable shield, and now her muscles shook as she chased Keen through the ruined catacombs beyond the fallen barrier. The fact that she was letting Keen lead spoke to her diminished capacity, but the "needle" she'd driven into the dragon's heart had required a concentration of her formidable power. Brute strength alone wouldn't have brought down the shield, only precision and absolute focus.

Her blade, white hot and razor sharp, had carved a line of fire down the invisible barrier. It had pushed back against it, but she'd held fast even as her palms burned on the hilt and her muscles started to tear, wishing she could have summoned her beast aspect to boost her strength. Her tall, angular form bent with the effort of forcing her sword downward, slicing inch by inch, until finally the barrier gave way.

Hero stumbled forward, her sword no longer afire. Darkness and silence swallowed the catacombs with shocking abruptness, broken only by the fiery glow of her eyes. Panting, heart thundering, she stood breathless, her sword in her hands.

"The veil is lifted," she said into the silence.

Keen answered, his voice high with excitement. "They know we're coming now."

She grinned, calling up a new wreath of fire to light their way. "Good."

The confidence she'd felt in that moment faded almost immediately. A few steps into the new passageway, she knew she was drained down to the dregs, and Keen took point when she had to stop and rest. He was like a hound on a scent, all his energy focused on what awaited them. If he was afraid of this Devourer, whatever it was, he wasn't showing it. As for her, she wasn't so much afraid as sick with doubt. She hadn't expected to face cosmic-level evil on an empty tank.

She stumbled on a pile of scattered bones. *Fuck*. It took her longer than she cared for to recover and Keen pulled ahead of her. "Wait!" she hissed. They couldn't charge headlong into this creature's lair.

He paused for a moment, glancing back at her, eyes reflecting the flames she'd called. "I intend to strike quickly," he said urgently. "Catch it by surprise."

He seemed profoundly confident, and maybe with good reason. After all, they'd made it this far without triggering the protections they'd encountered the first time. She wasn't sure what that meant; the Devourer might have started devouring its guardian elemental demons, or the creatures may have fled to the hills. Keen held his blunderbuss primed and ready in one hand and a glowing potion in the other, his saber sheathed for now. Perhaps he thought he could take the thing out with one shot?

Still a damned squirrel.

"We don't—"

But he was gone. Dashing down the final stretch of broken tunnel toward a light at the end, red and threatening. Suddenly, she felt too tired to move. She needed to rest, just for a moment.

The blast of Keen's blunderbuss echoed down the corridor. She groaned and pushed herself upright. Another blast, then explosions. Damn it, she was going to miss the whole thing! She staggered into a run.

The tunnel opened into a vast cavern. Jagged rock floors edged a deep pit – a pit that, judging by the pulsing heat and foul stench of brimstone, cut straight to the depths of the Underworld. It felt as if she'd opened the Gate and her blood sang, a surge of strength flooding her flagging muscles.

This was no mere summoning. Someone was trying to punch a hole through reality straight to Pandemonium.

It explained how those guardian demons, the sylphs and fire wraiths, had appeared on this plane: they had slipped through the burgeoning cracks – cracks she could now see spearing like jagged lightning all over the walls of the pit.

What awaited behind this final layer, swiftly buckling under an onslaught of life energy that snapped in the air like static electricity, must be the Devourer her father had warned her about – an ancient being banished to Pandemonium by the Goddess Herself, chained at the beginning of Time. A creature older than demons, yearning for freedom.

For absolute destruction.

Hero quailed, skidding to a halt just beyond the end of the tunnel, overwhelmed by the sheer power of her enemy. She couldn't fight this thing, even at full strength! She nearly turned and dashed back the way she'd come, frozen by unexpected and unfamiliar terror, chagrined at the thought that her partner – her *human* partner – had charged headlong to the edge of the pit even in the face of dreadful danger. Only one thing stood in his way: a slim, black-haired woman in a gauzy robe. Her eyes were turned up to Keen, wide and pleading. A delicate hand reached out to him, so seemingly innocent, so helpless…

His blunderbuss was lowered, the flaring barrel aimed at the ground, and he held the potion in his other hand as if not quite sure what to do with it. His whole body seemed to lean toward her, drawn inexorably into her orbit.

"You're here," Abigail Hollander said to him, red lips parted seductively, cheeks bright. Her soft voice reached Hero's ears as if she had whispered directly into them. "My hero."

Abigail stepped closer, and the hand she'd kept hidden in her robes swung at Keen from the left, fast as a striking snake. Keen jerked as she buried a wicked, jagged blade in his side. He stumbled forward, nearly falling on her, but she slipped aside and there was nothing between him and the pit to Hell.

Hero leapt forward, but her movements were slow, the air thick around her. Flame and shadow billowed from the pit, along with low, hideous laughter. For a moment, Keen was a dark silhouette against the hellish backdrop, hunched over in pain, teetering, the hilt of a knife protruding from his flank.

And then he tumbled over the edge.

CHAPTER THIRTY-EIGHT

"KEEN!"

His name tore raggedly from her throat. Suddenly, she could move again. Her mind blank with shock, she lunged at Abigail, prepared to skewer the woman. A few charred bodies blocked her way and she trampled over them.

She stabbed him! She killed him! Fucking bitch!
Damn squirrel. I should have protected him.
What am I going to tell his mother?

These thoughts flitted through her mind, insubstantial as moths against the glare of the killing rage rising in her gut. Keen's hesitation had cost him dearly. She wouldn't make the same mistake.

But Abigail was no easy target, dodging her sword with preternatural swiftness and grace. If Hero didn't know better, she'd think Abigail was part demon.

Fucking Hell, Viridian, you dolt! Realization flooded her. Abigail was like her – a half demon! How was that even possible? How had she kept it so well hidden, both from her and from a demonhunter? Astounding!

"Now, now, Inspector," Abigail chided, dancing away from Hero's furious blade. "You can't kill a helpless woman. Don't you peacekeepers have a code?"

"This is my code," Hero growled and lunged at her, advancing relentlessly. "You murdering bitch. No one will care if I eviscerate a fucking nun-killer."

Abigail laughed. Her feet lifted from the rocky ground, *en pointe* like a ballerina, and she rose gracefully into the air and flew backward over the pit, out of reach.

Hero followed as far as she could, then stopped sharply, balancing at the edge of the pit. She contemplated a wild leap.

Her gaze was drawn down to where the bottom of the pit writhed with fire and thick shadows, overlain with those lightning cracks. At the center, the shadows held a mouth, full of teeth, and eyes. The skin of the beast seemed made of stars. The mouth opened wide, inviting her inside. It had already swallowed Keen; she should surely follow.

The urge to jump gripped her. To be consumed would be a glorious honor, a magnificent end–

With a gasp, she backpedaled, horrified by how close she'd come to submitting to its inexorable pull. This thing was *powerful*.

She dragged her eyes away from the pit and looked toward Abigail, refusing to gaze into Oblivion again. She took heart in the fact that the creature wasn't yet free. If she could disrupt the summoning – or whatever the hell this was – she might stop the Devourer from breaking free. Let it rot in Pandemonium where it belonged!

Abigail floated above the pit, serene in her fluttering robe. Her black hair slithered around her head and her already fair skin had turned white. She smiled with lips the color of blood. Her slim, pale hands became long, sinewy and tipped with claws. Almost everything about her became a little less human as her true aspect was revealed. Only her eyes remained unchanged: cornflower blue, cold and cruel yet heartbreakingly beautiful. Hero seethed at the unfairness of it and gathered herself for a suicidal leap.

"I'll never understand why Father treasured you as he did."

Hero wavered as Abigail's voice filled the cavern, bitter and jealous. She should have been shocked by the implications of her words, but she knew her father; his lust was inexhaustible. How many other children had he spawned? Hundreds, probably, though she suspected fewer than a handful would have made it to adulthood. Having some demon heritage in your family history was one thing, being half demon quite another, and such children were often killed at birth – possibly with good reason, she realized, considering this one was trying to destroy a goodly portion of the Realm.

Her *sister*. The word was a vile hiss in her head.

"*Treasured* me?" Hero raged. "No one spit on you in the streets, I'd wager. Your mother didn't gouge out *those* eyes, no doubt! Or ship you off to a deranged abbess! *How dare you?!*"

Suddenly, the eldritch horror clawing its way up from Hell no longer interested her. Let it swallow this whole Goddess-forsaken world.

Abigail snorted in disgust. "Father nurtured your power, you ungrateful brat. He forged you in Hellfire while he left me to languish, the pampered pet of a weak and pathetic human family who craved power like ours. They shielded me from scrutiny, kept me safe with their money and vile potions." She glared at Hero, her cobalt eyes full of resentment. "For you, he killed your true mother – a weak, soft woman – and you, the favorite, were given the gift of a cruel one. She made you strong, made you powerful!"

Hero reeled, barely absorbing anything beyond *He killed your true mother.* Could it be? Was her mother not her mother? Or was this merely another of her father's many lies?

Somehow, she didn't think so. A strange mix of joy and hatred swelled in her heart. One more debt she needed to settle with dear old Pop.

Abigail sneered at her, revealing fangs the color of old ivory. "But look where we are now, sister. Who's the stronger of us? Who deserves a throne in Pandemonium? You, the traitor, or me, the loyal daughter, ever faithful despite his neglect? See what I have wrought." Her arms spread wide, encompassing the vast cavern, wreathed in fire and brimstone, a primordial birthplace of pure evil. "I have *earned* a place at his side!"

Hero started. *That* was what she desired? All this just to please their leech of a father?

"You can have it!" she shouted. "I never wanted it. I'd rather face oblivion than spend eternity with that rotten bastard."

"That was always the plan, sister." Abigail's clawed hands closed into fists as if pulling invisible strings. A sudden pulsing of power thrummed from points all around the edges of the cavern. Gleaming energy flowed toward the center, toward Abigail. She grew brighter, larger. Light shone from her eyes. Far beneath her, the star-dusted shadows heaved and the cracks spread, growing wider and wider, fed by the power she was collecting.

From children. From the students of Bright Renewal Academy, now chained like beasts awaiting sacrifice – and not the slow, torturous sacrifice of Sister Catarine. It would not take six days to drain them; it was happening far more quickly. Abigail was the conduit, siphoning all that pure power into the breach. At any moment, the egg would crack and the Devourer would rise.

Hero gathered herself, calling upon the final dregs of her power for a great, suicidal leap. If she could grab hold of Abigail, she might be able to drag her down into Hell and close this potential gateway behind them both. Together, they would burn for eternity – a fitting end to demon spawn.

And if she missed? If she failed to drag them both to Hell?

Then all was lost.

She had no choice. Digging deep, Hero reached for the fires of Hell–

"Auntie Hero!"

The scream was faint, desperate, the voice ragged and young. Hero recognized it immediately.

She found Molly across the pit, small and pathetic, crouched on her knees, anchored to the ground by a bright chain – and she wasn't alone. Hero picked out a dozen or so others, boys and girls, all dressed in a similar uniform – not Clem Prep garb; Bright Renewal Academy had been the funnel for this place, sending "troubled" children to their doom with the enthusiastic consent of the entire town.

Suddenly, another solution crystallized in her mind.

Break the fucking chains, Viridian!

She bared her teeth in a wicked grin and gave her sword a spin. "See you in Hell, sister," she told the floating woman, then winked and blew her a kiss, pleased to see the triumphant gleam in Abigail's eyes turn to suspicion. Then she dashed to her right, moving with demonic speed, leaving a trail of fire in her wake.

She reached the first child and barely paused, her sword shattering the strange material of the chain like it was made of glass, links flying. She flew past the child that had been tethered by it – a boy in a ragged school jacket, bright eyes staring, mouth open in shock – and yelled back over her shoulder, "Run!"

Abigail's angry screech echoed the ringing of Hero's sword through the next strand of shimmering chain links. The child she freed had been ready for her, on his feet, chain stretched tight, and he didn't need to be told to run. Same with the next one, a thin girl of about fifteen, dirty cheeks streaked with tears. Her face was a blur as Hero broke through the chain with an up hand swing.

"Look out!" the girl cried a moment before a streak of lightning crashed into the ground practically at Hero's feet. She twisted and leapt high, racing along the wall of the cavern to avoid a crumbling crevasse forming where the blast had hit. She glanced back briefly and was glad to see the girl running after her friends, toward the tunnel she and Keen had taken from the catacombs.

Another child, another chain. More lightning slammed into the rocks, but Hero was moving too fast to hit. Her demonic speed was all she had right now. She freed two more children and could only hope they'd find their way out and avoid Abigail's fury at the same time.

A low hum emerged from the pit, a deep rumble of rage. Abigail's Devourer had to understand that its way out was narrowing. She hoped it was split in half by the closing of the summoning.

Molly was next – finally – and her niece was ready for her, on her feet, chain pulled taut. Hero wasted no time in breaking her free, but she stopped her headlong dash for this particular child. "Are you all right?" she demanded, her voice harsh with adrenaline. "Can you find your way out?"

Looking startled and unsure, the girl managed to nod. Her hands flew to the collar around her neck and it came away in her hands, dissolving like it was made of sugar. Relief filled her filthy face. "Y-y-yes." Molly's eyes lifted up to hers with naked gratitude. "Auntie–"

"Go!" Hero gave her a little shove. She didn't have time for thanks. "Now! Get your father, the PKs – all of them!"

After a second's hesitation, Molly nodded and dashed away over the shaking, crumbling rocks. Shadows had risen from the pit, obscuring the edge of the cavern, but the girl ran with surefooted grace. Hero turned her back on her niece, racing toward the next chained child, a boy with red curls and a bruised, puffy face. He was gazing into the pit and the darkness residing there, but he must have been aware she was coming as he was stretching out his chain in expectation of her sword.

A violent trembling lifted the rocks beneath her feet, forcing her to stop and fight for balance. Her legs wobbled dangerously. She'd used up so much strength already; she didn't have much left. It would take everything she had just to complete the circuit, but she wasn't about to let a single child remained chained in this hellhole.

A flurry of pale fabric landed in front of her – Abigail, hands raised, fangs out. "You weren't supposed to live! Your family should have strangled you at birth!"

Hero snarled, sword raised, attempting to cover her weakness with bravado. "They tried – and failed, time and time again. Just as you'll fail, sister!"

Hero lunged to the side, attempting to skirt around Abigail. It was too big of a risk to attack her directly. Speed was still her best weapon.

But Abigail was having none of it. She gestured sharply, sending bursts of lightning at Hero with a malicious grin. The blasts caught Hero in the midsection. She gasped, momentarily blinded by pain. Something hit the back of her head, hard, and she dropped to her knees, her ears ringing. Goddess help her, this bitch was strong!

Abigail's maniacal laughter rang throughout the cavern. Doubled over, Hero could only clutch her midsection, her sword hanging from limp fingers, and desperately shake her head, trying to clear it. One more blow and she'd be finished.

But the blow didn't come. She took a breath, and another. Her vision cleared and the ringing faded. She began to pick up strangled sounds – shuffling feet and a low, angry buzzing. Blinking, she looked up to see Abigail struggling, her slippered feet kicking at the air. Thick, bright links were tight across her throat. A red-headed boy stood behind her, strangling her with his own chain. He was easily a head taller than Abigail, but she was still a half demon. He didn't have much chance–

His gaze locked onto Hero's, eyes bright with resolve as he held the writhing demon. "Save the others," he said, and then dragged Abigail to the edge of the pit, looping another length of chain around her neck as he went. Without another glance in her direction, he jumped, pulling Abigail with him over the edge.

A roar of rage rose from the shadows and brimstone below. Hero forced herself to her feet and ran. She had a job to do, and that boy – Cole Graham, she belatedly realized – had given her the time she needed to do it. She would remember him.

Rocks began to tumble from the ceiling of the cavern, and the trembling grew into full-on shaking. The whole place was going to collapse on her head! The remaining chains glowed like beacons in the rising dark.

Five more. Five more lives to save.

CHAPTER THIRTY-NINE

The alarm rattled through the town an hour before dawn, sending PKs tumbling from their beds and dashing to the firehouse. Bright Renewal Academy was on fire!

Sergeant Liam Franke was one of the first to answer the call, tall and broad-shouldered in his crisp uniform, directing his squad with masterful calm from his seat on the lead wagon. Molly shook with relief at the sight of her father, certain he would make everything right despite all that had happened. He'd been tricked; the whole town had been bespelled. Her aunt had broken it, though Molly had no idea how or what Hero Viridian had done. She just knew it to be true, just like she'd known her father would come running if she lit the school on fire.

Barefoot, her uniform not nearly warm enough for the chill autumn air, she'd escaped the cavern like her aunt had ordered her to, but she hadn't immediately gone to find her father. Instead, she'd crawled up out of the catacombs and returned to the dormitory, screaming from the top of her lungs the entire time. The cavern beneath the Academy was going to collapse! Or worse, the creature Abigail had been summoning was going to break through! Either way, all the kids in the school were doomed if she didn't get them out. The first torch she'd come across had inspired her next move. Setting fire to the new construction, built atop the old bones of an abandoned building, had given her a bit of trouble, but a thrown oil lamp had helped considerably.

"Fire!" Molly had shrieked as she'd run through the halls, evading adults as best she could, the lack of dorm-room doors working to her advantage for once. Spurred by terror, the students rose together and pushed for the exits. The guardians tried their best to beat them back, but smoke and flames were surer encouragement than clubs and whips and they were overwhelmed quickly. Some of their ranks began unlocking the doors to the outside in a moment of clarity. Evacuation was the only sensible reaction to fire.

Her job done, Molly stumbled out with her coughing, panic-stricken classmates. She was beyond thankful to catch sight of Rebecca's auburn hair in the milling crowd. Molly grabbed her by the hand and pulled the girl away from the building.

"Hurry!" she gasped. The distant alarms from town had begun to sound. "We have to get away!"

She couldn't explain or even begin to articulate the impending danger, but thankfully Rebecca didn't fight. She ran with Molly, eyes wild with terror and confusion, gripping her hand like a lifeline.

They'd stumbled to a halt near the road. Wagons raced up it, pulled by heaving draft horses, lanterns lighting their way. That was when Molly had caught sight of her father and her heart had lodged in her throat. She wanted to shout to him, but she was too far away and he was moving too quickly. The thundering horses carried the fire wagons past them, clanking bells and sirens splitting the night. Men clung to the sides of the wagons dressed in oiled, waterproof fishermen's jackets the color of dull ivory. Some were professional firefighters, but most were volunteers from the PK ranks and city tradesmen.

The girls turned to watch the wagons race up the hill to the Academy. Beside her, Rebecca let out a small, astonished gasp as she caught sight of it, and Molly could hardly blame her. Fire engulfed the miserable place, eating at the dormitory and the fieldhouse where so much terror and abuse had occurred.

"How?" Rebecca exclaimed. "What happened to the Academy?"

Molly shook her head, her lips pressed tight. She couldn't admit her part in it, not yet. Right now, it would look like she was a crazed arsonist.

A half demon, disgraced ex-nun arsonist happened to it.
Auntie Hero.

As if the thought of her aunt summoned destruction, the center of the complex of buildings collapsed in a deafening roar, sending flames and sparks skyward. Molly's breath snagged in her chest and dread snaked through her belly, leaving her chilled. Was her aunt still inside? Or had she fought her way free already?

"Stay here," she told Rebecca, and ran back toward the burning school, her friend calling after her, begging her to stop. Molly ignored her. She had to know!

The firemen had pulled up to the fire in orderly fashion, jumping from the wagons and uncoiling long hoses. They'd cut through the barbed-wire fence surrounding the Academy and their vehicles were parked on the vast lawn. The red tanks gleamed in the flickering flames while the draft horses stood stolidly. Shouted commands and orders laid some organization through the seeming chaos. Men moved in teams: a pair on the hand operated pumps, three handling the hoses and directing bursts of water toward the conflagration.

More men arrived on horseback, dressed in peacekeeper uniforms. They herded the confused mob of students and guardians away from the buildings.

A few dark figures emerged from the flaming wreckage, stumbling across the lawn, most of them students. A tall, silver-haired figure was herding them forward towards safety, a slim sword in one hand. Molly went shaky with relief at the sight of her aunt, clinging on to the side of one of the firewagons lest her knees give out.

"It's Viridian!" The cry rose from one of the PKs on horseback. He steadied his dancing mount and pointed toward Hero, standing in his stirrups.

"The demon!" cried another man nearby, scrambling for the pistol at his belt. "Goddess save us!"

"Wait!" ordered the man on horseback – Chief Dewey, Molly realized vaguely – but his order came too late. The uniform PK aimed his pistol at the distant figure and fired.

The gunshot seemed deafening. Hero lurched, one shoulder jerking back as the lead ball pierced her. She stumbled and went to her knee, shoving one of the students ahead of her down the hill as she fell.

Molly screamed, but her cry of horror was drowned out by the horrendous cracking of wooden beams and walls as *something* emerged from the center of the burning complex. Risen from the depths, a mass of twisting, spidery appendages attached to a fat, sluglike belly, raw and glistening. A head rose above its misshapen form, wizened and withered, wisps of white hair clinging to its charred scalp. It was as tall as the trees and roaring with rage.

The Devourer.

One of its impossibly long legs thrust forward, a clawed foot gouging deep into the grass, bringing the beast outside the circle of burning buildings and landing beside her struggling aunt, looking pathetically small next to the massive talons.

Nevertheless, Hero scrambled back, crablike, her sword trailing in one hand, her other arm buckling beneath her. She managed to pull herself to her knees, but then abruptly sagged back on her heels, her head tipped up toward the approaching fiend. Inexplicably, she laid her sword on the ground before as if it were an offering. Head thrown back, her shoulders slumped, she appeared to be waiting, resignation and submission in every line of her body.

The Devourer was quite pathetic, in the end, not much of an eldritch monster after all. Disrupting the summoning had left it weakened, and only this remnant had managed to squeeze through the quickly diminishing gateway Abigail had provided, a skinny-limbed giant with a protruding belly, no more destructive than your average lord of Pandemonium. Normally, she could handle something like this in her sleep. Hell, even Keen could have taken it on his own.

Hero winced as her small chuckle sent searing pain through her shoulder. Damn PK shot her, the bastard. She'd have his badge if she survived this.

She had nothing left. No fight. No strength. All she could do was watch and wait, and hope the PKs stopped the beast once it was finished with her.

The giant demon glared down at her, tusks protruding from its bottom jaw, fiery red eyes even more impressive than her own. It had to know she was responsible for its diminished state. She felt some regret that she hadn't managed to stop it completely; as weak as it was, it could still wreak havoc on Havenside before the ill-prepared PKs managed to bring it down. It would take more than a few bullets to stop it.

There was a sharp crack and the creature roared. More cracks followed – a barrage of bullets that seemed to accomplish little but make it more enraged. Its other leg lifted, its clawed foot moving in slow motion, hovering above her head as if mocking her.

"Come on!" she screamed at it. Goddess damn the thing. What was it waiting for?

A low boom rattled through it. The creature wavered, its eyes spinning wildly. Then its mouth opened in a wide, startled *O*.

Its foot came down hard right next to her, shaking the ground, coming close to smashing her flat. Hero stared up at the beast, at its fat stomach jiggling above her – moving strangely, now that she thought about it.

There was another dim boom, and she saw a flash beneath its skin – an explosion somewhere in its fat belly.

"Shit!" she muttered and threw herself to the side, shielding the back of her head with her good arm.

It can't be. It can't be!

She risked a peek up at it just as there was another boom and another impact tore the thing open. Its jiggling gut exploded and its long limbs flew apart with nothing to hold them together. Hero hunched into a tight ball as hunks of demon flesh and blood rained down upon her, the smell of rot and brimstone nearly suffocating her. The fall of debris seemed to go on forever, but finally it stopped. Struggling upright, she swiped at the fluids and charred flesh blinding her.

Against the backdrop of the burning academy, a figure emerged from the ruined corpse, covered in bile and demon innards. Effluvium coated him, slicking his hair to his scalp, making his too-big ears all the more obvious. There was a blunderbuss in his hand, smoke trickling from its muzzle.

"Keen."

Her partner's head swung toward her, his face painted with shadows, and he took a staggering step. Another. Hero rose to meet him, a trickle of hot blood oozing from her shoulder. The wound wouldn't heal until she could get the damnable bullet out.

"DH Keen!" she cried, swaying, even as joy bubbled up inside her, light as air. "Commendable work!"

He stumbled closer, his free hand clamped to his side, just below the protruding hilt of a dagger. "I told you," he said, his voice ragged and hoarse. "The element of surprise. Works every time."

A laugh broke from her. Then she went to her knees again on the soft ground. With two more stumbling steps, Keen was beside her.

"Next time," he said, starting to lower himself to the earth and falling onto his belly instead when his knees gave out. Stretched out prone, he reached out and patted her knee. "You go first."

This time, Hero's laugh was soundless. She hadn't the strength for much more.

"Inspector Viridian!"

She roused at the fierce shout. The voice sounded vaguely familiar, and she felt the ground vibrate through her legs, a thrumming of running feet coming closer. She could hardly bring herself to give a damn before she and her partner were surrounded by peacekeepers. Beside her, his hand still settled on her knee, Keen was limp and unconscious, probably from blood loss due to the knife wound, though being swallowed by an ancient demon probably hadn't helped.

One of the PKs took a knee next to her and lifted her face by the chin, turning it toward him.

"Helen," Liam said softly. "Can you stand? How can I help?"

She gestured vaguely. "My partner…"

Liam's expression hardened and he looked back at the others. "Get the medics. Now!"

Immediately, half of them took off at a run, leaving Hero with her brother, alone except for two uncomfortable-looking PKs. She recognized one as the idiot who'd shot her. He was lucky she was about to pass out.

"Mother is not our mother, Liam," she said woozily, right before slumping over her unconscious partner. Another warm wash of blood soaked through her clothes, but by then she was beyond caring.

CHAPTER FORTY

When First Rank DH Oleander Keen was finally released from the sanatorium, his partner was waiting for him. Though she'd drained herself of every scrap of power during the battle in the catacombs and had subsequently been shot, she had recovered far faster than he had – a failure of his fragile human body. The knife Abigail had buried in his side had led to massive internal bleeding, and being swallowed whole by an eldritch horror had ravaged his skin and lungs. Even now, breathing still hurt and a soft breeze felt like needles across his skin, though the doctors assured him the damage would heal – eventually.

As for Hero Viridian – leaning casually against the wall outside the hospital, cane in hand, tiny hat perched on her sleek silver hair, wearing her bastardized nun garb, the sun catching threads of gold in her emerald harem pants, fiery eyes shielded by green-tinted glasses – she looked the same as she had the first day he'd met her. Of course, this time he wasn't gripped by the instinctual urge to attack her. By now, he'd grown rather used to her demon half, even... well, appreciative.

Keen paused at the top of the broad steps outside the hospital, keeping to the shadows cast by the impressive edifice – like all things in Havenside, Merciful Souls Hospital had been built to project wealth and beauty – and watched his partner spin her cane. Yes, she seemed much the same, but no one came through what they had unscathed, not even an unrepentant ex-nun half-demon arsonist.

He rubbed his arm where the cannula had been embedded until only a few days ago, delivering the transfused blood and other fluids needed to keep him alive. The knife wound, still red but healing well, was hidden beneath his shirt – a civvy shirt. He twitched his shoulders, finding the clothes ill-fitting. Too new and too stiff.

Everything he owned had burned up in the fire that destroyed his house. Donations from citizens had helped him recoup some of the losses. He was grateful, yes, but he couldn't help feeling like a charity case again.

Good old Charity Keen!

The stray thought was in Dirk's voice, and Keen shuddered, tugged his sleeves down to his wrists, then sighed. He had too many regrets, killing Dirk being one of the biggest, but there wasn't much he could do about that. He could only carry on like a good PK would, a servant of the Realm.

At least, as far as he knew, he was still a servant of the Realm.

While he'd been bed-bound at the hospital, his fellow PKs had been in and out of his room, offering sympathy, bringing small gifts and sneaking in flasks he pretended to drink. Suddenly, they were all friends and he was the most popular guy in the precinct – a strange turn of events, considering they'd been trying to kill him not long before, though everyone assured him that had been due to the Fog spell engulfing the town. Now, he was a hero. His actions had saved the town. Hell, he'd saved the eastern coast of the Realm and every PK and demonhunter living there. No wonder they all loved him now.

Immediately after the destruction of Bright Renewal, things hadn't been so chummy. The PKs had only just been coming out of the effects of the spell and were confused to say the least. Even wounded and only just clinging on to life, Keen had been subjected to fierce questioning, forced to repeat every detail of the events leading up to that final, cataclysmic confrontation until his voice failed and he fell back into delirium. They hadn't gone easy on him, not at all. He could only imagine what Hero had gone through, the half-demon firestarter.

Nevertheless, he'd been more than happy to explain all he knew, and eventually they'd ceased their interrogations. Chief Roger Dewey had paid him a visit soon after the last of his questioners pronounced his interview complete, looking apologetic and vaguely ashamed.

"You did well, son," he'd said, twisting his captain's hat in his hands as he stood at the foot of Keen's narrow hospital bed.

His gaze kept switching to the nurses and other patients in the crowded ward, not a few of whom were injured youths who'd escaped the flames at Bright Renewal, before coming back to him. "I'm recommending you for a commendation."

Before, Keen would have swelled with pride at his commanding officer's praise, but now, with his skin feeling like it was being attacked by a cheese grater and every breath a struggle, he couldn't bring himself to care much.

"Thank you, sir," he said. Then he cleared his throat, wincing at the sharp pain, and asked what he'd asked every PK who'd darkened his door: "Where is Inspector Viridian? Is she allowed to visit? I would very much like to see her." No one else had given him anything other than vague assurances, but he wasn't about to let Dewey off so easily.

Again, a shifting of his gaze. "Inspector Viridian is not your concern."

"She's my partner." Keen struggled to sit up, confounded by the monumental effort of moving a thin sheet. He fell back, exhausted and angry. "Tell me! If it weren't for Hero Viridian we'd all be dead. *Where is she?*"

Lips pressed into a line, Dewey closed the curtains to given them some semblance of privacy before he settled himself on a stool near Keen's head.

"I know that, Keen," he said sharply. "I know it better than anyone. But I don't run this town, and lots of very powerful people just watched their considerable investment go up in smoke and flames. They're still grappling with the fact that Abigail Primm was half demon and the entire Primm clan a bunch of Pandemonium shills. Needless to say, respectable Havenside is rocked to the core. They came looking for a scapegoat and Hero Viridian seemed an easy target. Right now, she's cooling in a cell, safe and sound, under my protection and the protection of every peacekeeper who knows the truth and understands what we owe her."

Keen didn't know if he was shaking from weakness or anger at Dewey's confession. No wonder none of the others would tell him anything. "You *arrested* her?" he hissed. "You're letting the damn country-club set decide her guilt or innocence?"

"She's not under arrest, not technically, just... being held for questioning as a person of interest."

"Goddess damn you all!"

"She's fine, Keen," Dewey said with an admonishing look. "Better than you, anyway." He stood, slapping his hat back on his head. "We all owe Viridian. No one denies it, not among the peacekeepers, at least. By the Goddess, you owe her more than anyone. Her blood saved you when she hardly had a drop to spare."

Keen started, his eyes going to the tube snaking into his arm. It contained clear fluid at the moment, but he had vague memories of bright blood filling it, and of Hero's fiercely whispered encouragement as he lay dying: "Hang on, Keen. Avoid bright lights, kid. Come on..."

"You have to trust me, son. For now, just focus on getting better."

At the time, Keen had had little choice but to comply. Worry for his partner kept him from an easy rest, and nightmares plagued him when he did manage to sleep. The sensation of falling would grip him as he drifted off, shocking him awake to lie in a cold sweat. When his eyes closed, all he could see were teeth and a gaping mouth waiting for him.

The Devourer had swallowed him whole, sucking him down its tight gullet, so tight he'd thought he'd be crushed to death right there. But he hadn't. Instead, he'd landed in a pool of stink and searing acid, hot and dark and horrifying. In his nightmares, he was still there, fighting for his life, panicked and terrified.

Most times, in those dreams, Hero died fighting the Devourer and he was digested.

Sometimes, he dreamed that Abigail killed him, driving the knife deep into his heart. He never slept another wink on the nights he had that particular dream.

His deep feelings for Abigail Hollander had faded during his recovery, as if he'd been slowly freed of his own, personal Fog spell. It made him think her demonic power had been influencing him. It didn't excuse his mistakes, but he felt slightly mollified to think it wasn't entirely his fault.

Her small, shriveled corpse had been recovered in the embrace of the unfortunate Cole Graham, who had been sent to Bright Renewal as a sacrifice. Now the nuns had her body and were studying it, dissecting it, learning how to better kill demons like her in the future. The news of her demise had made him angry; angry for all her victims. The letter Cole had written to his sister had been found buried in the evidence file Smith and Coates had compiled – to their deep embarrassment – detailing how Bright Renewal Academy was feeding students cursed with demon blood to an eldritch entity in an attempt to raise it from the deepest reaches of Pandemonium. They also knew from Molly Franke that Abigail had been the one who'd chased Cassie Graham to her death off the clock tower, enraged that the girl hadn't kept her mouth shut.

Luckily, his agony over Hero's fate had been mitigated by the news that she'd been released at the behest of a certain Captain Culpepper from New Savage City, who was arriving soon with Keen's mother in tow. He'd sent Dewey a strongly worded letter ripe with threats and less-than-subtle implications. Soon after, Hero had been fully exonerated and restored to her full rank and station among the inspector peacekeepers.

That had been good news, and it had given him strength, which had sped his recovery. And now, fresh from his sick bed, looking down upon Hero Viridian from the top of the hospital steps, Keen felt a strange disconnect from reality. It seemed that no time had passed since he'd first laid eyes on her, while at the same time eons had come and gone. Baffling. Carefully, he made his way down the steps, his legs stiff and his gait unsteady, frustrated by having to move so slowly, like an old man. He supposed it could have been worse. By rights, he should be dead, a snack for the Devourer.

The stray thought made his lips quirk just as Hero looked up and caught sight of him. She pushed off from the wall, a very normal grin lighting her face, fangs and all, and tapped the brim of her hat with her ebony cane. "Finally," she exclaimed. "I've been out here all day."

"I don't move as fast as I used to," he said, trying to sound lighthearted even as his lungs burned from the effort of walking. He stopped a few steps above her and attempted to catch his breath without her noticing.

Her expression smoothed and she peered up at him. "You don't look so great, Keen. You sure they should have released you?"

He lifted a shoulder. "I'll be right as rain in a few days."

She *tsk*ed. "Of course you will." She copied his one-shouldered shrug. "Or we'll all be dead. Who knows?"

"Only the Goddess."

Her grin returned, disconcertingly broad. "You have any plans right now?"

He shook his head. "I'm not even sure where I'm going, to be honest, but I couldn't stay back there any longer. Besides, Mother's on her way home. I'll have to find somewhere for the both of us."

Hero scoffed and waved a dismissive hand. "We'll figure that out later." She swung her cane with a flourish, then started down the steps, swishing crinkling oak leaves out of her way. "First, we have a funeral to go to."

A light, misting rain began to fall on the way to the cemetery. Normally, it would have compelled Hero to quicken her pace, but Keen was so obviously struggling that she kept herself to an amble. A little rain wouldn't hurt her. Besides, she was in no great hurry to get to the graveyard near Clementine Preparatory. Her not-father was buried there – not that she'd ever visited his grave. She'd missed his funeral, too. At the time, the nuns wouldn't let her leave the abbey, fearing she'd never return. So she'd missed the funeral of one parent, but she didn't plan to miss the funeral of the second – another not-parent, a not-mother this time.

Hero blew a breath between her lips and twirled her cane as the deceptively soft mist gathered on its ebony surface and made the brick sidewalk grow slick. She felt a small trickle down the back of her neck, creeping down her spine and beneath her shirt. Damn little hat was useless as always, but she liked how it looked, so ridiculously small.

"I'm sorry I'm slowing you down," Keen said, huffing far too hard for the pace.

Hero slowed, reining in her long stride even further. "I'm in no rush to get there," she said. It was true: she wasn't going to miss seeing the old hag consigned to the cold, dark earth. There was time. If anything, she'd miss the priest's sermon and the nuns' blessing. Maybe even a few words from Liam. Her brother knew the truth now, but as he told Hero, the woman had raised him. He owed her his respect and would honor her in death. By all rights, she had been his mother.

Not mine. Never mine.

"The revered mother visited me in my cell," she said casually as they turned off Main Street and started down the broad, tree-lined avenue toward Clementine Prep. There was only a little traffic on the road and relatively few pedestrians out and about, driven inside by the chill rain. A woman walking her small white dog stopped to let it do its business, but she hastily dragged it across the street when she spotted Hero. Gratitude had worn thin already. She'd ruined a number of respected families with her actions, after all. "She apologized, if you can believe it, sincerely I think, but I could tell it hurt her physically to have to do it. She was fit to crack her teeth with all the grinding."

"So, she wasn't in on it? Not willingly?"

Hero shook her head. As much as she'd wanted to go after those fucking nuns, in the end they'd been innocent bystanders, ensnared by an evil much more powerful than even they were capable of dealing with. It was almost unforgivable, really. The Order of the Shield was supposed to be the first line of defense against Pandemonium. When they'd needed to be aware, when they'd needed to be strong, they had failed. Miserably.

"They lost their way," she said. "Too busy maintaining their image of superiority. I've seen it happen far too often. The battle nuns will face a reckoning one of these days. They almost did this time around, but fate intervened. They'll live to fight another day."

Keen snorted softly. "Are we fate now, Viridian? A bit pretentious, isn't it?"

"It's not pretension, merely the truth. We saved this town, Keen, when everyone did everything they could to stop us."

"They were ensorcelled."

"Not at the start. Too many went into the idea of Bright Renewal with eyes open, seeing profit in taking advantage of vulnerable children." She side-eyed him. "I found the charter in City Hall, the signatures—business deals for supplies, uniforms, what have you. The tuition fees, Goddess save us. Maybe they were fooled into thinking the Academy had always been there, but they knew what was happening behind those walls. And they didn't care because it wasn't their kids."

Keen was silent for a few more slow steps. Then he asked softly, "What *was* happening behind those walls?"

Hero's teeth clenched. She couldn't speak of it without losing her temper and she had no desire to call up Hell in the middle of the street. "My niece told me some of it. Let's leave it at that."

"As you wish."

They strolled along companionably for a moment. The mist developed a little backbone and Hero wished she'd brought an umbrella.

Then Keen asked, "What else did the revered mother say to you? Did she know about Abigail? Did she know what happened to Catarine this whole time?"

"No. I mean, she knew Abigail was off. Maybe she even knew the woman was half demon, but not that she was a cold-blooded killer. Only a few of the nuns were in Abigail's inner cabal – Catarine's roommate, for one."

Keen let out a low whistle. "I suspected Sister Agnes, but not her. She seemed so distraught and, well, not a little… vapid."

"You can call her stupid, Keen. She did allow Catarine to be lured to her doom, after all."

"Right." He winced, adding, "But she couldn't have been that stupid. She fooled us, didn't she?"

Hero swept a pile of soggy leaves out of her path with her cane. "She played us, all right, like a good little psychopath. Put our focus on Father Kellan and acted all reluctant about it, too. I should have seen through her, but I was so… I don't know. I feel like we could have solved this on day one if we'd been just a little more clearheaded."

Keen chuckled and gave her a chiding look. "Every PK says that after the job is done. Hindsight is the clearest sight. Maybe we could have done a better job, run a tighter case, but we did have an entire cabal and an eldritch demonic entity manipulating reality. Fair to say we did remarkably, all told."

"Don't forget a half-demon sister I never knew I had."

That part was hard for them both to accept, though of course for different reasons. Hero had learned after questioning Novice Eleanor that Catarine had always known Abigail's secret. It was why she'd been so determined to remove the stigma attached to those with demon heritage. Abigail had been her best friend, and Catarine had loved the miserable bitch. She hadn't cared that Abby had had demon blood, but she *had* cared that Abigail was sacrificing children to her dark lord. And confronting Abby about it, down in the catacombs, had gotten her killed.

Keen's expression turned dark, brooding. Did he still pine for the girl he thought he'd known?

"Abigail had everything handed to her in life," he said at last, speaking slowly, as if working out what he wanted to say as he was saying it. "She was beautiful, smart, popular. Exceedingly wealthy. Though now we know how her family generated their wealth."

"Demon worship and summoning can be quite lucrative," Hero agreed, wondering what he was getting at. "But it always comes with a price."

"True." His eyes cut to her. "Still, by every measure, she should have ended up a good person, even with demon heritage." His tone softened. "You did, despite everything thrown at you."

Forged in fire. He killed your true mother.

Her demon-father had wisely absented himself from Havenside following the destruction of the Academy, but she had no doubt he would come looking for her at some point. Her cane thunked rhythmically on the bricks as she imagined spearing him like a wriggling fish. "We all choose our own paths, no matter what our upbringing. Though, honestly, wealth does something to people even demons look upon with envy."

A strained huff of laughter burst from Keen, then he stopped abruptly to draw in deep breaths. Hero stopped, too, to brush raindrops from her scapular, giving him a moment. He gave her a smile through his struggle that was more of a grimace. "I'll be glad... when I can... breathe again."

"No rush, DH Keen. No rush."

After he had straightened and taken a moment to adjust his civvies, they resumed their journey, crossing the street and taking the sidewalk that led around school grounds. The cemetery behind Clem Prep was a public space, older than Havenside itself, so old that some of its tombstones were nothing but weathered slabs of rock, their carved inscriptions worn to nothing. All the town's prestigious families had members buried there, having long eschewed the dismal catacombs beneath all the churches in town. Yet Hero had a new fondness for those crooked tunnels of dead. Without them, they wouldn't have been able to strike at Bright Renewal as quickly as they had.

They entered through the open gates of iron filigree and Hero led them across the graves rather than taking the meandering paths. She knew where she was going. Her not-mother would be laid to rest beside her dead husband.

And where is my real mother buried?

It didn't really matter. The woman was dust and bones by now.

Hero paused to help Keen navigate a hummock of turf. He had to hoist himself forward with a hand on a tombstone, but he didn't complain.

Soon, a group of mourners came into view, above them on a low hill, exposed to the rain. It was a rather small group: a tall man, a woman beside him, and two teenaged girls standing arm in arm – Liam, his wife and Hero's niece, Molly, with... a friend? She didn't know the auburn-haired girl, but the two leaned on each other as if they were all they had in the world.

A few others stood across the grave from the bereaved family, mostly nuns from Clementine, attending as a courtesy. A clergyman stood at the head of the grave in elaborate vestments, a crimson-and-gold stole over his ivory robes, bald-headed and ancient-looking, his face scarred and pockmarked.

Not a priest. A bishop.

Hero sucked in a breath. She knew this bishop. She'd tried to kill him once.

"We aren't really dressed for a funeral," Keen remarked, keeping his voice low as they took shelter beneath a broad-canopied beech tree that still held enough deep-yellow leaves to stop much of the rain, which had by now grown irritatingly steady.

"This is as close as I plan on getting," she said, staring at the man who'd abused countless girls at her former abbey and gotten away with it. His craggy face still bore the marks of the fire she'd set to kill him.

She could kill him now. Easily. Her hand tightened on her cane.

Too much to lose, Viridian.

Hero relaxed. A person had to specially request a bishop to give funeral rites. This was no doubt merely one more way her not-mother was attempting to goad her. So instead of flying into a killing rage, she stood with her partner in silence. The droning of the bishop reached them like a buzz in the air.

"Whose funeral is it?" Keen asked after a moment.

"The woman who raised me," she said, unwilling to say the word *mother* to describe her. "Elizabeth Donovan Franke."

"I'm sorry."

"Don't be. She was a miserable cunt who tortured me every day of my life before sending me off to Blackstone Abbey in Plainfield. That man" – she pointed a long, pale finger at the bishop – "was our priest back then. He molested half the novices there and the sisters all turned a blind eye to his crimes. Even the abbess protected him. If not for her, the fire I set might have erased his blight from the world forever."

"Goddess!" Keen sounded horrified. "So that's why you burned down your abbey!"

Hero said nothing, merely watched as the coffin was lowered into the damp earth by the grave workers and held her breath. Not until she heard the clumps of dirt strike the lid did she dare breathe out, long and slow.

"There. It's done." She turned away and reached out a helping hand toward her partner. "Let's go." He took her hand in a grip stronger than she expected.

"Where to, Inspector?"

She tapped her cane to her hat brim. "Out of the rain, DH Keen." She grinned, letting her glasses slip down her nose ever so slightly. "How far away is Grantham House? I could use a drink."

ACKNOWLEDGEMENTS

As always, I have a multitude of people to thank. No book gets published without a team behind it - professionals, friends and loved ones. First, I have to thank my agent John Baker, whose unbridled enthusiasm and keen instincts make him the absolute best person to have in my corner. I owe the entire Angry Robot team a debt of gratitude: My editor Simon Spanton Walker for understanding what I was trying to do better than I did. Gemma Creffield, who gave me the go ahead to write about an ex-nun half demon detective. Alan Heal and his supreme skills as a copyeditor which made this book absolutely sing IMHO. Desola Coker for all her hard work herding the various cats involved in this project. I also want to thank Sarah O'Flaherty for producing such a stunning, hell-worthy cover. Like I said, it takes a team and AR has one of the best.

To my many author friends, I owe you most of all. For your enthusiasm and support and an inexhaustible supply of encouragement. In particular, my Transpatial Tavern friends who've been with me practically from the beginning, always offering great advice, but also love and kindness and a safe space. You showed me this doesn't need to be a solitary sport!

I want to give a very special thanks to my ride-or-die writing sprint partner, Sarah Jean Horwitz. I think I wrote most of this book on our zoom calls! Looking forward to many more sessions in the future.

I want to thank my family, too. My parents and all my sisters. Reading was essential in our house, and it's the reason

I wanted to write. My dad passed away before I sold my first book, but I know how proud he would have been to see my name in print. I owe my husband Bob a special thanks for his support and encouragement. I wouldn't be able to do this without him. Thanks to my kids, Emily, Audrey, Quinn and Tim, for believing in me. I hope I've made you all proud.

CRAVING MORE FROM SARAH J DALEY?

READ THE FIRST CHAPTER OF WINGS OF STEEL AND FURY NOW!

CHAPTER ONE

The great dome of Upper Splendour stretched clear in all directions, save one. To the east, toward the Keeper's Archon, stood the thick purplish bank of a miles-deep nebula. The detritus of dead stars, the nebulae were the favored haunt of the creatures they'd come to harvest, and as Eleazar squinted toward the mountainous swirl of luminous clouds a glimmer of leviathans skipped into view. Blessed Sol set fire to their fine scales and dragonfly wings as they rose as one into the perfect-day blue of the heavens. His heart swelled at their beauty, and then abruptly sank to his toes. How could he bring himself to kill one of them?

The blast of a trumpet sliced through his skull – others had spotted the glimmer. Beneath his bare feet, the deck of the royal drachen thrummed as the Mithran-powered engines roared. Above him, the battened sails unfolded with a resounding snap to catch the wind and give pursuit. Excitement shivered through him despite his reticence, a primal response to the call of the hunt. His kind had been hunting the leviathans since the First Creation; their blood and bones, skin and flesh sustained the blessed world of Splendour. It was a hallowed communion.

Eleazar Starson knew this but the idea of plunging a lance through living flesh like a barbarian from the Below made his belly churn. It was savagery, this ritual, more symbolic than necessary since they farmed leviathans like cattle to fulfill their needs. These hunts were a cruel paean to the distant past.

It is a vanity. A game for callow youths, this barbaric hunt. Why not let these few wild beasts live in peace?

"Do you think they might have the minds of men?" Eleazar mused aloud to his shivering page. At the boy's peculiar look, he hastily added, "Not of Angelus, of course, but base thoughts and feelings like the Beasts of the Below? The barest sentience…"

The youth gawped at him. Eleazar cursed silently. He should have kept his thoughts to himself. His page's nonsense answer confirmed it: "The Flaying of the Blessed Leviathans formed the firmament of Splendour; they are Holy beyond measure, milord."

"Yes, that is so, good Verity."

His grave nod made the boy beam with pleasure, but he was still cursing himself. It was nerves prompting him to give voice to his soft-hearted flights of fancy, or so his brother would call his ponderings. Foolish, pointless, and entirely inappropriate, today of all days especially. Today, the heir to the Solaire Throne must prove himself in the Blessed Harvest or lose the respect of every Archon in Splendour. Even the piniored might look upon him in disdain if he failed.

Resigned, Eleazar flung off his heavy cloak and let it slither to the deck. Instantly, his skin rose in gooseflesh as the chill air of Upper Splendour lashed him. He wore only a loincloth of deep purple and an elaborate harness across his chest and torso of matching leviathan skin which did little to shield him from the cold. But this was what the original Angelus wore to hunt the first leviathan. It was tradition, and, he had to admit, it exposed his bronzed skin in delightful fashion. After the hunt, he might just wear it to his favorite joint in Lower Splendour.

Imperiously, Eleazar threw his arm to the side and his page slapped an iron harpoon into his open palm. The slim boy gave him a grin and a cheeky wink, stepping back a mere instant before Eleazar spread his wings in a mighty whoosh of white and silver feathers. His wingless page went to his knees in adoration, his eyes boggling. Eleazar smirked. It never hurt to remind the pinioned of their place.

Almost immediately, he arranged his wings tight to his back, feeling a twinge of shame. Was he his brother, to torment a servant so? The boy was a good page. And as pretty as the sun. Which was why he forgave his cheek more often than not.

"Go to the hawk's nest for a good view, Verity," he said, giving the youth a benevolent smile. "Your prince becomes a king today."

Verity's eyes shone, and he scrambled to his feet. "Aye, milord! May the Luminous One bless you this day!"

"Bless the One makes this quick," Eleazar muttered to himself as his page skipped away. His heart full of thunder, he leapt to the railing of the drachen for his own good view. Spreading his wings against the fierce crosswinds, he grasped the rigging and leaned forward as far as he dared, the harpoon hanging in his grip. The drachen was over the vast nebula, closing the distance to the glimmer with ease. The leviathans were vulnerable when they skipped from cloud to cloud, seeking the freshest dust of the cosmos. The dense cloud banks provided good cover, but the open air of Splendour left them nowhere to hide.

In moments, the glimmer was beyond the deep cloudbank, the drachen in swift pursuit. Eleazar scanned the cluster of leviathans for a likely target. There would be no avoiding this unpleasant task; he might as well do it right. There. One smaller beast struggled to keep up, its tail curved beneath it like a hook and its four wings buzzing frantically. A juvenile, if he had to guess. Another far larger creature slowed to match its pace. The mother, unwilling to leave her child. His heart cracked. Her love would be her doom.

Just your bad luck to skip when a drachen is near. Poor beast, if it were my choice–

A sudden upthrust of wind nearly ripped him from his perch. The thick, braided line tore at his palm, but he kept his grip. Barely. His feet clenched the ornate railing hard enough to make his toes cramp, and he managed not to tumble over the side.

Unwillingly, his gaze dipped downward, drawn by a morbid curiosity and an atavistic fear. Far, far below him through layers of wispy clouds and open sky swirled a perpetual storm of black, charcoal grey and silver: The Black Silence, a gateway separating the world of Light from the world of Darkness. It shielded Splendour from the dismal world of Below. Only Mithran-armored drachens could survive the passage to that violent, dangerous place. That *human* place.

They dared the maelstrom to collect the Hallow Tithe, as necessary to Splendour's survival as harvesting leviathans. The angels who crewed those ships were legends among Splendour's inhabitants. Heroes to be adored. But Eleazar envied them not at all. *Leave me to my books and my poems and my sweetest loves…*

Another updraft wrapped around him, tugging at his wings, ruffling his feathers in dramatic fashion. It pulled his gaze from the Silence, thankfully, and he tried to focus on the task at hand. *The fucking hunt, Lee. Do your stupid duty.*

Cries of worry and fear erupted behind him. His momentary falter had not gone unnoticed. The crew and captain reacted with decided alarm to see him perched so precariously. Winged though he was – as all the Angelus were – dangerous, unexpected gusts could potentially send him into an uncontrolled tumble. This far from the safety of any Archon Aerie, he'd be sucked into the Black Silence long before he found a perch. And his safety was their responsibility. They might all be hanged if he were lost.

"Oh! Be careful, my prince!"

Eleazar steadied himself against the buffeting winds then glanced over his shoulder to find the source of the high, feminine cry. His betrothed, the Lady Maurissa Chrystos, stood on the deck far back from the railing, dressed in warm, black hunting leathers which wrapped her from neck to wrists to ankles. Even her long, raven-black hair was contained beneath a scarf, only a few winding coils escaping. Her face and hands were the only bits of her alabaster skin exposed. Modest clothing for a modest woman. She carried a crossbow – a far more manageable weapon for her slim frame than a heavy harpoon – and looked entirely capable of using it. He met her wide, crystal-blue eyes and managed an awkward nod. Her wings, as black as her clothes and hair, were half-raised behind her as if she intended to take flight and grab him should he falter again.

And wouldn't that be peachy? To be snatched from danger like a naughty child? Eleazar gave her a stiff smile. But he dropped down from the railing. He was weary of fighting the wind, anyway. Once the drachen was close enough for him to launch, he'd need all his strength.

More hunters joined them on the foredeck of the drachen, led by Eleazar's half-brother, Duke Rastaphar Mikalson. Tall and broad-shouldered, his wings tinged rare and beautiful emerald, Rast was everything their mother wanted in a son: A warrior, a hunter, an ascetic, a monk, and the Queen Regent's most trusted adviser. He was also the son of her first husband, the late Duke of Arcadia, and not in line to take the Solaire Throne. There were whispers among the more devout Angelus that perhaps the Luminous One had made a mistake in the birth order of Queen Lucretia's sons. Eleazar could hardly blame them. Sometimes even he thought the Kosmos had made a mistake.

But. The Angelus who became the Great King of Honour, the One who Guarded the Gates to the Ten Worlds, the One who brought balance and peace to Splendour was part of an unbroken line stretching back to the First Creation. His father had reigned a thousand years before he'd broken his neck slipping on the steps outside the Hoary Frog. He'd been celebrating the birth of his first son. The entirety of Splendour had been mourning him for twenty-five years, the same amount of time Eleazar Starson had been disappointing them. On the bright side, as king, he might disappoint them for eons.

"You should know by now, Lady Maurissa," Rast said, with a reserved, proper smile for the slim woman. "Cautioning Prince Eleazar is a fool's errand."

Maurissa pursed her lips, but Eleazar caught the flash of her bright eyes slipping toward Rast then away just as quickly. A strange look from a strange woman. At least to him. Beautiful, yes, sharply intelligent, certainly, but as dogmatic as a Maiden of Light and as cold and inscrutable as the Crystal Cliffs with their shifting colors and fierce winds. He was as excited to marry her as he was to kill a leviathan nymph. One more unpleasant task on the path to the throne.

Still. He harbored a hope that perhaps she would reveal a secret fire on their wedding night. A hope as slim as a feather.

And maybe the Black Silence will swallow all of Splendour by morning…

It was a joke that his mother had chosen such a woman for him. Or perhaps a censure for his decadent ways. Saying she was disappointed in his enjoyment of all things sensual was a wild understatement. Well, the joke was on her. A frigid wife wouldn't keep him from the brothels and haunts in the Lower Firmament. Not even the Luminous One could turn him into a proper Elect. Leave the moral authority and judgement to men like Rast and his entourage of second sons and the wealthy children of mighty Archons. They spent their days preparing for the hunt, meditating, praying, and *supposedly* eschewing liquor and meat and sex.

Why live at all?

Rast, son of Mikalas, cocked his head and regarded him. He held a harpoon, one half as long as Eleazar's and made of sleek and deadly steel. Below-made, if Eleazar had to guess. Human-made. They were clever, those Beasts of the Below. Savage and homicidal, but clever, nonetheless. Eleazar wished his own harpoon was steel, but iron, just like his clothing, was traditional. Only a weak, ill-favored Angelus would demand an edge in the sacred hunt.

I suppose my father used his bare hands to bring down his first leviathan…

"You're awfully eager, brother," Rast said, the barest hint of mockery in his voice. "Are you going to fly into the firmament without the crew and before the ship can heave to?"

Eleazar tried a casual shrug but felt as though his shoulders squeezed his ears. Quickly, he straightened, unfurling his wings. He might be slender, perhaps even frail, compared to Rast, but his silver and white feathers were unmatched among the Angelus. They were his greatest pride, and he wasn't beneath flaunting them. Even among the highborn, plumaged as they were in a glorious range of colors, his glossy whites were unique and uniquely gorgeous. His gaze skipped beyond Rast, drawn to his raven-winged betrothed, wondering how much she was paying attention. Her eyes were upon him, studying his wings. His chest swelled. For a moment, he let himself admire her beauty. He supposed they made a handsome match, at the least.

Abruptly, the girl caught his scrutiny, and ducked her head, a spot of red on her pale cheek. Surprised, Eleazar wondered if he'd been wrong about her if she could blush like a normal girl.

"Oh, leave him be, Rast," spoke up one of Rast's entourage, a skinny fellow from a minor noble family with purple-dipped wings. Eleazar thought his name was Alexi but couldn't be sure. They didn't exactly frequent the same beerhalls or gin haunts or houses of ill-repute.

The one whose name was probably Alexi gave Eleazar an encouraging smile, and Eleazar deigned to return it though with a thin-lipped lack of graciousness. Alexi's smile faltered a bit, but he added in a hearty tone, "Don't you remember the first time you had a chance for a solo kill?"

Rast nodded, laughing. "I was ten years younger than this one. No wonder he's so eager."

Eleazar bristled as the rest of the entourage echoed Rast's laughter. Suddenly, the drachen lurched beneath them, picking up speed. Only Eleazar stumbled from the sudden shift, his brother catching his arm to steady him. The ship veered hard to starboard, the sails rippling in the constant winds. They all dashed to the railing. The mother leviathan and her flagging calf were within the sights of the drachen's colossal, mounted harpoons. Eleazar sucked in a breath. Would they take the beasts for him? He wasn't sure whether to be upset or relieved.

"They won't shoot," Rast said briskly, gripping his bicep encouragingly. He was grinning and Eleazar forgot his earlier mockery. After today, would Rast finally be proud of him? He found himself grinning back at his elder brother. "They won't shoot without my order," he continued breathlessly. "Take your position on the rail, and I'll tell you when to fly. You must time it well, brother. Aim for the nymph."

He urged Eleazar back onto the railing, who clambered into place, the harpoon heavy in his sweaty grip. A thin line lay curled in coils on the deck which tethered the harpoon to the ship. It was pure Mithran, the gods' metal, but it seemed a slim thread when compared with the wild vastness of Upper Splendour.

"Hold fast, Eleazar. Slow your breath and trust in your wings. Be ready to dive."

"Yes, brother." Breathless with excitement, his eyes locked on the struggling nymph and shrieking mother leviathan, Eleazar opened his wings wide to feel the currents. His harpoon suddenly felt light as a feather and his body snapped with energy and strength. Today, he would prove himself at last. The doubts in his heart were overwhelmed by adrenaline. His dive would be everything. If he missed the nymph, he failed.

"Get ready, brother! Soon. Wait until we are over them, and slightly ahead. Drive your spike into the young one's heart! It will be a good death – quick and clean!"

"Yes! I know!" Eleazar readied himself to jump, his muscles bunching and tightening. The ship tilted sharply; he found himself staring down at a green-backed leviathan nymph silhouetted against the deep blue sky, its wings shivering rapidly. Did it know what was about to happen? Did it know what was about to fall upon it? Sudden vertigo gripped him. What if he jumped and missed? Only the thin filament of Mithran attached to his harpoon kept him tethered to the drachen. The winds here were strong enough to tear him apart.

"Now, Eleazar! Dive now and take him!"

Rast's command compelled him off the railing. The wind buffeted him, straining his wings and shoulder muscles; he caught the updrafts and rode them clear of the ship. Then he folded his great white wings and dove.

The rush of air deafened him, but still he heard the shrieking fury of the beast's mother – like a teakettle left on the fire. There was nothing she could do to stop him, however. She moved too slowly to halt a diving Angelus. Eleazar snapped open his wings before he slammed into the hard, slick scales of the smaller beast, his harpoon hurtling forward with all the momentum of his dive. When it struck flesh, it was like stabbing solid rock. Pain lanced through his arm, into his shoulder. He cried out, clutching the quivering harpoon so he didn't slide off the beast. Its point held, thankfully. Vibrant violet blood poured from the wound and the nymph bugled in pain.

Gasping, Eleazar clung to his harpoon, dazed, his legs folded beneath him and his wings askew as blood splashed across his skin, onto his face, into his eyes. The creature was three times his size, much larger than he expected. He'd impaled the creature's spine, he realized through a fog of pain. It hadn't been a killing blow. Its heart still pumped ferociously, and his harpoon was lodged in leviathan bone – pure gods' metal.

The wild blasts from the mother suddenly changed in tone. The high shrill became a low bellow, a sound of pain and anger that battered his ears. He looked up, fighting wind and the nymph's desperate bucking – its attempt to dislodge him – and saw lines attaching the mother leviathan to the royal airship. Ah. They'd cast their harpoons. The mother was finished; she was already being drawn up to the drachen, leaving her child alone.

He braced his feet against the sleek back of his prey and stood. The beast gave a final, pleading squeak to its doomed parent – the sound slid into Eleazar like a knife. It shuddered and nearly tossed him off, but Eleazar held on with desperate strength.

Bright blood spewed from the deep wound, spraying into the air in shimmering ropes. He tried shifting to avoid it. It was so warm, almost hot, and it tingled on his skin. Most of it flew upward, floating as if in water, the creature's blood imbued with deep magic. He spat it from his mouth, horrified as it clung to him like a living thing. He looked up toward the airship, hoping for its great harpoon to do his work for him, but the royal drachen was occupied with the mother leviathan. He had to kill the calf himself.

How? With what?

The nymph hovered in the shadow of its mother, not even attempting to flee. The buzz of its wings had slowed dramatically and it was beginning to sink. The magic which kept its mother afloat was nascent in one so young. It needed her strength and that of their glimmer to protect it. Only the thin line of Mithran attached to his harpoon would keep it from falling into the void when its strength failed entirely.

Eleazar peered upward, his chest heaving. The crew crawled across the scaled surface of the mother, securing hooks and lines to tether the beast to the ship. He spotted Maurissa sliding down a rope to reach its underside, her wings tucked tight to her back. She waved at him, staring at him intensely as she hung from the harness. He returned the wave, puffing his chest and setting his jaw, hoping he looked like a conquering hero and not a fool. She had no interest in the butchering, only in him.

A rush of wind and the heavy beat of wings warned him others had taken an interest in his safety, as well. He knew it was Rast before he turned, shame filling him. Blood rushed to his cheeks and his palms grew wet where he gripped the wooden haft of the harpoon.

"Brother!" Eleazar cried, pretending he hadn't a care in the world. "I've severed its spine. Not quite a killing blow, but close enough." He gave his harpoon a twist which only ground splinters into his palm. "If you could finish him off, I'd be in your debt."

Rast stared at him, his face like stone. "You failed," he said simply. "You cannot sever a leviathan's spine with iron. It is pure Mithran."

"Yes, well, but the beast is dying. Surely. The blood…"

Rast interrupted him with a sigh, hefting his slim steel spike and walking across the nymph's back with practiced surety. His wings tight against his back to avoid the ever-violent updrafts swirling, Rast drew abreast of him and dealt the killing blow to the unfortunate animal. It gave a last shudder and its thrumming heart stilled. Eleazar blew out a breath.

"You never cease to disappoint me, Eleazar."

Eleazar started. "Pardon?" Their relationship had often been fraught, but Eleazar couldn't recall Rast ever speaking to him in such a manner. It was shocking. His shock turned to pique. He was sore and tired and covered in blood. And all for nothing. "I never wanted to participate in this barbarity from the start," he snapped. "It is a stupid way to prove one's worth."

"Stupid and barbaric? Our most sacred tradition?" Rast shook his head mournfully. He backed up a few feet, facing Eleazar. "This was your chance, brother, your last chance. It gives me no joy that you have failed yet again to live up to the memory of your blessed father. An Angelus I greatly admired. One who always treated me as a son."

Eleazar bared his teeth. "But you're not his son, Rast. I am!"

"And what do you do to honor him? What do you do to deserve the Solaire Throne?"

"Deserve? It is my destiny!" Eleazar gripped his locked harpoon. Above them, the mother leviathan was secured, and the butchering had begun in earnest. It had captured the attention of everyone on the ship, including those meant to guard him. A fine bloody mist clouded the air around her. A feeling of dread stirred in his belly as he faced his elder brother once more. "By fate and the will of the Luminous One!"